MW01132097

RIVER ANGELS

An O'Brien Tale

Stacey Reynolds

River Angels: An O'Brien Tale © Copyright: Stacey Reynolds
December 24, 2017
Published by
Createspace Independent Publishing and Kindle Direct Publishing
*This book is the intellectual property of the author. This book is licensed for your personal enjoyment only. All rights reserved. No part may be copied, reproduced, or transmitted without the written permission of the author. You must not circulate this book in any format. Cover art was purchased legally through iStock photos. Any characters in the book are fictional from the author's own imagination. Any similarity to real people is coincidental. The businesses that are mentioned are purely to add to the ambiance and authenticity of the setting.

ISBN: 1981316663
ISBN 13: 9781981316663

Other books by the author

<u>**Novels**</u>
Raven of the Sea: An O'Brien Tale (Book One)
A Lantern in the Dark: An O'Brien Tale (Book Two)
Shadow Guardian: An O'Brien Tale (Book Three)

<u>**Novellas**</u>
Fio: An O'Brien Novella (A Spin-off Novella of The O'Brien Tales)

This book is dedicated to my big brother, Randy. He made my childhood one big adventure. I lost him too soon. I hope there's deer hunting in heaven, brother. I'll see you again, someday.

List of Characters from The O'Brien Tales Series

Sean O'Brien- Married to Sorcha (Mullen), father to Aidan, Michael, Brigid, Patrick, Liam, Seany (Sean Jr.), brother of William (deceased) and Maeve, son of Aoife and David. Retired and Reserve Garda officer. Native to Doolin, Co. Clare, Ireland.

Sorcha O'Brien- Maiden name of Mullen. Daughter of Michael and Edith Mullen. Sister of John (deceased). Native to Belfast, Northern Ireland. Married to Sean O'Brien with whom she has six children and eight grandchildren. A nurse midwife for over thirty years.

Michael O'Brien- Son of Sean and Sorcha, married to Branna (O'Mara), three children Brian, Halley, and Ian. Rescue swimmer for the Irish Coast Guard. Twin to Brigid.

Branna (O'Mara) O'Brien- American, married to Michael. Orphaned when her father was killed in the 2nd Battle of Fallujah (Major Brian O'Mara, USMC) and then lost her mother, Meghan (Kelly) O'Mara to breast cancer six years later. Mother to Brian, Halley, and Ian. Real Estate investor.

Capt. Aidan O'Brien, Royal Irish Regiment- Son and eldest child of Sean and Sorcha O'Brien. Married to Alanna (Falk). Father of two children, David (Davey) and Isla. Serves active duty in the Royal Irish Regiment and currently living in Shropshire, England.

Alanna (Falk) O'Brien- American, married to Aidan, daughter of Hans Falk and Felicity Richards (divorced). Stepdaughter of Doctor Mary Flynn of Co. Clare. Mother to Davey and Isla. Best friend to Branna. Clinical Psychologist working with British military families battling PTSD and traumatic brain injuries.

Brigid (O'Brien) Murphy- Daughter of Sean and Sorcha, Michael's twin, married to Finn Murphy. Mother to Cora, Colin, and Declan.

Finn Murphy- Husband to Brigid. Father of Cora, Colin, and Declan. I.T. expert who works in Ennis but does consulting work with the Garda on occasion.

Cora Murphy- Daughter of Brigid and Finn. Has emerging gifts of pre-cognition and other psychic abilities. Oldest grandchild of Sean and Sorcha.

Patrick O'Brien- Son of Sean and Sorcha. Married to Caitlyn (Nagle). Currently residing in Dublin after joining the Garda. Serving on the National Security Surveillance Unit on the Armed Response Team.

Caitlyn (Nagle) O'Brien- Daughter of Ronan and Bernadette Nagle, sister to Madeline and Mary. Married to Patrick. Early education teacher. English as a second language teacher for small children. No children of her own as she has fertility issues. Native to Co. Clare.

Dr. Liam O'Brien- Second youngest child of Sean and Sorcha. Currently abroad and unresponsive to the family's attempts to communicate with him. This is following a tragedy involving his girlfriend, Eve Doherty (now deceased). Finishing medical residency while on a medical mission in Manaus, Brazil. Internal medicine and infectious disease. Unmarried with no children.

Sean (Seany) O'Brien Jr.- Youngest child of Sean and Sorcha. Serving with the fire services in Dublin. Trained paramedic and fireman. Unmarried and no children.

Tadgh O'Brien- Only son of William (deceased) and Katie (Donoghue) O'Brien. Special Detectives Unit of the Garda. Married to Charlie Ryan.

Charlotte aka Charlie (Ryan) O'Brien- American FBI Agent with the International Human Rights Crime Division. Married to Tadgh. Sister to Josh. Currently working in Europe as the liaison to Interpol.

Josh O'Brien- Formerly Joshua Albert Ryan until he changed his name. Lives in Dublin with his sister Charlie and his brother-in-law Tadgh. Attending junior college for Maritime Studies.

Dr. Mary Flynn-Falk- Retired M.D., wife of Hans Falk. Stepmother to Alanna O'Brien and Captain Erik Falk, USMC.

Sgt. Major Hans Falk, USMC Ret.- American, father of Alanna and Erik. Married to Doc Mary. Retired from the United States Marine Corps.

Daniel McPherson- Son of Molly Price and Jonathan (John) Mullen. Just recently found the Mullen family. Was an unknown offspring of John, who never knew he had a son. Raised in the Scottish borderlands by his English mother. Molly Price married an old friend who claimed Daniel as his son.

Maeve (O'Brien) Carrington- Daughter of David and Aoife. Wife to Nolan, mother to Cian and Cormac. Sister of Sean Sr..

Katie (Donoghue) O'Brien- Native to Inis Oirr, Aran Islands. Widow of William O'Brien. Mother of Tadgh O'Brien.

Aoife (Kerr) O'Brien- Wife of David O'Brien, mother of Sean, William, and Maeve. Originally from Co. Donegal.

David O'Brien- Husband of Aoife, father of Sean, William, and Maeve. The oldest living patriarch of the O'Brien family.

Michael Mullen- Native to Belfast, Northern Ireland, married to Edith (Kavanagh). Father of Sorcha and John.

Edith (Kavanagh) Mullen- Married to Michael Mullen, mother of Sorcha and John.

Lt. Izzy Collier, USN- Doctor/Surgeon in the United States Navy. Originally born in Wilcox, Arizona. Close friend to Alanna O'Brien. Daughter of Rhys and Donna Collier, apricot and apple farmers in eastern Arizona.

Jenny- Daytime barmaid at Gus O'Connor's Pub.

PROLOGUE

*The lofty and matted forest rose like a green
wall on either hand...*

Theodore Roosevelt

Manaus, capital city in the State of Amazonas, Brazil

Dr. Liam O'Brien stepped off the boat at the eastern end of Manaus. The winter season had just begun, bringing the rain, cooler temperatures, and flooding. It rained all year in Brazil, but December and January were the months when the fun really started. During this time of year, boat traffic was high, and anything without four-wheel drive stayed in the city. The boat captain, of sorts, pulled his one-man operation onto the rickety dock, where another man waited with an ATV. The vehicle was impressive in that it was surprising that the thing actually ran. Mismatched panels made up the body, smoke came out of the exhaust with a loud grumble, and the trailer attached to the back was empty, but had vines and discarded weeds clinging to the hinges of the tailgate. Liam assumed that this was Paolo, the groundskeeper for the abbey.

He didn't speak much, but he assisted Liam with his luggage and the supplies he'd brought from the sister abbey in Dublin. All mooched from the local hospitals, of course. As they finished the

unloading and reloading, Liam attempted to hand the boat captain a tip, but he waved it away.

"Não, obrigado." he said, continuing in Portuguese as he pointed up the path that would lead to St. Clare's Charity Hospital.

Liam had taken an intense, abbreviated course in conversational Portuguese. He was nowhere near fluent, but he followed along most of the time. He understood it better than he spoke it. The gist of it was that the man was grateful for the doctors and the abbey full of do-gooders, and he wasn't going to take Liam's money.

St. Clare's was located east of the city, on a visually spectacular stretch of the Amazon River. The Rio Negro and the Solimões River merged and flowed into the Amazon. One river was dark and one was a lighter tone, clouded with muddy sediment. As the two joined at Manaus and flowed into the Amazon, it appeared to split the river down the middle, each refusing to submit to the other. A little farther east, north of the abbey, was where the Rio Puraquequara started, with a strip of land between it and the Amazon. All four rivers had multiple tributaries branching out on either bank of the rivers. Just outside the city was rainforest. Dense jungle in every direction, which is why Manaus was a staging point for a lot of activity and access in and out of the rainforest.

As Liam mounted the ATV, Paolo carefully turned it around and headed away from the river and the departing boat. Liam immediately felt the sensation of being swallowed whole. The lush, wet, green landscape surrounded them. Birds and insects, and God knows what else, fluttered around them. It was as if everything he'd ever known had left with that boat. This was good. This was exactly what he needed.

In the wake of Eve's murder in Dublin, the instinct to flee had been overwhelming. Everything in the city reminded him of her. Cafes where they would sit and drink coffee, the different nooks of Trinity College where they'd meet between classes, the dormitory she'd lived in all three years that they'd been together. The dance studio where he'd first watched her graceful limbs and quiet beauty.

So, he'd taken off early. Three months before his departure date, as a matter of fact.

The only personal belongings he'd brought were currently stuffed in his duffel. Clothes, a couple of medical books and Portuguese cheaters, his toiletry kit, and his iPod. He laughed at the thought of his last-minute additions. The little gifts that Alanna's friend Izzy had given him. She'd mailed him a treasure box of silly little gifts. A bottle of bug repellent, a bottle of water, a potty humor book in case he got dysentery and was stuck on the toilet, and a condom...that one had thrown him for a minute until he'd read the note. Oh, and a beard comb, even though he'd never had a beard. All the gifts had come with humorous little notes of explanation. He'd brought everything with him but the condom.

It was a kind gesture, meant to cheer him up and to prepare him for this journey. To divert his attention to other things. It was the first time he'd laughed in weeks. The last gift had been a calling card, with instructions to call his mother regularly. Included in the note was a threat to show up and put him in a headlock if he didn't call home. Izzy Collier was a trip. Unapologetically American, a U.S. Navy doctor. A surgeon, actually. Eve had liked her. Thought she was tough and funny and smart.

He thought back, again, to the calling card. He'd pondered long and hard about how much to isolate himself, and he had come to the conclusion that he needed to put Ireland behind him. For now, at least. He needed to dive head first into this culture, this new environment, this challenging work. This place was second only to Africa with regard to infectious disease work, and these people needed his head in the game. The CDC in America, as well as other countries, were testing vaccines for Zika, and thus he was right in the middle of medical history being made.

He needed to be consumed with something other than grief. What he didn't need were updates about the latest happy news from the rest of the O'Brien clan. He didn't need to be reminded of all that they had, and of all that he'd lost. He didn't need their pitying looks

or understanding platitudes. His mate was gone. His heart was dead in his chest and he wasn't going to go back to that life until he was good and goddamn ready.

The trip took about five minutes. Paolo took care not so much with his passenger, as with the medical supplies in the trailer. The trail opened up dramatically to a sweeping estate that was surrounded on all sides by a four-foot tall fence. The barrier was built of clay and river stones, and he wondered why they bothered, as the fence could be easily cleared by anyone bigger than a six-year-old.

As Liam looked up at the simple clay structures, he realized it wasn't just a hospital. There were bilingual signs in Portuguese and English. He dismounted from the vehicle and took it all in. He looked at the main building which was the hospital. Small by western standards, and in comparison to some of the bigger hospitals in Manaus, but large enough to be self-sufficient. It was strategically placed outside of the city, in order to cut down travel time for the people who lived on the eastern fringes of the city and the indigenous tribes that lived in remote areas off of the tributaries.

To the left of the hospital was what appeared to be a school that included some sort of dormitory. *Orfanato... Jesus,* he thought. *An orphanage.* Children ran around the area, a rusty swing set was the only playground equipment. There was a small half field for football, where the boys chased each other and kicked the ball back and forth toward a homemade goal.

He looked at the building to the right, which had to be the abbey. There was a chapel and another dormitory type structure where the sisters must live. The only part of this place that he'd read up on was the hospital. The three-page pamphlet highlighted information about the medical mission. There were staff quarters for himself and any other visiting doctors, nurses, and midwives. Segregated, of course, by gender.

There was one more building off to the far right. The cantina was in a separate building, which made sense. Separated due to the heat and the fire risk for the other buildings. He looked at his watch, and he

hoped that whatever the smell was coming out of there was almost ready. He hadn't eaten since the rubbish they'd fed him on the plane. He had no idea what time it was in Ireland, but it was almost noon in Brazil.

"I see you found your way, Dr. O'Brien." Liam turned around to find a stern looking Irish woman in full habit. It wasn't the penguin effect of his youth, with the black robe and white collar. She was dressed in a cream-colored robe and white head piece. Pretty gutsy considering the mud. The other sisters he saw milling around wore a rougher weave, linen perhaps, with a brown-colored overdress, which seemed more practical given the terrain and the climate.

"Dia duit, you must be the abbess." The sternness softened a bit, the corner of her mouth coming up. He estimated her to be in her late sixties, but it was hard to tell under the habit and robes. Her blue eyes and fair skin told him as much about her heritage as her accent. Lined and marked with the passing of time. Her eyes reflected intelligence and a quiet strength. She was tall for a woman, but her frame was thin and elegant, almost frail. Like a woman who had few excesses and had lived a disciplined life.

"You may call me Reverend Mother Faith if you prefer, or Abbess is fine as well. It's good to hear the young folk speaking the old tongue. I'm from County Sligo. Reverend Mother Mary Magdalene at the Dublin abbey said you were from County Clare. I am surprised you came early. Brave man, coming in the rainy season. Is there any reason for the early departure?"

The abbess was sharp, and Liam suspected that she often asked questions she already knew the answer to. He said nothing, afraid that his O'Brien temper might flare. She looked prepared to send him right back home on that little boat. He answered her question with a question. "I didn't know there was a Saint Faith."

"Yes, well she's an old one. St. Faith of Conques or Sainte-Foy in French. She was from Aquitaine. I'm afraid she was tortured to death by pagans. But we Irish do love a dark tale, don't we? Which brings me back to your early arrival. Tell me, lad. Are you running to something or away from something?" she asked.

He almost bit his tongue, but answered cooly. "I'm just here to do some good. I've got three months left on my residency, but I am prepared to stay as long as you need me."

Her brows went up at that. "Are ye now? Well, we'll see how you get on. Don't over commit yourself, lad. I'll hold you to it. Now...did my sister also tell you our conditions for your early arrival?"

He ground his teeth. "I assure you, Reverend Mother, I'm of sound mind and ready to work. I'm sure you are a busy woman."

"Aye, I am. Very busy, as you can see." She spread an arm out over the estate. "St. Clare's is much more than a hospital. This mission takes in orphaned children and tries to place them with adoptive families, and operates as a school for them and a few of the children from the more remote indigenous tribes and villages. We run on almost all volunteers, with a few paid local staff that we employ out of necessity."

She took a breath and gave him a direct stare. "All that aside, I assure you, young man, that I am not too busy for you. You may not think you need my counsel but I must insist you submit to the arrangement. I'm sure Reverend Mother Mary told you that my background was in psychology before I took the veil." Her brow was up, and her blue eyes looked right through him.

She turned abruptly and began walking. "Every Monday you will take your tea with me for one hour. Now, I will give you a tour of the facilities." She turned to the groundskeeper and spoke in perfect Portuguese. "Paolo, please take the luggage into the male staff quarters and the supplies into the family clinic office." Then she turned back, her robes swinging. She had the gait of a woman half her age. Liam was going to need a translator. His Portuguese was primary school level. His shoulders slumped. *Shit*. This nun was going to be a real ball breaker.

1

*But when hunter meets with husbands, each confirms the
other's tale—
The female of the species is more deadly than the male.*

Rudyard Kipling

Naval Medical Center Portsmouth, Virginia, USA
Nine months later...

The voice over the intercom was deep, male, and slightly put
out. "Paging Lieutenant Collier. Paging one Doctor Izzy
Collier. Only a total doucher would schedule a surgery during her hail and farewell party."

The nurses and assisting surgeon grumbled with laughter as Izzy
sighed into her surgical mask. "I didn't schedule it. It's a trauma case,
numb nuts... and I'm closing! Tell everyone I'm closing! I'll be done
in ten!"

"Excuse me, Dr. Collier," the voice continued over the intercom.
"I know you didn't just call a superior officer numb nuts."

More laughter. He was only her superior by about 30 seconds,
having just recently been promoted. "Sorry, I meant Lieutenant
Commander Numb Nuts. Now let me get this guy closed." She nodded to the nurse. "Kill the intercom, Ensign. Thanks."

"Yes, ma'am."

"You can go, Izzy. I can take it from here." The doctor across from Izzy was a civilian doctor and a damn fine surgeon, but this was her patient. She wasn't bailing on him right at the finish line. She finished the last staple, checked his vitals, counted sponges, cleaned up the incision, and voila! She leaned down by the patient's face. He was young, handsome, and an infantry Marine. Real poster boy material.

"You only get issued one spleen, Corporal, and one life. Take it easy on the bike from now on. Grow up, get a honey, have babies. Do you copy?"

As she cleaned herself up in the locker room, she took a hard look at herself in the mirror over the sink. She turned thirty last month. As she looked over the lines of her face, she felt confident that she looked good for her age. She stayed healthy, lived cleanly, and she was an athlete. Always had been. But inside? She felt old.

That kid on her table was practically a baby. Probably not old enough to buy beer, but old enough to die on the battlefield. Old enough to come home from war with adrenaline withdrawal and a full bank account…hence the crotch rocket. At least he'd worn a helmet and leathers, so he didn't look like he'd been through a cheese grater. He was still beautiful and young…just a little more banged up. Small favors. He'd recover. She'd managed to salvage part of the spleen, and a partial was all he needed. The broken ulna would also heal. It was a minor break that their orthopedic guy would set and cast in the morning. The surgery had gone well. A great last call, as it were.

"Collier, move your ass!" Another pushy colleague, this time a male nurse she'd befriended in the ER.

"I'm coming, Warren! Don't get your panties in a wad!" She pulled the linen dress over her head, forgoing her PT gear for party attire, slipped on some leather sandals, and grabbed her duffel bag. She looked at the nameplate on her locker as she closed it. *LT I. Collier, USN.* She plucked it off the metal door and left, bag slung over her shoulder.

♉

Izzy looked around the Navy-themed pub and smiled. She'd insisted on an all ranks event instead of one at the officer's club on base. The main reason being that she didn't want to exclude the enlisted staff and volunteers, Hospital Corpsmen, spouses of enlisted sailors and Marines that volunteered at the hospital, and some of the other medics she'd worked with from time to time. A hail and farewell was exactly that. A celebration of those coming aboard and those who were leaving. Leaving due to retirement, reassignment, or separation from active duty. She was the latter. She'd done six years in the Navy, and although she knew this was the right path for her, she was really going to miss the people.

Her commanding officer had said a few kind words about a Corpsman who was leaving for Yemen with a platoon of Marines. Then he welcomed the new surgeon who would be taking Izzy's place. He was older than her by at least five years, having joined after his medical training was completely done and he'd worked a couple of years in the civilian sector. He'd done hard time in a high traffic ER in Los Angeles. He was a good choice, and she felt right passing the baton to him.

"Last but certainly not least, Lieutenant Collier, please get your butt up here and let me farewell you properly." Her Lieutenant Commander had insisted on doing the speech, although he wasn't the highest ranking person in attendance. She'd worked with him more than anyone else, and he knew her better than the higher-ups. She approached the front of the room, dodging pub chairs and tables filled with her colleagues.

He spoke at length about the path of her career, and she was both proud of and humbled by his praise. It was her seven month tour that started in Germany and then to the Army Hospital in Al Asad that had her tearing up, choking down the wave of emotions. The draw down of troops had been happening in stages, but they still needed doctors to see the troops through until the withdrawal was complete and the hospital was completely closed down. She'd been fresh out of training, and they were looking for new blood in order to give the senior surgeons a break from deployments. She'd had an overseeing surgeon with her, of course, and it was a chance to get her residency completed in a combat zone and come home ready to launch a promising career as a Naval surgeon. They were operating on a skeleton crew, just like all of the forces that were left in theater. The media would boast daily that the war in Iraq had ended, but she saw the reality. The withdrawal was fast, politically motivated, and it emboldened the enemy at a time when the reinforcements weren't there for back-up.

She'll never forget the roadside bomb attack...not until her dying day. The Army platoon had taken casualties not only among their soldiers but their one medic had been injured as well. She'd gone with the medical chopper, leaving her boss and the small team of surgeons and nurses to get ready for the incoming wounded. Nothing had prepared her for the carnage. She vividly remembered the smell of blood and charred flesh. She remembered the stifled moans of the wounded men. She'd gone on auto-pilot, along with the two medics who flew with her. They'd been amazing, and what looked like inevitable fatalities had ended in a 100% survival rate. One foot amputation, burns, head traumas, and two gun shot wounds. One to the thigh, and the other to the shoulder, from a sniper who'd lain in wait. She'd received the Navy Achievement Medal for her actions that day and she'd nominated her two medics for a bronze star because those crazy bastards actually had to get out of the helicopter. She'd been forbidden, with threat of duct tape, to get out of the aircraft. Where they landed, it was not safe or secure, but those men couldn't wait. Especially with their medic among the wounded.

Izzy came back to herself as grumbles of laughter went through the crowd of well-wishers. They chuckled at the thought of anyone trying to duct tape Izzy Collier into submission. She smiled, "Well, I was new. I behaved for that first year." Everyone laughed again. They all knew her well enough to know that she didn't take any shit, loved to be in the middle of the action, and was also a black belt in Hapkido.

Her boss turned to her. "We'll miss you, Lieutenant, and the Navy will feel your absence." He turned to the crowd. "Many of you know that she has a nice little vacation planned starting this weekend. She doesn't seem to be worried about getting back to those three different civilian hospitals that are currently vying for her attention. What you all may not know is that after her brief trip to the Emerald Isle, our little do-gooder has signed on for a three-month stint with a medical mission in Brazil."

The group gave a collective gasp, but a few of Izzy's nearest and dearest already knew. They smiled at her. As the LT CDR presented her with a going away gift, she shook with laughter. Many military members received shadow boxes with a folded flag and a weapon of choice. A Marine K-Bar, an Officer's sword, and the like. Her display, however, had a scalpel under the flag, mounted in the velvet-lined shadow box. As she read the inscription, she barked out another laugh. The inscription plate read,

LT "Izzy" Collier, MD. No better friend, no worse enemy.

As the ceremony ended, and the drinks were poured, a group of her lady friends approached. Nurses, midwives, fellow doctors of different disciplines, and a couple of Navy spouses. She loved her male colleagues, but she needed her female tribe. Serving in the military could be isolating for a woman. They were giggling and nudging each other as they approached.

"Okay, what are you girls up to? I smell mischief." Her friend Tanya, the Ensign that assisted her in her last surgery, had a look of pure innocence and good intentions on her face as she handed Izzy a gift bag. Izzy didn't buy it for a minute. These ladies were as unruly as they were sweet.

"It's just a little something for you to pamper yourself, before your trip to Brazil."

Izzy pulled out an envelope that had the emblem of a very nice day spa in Norfolk. She'd gone there for a lady-date with her girlfriends once, but couldn't afford it on a regular basis. Then she saw the handwritten note on the back of the envelope.

When in Rome...

She opened the envelope and burst out laughing. A gift certificate for a full Brazilian wax. Ouchy. The women all started clapping, the tears started pouring, and the vows to keep in touch were exchanged.

As she left the pub, one glass of bourbon later, she started thinking about what was in store for her. Which made her think about that tear-soaked phone call she'd received from Alanna several weeks ago. Liam had been gone for nine months, going into his tenth. They hadn't heard from him since the first week he arrived in Brazil. He'd changed his contact information and sent word that he needed to focus on his work, free of distractions. He needed to grieve in his own way, and that they weren't to worry about him.

Now, the only time they got word was through the abbey in Dublin. Once his commitment was up, they'd expected him to return. The only thing the abbess had told them was that he was okay and that he'd extended his work in Brazil indefinitely. She'd also periodically passed on letters from her sister abbess in Brazil. Always brief and to the point. Liam was fine. He was a great asset to the hospital. He was doing God's work. Yadda yadda yadda.

The O'Briens were good people. As good as it gets. As good as her own family of farmers and ranchers. According to Alanna, Sorcha was a mess. Like a mother bear who'd lost one of her cubs. Sean was worse. After the death of Liam's girlfriend, Sean blamed himself. He thought that maybe Liam blamed him as well, and that was why he'd cut the family off. The whole family felt the loss keenly, his absence shadowing every gathering. It was a close-knit family and they were coming unraveled.

So, she accepted an opportunity to go on a medical mission to St. Clare's Charity Hospital in Manaus. She had a lot of leave accumulated that she had to burn or lose. Two months of being in the Navy, but no longer working. So her terminal leave would be spent volunteering at a small charity hospital on the Amazon River. They'd been absent an on-site surgeon for three years, and depended on the local hospitals to cough up a volunteer once a month for minor, scheduled surgical procedures. No trauma patients could be treated there or emergency surgeries. So the time in transit to a hospital within the city made for delayed treatment and dangerous complications. They had the facility, just not the staff. She loved the idea of stepping in for a three month period and getting an emergency surgical team trained. Maybe she could even help with recruiting some more doctors to the area. This was a small operation run by the Catholic church. This wasn't a *Doctors Without Borders* funded operation. They had no real press, no global marketing, and operated on a shoestring budget. She doubted she could make the situation any worse.

The secondary mission was Liam. It was time for him to cut the shit. She'd threatened to show up and put him in a headlock if he didn't call his mother. Obviously, Dr. Liam O'Brien didn't realize that Izzy Collier didn't bluff.

2

St. Clare's Charity Mission
Manaus, State of Amazonas, Brazil

"Dr. O'Brien, the Reverend Mother has asked me to remind you that it's time for tea." Sister Agatha was a sweet, amiable lass. Liam didn't mean to get testy with her. But he was kind of an asshole, so he was all about shooting the messenger.

He yelled toward the door. "Well, that's just grand, Sister Agatha. Could you pass along to the abbess that I'm helping Sister Catherine deliver a placenta at the moment, but she's welcome to roll the tea service right in." Sister Agatha crossed herself and ducked out of the exam room.

Sister Catherine gave him a chiding look. She was not just a sister. She was a trained nurse midwife. "You shouldn't scold her that way. She's a gentle soul. If you need to leave…"

"I don't have to leave, but thank you. The Reverend Mother will understand. It's not like she's got anything new to say."

"Shame on you, lad. If you'd spend less time fighting her, and more time listening, you might not have to go to those sessions. She never told us why, but she must have her reasons."

Liam ignored her and spoke to the nurse who was assisting. "Margaritte, any word on that blood work? Page Pedro in the lab and get a report from Alyssa on how the baby is doing."

The patient in front of him had come in with a high fever. She'd been a little out of her head. She'd assumed that the cramping had been due to her illness. She was not only sick; she was dilated eight centimeters and fully effaced. He feared malaria, but he needed her labs. Malaria was very dangerous for the mother and the unborn child.

Sister Catherine cleaned up the mother as Liam took her vitals again. Diarrhea, vomiting, fever, weakness. *God, please don't let it be malaria.* As if on cue, the local nurse, Margaritte, re-entered the room. "Pedro says no on the malaria screening. It's bacterial."

Liam and the others in the room let out a breath. Probably cryptosporidium or giardia, but the treatments were the same for a nursing mother. Alyssa, an Irish nurse from County Mayo, popped her head in the room, "The baby is fine. No fever or jaundice. He's a bit underweight by our standards but healthy. An eight on the Apgar scale both times I tested him. Doctor Watt has been paged, but the boy looks good."

"All right, thank you, Alyssa. Take a blood draw and make sure she didn't pass the bacterial infection to him, just to be safe. And could you feed him? She's not well enough to nurse just yet. We'll get her fever down, get her hydrated, get the antibiotics started in her IV, and then you can bring him to Sister Catherine. Give her a couple of hours." He'd filled a lot of roles at this hospital, but lactation consultant wasn't one of them.

If anyone had told him nine months ago that he'd be doing everything from delivering placentas to stitching up football injuries on orphans, he'd have thought them insane. He'd done the regular rotations in medical school, but his specialty was internal medicine. The study of human diseases. He'd also studied infectious disease, hence the assignment. He'd done plenty of that. Testing water, identifying bacterial colonies and parasites. He'd also treated everything from hookworm to dengue fever within his own specialized practice within the hospital.

The reality, however, was that if you could pitch in, you did. The hospital worked on a skeleton crew. They had no surgeon other than Antonio, an Italian doctor that volunteered once a month. He worked for one of the wealthy, private hospitals, was well paid, had a great staff, and had plenty of up-to-date equipment. He was a good guy, though, and he helped as often as he could. Alyssa was a trained nurse anesthetist, but she was sorely underused due to the lack of a full-time surgeon.

They'd lost three patients that could be considered emergency cases since Liam had been with St. Clare's. They'd done all they could to stabilize the patients before transporting them but none of the in-house doctors were surgeons. One injury had been a jaguar attack, giving the patient multiple lacerations and an open artery at the neck. He was a minute from death when his family had reached St. Clare's. The gap of time between the injury and reaching help had been too long. The other fatalities had been during childbirth. The woman was infected with malaria and the baby was breach. He could do a lot as a doctor but he wasn't qualified or certified to do a c-section. The baby was dead in utero by the time they got the woman to a city hospital. The mother died two days later. It was the harsh reality of medicine in developing nations.

Liam took his gloves off first, relieved to give his hands some air. Next came the mask, goggles, and finally the cap that he put in the laundry bin for the housekeeping staff to bleach. He left the hospital and headed to meet the Reverend Mother and her all-knowing eyes.

"Have a seat, lad. I've just made a fresh pot of tea." Reverend Mother Faith was in her linen habit today, having walked the grounds with Paolo, assessing some work that needed to be done to the abbey's exterior. Liam sat, suddenly tired and in need of the sustenance she offered. "I heard you had some excitement with the febrile patient. Placenta, was it? I'm afraid Sister Agatha was quite taken aback by your candor." She gave him a chiding look. He was quite accustomed to that look.

"Aye, sorry about that. She caught me at a bad moment. The mother's going to be fine, by the way. The babe is healthy. Adam will give him a thorough exam later today." Liam's voice was low, fatigued.

"Well done. Not exactly what you thought you were signing up for, I take it. You thought you'd be staring into a microscope lens more often than not." She poured the tea as she spoke.

Liam grinned slightly, rubbing his beard. "Aye, well, it's been good experience for me. I can't let Antonio have all the fun, now can I?" He accepted the cup gratefully, along with a plate of biscuits.

"Speaking of surgeons, we've had a run of good luck. We have a surgeon coming on board in the next two weeks. The doctor was recruited through Reverend Mother Mary's office in Dublin. A three-month commitment in an attempt to get the surgery up and operating again."

Liam sighed with relief. This was excellent news. They needed all the help they could get.

She changed subjects abruptly, catching him off guard. "So, have you contacted your family in Ireland?" the Abbess asked, already knowing the answer. Liam groaned. *Here we go again.*

"I think you know the answer to that. Why do you bother asking?"

"Why do you punish them, Liam?" Her tone was soft. She really thought that was it. She thought he was trying to punish his family.

"I'm not punishing them. Jesus, we've been over this."

"Well then explain it. You've told me about this large, wonderful family. About the family lore. How blessed they've all been to find what they believe to be their mates. Do you resent their happiness? It doesn't seem as simple as all that," she said.

How could he make her understand? He'd been the fun-loving O'Brien. The one full of easy laughter. The one for whom everything came so easily. What had Izzy said? "The charmed O'Brien man."

"Who, Liam? Who is the charmed one?" He hadn't realized he'd spoken out loud.

"I was. I was the charmed one. I was the happy, fun son. The one they never had to worry about. I'm not that man anymore. Losing Eve changed all that. They aren't ready for who I've become."

The abbess snorted. "For heaven's sake, lad. You're a bit broody, I'll admit, but you haven't transformed into Dark Vader."

Liam choked down a laugh. "Darth, Reverend Mother. It's Darth Vader."

She waved a dismissive hand, "Aye, you get my meaning. You aren't even giving them a chance to see you through this. It's been months, dear boy. Your family calls the Dublin abbey at least once a week. Your mother broke down sobbing in the abbess's office." Liam shut his eyes, overcome with sadness. "You've had a good life. This thing with your girlfriend, it was tragic. Unbelievably so. But you've chosen to keep moving, keep breathing. You can't just erase the rest of your twenty-eight years. You have a family. You have a home. I don't want you to leave, but you can't go on pretending you live in a bubble. You have stewed in your grief for months. You've worked non-stop, you've lost weight. You can't keep this up. Tell me how to help you."

After not receiving a response, she added, "I finally broke down and sent a letter to your parents." Liam stiffened. "And before you say a word, it was short and to the point. They know you're alive and well and working. I didn't betray any confidences. Your mother has a right to know that you're okay. If you're going to abandon her to think the worst, as mothers do, then someone had to step in."

"How do you know what a mother feels? You're a nun, hiding in this bloody abbey!" After ten months, nothing that came out of Liam's mouth had an effect on Reverend Mother Faith. She swallowed her tea, her face tight, and Liam knew he'd finally hit a nerve. He just wasn't sure why.

"Don't make assumptions, Dr. O'Brien. I wasn't always a nun." She stood. "Now, you've had a long day. Go have a lie down before supper."

Liam sighed. "I'm sorry, Reverend Mother. My mother's a sore spot. I...I'm sorry if I said something out of line."

"Not at all. You look tired. Go sneak off to that bungalow you all think I don't know about." Liam barked out a laugh, shaking his head. The woman missed nothing. The corner of her mouth lifted just a bit. "Get some rest. Gabriela is making Tucunaré tonight. We don't get it very often." Liam had only known Gabriella to make the dish, peacock bass, twice since he'd been there. It was very good and there were never any leftovers.

"Yes, she was cleaning the fish when I went in for some of her good coffee this morning. I'll see you at six. And it's great news to be sure. About the surgeon, I mean. That birth could have gone poorly today if she'd needed a c-section. Time wasn't our friend."

"Aye, well then you'll be thrilled to hear that I think I've snared an obstetrician from Tipperary. He should arrive with the surgeon if I can get him to commit. We've been blessed this year, I think. Hopefully, it's a trend." Liam nodded and headed out of her office, and toward the secret bungalow, west of the abbey.

It was within a small cluster of four houses, all temporary huts with hammocks for fishermen who traveled from the jungle or deep within the city. The place was a bit of a secret, though, and they were usually empty. Every once in a while a couple of men would be seen dropping off their gear and heading out on a boat.

A wealthy doctor had come to do some philanthropic work about ten years ago and acquired the little house. No bigger than an efficiency flat, he'd paid local workers to enclose it, wire it, and dig a cistern with a water filter. Then they'd hooked the house to a local sewer drain. Liam never trusted the water for consumption but the toilet flushed. Plumbing in Brazil was archaic by western standards and sewage sometimes made it into the river system. Peru was even worse and unfortunately, they were upriver from the Brazilians. The house had a big bed with a semi-clean mattress, sealed windows, and a wall mounted AC unit, which made it a comfortable oasis. The owner had a local handyman come and check on it quarterly, to keep everything running.

It was this aging, wealthy doctor's legacy. A place for the volunteer doctors to go and get some rest. Maybe have a tryst away from the watchful eyes of the sisters of St. Clare. No one on the current staff used it except him. Alyssa was happily married, as was Adam, and they just stayed in the staff quarters of the hospital. Liam liked it, though. It was quiet and cool. Back at the mission, it was hard to get sleep during the day with the orphanage nearby and the heat of the day coming through the windows. After his initial three months was over, his overseeing doctor, a man from Australia, had bequeathed him the key and returned home to his normal job.

He walked the path west, breathing in the scent of the rainforest air. It was warm and wet; so fresh and alive. So different from the smells inside the hospital or coming out of the cantina. It was raw and slightly peppery, smelling like leaves, both dead and alive. The air was thick and dense, almost creamy. And that moisture would gather and hang in the air for only so long, until it could hold it no longer, and then the rain would begin. It was a fifteen-minute walk if he took his time, and he did. The rain began, as he knew it would, but he didn't care. It made him feel clean, coated his skin like a touch. He missed being touched.

When he finally made it to the opening, he climbed the stairs to the small oasis, using his key to walk into the cool, dim house. Unlike the cottages in Ireland, it was on stilts, due to the flooding. He left his shoes on the mat inside the door. He'd been warned not to leave them on the porch, which was sound advice. He didn't need a wandering spider making a home in there while he slept, or a bullet ant. Two of Brazil's deadliest creepy crawlers. He replaced the rolled up towel that stopped up the crack under the door. Next, he took a stick and checked the rafters and under the furniture for snakes, and he checked the bedding for scorpions or spiders as well. It was a ritual that had to be observed because some of these creatures would kill him before he managed to get himself to the hospital. He always went liberal with the pesticides before he left the house, as he only managed to get down here maybe once or twice a week. Better to die slowly over a fifty year period from pesticide exposure than to die writhing in pain from some poisonous little bastard lying in wait.

He stripped, walking nude to the small bathroom as the AC washed over his whole body, making his skin tingle and his muscles tighten. He looked at himself in the mirror, thinking about what the abbess had said. He hadn't lost weight. When his clothes had become a little baggy, he'd weighed himself in the clinic. He was actually up a couple of pounds. Gone was the soft, boyish remnants of a life spent in the library. He'd led the life of a student. Out of all the O'Brien men, he'd been the slimmest. Never chubby, just smooth and slim because he didn't have the physically taxing jobs that they did. He'd been the brainy one that liked to hit the pub.

While at school, he'd squeezed in a run twice a week just to clear his head, or played football in the yard with some of his mates. Now his body was strong, muscular, tanner than he'd ever been on his arms and legs. He did a lot of work around the abbey. When he didn't have patients, he pitched in with the more physically demanding jobs. He unloaded supplies, helped Paolo outside, chopped wood for the cantina. The Reverend Mother was probably around seventy. The other sisters were varying ages but all small of stature. As a long-term staff member, it was only right that he pitched in.

After his six-month commitment was up, the abbess had begun giving him a weekly stipend. It was modest, but it was a gesture. The average salary per month in Brazil was equivalent to about six hundred euro. Sure, some aspects of the cost of living were way less expensive than Europe, but it was still drastically low wages. She'd given him a stipend of five hundred Brazilian Real a week, which was just about a hundred and thirty Euro. Slave wages, but it was more than most of the full-time, local staff made. Only Margaritte, a nurse who had worked there for eight years, made more than he did. Pedro, his lab assistant, had a wife and child at home and survived on less, but he loved his work. Loved working for the abbey.

He didn't want to take the salary, but the abbess was as stubborn as any Mullen or O'Brien he'd ever met. She was showing him that he was no longer a visiting doctor who was scratching that philanthropic itch. He'd shown his worth, he'd stayed because he knew they needed him, and she'd insisted on him taking a small wage. The first thing he'd done was replace the AC units in the treatment rooms they used most often. The old ones dripped, which was a sterilization issue if they ever wanted to get this hospital up to par. Then he'd bought a new swing set for the orphanage, one that wasn't a tetanus shot waiting to happen.

He didn't need the money. They fed and housed him and gave him a burner phone. His only indulgence was a lager and a meal at a local restaurant once a week. It was on the river and was little more than a shack, but the beer was cold.

He continued to study himself in the mirror. His reflection was so strange to him because he didn't really bother to look in the mirror very often. His body was a vehicle that got him from place to place. His eyes and hands were tools. He'd toned his body almost by accident, but the rest of him was a little rough around the edges. His hair was long and had golden highlights from the sun. His beard was brown and tinged with a bit of red, similar to his brother Patrick's hair. It covered the handsome face and quick smile that had charmed more than a few lasses out of their knickers in his youth. His face had changed, though, hadn't it? He looked older and meaner. If his family saw him now, they wouldn't recognize him. He ran his hand over the beard again. He should shave it. It was hot in the warmer months. It wasn't one of those lumbersexual, Instagram beards. He gave himself some credit. He kept it trimmed. He shook himself, needing to get cleaned up so he could get a nap.

He used bottled water to brush his teeth and wash his face. Then he took the beard comb he'd been gifted and used it to scratch under his beard. It felt good. Smelled good as well, the cedar smell coming through the pores of the wooden comb. He set the comb back down and ran his fingers through his unruly hair. It was down to his shoulders now. He marveled at the resemblance to his little brother before

Seany had cut his hair. The same blue eyes, just like their father. Sean Jr. must be twenty-one now. Living in Liam's flat in Dublin. The thought of the youngest brother threatened to break through his defenses, so he switched his mind off. He went to the bed, stretched out onto the soft, cotton bedding, and fell into a deep, dreamless sleep.

3

Dublin, Ireland

Seany stood in the arrivals area, watching for a familiar face. Izzy Collier was hard to miss. She was gorgeous, taller than the petite women in his family, and she had a mane of caramel-colored hair. She was easily ten years older than him, but that didn't diminish her effect. She was hands-off, of course. His sister-in-law Alanna, another beauty, was pinned down at his mother's house with a sick toddler and infant. So, she'd called him in a panic, asking him to pick her friend up at the airport. Just when he started thinking that she'd missed her connection, he saw her. She did a double take before a grin spread across her pretty face.

"I didn't know she'd send a hot fireman to pick me up," Izzy said as she winked at him. He pulled her into his arms for a hug and a kiss.

"It's good to see you, lass." Seany cupped her hair in his hands. "You're about ten inches lighter. It looks lovely on you."

"Yes, I donated it. It was a good time for a change."

"Beautiful and kind. Are you sure you don't like younger men?" he teased. She laughed as he helped her with her bags. "Christ, Izzy. How long are you staying? You've got enough luggage to clothe a village." She ignored the question and he cocked a brow at her.

"It's a long story."

"It's a two-hour drive," he fired back, suppressing a grin that was pure O'Brien charm.

She sighed. "Right. Let's get on the road and I'll spill." He looked at her, not getting the slang. "Spill my guts. Confess all."

"Ah, best get to it, then." Seany handed her the smaller bag with wheels and slung the large, military duffel over his shoulder.

"Jesus, Izzy. Does Alanna know you're doing this?" Sean Jr. was shaking his head, hardly believing what Izzy had done.

"No, not yet. I thought I'd tell everyone when I got to town. I didn't want them trying to talk me out of it. Liam sent word, I know. He's alive and kicking and has requested that the family give him his space and not try to come after him, but this not calling shit...not even when he didn't come home, not even when Brigid and Branna had their babies." She shook her head. "This is bullshit. Someone's got to yank a knot in his tail. This is killing your mother. And I'm not family. I'm just me. I can do whatever the hell I please." Seany swallowed hard. Then he abruptly pulled the car over on the side of the road, slammed it in park, got out of the car before Izzy knew what was happening, and yanked her door open. He pulled her out of the passenger seat and hugged her so hard, she thought he was going to break a rib.

"Thank you. Oh, God Izzy. Thank you." Izzy melted into the hug, putting her arms around his waist. "This is killing my parents. All of us. It's like a shadow over the family." He let her go and she saw he was fighting tears. So was she.

"It's not that big of a deal, Seany. The mission really needed a surgeon and I'm on terminal leave," she explained. Not wanting the hero worship she saw in his eyes. "I just saw an opportunity to help your family and it worked out."

"Don't even try it, lass. If this was just about charity work, you could have done that from the States." She shut her eyes, willing herself to stay composed. These O'Briens were an emotional bunch, and that hug had thrown her for a loop. Seany was way too young, and she didn't feel that way about him. It was just that she hadn't been held in a long time, and even at twenty-one, she felt the passion in him. Not for her, not sexually, but the innate passion that ran through his bloodline.

"Just get back on the road, Seany. I need to get to Alanna…and Sorcha. I want to be with them when I explain it all. I can only stay through the weekend because the abbess needs to meet with me. I've got supplies to haul, arrangements that need to be finalized."

Seany gave her a shy smile and said, "You can stay with me. Tadgh's got a full house, but Liam's room is empty. I move out next month, but we've got it for now. No funny business, I promise. I realize that I tease you a lot, but I know when to behave. You could stay with Patrick and Caitlyn if you aren't comfortable." He was blushing. This big, hunky fireman was actually blushing.

Izzy smiled at that. "I never doubted you were a gentleman. Thanks for the offer. I think Alanna will want to drive me back, but I'll take the room offer once I get back to Dublin on Monday. I know you have to work tomorrow night. I appreciate the lift. Why do you have to move out of your apartment?"

"Well, the arrangement was for six months, wasn't it? Liam put the funds aside, but the money ran out. The landlord isn't as civic-minded as the man who owns Tadgh and Patrick's building. I can't afford the full rent. I tried to find a roommate within the fire department, but most of them are married. I didn't want to live with a stranger. I'll live with Patrick until something opens up in his building. Besides, I may not stay in Dublin. I miss the West coast. Dublin's a bit fast for me, and it has some bad memories."

"You mean about Eve?" She said softly.

He nodded. "Partly, but being in Liam's apartment has been hard. He lived there for six years, his stuff is everywhere. When he left early, he didn't tell anyone. Honestly, after a few days of no one hearing from him, I feared the worst. Tadgh and I went to the apartment. It was before I'd moved in, ye see." He swallowed, grinding his jaw. "I thought I was going to find him hanging. We walked into the apartment and it was spotless. Everything was in order. There was a note on the coffee table. I ran to the bath…"

"Oh Jesus, honey. I'm so sorry you had to deal with that. You and Tadgh. He just wasn't thinking. You know that, right? He just fled. He wasn't thinking clearly. He probably thought you all would try to talk him out of it."

Seany nodded. "Aye, I know. I get it. Losing Eve like that? I can't even imagine. O'Brien men fall hard. They love deeply, they don't stray, they protect their women. I'm not sure he'll ever get over it." He cleared his throat. "But I miss him. I need to get out of that apartment, for my own sake. Da is renting a truck to haul his stuff to Doolin. They'll store it for him. I can't wait him out on this. I have to take care of myself."

"Of course you do. It's the right thing to do. And who knows, maybe I'll do some good. Maybe I can get him to video conference you or something. And I wasn't bullshitting about the job. It's a great opportunity. A once in a lifetime chance to do something really great with my talent. Soon I'll be working in some hospital with three bosses and malpractice insurance. I'm really looking forward to helping St. Clare's. Don't underestimate how self-serving I am."

But Seany knew. She was doing this for them. For his mother. The affection he felt for her bloomed into something almost brotherly, replacing the tiny crush he had on her. He felt like she belonged with them as if he were taking her home.

Doolin, Co. Clare, Ireland
The house was full, packed with O'Briens and Murphys. Izzy held baby Isla while Alanna changed Davey's pull-up. "Okay, little man. Remember, you need to tell momma if you have to go potty. Got it? That pull-up is just a safety net. Big boys go on the potty." She stood

up, washed her hands, and took Isla from her friend, handing the baby off to her husband. Aidan crooned endearments to the little girl, completely in love. Then Izzy watched as he looked at her friend. Stars in his eyes. They'd been married almost four years, and he was still besotted.

Alanna was a beautiful woman. Smart, too. And she was passionate about her work with wounded veterans. They were a beautiful couple who made gorgeous babies. As happy as she was for them, she envied them, too. She hadn't ever managed to make the relationship thing stick. Too much work, too much moving.

Caitlyn spoke up from across the room, interrupting her pity roll. "Izzy, love. Alanna never told us how you two met. Did you work at the hospital together?"

Izzy laughed, "No, not so dignified as all that." She gave Alanna a sideways glance. Caitlyn looked at Alanna for an explanation.

Alanna spread her hands dramatically. "Picture this, I'm teaching my first Zumba class." Izzy was stifling her giggles. "I've memorized the routine, all ready to wow the class with my teaching skills and my moves. But you know how those classes are. Anytime the teacher or the routine changes, or you get a new student, someone's off rhythm. They don't know the moves yet. So, I'm trying my best to keep everyone with me. Then I see this one." She points a thumb at Izzy. "She tried to play along for a while, but finally she just gave up and started doing her own thing. And she wasn't discreet about it. She was shaking her moneymaker, letting out a whoop or two, hands in the air. The Marines in the class were mesmerized….I mean….y'all have seen her booty in action." Caitlyn was holding her stomach, tears coming down. Everyone was laughing.

"Hey, I can't help who I am! I can't sit still when there's a good beat going!" Izzy was smiling.

"So, it kind of broke the tension of me trying to host the perfect class. It started being fun, and I knew without a doubt that I had to have some more Izzy in my future." She threw her arms around Izzy's neck, giving her a big, messy kiss on the cheek.

Caitlyn's laughing died down, and she took a deep breath. "I think I've got a stitch in my side. I haven't had a good laugh in a while."

Sorcha smiled at her and put a hand on her tummy. "It's those muscles stretching. It's a good sign."

That's when Izzy saw a barely noticeable bulge. "Oh! Oh my God! Congratulations!" She knew how much trouble Caitlyn had had. Two miscarriages early in the first trimester, and a lot of trouble conceiving in between. "How far along are you, sweetie?"

Caitlyn's smile turned fragile, fear striking a blow to her mood. "Sixteen weeks. I've made it to the second trimester."

"Well, that's some great news." Izzy's voice was uncharacteristically gentle.

"Speaking of good news," Seany said, giving her a pointed look. This didn't escape Alanna's notice.

"You have something to tell us." It wasn't a question. So Izzy asked everyone to sit down and she started.

"As you all know, I've just separated from the Navy. I'm on terminal leave as of midnight last night. I have sixty days of leave to burn before I'm officially out." Izzy looked at Alanna, and her friend clapped her hands together.

"Are you staying with us for two months? Oh, Izzy! You can come back to England with me!"

Izzy shook her head. "No, no. Sorry. That's not the plan."

"What is the plan then, lass?" Sean Sr., the patriarch of the group, was as smart as he was handsome. His eyes were serious.

"I've signed up for a three month medical mission. I...I'm going to Brazil. I'm going to be the surgeon for St. Clare's Charity Mission in Manaus." The group just stared at her. Sorcha spoke first.

"St. Clare's? That's where..."

Izzy finished, "Where Liam is. Yes."

"Have you spoken to him? Did he set this up?" Sean asked.

Izzy let out a big sigh. "No, he doesn't know I'm coming and the abbess has agreed not to tell him. They need a surgeon, and it was one of my conditions."

"Jesus Christ, you're setting up an ambush," Patrick said, a large grin spreading across his face.

"I know you all agreed to leave him be, that you're giving him space. I know you're afraid to push. I never agreed to any of that, however. I know the toll this has taken on Aidan and Alanna...and Seany." She gave him a knowing look. "And that can't even begin to compare with what his parents are going through." She heard a soft sob come from Sorcha as Sean put his arm around her.

Michael spoke now, holding his sleeping son in his arms. Brigid was next to him holding her son as well, starting to cry silently. Finn kissed her on the temple. Michael said, "You're taking the last paid leave you have in the Navy to go find my brother?" His eyes misted.

Aidan spoke next. "Izzy, this is your time to adjust and transition out of the military. To look for a job. We can't ask you to do this."

Izzy smiled. "Don't worry Captain, I've got three job offers waiting. I told them all that I had this thing I needed to do first. I'd make my decision soon, but that I needed this time to do some philanthropic work. It actually worked it to my advantage. Two of the hospitals, that really want me, offered to send supplies to the mission. I managed to mooch some surgical equipment, field trauma kits, and a mobile defibrillator. The supplier freighted it right to Brazil. Reverend Mother Faith was more than willing to throw your brother under the bus for better equipment."

Patrick barked out a laugh. "Sneaky lass. Remind me not to make an enemy of you." She smiled, but her eyes were still on Sorcha.

Sorcha stood and walked to her, kneeling down and taking Izzy's hands in hers. "I know you can't make him come home, but I love you for doing this. If I could just see his face and talk to him. See his eyes." She sobbed, "My lad. Oh, my sweet boy."

Izzy held her, comforting her.

"Why would you do this for us? It seems like too much to ask." Michael said.

"You didn't ask. And I didn't ask y'all for permission. Look, I know you don't know me that well. Honestly, this isn't as selfless as you might think. This is a great opportunity. I can come home and take some job in a nice, sterile hospital with all the equipment I could possibly need. Backing from big pharm, big insurance, and that's all okay. But this…this is a challenge. It's a chance to step into a situation where I'm really needed. I can make things better for this place, train a surgical team, use what I learned in field medicine, improve the medical care at St. Clare's. This thing with Liam, it's only part of it. A big part, yes. But where I come from, if you can do something to help, then it's your duty to help. I can step into this situation on a level that you all can't. Listen, I liked Eve. She was a sweet lady. What happened to her was beyond tragic. It's like a nightmare. I didn't know her that well, but she loved your boy. If she was standing here right now, I feel like she'd be cheering me on. Someone's got to go. I'm not family. I'm able to separate myself emotionally. Liam and I don't have any history to speak of. Maybe I'll be able to talk some sense into him, where others have failed. All I want to do is try."

Izzy walked into the kitchen where Sorcha was doing dishes. "Where do you want me, momma?" She'd agreed to stay one night with the O'Briens, but Hans and Mary had threatened to come drag her out if she didn't stay one night with them. Hans was such a good man. A single father and hard ass Marine. When she'd met him, he'd still been active duty. He'd also been handsome and tragically single. Doc Mary was pretty much perfect for him.

Sorcha turned to her and Izzy saw the tears. "I'm sorry, Sorcha. I'm so sorry you're hurting." Sorcha wiped her hand over her cheeks. Then she took Izzy's hand and led her into the bedroom.

She sat on the bed and pulled Izzy down next to her. "This was Liam and Seany's room. There used to be bunk beds in here. Sean Jr. was a bit of a surprise, so you can imagine what it was like when Patrick moved to Aidan and Michael's room. Patrick and Liam were so close in age, so Liam was mortified when we set up the crib in his room. Thought we were sticking him in the baby room. He wanted to go with the other lads."

She shook her head. "But when I came home with little Seany, Liam never said another word. It had occurred to him that he wasn't the youngest anymore. That he would be a big brother, just like his brothers. He said, *I'll watch over him. You don't have to worry. I'll teach him how to play football and the guitar. I'll be a good big brother, Mammy.*" Sorcha's tears still fell, and Izzy felt her own tears well up. "And he was right. He was a good big brother. He's been good at everything he's ever done. Everything always came so easily. But this loss, this grief? It's like the earth dropped out from under him. It wasn't something he could fix, or work hard and overcome. It was soul-sucking. I don't know how to help him. I've failed him."

Izzy hugged her, offering what words she could in support. But inside of her, there was a battle going on. Suddenly she was pissed at Liam. He wasn't the only one who'd lost something on that Dublin street. Indirectly, the O'Brien's had lost a son. He'd fled and not looked back. Suddenly she couldn't wait to get to Brazil. She was going to have a *come to Jesus* meeting with Liam O'Brien.

Izzy was changing into her pajamas after she washed her face. She heard a knock on her bedroom door. Cora stepped in shyly, unsure about the intrusion. "There's my girl! Come give Auntie Izzy a hug!" Cora ran to her.

"How was school?"

Cora sighed dramatically as she plopped on the bed. "Ghastly. There are some new girls, blow-ins from County Limerick. They aren't very nice."

"You want me to beat 'em up for you. I got your back, little sister." Izzy nudged her, making her smile.

"No, I can handle them. They just think they're terribly clever and smart, and they heard some things about me." She looked sideways at Izzy. "About what I can do. About the dreams."

"Ah, I gotcha. Did you threaten to put a spell on them?" This made Cora laugh, as she'd meant it to.

"Heavens, no. Sister Francis would have a stroke. I just ignored them. They're not the first." Cora paused. "You're not family, so you'd tell me the truth, right?"

"Of course. I'm known for being overly blunt. What's the question?" Izzy prodded.

"Do you think I'm a freak?"

Izzy was taken aback. "God, no! Of course not. I think you're amazing, Cora. I'd give anything to have that kind of gift."

"Really? Truly?"

"Absolutely, little sister. You are the shit, Cora Murphy. Don't ever doubt it." Cora popped a hand over her mouth and giggled. Izzy blushed. "Sorry, that one popped out."

Cora gave her a dry look. "Ye've met my mother. She curses like a bloody sailor. But I'm glad. I'm glad you don't think I'm a freak. I need my lady tribe." Izzy bit her cheek, not wanting Cora to think she was laughing at her. A nine-year-old saying she needed a lady tribe was just about the best thing she'd heard all year.

"You've got one, Miss Thing. Always."

"Ma said I could stay here if you didn't mind. I could help Auntie Alanna with the babies."

"Of course I don't mind. You can bunk in with me. I'm anticipating one of those big Sorcha breakfast spreads. Did you bring your dance game?" Cora nodded excitedly.

"Okay, baby girl. Bring on girls' night!"

4

I t was the middle of the night when Izzy heard Cora stirring. She opened her eyes, and Cora was still asleep. She was dreaming. "Cora, honey, wake up. You're dreaming." Cora's eyes popped open, and a single tear came down her cheek.

"You wanna tell me about it?" She said, both their faces lit by the moonlight.

"I saw Auntie Eve."

Izzy swallowed hard, the hair standing up all over her body. "Yeah. Were you scared?"

Cora shook her head. "No, but…" Another tear came down and her face got a determined look. She put her hand on Izzy's cheek. "You must follow the river. Eve said, when the time comes, you must remember to follow the river. It's important. She wouldn't have come to me otherwise. Do you understand?"

"Yes, baby. I understand. I promise I'll remember."

The breakfast crowd was huge. Michael and Branna were absent, but Tadgh, Charlie, and Josh were all there bright and early. They'd been to the island to see Tadgh's mother. "Can I ride back with Seany?" Josh asked.

Charlie's mouth was full of pastry, so Tadgh answered. "Of course you can. You don't have to ask, Josh. Just have the hookers out by Sunday night and don't be late for class."

Charlie smacked him and he winked at Josh. "Sorry, she's right. Don't pay for it. There's plenty of young lasses that'll give it up for free, as you know."

"Tadgh!" Charlie chided. Seany, Josh, and Tadgh were all laughing now. Aidan was shaking his head, trying to suppress a grin. "You aren't funny. I was traumatized!"

Izzy gave Tadgh a questioning look and Josh was turning red. "Aye, well. Josh has been quite the novelty at the school, you know, with that Yank accent and those big swimmer muscles. Charlie had the unfortunate luck of walking into the apartment while he was getting to second base with a film student from Trinity."

"Third base," Josh corrected. Which prompted Seany to say, "Niiiiiiice," and give him a fist bump.

Sorcha interrupted. "Excuse me, lads. I hate to interrupt your bragging and conquests, but we have ladies present. Behave or I'll box your ears." Then she pointed her spatula at Josh. "And you, lad. Do I need to have the condom talk with you?"

Josh covered his ears. "No, Auntie Sorcha. God, I'll behave. No more sex talk!"

Alanna put her arm around Izzy as the group settled into the morning. Izzy said, "Where's Cora? With the babies?"

Izzy nodded. "That was sweet of you to let her hang out with you last night. She's an amazing kid."

Izzy rubbed the top of her lip nervously. "Yeah, about that. She had a dream last night."

Alanna stiffened. "A regular dream or a Cora dream?" But Alanna could tell the answer before Izzy gave it.

"She said Eve came to her." Alanna's breath shot out. "I'm not going to lie. It rattled me."

Alanna thought before she spoke. "I come from a psychology background. I never gave parapsychology a second thought. A lot of

29

my colleagues mocked it outright. I just didn't think one way or the other. I try to use the logical approach that I was taught. But I'm going to tell you something, Izzy Collier, Cora doesn't make stuff up and she's not comfortable sharing her gift. It's been a blessing and a curse to her." She put her hand on Izzy's arm and looked her square in the eye. "If she told you something, she did it for a reason. You heed what she said. You bet your life on it."

The goosebumps were back. "All right. I hear you, sister. I'll remember."

Hans slid a cup of tea in front of Izzy as Mary took some warm bread out of the oven. "It's got walnuts and cranberries. I didn't think to ask about nut allergies."

"No worries, Mary. I'm allergy free." Hans sat at the table, giving her a hard stare. "Come out with it big Daddy. Get the safety brief out of the way." Laughter burst out of his chest and he just shook his head. "Izzy, do you have to be such a hard-ass?" He put his hands up, "I mean, we know I love the tough ones, that one's going to be the death of me," he said as he pointed a thumb in Mary's direction.

"I'm going to be careful. This is a medical mission. I'm not landing in a hot zone."

He got serious fast. "Listen to me, and pay attention. The drug cartels, the disease, the poverty, illegal logging, illegal miners, fucking cheetahs."

"Jaguars, my love. Wrong continent," Mary said sweetly.

He threw a hand up. "Whatever. You catch my meaning. Arguably a hot zone would be safer. You'd have a platoon of Marines watching your ass. Not a bunch of nuns and nurses. Did your parents agree to this?" Now it was Izzy's turn to laugh.

"Hans, honey, I'm thirty years old. They didn't get a vote." He twisted his mouth, trying not to dig himself in any deeper.

Mary sat down with a plate of steaming bread and butter. "I think it's grand altogether. I'd love to join you. It took six months of sitting on my ass and five unwanted pounds for me to go back to work part-time."

Hans grinned. "I like those extra five pounds just where they are." Izzy was giggling with a mouth full of bread.

Mary gave him a sideways grin. "Aye, I've noticed. That aside, consider yourself on an intel gathering mission. Perhaps we can recruit from my contacts. It sounds like they are short-handed."

Hans gave her a look. "Not for me, for other people." She patted his cheek, but the narrowed gaze stayed fixed.

St. Clare's Charity Hospital- Manaus, State of Amazonas, Brazil
Liam had Margaritte wipe his brow as he looked down at the current dilemma before him. "How far out is Antonio? Did he come from bloody Rio? I need him!"

Alyssa spoke up. "He just called and he's three minutes away. Paolo has him in the Jeep."

Liam cursed, looking at the man on his table. The deep laceration was holding under the pressure, but he'd lost a lot of blood. He'd missed the artery, but his trapezius muscle was severed. They'd doped him up on as much morphine as they dared, but they needed a surgeon. "When the hell does that new surgeon arrive? This shit is happening too often. I could sew him up, but these muscles and nerves are severed. It's going to need some finesse. I need Antonio yesterday. How's that O-neg coming?"

Margaritte switched out the bag, nodding to him. "That's the last one, médico."

Just then, someone busted through the swinging doors. "Antonio, Jesus. Get your ass over here with that needle and thread."

Izzy de-boarded the plane, walking into a blast of humidity. "Whew, that'll get your attention." The man next to her laughed.

"Aye, a bit balmier than Tipperary. Now, what's the chap's name again who's meeting us?"

"Raphael. He's short, brown hair, brown eyes, tan skin." She said, hiding her smile.

"Ye've just described half the bloody airport."

"The abbess said he'd have a sign. We need to worry about our luggage. I paid top dollar for my oversized luggage to get here, and I'm going to be pissed if it's not waiting for me."

It was there, thankfully, along with some supplies that the abbey in Dublin had sent with Dr. O'Keefe. Izzy sighed in relief when she saw a man standing with a sign for Dr. Collier and Dr. O'Keefe. She approached him and stuck out her hand. "You must be Raphael."

He shook her hand and smiled, his sun-baked face looking almost sweet. "Boa tarde, Médica."

"Obrigado, Senhor," she answered.

O'Keefe said, "I thought ye said you had no Portuguese?"

"That's the extent of my knowledge unless I'm looking for the head."

He laughed. "I can't believe you took this job if you didn't speak the language. Why didn't you go to Columbia or Peru? They speak Spanish."

"I had my reasons. I'll hire an interpreter." That's when she realized Raphael was listening to them both. He smiled. "Well then, Dr. Collier. You're in luck on this day. My English is very good."

They loaded the gear into the Jeep. The top was up but the doors were off. "So, besides the Brazilian form of Uber, what do you do, Raphael?"

He shrugged. "This is temporary. I give the sisters at St. Clare's a discount because it's the right thing, yes? I was in the Army." He turned onto the main road and continued. "I was good with languages. I can follow some of the tribal languages as well. Then I got injured in my shoulder." He thumped his left shoulder. "They made me auxiliary forces. I am strong now, I have surgery from Dr. Antonio, who you will meet. He's a bom médico. I wish to go back, be in the Army again, but it's not so easy once you leave. For now, I am serving in the auxiliary forces. Like your reserves."

"A military man, eh? That's a coincidence. I just got out of the Navy. I get what you're saying. It was a big decision. They don't often let you change your mind, and I had to be sure it's what I wanted."

"Yes, a Navy doctor. Very good. I meet some of your Marines in training. They are good fighters."

"So how about it Raphael, are you looking for work? I need an interpreter and a tutor. I need to get conversational fast. What's the going rate?"

"Now you've done it. You've got to learn to haggle in this country, lass." O'Keefe finally interrupted from the backseat.

"Raphael wouldn't cheat another military member, would you?"

"Well, you'll have some help at the abbey if you need it. Some of the sisters and doctors are bilingual, but I can work with you if you really need it. Ten Real an hour and I will be at your command, Dr. Collier. The wet season is coming, and that cuts down my driving. Too many drivers inside the city and fewer tourists. Can you pay this wage?"

O'Keefe raised his brows. "That's not bad, lass. I'd take it."

It was robbery. It was a little over three dollars an hour. "Do you have a family, Raphael?" His smile transformed his face. "Yes, I have my beautiful Milena. She give me two boys. Eduardo and Marcos. Bons rapazes, good boys." He was already teaching her. She repeated the phrase. Then she said, "Make it twelve an hour plus meals. I'll work it out with Reverend Mother Faith." It was about $600 a month to be at her beck and call. She was living with free room and board while the Navy was paying her housing allowance and a full salary, at least for the next two months. She could afford to pay this guy for his help. "We'll take it week by week and see how good of a student I am. Fair enough?" She put her palm out, making eye contact over her aviator sunglasses.

"Sim, Medica. It's very much fair enough."

Izzy looked around. They were out of the main city center. There were houses stacked on top of each other; shacks really. They were right at the river's edge. "The slums, lass. St. Clare's does a mobile clinic once a week. Get used to the smell." Izzy bounced in the Jeep, staring at the poverty. Then they were away from it, the shacks giving way to green. Raphael pulled off onto an access road, and they were consumed by rainforest on all sides.

Liam walked down the hallway of the hospital, toward the lab. As he rounded the corner, he almost went ass over tea kettle as he tripped on some boxes that were stacked in the hall. Big boxes. "For feck sake, Pedro. Get these boxes put away! Someone's going to break their neck!"

Pedro, Liam's lab assistant, poked his head out of the lab. "Sister Catherine said to leave them there until the new doctor comes." Pedro studied in America for six years, so his English was excellent. Better even than Margaritte and Sister Maria, the Brazilian nurse and the sister that helped in the orphanage.

"Have you had a look at the cultures from the woman who came in pregnant and the newborn? Did the baby grow anything?"

"O bebê is clear. We checked the blood, urine, and stool. A mãe is positive for giardia and negative for schistosomiasis, hookworm, malaria, dengue, Zika, and cryptosporidium."

Liam sighed. That didn't explain why he couldn't keep her fever from going up and down. He said, testily, "Portuguese or English, Pedro. Pick one."

Pedro laughed, "Why? You understood me, didn't you?"

"Not the point. The new doctors may not be as proficient and you're going to confuse them. Can you go call our city lab and check on that biopsy I sent in last week? I see the patient this week and I need a definitive answer." He knew the answer. It was cancer. But he needed the results before they could put the mother of three on a waitlist for an oncologist. She also needed scans done. Another waitlist. Only the wealthy got fast treatment in this country.

"Sim, I'll go to the office and call right now." Pedro left and Liam put a slide into his microscope, checking the water samples he'd taken in the cantina. They'd had a couple of sick kids this week, and he wanted to make sure the water supply was still sound. Gabriella rinsed raw stuff with bottled water, per his instructions, and she was good about her cooking heat, but he needed to make sure. One of the kids had been a toddler, and that could go bad fast when you couldn't keep the child hydrated. He didn't look up as the door opened again. "Back so soon? I really need those feckin' results, brother. And tell the abbess those boxes can't stay in the hall. I don't give a shite what the new doctor says about it."

"That new doctor would love them moved. Into the surgery if you're offering." Izzy stood in the doorway, almost unable to get the words out. He looked so different.

Liam looked up, his eyes shooting in the direction of the voice. Something was slightly familiar about it. The woman was about 5' 6", loose, caramel curls cropped above the shoulders around a pretty face. And the eyes… "You cut your hair."

Izzy was propped comfortably against the door frame. "You didn't," she said with a smile.

"The length suits you."

"Ditto, although I was kidding about the beard," she said. That made the corner of his mouth turn up.

"Well, you can feel free to tell the family I'm alive and well. Now, I have work to do. Goodbye, Izzy. Go back to Virginia."

She laughed. The blasted woman actually laughed. "Sorry, Senhor. I'm afraid I can't do that. See, I promised the abbess three months and some nice new equipment. So, maybe you should be the one to go back home."

He narrowed his eyes at her. "The reverend mother knew about this? That I knew you?"

A voice came from behind Izzy. "Yes, Dr. O'Brien. I did. Dr. Collier contacted the Dublin abbey and we were thrilled to get someone of her caliber here to get the surgery up and running."

Liam sighed. One stubborn woman was a piece of cake. He knew from experience that two was a whole different ballgame. "And your job? No way the Navy let you have three months off."

Izzy came off the door frame, straightening. "I'm out. I have two months of leave left then I'm done. So, where's my hug O'Brien? That is…if you're done being all broody and aloof."

"I'll leave you two to catch up," the Reverend Mother said, suppressing a smile. Then she ghosted back down the hall.

Izzy came into the room, and Liam stared down at his microscope. "They're all okay. I'll tell you everything when you're ready." He shut his eyes. Her voice was uncharacteristically even and calm."Maybe later, then. Now, Dr. O'Brien. How about a tour?" She hooked her arm in his, pulling him off the stool. "That slide can wait, right? Show me around." He stood in place. She cocked a brow. "I brought duty-free." Her toothy grin disarmed him and he coughed out a laugh. That's when she hugged him. The contact was unexpected. Not because Izzy wasn't a hugger. She was, and he had been one once as well. Especially when the squeezing involved a pretty lass. It's just that he hadn't been hugged in almost a year. Not since his mother had held him. A few hugs around the neck from the children at the orphanage, sure. But he hadn't been in someone's arms for a long time. He wasn't sure what to do, but his body took over. He sank into her, returning the hug.

"I'm just here to help. I'm here to help St. Clare's and you." She pulled back, looking at him. "You look good. I was afraid of what I'd find. Almost unrecognizable, but good."

"Don't try the honeyed tongue with me, Isabelle Collier. I'm not done with you."

"It's Izzy, and I had no doubts. Now help me get this stuff into my new O.R."

"You don't like Isabelle?" he said as they walked and started moving boxes.

"It's not my name."

"Isabella," he said confidently.

"Wrong, and Izzy will be fine unless you want to call me Dr. Collier."

"Elizabeth?"

"Izzy."

He laughed on his way into the surgical room. "You know I'm going to find out." But she'd stopped playing along. She stared at the room as she put the box on the floor.

"Wow, this is it?" she asked.

"Yep, you aren't in Virginia anymore. Ready to go home?" Liam jibed.

"Bite me, O'Brien," she said casually as she looked around. The room was small, the equipment old. The only thing up to date in the room was the AC unit.

Liam noticed her gaze. "I replaced it. It was leaking and I thought that was a sterility issue. Antonio only uses the surgery once or twice a month, but it needs to be cool and clean."

Izzy looked around. It was clean, but she left nothing to chance. She'd do a full scrub down before she put the new equipment in place. "I brought compact trauma kits for the mobile unit. Where is the storage?"

"I'll show you. Let's get the rest of the boxes in. What did you bring?"

"New surgical tools, a replacement overhead light, an IV med. pump for recovery, and a case of face shields. Oh, and a mobile defibrillator."

"Jesus, Izzy. Did you steal stuff on the way out?" he teased.

"No, I squeezed the donations out of two of the three hospitals that want to hire me. The third is underfunded, so I decided not to hold it against them."

"In demand, but still you took three months in Brazil. Will they hold the positions?"

"I have to pick one by January first. They have doctors leaving after the holidays or retiring. One of the hospitals built a new surgical wing and needs more surgeons on staff when it opens. Construction is not done yet. It'll hold. If it doesn't, I will find something else. I can work as a civilian doc in a military hospital if I can't find something right away."

"Well, this isn't going to be what you're used to, Izzy. Let's get your supplies into storage and then I'll give you the full tour. You may not find it up to your standards."

She laughed softly, shaking her head. "Quit trying to get me to leave, Liam. I don't bail on obligations. You're going to hurt my little feelings if you keep it up."

He gave her a sideways glance, then opened a door. Izzy was pleasantly surprised to see that there were no supplies stored on the floor. Given the annual rainfall and pest problems, it was good. The door had a good seal as well. "Where do you keep the perishables? Vaccines, IV meds, banana bags, blood?"

"In the lab. We don't keep a lot of blood on hand since we don't do trauma patients. There's room for a bigger supply if the need arises." Izzy nodded, not feeling the need to comment.

Once she'd toured the entire hospital, they left through the front door. Liam waved at the Brazilian sister who manned the patient intake desk.

"So, it's small but self-sufficient. Undermanned, under-equipped. Still want to stay?" Liam asked. But he knew the answer. She had a spark in her eye. She liked a challenge.

"No less than some of the hospitals in combat zones. That x-ray machine is the only problem. It's archaic. Have they made sure it's safe?"

Liam nodded. "We don't fancy radiation poisoning. It is sound. It was donated from a veterinary clinic that was closing. The reason you think it's old is that it's a model that usually x-rays dogs and cats. It's not actually all that old."

Izzy laughed. "Ah, that explains it. The ultrasound machine is basic as well. O'Keefe is going to be missing that one in Tipperary."

"Yes, the OB-GYN. Excellent. We have a midwife, but no one to step in if it gets hairy. We lost a mother and child a few months back."

"I'm sorry. That must have been hard on the team. Sounds like you've been doing more than water samples and parasite research."

He threw his head back and laughed. "You have no idea. We just had an unexpected birth last week. Came in with a high fever, next thing you know I am helping deliver a baby."

She smiled, looking him in the eyes. "Your mother would absolutely love that. You should call her and tell her all about it." Sorcha had been working as a midwife for over thirty years.

Liam stiffened, then turned toward the orphanage. "The kids are this way. I'll introduce you."

"Liam, you should call home. We can video chat. I have my laptop."

He turned on her abruptly and pointed a finger at her. To her credit, she didn't take a step back. *Here we go. Bring it on, asshole.*

"You are welcome here in every professional capacity, Izzy. We need a surgeon. But my personal affairs are off limits. Not negotiable, or you can get right back on that feckin' plane."

She folded her arms over her chest like a man twice her size. Like she was thinking about which side of his face to smash. "Is that so?" Her voice was deceptively calm, almost husky. "Well, Dr. O'Brien. That shit might work on your family, maybe even on the abbess, but I am a whole different animal."

"You think you are going to come here and fix something? Be the family hero and return the prodigal son? Forget it. This is my personal shit-show and I get to choose how to run it."

"Is that what Eve would have wanted?"

"Watch it, Collier. I mean it." Liam's voice held a warning. "You don't know shit. You met Eve a couple of times, so you can keep your opinions about what she'd want to yourself."

She didn't even flinch, and Liam cringed a bit at how much of a dick he was being to her. Almost aggressive. His father would be ashamed. But that was him, now. The new Liam. Like it or not.

"You're right. I didn't know her that well. You did. So what would she have wanted, Liam? You need to think about that. The grieving lover thing worked ten months ago, even on me. Everyone bled for you. But it's been ten months! Would she have wanted you to hide here and cut everyone off? I know you haven't contacted your family. Have you contacted hers? You had her for three years, Liam. They had her for a lifetime, you arrogant prick! Have you checked on her siblings? I know you left your little brother to the wolves, so I can't imagine you're worried about them either." *Damn, Izzy. That was cold,* she thought to herself. He had her blood up, though, and she was just going to let it rip. Get the blow-out, that she knew was coming, out of the way. The sooner the war, the sooner the peace.

He reared back like she'd stung him. "What the hell is that supposed to mean?"

Suddenly she was tired. She shook her head, "You know what, never mind. You've obviously had those months to scrape your family off your shoe like unwanted gum. Any problems they've been dealing with, any heartache, probably won't even break the squelch with you. Let's go see the orphans. I need a shower, a meal, and a nap."

He blocked her retreat with his body. Steam was coming out of his ears. "Oh no, sweetheart. You don't get to drop a turd in the punchbowl and leave the party. You started this, you're going to finish it. What in the hell did you mean about Seany?"

She was overwhelmed with the urge to sweep the leg, knock him on his pretty ass, and put him in a chokehold until he turned purple. "Did you even think about how your departure affected him? He was supposed to have a roommate. He's young, starting a new job, moving to a big city. He thought you had his back. Now he's homeless and moving into Patrick's spare room." He wasn't technically homeless but she was on a roll.

"I set aside my share of the rent for him. I paid it all up front!"

"Yes, you did. Six months of rent. How long have you been gone, again?"

The realization showed on his face. He rubbed his face, bringing his hand down over his beard. "He could have sent word."

"You are such an idiot! You didn't call when your sister or sister-in-law had a baby. Which is staggering to me, given what has happened to Caitlyn and Patrick. You didn't call when Tadgh got married. You didn't call to see how your mother's annual cancer screening went or to check on your elderly grandparents. No birthday calls for your nieces and nephews. Not a goddamn word from you for months. Like he's really going to send word and bug you for money?" She rubbed her temples, feeling a headache coming on. The heat of the day, the traveling, the anger she was feeling, all settling into her temples.

She let out a breath to calm herself. "Liam, he's been living in a missing man's apartment. You left with no word. You said you were working over the holidays so you didn't have to see them. But you lied, didn't you? You were gone before he even moved in. Tadgh and Seany went to your apartment and saw your car out front. They walked that last mile up the stairway to your flat, wondering what kind of condition your body was going to be in when they took it home to your mother." Liam's face was contorted, confused. "I think his exact words were, *I expected to find him hanging. I went into the apartment and it was spotless. He'd left a note. I ran to the bath...*"

"Jesus Christ." Liam cursed under his breath, rubbing his eyes. Finally some emotion other than anger showing on his face. "They should've known I'd never do that to them."

"How, Liam? They were weaned on stories about O'Brien men and their women. They've seen your dad when Sorcha had cancer. Aidan when he almost lost Alanna. What exactly was it about your horrific tragedy that would make them not worry about you heading off the deep end? I barely knew Eve, and I cried for two hours straight after Alanna called me! Pull your head out of your ass, O'Brien!"

A little voice interrupted them. "Médico Up! Up!" The little girl was about three years old. She was pulling on the hem of Liam's shorts. Suddenly Izzy realized they'd drawn a crowd. A Sister scurried over to retrieve the child, but Liam waived her off.

Izzy lowered her voice. "That's enough. We can do this later. I'm sorry. I can be too blunt, sometimes."

Liam was holding the child, now. She pulled on his beard, giggling. He didn't meet Izzy's eyes. "Brigid and Branna, how were the births?"

Izzy exhaled. "Branna was high risk, but she's great. She went early, but your mother was ready. They took her to Galway before it became an emergency. Ian...they named him Ian. Brigid had no problems. She and Finn named him Declan, after Finn's father. Your family has a lot of boys. No wonder Cora is so tough."

He met her eyes, pain creeping past his strongly fortified defenses. His voice was strained. "And my mother?"

"She's clear, Liam."

He nodded, then he adjusted the child on his hip. "This is Estela. She lives here at the mission with us." Then he spoke in Portuguese. "Estela, this is our new médica, Izzy." The little girl put her head shyly in Liam's neck. "Use your manners, lass." He spoke in English this time. The child was obviously taught both at the school. Small favors.

"Oi, Médica. I'm pleasing to meet you." And that's when Izzy melted.

5

Sister Agatha took Liam and Izzy into the school room. There were two rooms, actually. One for primary children from four years old to ten. The other room was for the older students who were pre-teens and teenagers. The rooms were set up to be bilingual. Most things in Portuguese with the English equivalent under it. This was, after all, an Irish foreign mission. It made sense that given the number of English speaking volunteers that floated in and out, teaching the children both was practical. More tools to aid them in what must be a difficult start to their young lives. Little Estela was dragging Liam over to her painting that was displayed on the wall, and Izzy's heart squeezed. His face, when she'd made the comment about Cora, showed pain. He missed his family. He just didn't know how to transition from this life in Brazil to the one he'd had before he lost Eve.

"It's a very good school, Sister Maria. Clean and organized. Your students are very lucky to have you. Who helps you between the two classes?"

"It can be a challenge. Sometimes we get a visiting missionary who will help in the school. Sometimes I depend on the older kids. This is Genoveva. She is one of my older students and she helps me a great deal. Genoveva, please stand up and say hello to the new médica, Dr. Collier."

Izzy was surprised when the girl stood. She was tall for her age. As tall as Izzy, if not an inch more. She couldn't be more than fourteen. Her body language spoke volumes. She wasn't comfortable in her own skin, tried to make herself smaller, but Izzy couldn't understand that. She was solidly built. She looked strong, if not in attitude, at least physically. Strength was to be celebrated, honed. The girl wore a sloppy, big shirt and track pants. She was taller than almost all of the boys. Izzy wondered if she had a European parent. "Hello, Genoveva. How old are you?"

The girl was awkward. Painfully shy. She had long hair that she kept in a ponytail. When she finally met Izzy's eyes, Izzy almost gasped. The child's eyes were extraordinary. Green and glowing, not a common eye color for the native people. "I'm fifteen, Senhora."

"It's Senhorita. I know I'm old, but no one has managed to marry me yet." Liam and the sister stifled a laugh. "Well, it's very nice of you to help the sister. Maybe if you aren't too busy, you can help me some time. I'm getting the surgical facility in order, and I could use some help with work and my Portuguese."

Sister Maria translated and the girl's face lit up. "Sim, Senhorita...I mean, yes, Doctor. I would help."

Izzy looked over at some older boys that were writing on the chalkboard. They were looking over their shoulders, snickering at the girl. And not in the flirty, you're going to be a knock-out when you're twenty, honey, please be my girlfriend, kind of way. It was in a mean little dickhead, bullying way. Right. "So, Sister Agatha. I can't read what the boys are writing over and over again. Could you help me with a translation?"

She smiled, catching Izzy's observations. "It says, *I will not behave like a heathen baboon during class.*" Izzy cracked off a laugh, and Liam smiled at her. He raised his brows as if to say, *Welcome to life in a Catholic school.*

"I could use some help scrubbing floors and walls in the surgery. Are you against labor as punishment?" If it wasn't too lowly for a young private in boot camp, then it wasn't too lowly for these guys.

"Muito bom, Médica. Very good," said Sister Maria "Now, let Dr. O'Brien take you to the staff quarters. I'm sure you would like to be settling into your room. I will send the boys to the surgery tomorrow, after morning prayers, and Genoveva as well, if she wishes."

As they started to leave, Izzy turned back and addressed the girl. "It's a beautiful name, Genoveva. What does it mean?"

The girl turned crimson, clearing her throat. "It means leader. The leader of the Tribe." Her accent was beautiful.

"Well, that doesn't surprise me. A strong name for a strong girl. I'll see you tomorrow, Genoveva."

Liam watched as Izzy immediately got to work putting her gear away. Like she was staying...for three months. *Shit.*

"Between Iraq and Arizona, I thought I was familiar with hot weather. This is different. Damn. It's like Virginia in the summer, add a lot of bugs and a few degrees." As if on cue, she smacked her forearm.

"Jesus, lass. Don't you have bug repellent on?"

"Yes, sort of," She said sheepishly.

"Not that essential oil shite, surely?" Liam said, like she was a child.

"I have deet, I just haven't unpacked it yet."

Liam left abruptly, and she heard him go down the hall to the male locker room. He came back with a can of deet. "Right out of the shower. No perfume, no scented deodorant, use antibacterial soap in the bath." He popped the lid off and started spraying her as she sputtered and hopped.

"I read the freaking booklet! I get it!"

He stopped spraying and got eye level. "No, obviously you don't get it. Mosquitos kill people in this country. They aren't just a mild irritant. That mosquito net on the top of the wardrobe is an absolute necessity. They don't have screens in the windows."

"Then put screens in the windows. This isn't the middle ages!" She was tired and hungry and being pissy. She knew this.

"Paolo is working on it. He ordered rolled screening and velcro. It's the best we can do without doing major construction. The Abbey can't afford it. Antonio, the visiting surgeon, picks up our supplies on the West side of the city. He comes tomorrow. We'll cover the windows for you and Dr. O'Keefe."

"Did I hear my name?"

Liam turned to see a middle aged man, tall and stout, smiling as he came down the hall. "You must be O'Brien. Seamus O'Keefe. OB-GYN. Glad to finally meet you." Liam shook his hand.

"Aye, Tipperary is it?"

"Yes, in the country. You can keep the city life. Full of travelers and cheats."

Izzy laughed. "Surely all travelers aren't cheats."

Liam turned to her. "Travelers are what we call…well, I guess you'd call them gypsies. They're nomadic. A lot of mischief seems to follow them. Tipperary has had their problems with them. The countryside is lovely, though. Glad to have another Irishman aboard. Adam, our pediatrician, is from Sidney, but we'll forgive him for that. The men are severely outnumbered."

"Well, I'm used to that. My ex-wife and I have three daughters together. They're mostly grown, of course. Having a house full of women was a blessing and a curse. Even the dog had ovaries. It hardly seemed fair."

Izzy laughed, which drew Seamus's attention. "Did you see your surgical wing? I'll need to have a look as well. Apparently, I can expect the occasional c-section. The midwife, Sister Catherine, gave me a tour of the exam rooms, birthing room, and nursery. It's occurred to me that we don't have a general practitioner or family practitioner among us. All specialists."

Liam nodded. "Well, it's a small crew. We take who we can get. My advice is to start recruiting. The sisters aren't overly proficient in the art of computers. The Reverend Mother still sends handwritten letters."

"Well, I'll see what I can do. At least they have WiFi in the abbey library. Now, I'm off for a shower. Can you point me to the men's bath?"

Liam pointed to the door at the end of the hall. "It's clean, but don't drink the water. Use the water bottle to the left of the sinks." Then he pointed to the hall that led to the female locker room. "Yours is down at the end."

When the men left, Izzy sat on the edge of her small cot. It was clean, albeit a little lumpy. She was here. It didn't seem real. She was actually sleeping in a freaking convent. Her mother was raised Catholic. That was the Italian side of her family. Her father was a Presbyterian. The German and Welsh side, and he'd had no intention of converting. Her mother had conceded, saving mass days for Saturdays when her father was harvesting or helping her grandfather at the ranch. Sundays, they'd gone to First Presbyterian together. She'd never thought much about the dueling denominations in her family. They made it work. She'd even gone to mass with her mother on occasion. But this...this was REALLY Catholic. Like fasting, morning mass every day, nuns in full habit type of Catholic. She was really going to have to rein in the swearing. Compared to most sailors, she was tame. Compared to most doctors, she was even more tame with the cursing. But she had a recollection of herself screaming at Liam O'Brien to pull his head out of his ass...right in front of a three-year-old and a nun. *Cringe.*

She put her things away, hung her mosquito net, and pulled out her toiletries and her stupid can of deet. She hated the smell and how it felt, but she knew it was a necessity. So was sunscreen. They were close to the equator, and burns could happen in minutes. She didn't mess around with skin cancer. She worked too hard at being healthy. She grabbed her towel, her shower items, and her fresh clothing and headed down to the women's locker room.

Total catastrophe. Izzy looked around the women's locker room and couldn't believe what she was seeing. It looked like it hadn't been used in thirty years. Rusty pipes, huge freaking spiders, and the smell coming out of the floor drains was unholy. She walked over to the faucet and turned on the shower. It coughed, sputtered, then released the water. It was brown. Where on earth had all of these women been showering? Because she knew no one was using this one. The large bottle water dispenser for tooth brushing was empty.

Screw this. She was checking out the men's locker room. She suspected Liam O'Brien liked to condition his freaking beard in a nice, clean shower. She marched down the hallway just as O'Keefe was coming out, all fresh as a daisy. "Is anyone in there?"

He cocked his head. "No, just me. Why?"

She didn't answer, she just pushed the door open. It was the same set up, yes. But it was clean and functioning. O'Keefe came in behind her, intrigued. "What's amiss, lass?"

She turned to him, fuming. He took a step back. Then she realized, this wasn't his fault. He just got here. "Come with me, would you? You need to see it to grasp the full effect."

He stood inside the women's locker room with his nose crinkled and his jaw dropped. "I thought the women outnumbered the men? Where the hell are they showering?"

"My thoughts exactly." She was not amused.

"Well, at least the toilets are private and working. You won't have to walk into the hospital to do your business."

"Do you have a tablet? Like paper and pen?" she asked.

"Aye, there's some in the desk in my room. You probably have it too."

She hadn't looked in the desk yet. She walked out, leaving him trailing behind. Once in her room, she yanked the drawer open. Perfect. She had basic office supplies. How thoughtful. Too bad she didn't have a shower down the hall from her room. She smiled...*Oh, but you do.*

Liam finished closing up the lab and headed back to the staff quarters. He could stand to have a shower as well. He'd given the new guy a good half hour to clear out. It was a communal shower, but he thought the man might appreciate a little privacy the first day out. He grabbed his shower bucket and clothes, getting closer to the locker room. He heard the shower still going. What kind of Paris Hilton showers did this guy take? He had five siblings. Ten minutes had been their limit in the shower, to save the hot water. Brigid never stuck to it, so he'd learned not to follow her in the line-up. As he went to press the door open, he noticed that there was a piece of paper stuck over the *Men's* sign. It said, *Co-ed.*

He laughed. He was going to like this Dr. O'Keefe. He pushed the door open. "Ho! O'Keefe! Are you trying to lure wife number two in with that sign? I don't think the women are going to…fall…for it." His words lost their momentum and volume as he saw that it was most certainly not Dr. O'Keefe in the shower. "Fucking hell!" He was struck stupid for a second. Only a second. But that was all he needed to get a full head to toe on Izzy Collier. He flipped around as she dove for the towel.

"Holy shit, Izzy!" He yelled it with his back turned just as she screamed, "Can't you read, O'Brien?"

"I'm sorry, I thought O'Keefe did it as a joke. Get down to your own feckin' shower!"

He could hear her scurrying with her clothes as he walked out. Ran out was more like it. Then he turned and stared at the door. *Always read the small print,* he thought to himself. *Co-Ed.* Underneath it, it said, *until repairs are made to the women's showers.* What, like she wanted a spa? If it was good enough for Alyssa, what was her problem? Alyssa never complained. Neither had the other nurses and docs that had come and gone in his time here. He walked down to the other hall, toward the women's locker room. He knocked, called out, but all he got was an echo. So he entered, and he couldn't believe his bloody eyes. Izzy, sopping wet, but dressed, came in behind him.

"Is this some kind of joke? I can't believe this is how you run your shop, O'Brien. You're the senior doctor here, if you are going by time served. This is unacceptable."

"I agree." He said. That surprised her. He continued. "I've never been in here. Alyssa never said a word. No one did. Where the hell have they been showering and getting their clean water?"

The voice behind them answered. "The patient shower in room seventeen. The one we rarely use because the bed motor is burned out."

They both turned to the nurse. "Hello, Dr. Collier. I'm so sorry I wasn't here to help welcome you. I was on rotation today, checking all of our admitted patients. Margaritte just relieved me. I'm also a nurse anesthetist, so I'll be assisting you in the surgery."

"Alyssa, why didn't you tell the Reverend Mother about the locker room?"

"I did. She said it needed a full plumbing overhaul and that they didn't have the funds. She offered the showers in the abbey, but then Alessandra showed me where the previous nurses had gone." She turned to Izzy. "Alessandra is a local nurse who works part time." Then she shrugged. "It's inconvenient, to be sure. We've just dealt with it. The women who don't live on the grounds have to use it as well, you know, if we've had a messy day. We have to rotate or head to the abbey."

"I'm sorry. That's not fair to the women. We'll trade. Seamus and I will shower at the hospital and you can have our locker room. The female staff are welcome to come in and use it as well. I wish you would have said something."

"I guess I should have. It was just how things were done for the last couple of years. How did you find out?" Alyssa asked. Then she looked at Liam's cheeks. "Dr. O'Brien. I don't think I've ever seen you blush." Then she looked at Izzy. She was sopping wet under her disheveled clothing.

Izzy shrugged. "I put up a sign. He obviously can't read." Alyssa's eyes bugged out, but Izzy rolled right over any response she might make. "And you don't have to trade one bad situation for another. We will share the locker room like adults. Women get it from six to seven in the morning, men seven to eight. At night, we'll reverse it. If you take a shower in between that time, leave a bigger sign." He grumbled and walked out of the room. That's when Alyssa and Izzy burst into giggles.

Holy shit, Liam thought. He should be trying to figure out a solution to the locker room deficit, but every time he thought about it, he saw Izzy. Buck ass nekkid. He scrubbed his face with his hands and decided to forgo the shower. There was no way he was getting anywhere near that shower right now. Nope. He might start taking his chances in the river with the snakes and parasites. *Holy shiiiiiiit.* He'd known she was an athlete. That made sense. She was military. She was a hard-ass. He'd never thought about her naked, but if he had, it would have been lean muscle and an admirable amount of tone.

God damn. That was not the half of it. She was in shape, yes. But under the karate clothes, the jeans and t-shirts, and other benign clothing he'd seen her in…*holy shit.* She was curvy. Not fat, but round in the right places. Those athletic bras women like her wore could squeeze a lot into submission. And all he wished right now was that he'd stopped at the breasts. Why the hell hadn't he turned around more quickly? Why hadn't she been quicker at grabbing that damn towel? He officially knew way more about Izzy Collier's grooming habits than he ever wanted to know.

Izzy walked into the cantina early, hoping to dodge the crowd. After the initial adrenaline had worn off, she was confronted with the fact that Liam O'Brien had seen her naked as a jaybird. As if thinking about this humiliating experience had teleported him, there he sat.

He was the only one besides the grounds worker who was eating. He'd probably come in early for the exact same reason. To avoid seeing her. His spoon stopped halfway to his mouth as he gave her a quick once over. It had been involuntary, because he immediately blushed and diverted his eyes. She was not going to apologize or make a big deal about it. It was an accident. He was a doctor, for God's sake. He'd just delivered a baby last week. The internal pep talk was not working. She was at a nunnery, and the first day on the job, it was all around the staff that she'd used the men's locker room and that the handsome Dr. O'Brien had walked in on her. Naked. She fought the urge to slink out the door. She walked past him.

"Izzy," he said as a greeting.

"Liam." After all, they were adults. First name basis was appropriate considering she was a friend of the family…oh…and since he'd already seen her naked. She approached the cafeteria window and a lovely, plump, older woman handed her a tray. It smelled good. Some sort of fish stew, a bowl of rice with beans, some sort of roll, and a bowl of fresh fruit. "Thank you, Ma'am." She turned with her tray, staring at Liam's back. If she didn't sit with him, it would look petty and immature. He was the only one in here besides Paolo, who was handing Gabriela his empty plate.

Liam knew she was coming to sit with him. Her pride demanded it. He'd just play it cool. The old Liam would have reveled in the teasing, but he was just here to do his job. Not see his co-workers naked. Really naked.

"Alyssa seems nice. Has she been here long?" she asked as she sat on the bench across from him. Small talk. Perfect.

"Three weeks. We've got her for another two months or so. She is a great lass. She's from County Mayo, to the north of us. Before Donegal on the coast." Liam was an idiot. Like she needed a geography lesson? He was quiet. He swallowed hard, because he was overcome with the urge to grin. That old Liam was trying to rear his stupid head right at the worst possible time.

"If you grin, I will stab you with this fork."

"I'm not. Not at all. It's no big deal. I'm a doctor, for God's sake." Too bad they both knew that doctors were just as perverted as the rest of the population.

She slammed her fork down and he jumped, looking up. She said, "It was a gift, from my friends before I left. Kind of a fun joke between girls. Because I was coming to Brazil." He looked confused. "You know, a spa gift certificate." She gritted her teeth. "For a full Brazilian wax. It was a gift."

He couldn't do it. He couldn't keep the grin off his face. "Izzy, you don't have to explain. Your personal grooming is your business. I didn't see a thing."

"You're lying."

"Yes, I am. What made you choose the triangle? Is there a chart of different shapes to choose from?" She reached over the table and cuffed his ear. "I'm just curious. Do they use a template or stencils?" Now they were both laughing. Gabriela leaned over the counter, watching them with her own grin.

"You are such an idiot!" she screamed, smacking him again on the shoulder.

He wiped his face with his hand. "I'm sorry. I tried to play it off. I'll take it to my grave, I promise. I won't think on it again."

That's when they noticed Dr. O'Keefe in the doorway. "How long have you been there?" Izzy barked out.

He put his hands up in defense. "All I saw was the physical assault. I'm certain he deserved it. I'm a feminist. Give him hell, sister."

6

Izzy lay in her cot, trying to will herself to sleep. The call with Sorcha had been brief. She just wanted to touch base and let her know that her son was indeed alive and unruly as ever. Now, as tired as she was, she could let go and surrender. Normally she was great at falling asleep fast. But she was hot. Really hot and sweaty. And there was a hole in her mosquito net. Liam had told her that the essential oil was good for nighttime, if she didn't want to sleep hosed down with poison. She used tape to seal up the hole after about the tenth bite. She couldn't do squat about the heat, though. It was ten thirty. She needed some sleep. The travel was catching up to her, even if the time change was minimal. She heard a knock on her door. It was Alyssa.

"Liam sent this down before he left." *Left? Like, left the property?* "I'm sorry. I got called back to the hospital." It was an electric fan. She had a ceiling fan, but it was insufficient for the task.

"Thank you, Baby Jesus." She took the fan, gratefully. "Anything at the hospital that I need to know about?" Alyssa shook her head.

"No, one of the children rolled out of bed. It was a broken clavicle. Adam, I mean Dr. Watt, he's the pediatrician, did a quick exam and x-ray and put the child in a brace."

"Who was it?" She was going to throw up if it was Estela.

"Cristiano. He's the little boy with glasses. Kind of sweet and nerdy."

She'd seen him in the older classroom. He was small for his age, obviously. "Okay, I'll look in on him tomorrow. Thanks for the fan." As soon as she fired the thing up, the chill settled beautifully over her skin. It was still hot as hell, but she had a breeze now. And it might blow those hell spawn mosquitos off her net.

Liam tossed and turned, trying to fall asleep. The first three months he'd been here, he'd stayed at the staff dorm every night. Now, he got a retreat, a couple of times a week. It was cool and peaceful. He hoped that Alyssa had given Izzy his fan. Nights were cooler, but in August it was still stifling in those little rooms. And he needed to enclose the windows. Hopefully, the supplies had come in.

He'd been plagued by dreams about Eve that first three months. Some were horrific. Some heartbreakingly real. Him above her, their bodies gliding. She was a dancer, slim and lean. Graceful. He'd always tried to be gentle with her. She just seemed so breakable. The guilt consumed him at night. He played that night over in his head, wanting to go back and leave work early. Pick her up himself. Or push harder for her to stay home, skip work that night.

As the months ticked by, the searing pain settled into a dull ache. He still hurt, but he started sleeping again. The dreams were not as often. That wasn't his problem tonight. That would have been familiar. No, what plagued him tonight was that scene in the locker room. He'd made a joke out of it, put her at ease, and vowed not to think on it again. But for Christ sake. He was a man. That was like telling a dog not to bark. Thinking about naked women was what they did. He hadn't had any impulse problems since he'd come here. He was grieving. Other than the normal piss boner in the morning, he'd been almost dead below the waist unless he'd had a dream.

Now, laying here in the dark, he had a perfect image of Izzy Collier all soaped up and wet. Swaying breasts as she washed her hair. And a thin little triangle, trimmed and perfect, like an arrow. Pointing right down to that spot that only women were blessed with. That heavenly little spot.

He sat up, abruptly. Damn her. Why did she have to prove a point by changing that sign and using his shower? She didn't seem like the type that would deliberately try to seduce a man. Especially him. She hadn't even flirted with him a tiny bit, which he was grateful for. O'Keefe? Nah, that didn't fit either. He was probably fifteen years older than her, kind of chubby, and she didn't flirt with him either. There was nothing calculating about her. She'd just been trying to get a shower and trying to prove her bloody point about inequality, and he'd not read the perfectly readable sign on the door. He closed his eyes as he leaned on the bathroom sink. *Stop thinking about the triangle. Stop thinking about the triangle.* The problem he had was that he was a virile twenty-eight-year-old man. His heart might still be dead in his chest, but it appeared that below the waist had suffered an abrupt resurrection.

Izzy looked up from her task as Sister Agatha escorted the children into the surgery. She was at her desk, a nook of an office off the eastern wall. Sister Agatha was quiet, petite. She was pretty, the little that she could see of her. "Hello, Sister Agatha. Is everyone ready to work?" She smiled, nodding. "Can I ask you something, Sister?"

"Yes, Doctor. How can I aid you?'

"I'm just curious. Why is your head covering different from the other women?"

The woman blushed, putting her hand to her veil. "I'm a novice, Dr. Collier. In training, so to speak. I've not yet taken my vows. It's a two year period when I explore the vocation."

Izzy understood. She'd imagine it would take that long to see if the strict, disciplined life of a nun was going to stick. Sometimes it didn't, even after the vows. The no marriage and no kids thing would keep a lot of women out. "I see. Thank you. My mother is Roman Catholic. Not my father. We didn't have any nuns or sisters where I'm from in Arizona. And there aren't any nuns in the Navy chaplaincy."

Sister Agatha nodded, "Well, you have them until lunch, and after if you need them." She turned to the children. "Now, do as you're told, or Sister Maria will hear of it." The children spoke a reply in Portuguese.

Izzy turned to Genoveva, who stood quietly, not fidgeting like the boys. "Okay, Gen! You ready to work these boys until they learn how to behave?"

Genoveva giggled under her hand. "Sim, Médica."

Liam sat at his desk, rubbing his eyes. *Well, that was awful.* He'd spent the morning telling his patient from one of the outlying villages that she had breast cancer. She'd found the lump herself. At her age, that was scary. She was still in child bearing years. Just like his mother had been. Sister Catherine had assisted him with the exam and the ultrasound. They didn't have a mammogram machine and she couldn't get waitlisted if there was a chance it was cancer. She was young enough that her breast tissue was still dense, and by the time the lump was noticeable, things may have gotten out of hand. He'd gone ahead and done a biopsy and it was malignant. She also needed a more thorough scan of her lungs, liver, and lymph nodes. Antonio pulled some strings with a local oncologist to bump her up on the radiology list. This couldn't go untreated. She had two kids and a distraught husband. As he stared across the room at the poor sod, all he could think about was his father. He'd been through this. Faced the same crucible every year, to make sure she was still cancer free.

Antonio came into the room. "So, I've done all I can. I can do the surgery here if it's just a lumpectomy." His English was fluid, dripping with that suave Italian accent.

"Thanks, but our new surgeon might want to have a look."

"Ah, he's arrived? Take me to meet him."

Liam just grinned. *Do I tell him? Nah, where's the fun in that?* "Come this way, Doctor Rinalto."

Liam and Antonio stood in the propped open doorway of the surgery, trying to decipher the tragedy at play. Three sullen boys were on their hands and knees. Goggles, rubber household gloves, and toothbrushes? They were scrubbing the grout of the tile floor, inch by monotonous inch. Izzy was standing over them. "Now boys, don't be lazy. Get in between every one. Do it in a pattern so that you don't skip any."

There was a short, Brazilian man next to her. He looked familiar. They used him as a driver sometimes. Raphael, perhaps? The man translated the instructions in perfect Portuguese, which told Liam a lot about how good his English was. Izzy bent over, showing the boy exactly what she meant. Liam heard a gurgle, like someone in distress, next to him. He looked over at Antonio's face. It was fixed on Izzy's scrubs, specifically the portion covering her ass. He thought it prudent not to tell him that the ass in question looked even better in the shower. Because he wasn't thinking about that anymore. It never happened.

He cleared his throat. "Dr. Collier, excuse us for a moment."

Izzy stood up, all business, and approached them. "Dr. O'Brien, good morning." Her voice was commanding. No hint of the teasing wild-child anywhere in sight. This was her work face. Her war face.

"This is Doctor Antonio Rinalto, the volunteer surgeon. He comes once a month from the private hospital. Antonio, this is Doctor Izzy Collier." Izzy shook his hand. "We were just going over my last patient's file. Stage two, possibly three. Tumor in her left breast. We sent her for scans and to see an oncologist."

"If it's a simple lumpectomy, will she be treated here?"

"Yes. Let's hope that's the case. I told him you'd want to weigh in on it."

Izzy looked at Antonio, and Liam was wondering if she was going to pull rank on him and try to take the case over.

"I'd like to assist, if you don't mind. I'm a bit rusty on the non-emergent surgical procedures. I've done them, but I was on the trauma team at the Naval hospital. Do you mind?"

"I'd consider it an honor. I'm a general surgeon, so I think we will complement each other nicely." Liam almost rolled his eyes. Antonio was smooth. "I see you are giving it a full scrubbing. This is molto bene."

"Grazie, Dottore. Spazzolino da denti?" She said as she offered him a toothbrush. He put his head back and laughed.

"Magnifico! I suspected as much, Isabella."

Liam grinned as she said, "It's just Izzy. How did you know I was Italian?"

Antonio said smoothly, "Ah, it's in the skin and the eyes. I suspect it's in the temper as well."

Liam was going to puke. "If you'd ever met a Welshman, you'd know that she didn't get her temper from her mother," he said dryly.

Izzy lifted a brow. "Touché, Dr. O'Brien. My mother is as sweet and docile as honey. My papa is another story. He's like an angry boar when he's tired or hungry."

"Well, Italians never let anyone go hungry. Perhaps you'd like to follow me back to the city for dinner."

Liam noticed that Raphael was watching this all with amusement. Intel gathering, because he understood every word. This flirting was getting old. But before he interrupted, Izzy changed the subject. "Have you all met Raphael?"

They both knew him, but not well. "He'll be working as my interpreter for at least the next two months."

Liam sputtered. "The abbess gave you your own interpreter?"

"No, I found him myself. He and I have a private arrangement." She didn't elaborate. "Now, I hate to break up the party, but I have a lot of work to do. Unless you want to help. I could use some long legs."

Antonio had a scheduled procedure in the other part of the hospital. Liam helped Izzy mount a second dry erase board next to the one in the surgery. She'd taken it out of her office. He watched as she put the names down of the entire medical staff. She made a column for drug allergies and one for blood type. "I need to know everyone's blood type who will be working on the team. Both mobile and hospital teams. I'd also like the same information on the sisters and the kids at the orphanage. If they don't know their type, then we need to type their blood in the lab." She put O Neg next to her name. Same as Liam's. "I'll keep a supply on hand for emergencies. If one of my team gets hurt, we need this information on hand. This cleaning will be done by lunch. After that, I will set up the new equipment and we will be open for business tomorrow morning. Tonight if we get an emergency."

Liam watched her as she spoke. Her hands were on her hips as she stared up at the dry erase boards. He looked around and noticed that she had Genoveva washing walls. She was thorough, confident, and commanding. He'd never considered typing the blood for the staff. She'd been in Iraq, though. She'd done field medicine on trauma cases, undoubtedly.

He thought back to one of the three fatalities they'd had in the hospital since he'd arrived. A jaguar attack. Beautiful, ruthless, deadly bastards. Maybe if they'd had a trained trauma surgeon on hand and plenty of blood stored, they wouldn't have lost him. Suddenly he wasn't so upset that she'd shown up to the abbey. Not that he was going to admit that to her.

She seemed to be hitting it off with the staff and the kids. Even the boys she was punishing didn't seem that put out. They kept stealing glances at her when she wasn't looking. Whispering and snickering the way that teenage boys did. He approached the lads and they fell quickly silent. "You like the new doctor, do ye?" They couldn't keep the grins off their faces. He said in Portuguese, so they caught his meaning. "Don't think that this is reward for bad behavior. Next time you are with me, washing bedpans."

Raphael laughed out loud. He turned, realizing he'd been listening. Izzy turned, brow raised. She looked at Raphael. "No worries, boss. This is…what's the phrase?" He looked at Liam. "It's man talk."

Izzy smirked. "Far be it from me to interfere with male bonding. Genoveva and I have our own secrets." She winked at the girl, who gave a shy grin. That's when all hell broke loose. Sister Catherine busted through the doorway. "Are ye ready for a patient?"

Liam watched as Izzy sprang into action. The patient upstairs, the woman who'd delivered in the throes of a gastric bacterial infection, was headed to the O.R. He hadn't released her or the child because she was continuing to battle a low grade fever, despite the antibiotics. Sister Catherine had continued to monitor her, seeing her through the childbirth recovery. She'd been worried about some abdominal pain, because the diarrhea had stopped. It would follow that if the diarrhea stopped, she shouldn't be having abdominal pains other than the normal postpartum cramps. This seemed too severe.

Izzy's adrenaline spiked. She started barking out orders. "Get a mop. A new one. Get this floor dry!" Raphael jumped to it, even though it wasn't his job."

Liam approached her. "What do you need?"

She let out a breath. "Get into the sterilizer and pull out my new surgical kit. Can you prep a surgical room?" He nodded. He'd helped Antonio. "Catherine, I need Alyssa here, stat. Do you have an intercom system here?" They didn't. Shit, she needed to be in contact with O'Keefe. She turned to the boys. "Go back to school."

The boys looked at Liam, thinking they should be helping. "Too many bodies in one room. Go, boys. I thank you, but you can go," Izzy said, not waiting for Liam to handle them. Raphael translated, and the boys left. Then Izzy said, "Genoveva, I need you to run up to the second floor and find Antonio. Tell him we need him to scrub in. After that, you can go back to school as well."

She looked at Liam. "Give me the history while you work."

He did, as she went to the sinks and started scrubbing. Catherine joined them again, with Alyssa behind them. The team was fast, Izzy thought. Efficient. "Dr. Collier, I spoke with Dr. O'Keefe. The patient didn't pass the entire placenta. There's just a small bit, and it's festered. Probably because she was already immune compromised. He asks that you assist."

"On it! Do we have laparoscopic equipment? He may want to go in vaginally." Catherine ran to the drawer and pulled out a new scope. That's when Dr. O'Keefe came through the door, wheeling a very pale, very pained young woman.

"I need a scope and a surgical kit!" Seamus yelled. Then he saw everything they'd already done. "Holy Mother, I love a good hospital team. We need IV Vancomycin started and an IV antacid. I don't want her aspirating on the table. Where's my nurse anesthetist?" Alyssa called over her shoulder, letting him know she was right there with him and ready. He came next to Izzy and started scrubbing, right on his heels was Antonio. Seamus said, "Antonio, go into my office and read the ultrasound. Make sure there's nothing else going on here. No tears, nothing with the bowel. I didn't see anything but I want two sets of eyes on it. That ultrasound machine is a piece of shite. Liam, go up and retrieve her blood work and take it down to the lab."

Liam said, "Okay, then I'll be back." Izzy shook her head at that, and he stiffened.

"We need you and Dr. Watt to cover that floor full of patients and intake. We can't all be tied up in the O.R. And you can't be in the surgery with that beard. It won't be covered by the mask. I'm not sure if we are going to have to open her up."

"She's my patient. I want to assist."

She turned, trying not to escalate the situation. "And we need a set of competent eyes on that blood work and her cultures. I know she's your patient, and I promise you that we will take good care of her."

Liam shut his eyes. He knew she was right. Why hadn't he shaved the fucking beard? "You're right." He went over, finished the prepping. Then he removed the face shields from their boxes. "You need these?"

She shook her head. "No, I haven't sterilized them. The goggles will do. Thank you, Dr. O'Brien. I can tell you know your way around a surgery. I'm glad you were here."

It chaffed a little that she was complimenting him like a school child, but he left, taking one more look at the patient's pale face. When he went out the door, he almost ran into Sister Catherine. She was crying.

She said, "I checked her. Twice a day, I checked her bleeding and examined her. She didn't present with this problem, but I should have thought to do an ultrasound when her fever didn't go down."

He put his hand on her shoulder. "I didn't catch it either. Her other infection was masking the symptoms. I'm as much to blame as you are."

Liam heard someone approach behind them. "Reverend Mother, you've heard?" he asked.

She nodded. "Yes, Genoveva came and told me there was a problem. Margaritte gave me the particulars. Go along, Dr. O'Brien. I'll have a moment with Sister Catherine in prayer. Then she'll go do her other job. Isn't that right, Sister? You have a job to do."

Catherine lifted her chin. "Yes, Reverend Mother. I'll do all I can for her."

7

Spirits were high around the dinner table. The staff, children, and sisters were all gathered in the hall of the cantina, celebrating the successes of the day. Gabriela was ecstatic to have a full house. The mother and child were both going to be fine, and she still had all of her baby making parts in tact. The husband had come in part way through the surgery, having been pulled off his job site with the unfortunate update on his wife's condition. Now he was letting her rest, walking around with his baby in the cantina. Raphael had departed after a quick meal. He'd spent the time that Izzy was in the O.R. making quiz cards for her. Medical related terms in Portuguese and English.

"He was Brazilian military. He got hurt, had to go auxillary or reserves or whatever they call it here. He's not making a lot of money driving a cab, and he's a good interpreter. I was lucky to find him."

O'Keefe interrupted. "Not just military. Counter narcotics. I think he may be a badass in disguise." He took a bite of his cheese bread and moaned. "That cook is a genius. It's nice to have a meal made with love. It's been a while."

Izzy smiled. The bread was really good. "So, how long have you been divorced and what did you do to piss her off?" Liam choked on his stew, but Seamus didn't seem to be offended.

"I've been divorced for eighteen months. As for my crimes? I bought her a membership to a very overpriced gym."

"So you insinuated she was fat?" Izzy said, offense creeping into her tone.

"God, no. She's never been fat. Even pregnant, she was slim. Not that it would matter to me. I don't mind a bit of curve. She asked me to buy her a year membership for her birthday. Bloody expensive for throwing around stuff you could find in an old garage. Tires and ropes and such. Anyway, I did it. I rarely denied her anything, honestly. We'd been together since we were twenty. I was an Army medic and she was a cashier at a department store. Two broke, starry-eyed kids. She gave me three daughters. I thought we were happy."

"So, what went wrong?"

He leaned down, lowering his voice. "What went wrong was that the trainer who was helping her in the gym accidentally tripped over the rope while nude, and landed cock first on top of my wife. Or something like that." Liam and Antonio were laughing now, and Seamus joined them.

"That is not funny! It's awful. After being together for over twenty years, she just dumped you for some poser at a crossfit gym?" Izzy looked stricken.

"It's okay. There were problems. I just didn't see it. I worked a lot. I'm almost fifty years old. I have a demanding job. I don't have time to hang out at the gym for two hours and talk about protein intake and coconut oil. I should have known, really. She was always trying to put me on a diet. Telling me that just because I was middle-aged, didn't mean I should just let myself go."

"Wow. No offense, Seamus, but your ex sounds like a piece of work." Liam was shaking his head. He couldn't imagine his mother treating his father that way.

"Yes, I see that now. She traded me in for a new, fitter model. Our girls are out of the house, now. The youngest at university. She's living in my house with some tosser. So, to answer your question, what

I did to piss her off was get old, enjoy a pint and some chips now and again, and spend too much money on a gym package for an ungrateful floozie."

Antonio waved a hand. "Life is too short to worry about such things. I was taught to savor good food and wine."

"Aye, says the Italian Stallion with the thirty-two inch waist," Seamus said dryly.

"I'll tell you what. Why don't we all go out for my birthday. It's in two weeks. Brazilian women love a man with some meat on his bones. They like the big men that come to visit from Europe and America. It's, you know, something different from what they have. A big strong Senhor like yourself with the blue eyes and the light hair, they'll love you." He turned to Izzy. "Do you like to dance? I'm afraid the American women have a hard time keeping up with the Brazilian girls. It's in the blood, the hips, but I think you'll have fun." There was a twinkle in Antonio's eyes, like he was deliberately baiting her.

"You think I can't keep up, eh?" She leaned in.

He shrugged. "It's science. Brazilian women move like no others."

"Well, I guess we're going out for your birthday, then. Alyssa, you in? I need a wingman. I'm not going out with all of these men by myself."

"I'm in. We'll try to drag Adam out as well. He never leaves the hospital. He misses his wife and baby."

Dr. O'Keefe looked sideways at Liam. "You're quiet."

"I won't be joining you. I'm busy," Liam got up, finished with his meal.

"You know that you're going to be busy two weeks from now?" O'Keefe asked.

"Absolutely. I'll make sure of it. I don't do dance clubs. But feel free to take video of Adam trying to cut a rug." He chuckled. "I'm headed back to the hospital to check on our patient."

Izzy got up as well. "I'll come with you. I'll see you all back at the barn. Antonio, thanks for your help today. Everyone really pulled it together. I promise, I'll have the new equipment in place by nine o'clock tomorrow morning."

॰

They walked in silence until Izzy smacked her arm. "Jesus, woman. Didn't you put your Deet on after you showered?"

"I did! The little bastards love me. They seek me out!"

He nodded. "Yes, some people are like that."

"Maybe I'm too sweet?" she asked with a grin. He laughed.

"Doubtful. I'll give you some of the stuff we keep in supply. Yours may not be strong enough. I want you to tell me immediately if you feel funny. The sniffles, griping guts, anything. I haven't been over your medical screening yet, but I'll do it tomorrow."

She stopped, "Why do you need to do that?"

"Because I need to check all of your vaccinations. There may be something you didn't think of. Something that isn't required, but that I think you should have. There's no vaccine for Zika, malaria, or dengue. Are you taking your malaria drugs?"

"Of course I am. They give me weird dreams."

"Did you take a pregnancy test before you came?" He didn't meet her eye with that question. "If there's even a chance, you shouldn't be..."

She laughed. "Believe me, there's no chance. Not unless I am some anomaly that has a two-year gestational period."

He said nothing at first, then added, "Aye, well be careful. You've seen the news. The birth defects."

She sighed. "Why don't you just come out with it? What are you worried about exactly?"

"Well, you're single. Three months is a long time. Antonio is certainly interested, and he won't be the last. You're a grown woman. I'm not trying to be intrusive."

"Yes, you are. To answer the question that you could've found the answer to in my medical file, I've had a hormonal IUD in place for three years. I have no intentions of having a Doc on Doc booty call with Antonio, but I'm covered if Bradley Cooper shows up and throws himself at my feet." She narrowed her eyes. "Did I pass muster?"

Liam started walking again and she fell in next to him. "Yes, but I'm serious about the bites. You need to self-monitor. You're no good to us if you fall ill."

"Yes, sir. Now, why don't you explain the clean-shaven face? I didn't mean to insinuate you had to shave."

Liam smoothed a hand over his chin. "It was time. It wasn't something I'd thought of, and I didn't like being where I was today."

"And where were you?"

"I wasn't there. I couldn't be there to help. I don't like that feeling. She was my patient."

"I would have sent you to the lab anyway. You were exactly where you were needed. We had two surgeons and an obstetrician."

"But what about next time? What happens if Antonio isn't here and it's not an issue for an obstetrician or a pediatrician? I don't want you to be on your own if you need me to scrub in with you. It's not that big of a deal. The damn thing itched, anyway."

"Yeah, I guess you're right. I don't need you dropping a face pube in my patient's surgical incision."

Liam burst out laughing, as she'd meant him to. "Face pube! I'll have you know that I looked amazing and manly with that beard!"

She was laughing lightly. "You did. No argument."

"And I kept it clean. I even used that wee comb you gave me."

"Ah, glad it came in handy. Have you used the other stuff? You didn't try to seduce Sister Agatha out of her vows did you?"

Liam smirked. "I left that particular gift for Seany in the medicine chest."

Izzy feigned insult. "You regifted my thoughtful condom?"

"I do use the oil at night, and the little book has been a hit in the men's toilet."

"How about the calling card? Are you planning on using that?" The teasing having gone out of her tone.

"Don't, Izzy."

Her tone was light when she answered. "Sorry, but I can't agree to that. I got a crash course in ball breaking from your sister, Brigid. She's expert level, as you know. She only had three days, but I'm a fast learner."

Liam gave a sad smile, looking very tired. "Yes, well she learned from the best. Nosey peahens."

"Yeah, well…a little bit of spark has gone out of your mother. I'll have to take your word on that."

Liam paused halfway through the hospital door. "Why? She's not ill, is she? You said her scans were clear." There was alarm creeping into his voice.

Suddenly Izzy's eyes were sad, too. "Her scans were clear. She's just got a broken heart." Liam swallowed hard, his jaw tightened, and he walked down the hall to see his patient.

8

The week flew by with little drama. The mother and baby were released to go home. The patients that were currently admitted and occupying hospital beds were mostly for malaria, an injury involving a machete to the trapezius muscle, and an elderly woman with a broken ankle.

Dr. O'Keefe had a full patient board since the word got out to the villages about a new OB-GYN on staff. Dr. Watt spent the week giving the kids at the orphanage annual physicals and vaccinations with Liam's help.

Izzy watched from the door of the cantina, a cup of coffee in her hand. She'd had time to settle in and make some observations. The Reverend Mother came alongside her. "I see you've learned our secret. Gabriela makes the finest coffee I've ever tasted." Izzy smiled at her over the rim of her cup.

"Yes, she really does. She seems to be here more often than not. Seven days a week. Does she have a family?"

"She's a widow. Her son is grown and moved away. We're all she has, really. Paolo drives her to the closest village. She rents a room from another widow. Now, I see your wheels turning, Dr. Collier. Who's caught your attention?"

"Genoveva, for a start," she nodded toward the play yard.

The abbess grunted. "Aye, she keeps to herself. I think the other children don't know what to do with her."

"Why? She's a great kid. I've seen how helpful she is. She unloads supplies, she helps with the smaller kids. She's an angel."

"To be sure, but she's different. She's bigger than most of the boys, she's got wide shoulders, those piercing green eyes. She doesn't fit the mold. Kids can be rather unkind, I'm afraid. We've tried talking to some of the older kids, but she said it only made things worse. I'm afraid I'm rusty at schoolhouse politics."

"Do you mind if I work with her, try to build up her confidence? I think she could use a friend."

The abbess's face lifted. "Why, I think that would be grand altogether. What did you have in mind?"

"Sweat therapy."

"Never heard of it."

"Yeah, well, just trust me. She needs to learn to celebrate what's different about her. I think I have just the thing," Izzy said. They both looked ahead as Raphael pulled his Jeep onto the property. Izzy waved to him.

"How is your Portuguese coming along?" the Reverend Mother asked.

Izzy gave her a sample of her newfound knowledge. She could do basic greetings and niceties, she could ask someone to show her where the pain was on their body, and she could ask if there was any blood in their stool or urine. "Well, it's practical. I'll give him that."

Liam approached the walled garden located behind the abbey. The sisters used it for a bit of quiet reflection. He liked it. It was like something out of a children's book. Lush vines and flowers. Benches to sit and read or just think. There was a statue in the corner, nestled in the vines and shrubbery. It was an angel. There were others around.

A figure of St. Clare taking prime billing, but other saints scattered in the greenery and messy, lush flower beds. The abbess came here before morning prayers to collect her thoughts and prepare for the day. She had a lot of responsibility. Then she'd come as the sun went below the tree line, taking another few moments to herself.

Right now, he heard Metallica buzzing through the hedge. He crept along the hedge, not wanting Izzy to see him. He thought she'd be alone, getting a workout. He was surprised to see that the teenage girl, Genoveva, was with her. They had a garden bench in front of them. They leaped in unison, with both feet and no hands, up onto the bench. He looked around. Raphael was using a bamboo staff to stretch out his bad shoulder. When Genoveva finished her tenth jump, Izzy gave her a fist bump. "Bem fieto, irmã!" *Well done, sister.*

Liam's heart squeezed. Genoveva had a hard time of it. She was half European. Different. She was bigger than the other kids, and kind of awkward. But right now she was glowing.

Izzy asked, "And what is our battle cry?"

"Strong is the new skinny!" Genoveva roared, her words thick with her Brazilian accent.

Raphael saw him first. "Oi, Dr. O'Brien! You want to come for some working out?"

Izzy turned, wiping the sweat off her forehead.

"No, thanks. I'm here to see Dr. Collier. Do ye have a minute?"

"What's up? Am I needed at the hospital?" She looked ready to move.

"No, not at all. I wanted you to know that we're taking the mobile unit into the eastern slum tomorrow. I'd like you to come along. You need to learn the way of it. Adam will come as well. The nurses and Seamus can manage, I think."

"Count me in. What time?" Izzy said, suddenly excited to get off the abbey grounds.

"Eight is fine. Get some breakfast. We'll have lunch in the city. I know where the safe places to eat are. Parasite free."

Izzy shuddered. "Good to know."

"How are the bug bites? Did the new stuff work?"

She turned her leg to show him. "Better, but they're still trying to eat me. I think I'm going to start sleeping with a garlic wreath around my bed."

He looked at the bites. Too many. "I've got one more thing to try. Paolo swears by it. He gets it from the medicine man in one of the indigenous villages. I'll bring it to you later." He turned to walk away but stopped. "It's nice, what you're doing with the lass. She's a good girl."

"She is, and she's strong and smart. She's also going to be a knock-out when she gets out of this awkward stage. Those boys are going to wish they'd been nicer to her."

"Are you speaking from experience, Isadora?"

"Izzy, and yes. I was a tomboy. I liked to climb trees and barrel race on my ornery appaloosa. It took the cowboys a while to catch up." She winked at him.

"You know I'm going to find out. Why don't you just tell me your full name?" He looked at Raphael and yelled, "Hey brother. Did she tell you her first name? Her real first name?"

"Oh Sim, Senhor. It's Boss-lady. That's the only name I need."

"Feel free to call me that, if you don't like Izzy. I am your elder," she goaded.

He closed in, looking down at her. "In your dreams, wee lass."

"Though she be wee, she be mighty." Her brow was cocked.

He smiled, "Aye, I've seen you in action. Don't give her that staff, Raphael. She'll kick your ass, brother."

Liam dug through the supply closet, finally finding the dark glass bottle that Paolo had given him. It was some sort of organic matter, a plant extract. That's all he knew. The medicine man didn't advertise his recipe. When Paolo had first given it to Liam, he'd tried it on himself. He assured him, in Portuguese of course, that if he dropped dead, then Liam shouldn't use it on anyone else. He was kidding, of course. Gabriela knew of the tonic as well and said it worked well for keeping flies and mosquitos away.

He walked to the women's quarters and ran into Alyssa coming out of her room. "Have you seen Izzy?"

"Last time I saw her, she was headed to the abbey library with her laptop."

He walked into the abbey's main entrance, the one closest to the library. Reverend Mother Faith was speaking to Sister Agatha, the young novice.

"But Reverend Mother, if you'd just let me show you the different social media outlets we can use, I could fundraise for the abbey online. We could get more exposure." Liam pitied the woman. He'd had the same conversation with the abbess. She was unreasonably anti-computer. The only way he'd even come across St. Clare's was through his scholarship. He'd dealt with the partner abbey in Dublin. St. Clare's was stuck in the seventies. The only reason they had any computers or WiFi was that the diocese had put their foot down and demanded it. They needed to be able to contact the abbey in this remote location, and the visiting doctors needed to be able to contact their families back home. He thought about what it would mean for the abbey to get social media exposure. YouTube could be a great tool. As he thought about it, he absently walked into the library. He hadn't been paying attention until it was too late. Izzy's back was to him, and his mother's face was on the computer screen. He froze as Izzy turned around.

"I didn't mean to interrupt. Sorry."

Izzy stood, and he could see his mother, her hand over her mouth. "Liam," she croaked. "Oh, God. Is that my lad?" His mother burst into tears. He couldn't just walk away. He wasn't, he reflected, as much of a bastard as he pretended to be.

"Don't cry, Mam. Please, don't cry," he said as he walked toward the desk where Izzy had been seated.

Izzy squeezed his arm. "I'll give you some privacy." As she crept out of the library, the Reverend Mother stood in the doorway.

"Well, miracles never cease. Well done, Dr. Collier."

Izzy took a shower, rubbing the stinging spots where she'd scratched her bug bites. Hell-spawn bloodsuckers. She toweled off, applying some salve to the affected areas. Hoping to quell the itch. She put on her clean shorts and a tank top, the clothing she slept in. She normally slept in a pair of panties and nothing else, but she wasn't at home. She never knew when someone would come busting in, with a trauma case, to get her out of bed.

She went to her small room, surprised to see Liam sitting on her bed. She paused in the doorway, unsure of his mood. She said, "I'm sorry. I didn't plan that. I wouldn't have just tricked you like that."

"I know, and it needed to happen eventually."

"Are you okay?" she asked.

"She cried a lot," he said sadly.

"I'm sure she did. That must have been very hard on you," she said softly. "You can use my laptop anytime. Did you get to talk to your dad?"

"I did. He seemed...relieved, I guess."

"Well, he has a lot of guilt about what happened. It's understandable. Charlie said Tadgh has nightmares every once in a while. Between Eve and what happened to his partner, it was very traumatic. Some things don't wipe off so easily."

"Yes, I'm sure you know about Aidan," he said.

"Alanna told me a little, but Aidan told me the rest. You forget that I was in Iraq. I didn't fight. I didn't carry a gun. I just cleaned up the messes."

"I'd like to hear about that sometime, but not tonight. It's late, and," he paused. "I'm a bit tired of feeling anything. We have a long day tomorrow. Anyway, I came to bring this." He handed her the juju

75

magic bug repellent. "I'm not sure exactly what it is, but it's safe. Some sort of tonic from the indigenous medicine man."

She pulled the cap off and smelled it. "Phew, like bark and mushrooms."

"It very well could be. Just try it. It's safe to sleep in as well. I sprayed your screen with deet. The velcro seems to be holding." Then he said, "Did you know Caitlyn is pregnant again?"

"Yes, I did. I'm sorry. I probably should have told you. I didn't think. Is she doing okay? She made it to the second trimester."

"So far, so good. She's taking it easy, sitting more at school, not picking up the little ones. I hope this one takes." He stood up to leave. Izzy put a hand on his arm.

"I'm glad for you, and your family, Liam."

"You must be pretty proud of yourself," he said dryly.

"Actually, I'm proud of you. I didn't do anything. You did the hard part. You stayed. You didn't run. It's a starting place."

He met her eyes then, taking in her face. "Good night, Izzy."

9

T he mobile unit was surprisingly well organized and main-
tained. The supplies were basic, so the mobile trauma kits
were very much a needed addition, as was the defibrillator.
It was a panel truck that had doors on one side which opened up to
a makeshift clinic. Paolo drove the large vehicle into the city with Dr.
Watt, the pediatrician, riding shotgun. Raphael transported Izzy and
Liam in his Jeep, carrying extra supplies and a cooler that Gabriela
had packed for them. Covered in sunscreen, varying bug repellents,
and carrying walkie-talkies in their white coat pockets, they were met
at the usual lot by a huge crowd of people that were waiting to be
seen.

Izzy looked around at the layers of shacks built one on top of the
other in a wall of wood, rolled asphalt, and corrugated metal, that
made up the architecture of the impoverished and underprivileged.
People talked about how great the socialized healthcare was in Brazil,
but that was more applicable to the south. Up here on the river, it was
a different story. According to Antonio, there was a shortage of x-ray
machines, and there were waitlists to even get a simple set of x-rays
done. The people on the outskirts, farther into the bush, depended
on small clinics and mobile units, as did the people in the slums that
couldn't spend all day in some public hospital waiting room, competing for a little attention.

Adam handled the children, most of the ailments minor. Liam helped him by checking the children's vaccine cards if they had one. Izzy took minor injuries, having Raphael interpret as needed. Right now she was sitting across from an old woman who'd suffered a nasty burn to her forearm. Before that, a young man had cut his hand with a fishing knife. It was wrapped, and the wound was two days old, but it needed to be cleaned. The laceration was infected and not closing properly. She gave him some lidocaine after cleaning the wound, even though he seemed to bear the pain with no protest. She stitched it up, redressed it, and gave him a tetanus shot. Then she gave him oral antibiotics and sent him on his way.

The burn, on the other hand, was painful. Granny had burned herself while boiling water for laundry. She was displeased when Izzy told her that under no circumstances was she to do laundry and get the dressing wet.

They worked non-stop, taking water and bathroom breaks in pairs. The bathroom situation was grim. Izzy was horrified to find that some of the toilets drained right out of the bottom of the house and into the river. The remaining patients sat along a fence, willing to stand by until they returned from a much needed break. There didn't seem to be an end to the need. Izzy had been prepared for the poverty, but not for the drug addiction she witnessed. It was South America. She knew that there was a big drug trafficking problem. What she hadn't been prepared for was the amount of the native population that was using. Cocaine use was a real problem in Brazil. When an addict came to the mobile unit, they would treat them for whatever issue they were having. She noticed that Raphael stood behind the doctors and nurses, putting himself between the patients and the pharmaceutical cabinet. They didn't carry narcotics, but that wouldn't stop someone who was desperate and prepared to do a smash and grab.

Paolo disappeared during the morning, going on foot to visit his family. He was back now, prepared to move to a lunch location. They sealed up the truck and drove to a small restaurant, away from both the slums and the tourist areas. Castelo do Rio was indeed not a castle. It had cheap plastic patio furniture, but the view was amazing. Liam said to Izzy, "I've done extensive research on which places are safe to eat. I love Gabriela's cooking, but I like to get off the abbey once a week. The statistical chance of getting any sort of nasty parasite or food pathogen is the lowest at this place when you stick to specific items on the menu. So, I'm not trying to *mansplain* you or *micro-aggress*, or whatever the hell they're calling it, but I suggest you let me order."

Adam laughed at the look on Raphael's face. "They didn't teach you those words in the Army?"

Izzy elbowed Adam. "Enough! I get it, I get it. One rule, I don't eat eyeballs."

The tanned, thirty-something man who seemed to do three different jobs at the place, came up with a pad of paper and looked at Liam for some direction. "Hello, Thomas. Dois bacalhau, três cassava chips, dois pão de queijo, e muito feijoada." Liam said, making a gesture that suggested he wanted plenty to feed the whole group. The man wrote it all down, and Liam thanked him as he dispersed bottled water. "Skol, Senhor?" Liam declined the offer of a round of lager.

"Translation, please? Any guts or eyeballs?" Izzy asked. Raphael laughed, but Liam answered.

"Salt cod fritters, yucca chips, cheese bread, and the national dish. That one has beans and various bits from pig or cow. He'll bring out a bowl of rice to go along with it. Best not to ask too many questions. Just eat it. His feijoada makes the angels weep." He was smiling and relaxed. More so than Izzy had seen him her entire time here.

They sat in the shade, sipping their bottled waters and discussing the work they'd done. Izzy asked, "Do you see this scale of drug use in the villages?"

"There's some in most villages, but the city seems to be where we see the highest percentage. In the indigenous tribal villages, not so much. The problem is that the farther out you get, the more you get into hidden airstrips, drug planes, trucks using the deforestation roads, and even riverboats. All transporting, and all including a gang of horrible bastards that protect the shipment. The cartels are nothing to play around with. Luckily, St. Clare's hasn't had any dealings with them."

The food arrived and the group ate with gusto. Liam wiped his mouth. "I'll get the bill. Just leave him a good tip. He works hard." At that, Liam went to settle the bill with Thomas. They all got back into the vehicles and headed to work.

They pulled into the abbey around tea time. Izzy was exhausted. Liam watched her as she leaned against her arm, trying not to nod off against the Jeep window. The doors were on today, so at least she wouldn't roll out. The mobile unit wasn't just hard work, it was emotionally draining. Poverty, addiction, malnourished children, and poor living conditions. "You need to go lie down. I'll finish the patient logs."

She turned to him as they unloaded the vehicles. She was smiling warmly. "That's a kind offer. I may shamelessly take you up on it." But it wasn't to be. An old pick-up came tearing into the estate. The men were screaming in Portuguese.

Raphael said quickly, "It is a spider bite." Liam jumped in the back of the truck while Adam ran for a gurney. He spoke fast to the men who brought the patient, and Raphael translated. "It's the wandering spider. Very dangerous, very painful. They ask if the médico have the cure?" Izzy understood, running toward the hospital to find the antivenin. The man was screaming and writhing in pain. The children and the sisters began pouring out to see what was going on. Adam and Liam loaded the twitching, moaning man onto the gurney and took him into the critical care wing of the hospital. Alyssa fell in beside them and began taking vitals. Margaritte ran an IV.

"Izzy, I need that vial!"

"Got it! Right into the IV?"

"Yes, the entire thing. And Margaritte, he needs morphine. He looks to weigh about ten stone." The team worked flawlessly, everyone weaving in and out, taking care of business. When they were finally done, the man's roaring simmered down to whimpers. It was an extremely painful bite and potentially deadly. The spiders weren't web builders. They wandered the jungle floor, hence the name, just waiting to fuck up someone's day.

Raphael was waiting when they came out of the treatment room. "I spoke with the men. They had to go back to work. They'll check back at sundown."

"Where are they working?"

"They are with a deforesting group. They were very worried about getting back. The foreman didn't want them to leave. The asshole actually told them to let him drive himself to the hospital."

"Sounds like that foreman needs his balls handed to him," Liam said. Izzy grunted approval and someone cleared their throat behind them. "Oh, sorry Reverend Mother."

"How is the patient. I heard the wailing from my office. Bullet ant?"

"No, Abbess. It was a wandering spider." Margaritte answered.

The abbess shivered. "Horrible, wee nasty creatures. Paolo does a daily sweep for them in the buildings. Last year we had a brown recluse nest in the abbey library, and we get the occasional snake wandering into the cantina. Paolo keeps that machete on him for more than the vines."

"That disaster zone of a locker room has a lot of spiders. I know no one uses it, but it needs to be bombed. That's way too close to my bedroom. I'll tell Paolo." Izzy was not going to forget because she considered herself a hard-ass, but spiders were her kryptonite. Spiders and snakes. *And what the flying fuck are bullet ants?* She looked at Liam, suddenly ready to clean his clock. He noticed the shift in mood and cocked his head.

"If you think this is under control, I'm in need of a shower. Everyone did great. You all were amazing."As Izzy walked through the hospital hall, Liam fell in step next to her. "I'm mad at you," she hissed.

"What the hell did I do?" He was laughing. She didn't hear the sound very often, and it was nice, but she was still mad.

"You came to Brazil. You couldn't find somewhere less infested with killer creepy crawlers? What the hell is a bullet ant?" When he explained that it was arguably the worst pain you could suffer from an animal bite, and that they looked like regular ants only ten times bigger, and multiple bites could be fatal, she punched him in the chest. "Jesus. Give me roadside bombs and missiles any day over this shit!"

"You're crabby, love. Do you need a cookie?" Liam's tone was indulgent.

A cookie suddenly sounded amazing. She stopped and looked at him, arms crossed. "If that is an empty gesture and you don't actually have a cookie, I'm going to beat the shit out of you."

The infernal man threw his head back and laughed. "Just go take your shower, hen. I'll find you a cookie. Then I have a surprise for you. You just need to stop threatening me or you won't get it."

She cocked her head. "Chocolate chip?"

He smiled. "I'll do my best."

Liam's chest still burned where Izzy had punched him, and not in a bad way. This was not good. He'd tried hard to put that little scene in the shower behind him. Izzy was a professional and an amazing doctor. She was a bit of a hard ass for his taste, but simple sensory deprivation had weakened him over the last several months. He hadn't seen a naked woman in longer unless you counted patients, which he didn't. He hadn't been touched either.

A wave of pain went through him, as he pictured his beloved Eve. So sweet. So innocent and lovely. He'd been with women before Eve. He'd had genuine affection for them all, but he couldn't say he'd loved any of them. It had been the youthful, carefree, exploration years of his life. Reveling in sex and the excitement of living away from home. Moving into a big city where he met new lasses that he hadn't grown up with, from diapers to school dances. Eve had changed that. Once he'd committed to her, which was almost immediately, he'd never strayed. Never even lusted in the privacy of his own thoughts. O'Brien men weren't wired that way. The shame of feeling even an ounce of sexual need almost buckled his knees. Eve was gone. That was it for him.

Even as he said this to himself, he found himself in Gabriela's kitchen. "Do you have any sweets? Dr. Collier is having a meltdown." She didn't understand, so he tried in Portuguese. She smiled knowingly. She rummaged through the cooler. She often made cakes and biscuits for the children, and for tea. She pulled out a lump of dough, unbaked. "Sim, biscoitos. Abóbora. Ten minutes." Her pumpkin cookies were fantastic.

He sat, willing to wait and maybe steal some dough when she wasn't looking. "Chocolate chips, por favor?"

Izzy washed off the stress and filth of the day, both mentally and physically. It was blazing and sticky, just at the end of the really hot season. The rain would come soon. Then the temperature would drop a bit. She soaped up her body, thinking about what she'd told Genoveva. *Strong is the new skinny.* She hoped so. She hoped she was strong enough to do this. The poverty was bad enough. The addicts, the hungry kids, the lack of clean water. It made her feel a sort of despair she hadn't felt in a long time. She hadn't ventured off the base in Iraq but once. The war-torn cities, the haunted eyes of the small children, the catastrophic injuries on both sides.

This was different though. This was systemic. It was ingrained in the culture. There were a lot of wealthy, privileged people in Brazil. There were also a lot of people who needed help. Liam had done this for months. The abbess was going on her twenty-third year. She'd rescued this abbey from being closed.

She thought, perhaps, that Reverend Mother Faith had a story. She didn't seem like she'd been cloistered from the world as much as one would think. She was too quick with a comeback, for starters. She had wise eyes. Not just about God, but about life.

Izzy rinsed off her hair, loving how the soap and water washed over her body. Out of nowhere, she thought about Liam seeing her in the shower. What had he thought about what he'd seen? His opinion shouldn't matter, but she suddenly wondered what he thought of her body. She was average height, fit, but she was pretty curvy. No amount of working out had rid her of her Mediterranean ass and thighs. It was genetic. She had an ass on her, and boobs that she'd constantly tried to press into submission with athletic wear. They got in the way, but most men liked a little T and A, right? Jesse certainly had. Her Texas cowboy turned Marine. The one she'd let go, because he needed someone a little less driven and selfish. But they'd had some amazing sex, and when he'd discovered what she was hiding under that well-pressed uniform, he'd loved every inch of her. She hadn't thought about Jesse in a long time. God, she hoped he was happy.

She remembered Eve. She'd really liked her. Thought she was beautiful in a very understated, graceful way. A waif of a girl, slim like all ballerinas. Long, pretty brown hair. Izzy ran her hand over her shorn bob. She didn't regret donating it. She just missed her long hair sometimes. The donation aside, this cut was easier, given her lifestyle. But the long hair had been feminine. The only feminine thing about her, really. She shook herself. What the hell did it matter what Liam thought of her naked? She needed to stop thinking about that right now. That was not a complication she needed. He was ruined in that regard. He didn't even think twice about her in that way.

Still, as she closed her eyes, she saw his face. His intense, blue eyes. The smooth skin where the beard had been. He was so different now. She hadn't given him a second glance when they'd met last year. He was with someone, and she didn't mack on other women's men.

Period. He'd been fun, happy, and friendly. Boyishly handsome, yes. But he was actually only two years younger than her, and life had aged him. He had an edge to him now that wasn't the old Liam. She hadn't even thought twice about him back in that Dublin bar. But now, that edge was... she cursed out loud. It was sexy as hell. He was corded with lean muscle, his face was leaner, his eyes more aggressive. And although she was military, and favored the clean cut look, that long hair was fantastic. *Dammit.* This was very inconvenient. If he brought her chocolate, she was done for.

10

iam's breath shot out of him when Izzy came out of the shower. *Dammit.* There was absolutely nothing remarkable about what she was wearing. A well worn, oversized, U.S. Navy t-shirt and a pair of old scrub bottoms with dried paint on them. Her tangle of wet curls just above her shoulders and she didn't have a stitch of make-up on. But she was flushed from the shower and her eyes were glossy. Maybe from fatigue. She stopped short. "Do you have cookies?"

He raised a brow. Still prickly as a porcupine. He'd stood in the hall, outside of her room. It was warm. The kids were squealing in the yard. Paolo was running some sort of landscaping equipment. A pang of guilt hit him about holding out on her. That bungalow had not been bequeathed to him alone. "Come, lass. Put some shoes and bug repellent on and follow me."

"I smell something. Do you have sweets in that bag?" He smiled and said nothing. She dove at him trying to grab his backpack.

He dodged her. "Come now, hen. Don't be like that. I promise, you will not hate me once you see my surprise."

She narrowed her eyes at him, but he'd piqued her interest. She dropped her shower gear at the foot of her bed, then grabbed the new bug tonic he'd given her. Liam looked away as she rubbed it all over her exposed skin. It smelled earthy. Not good, exactly. Just organic. "Is it working?"

She stopped, looking up. "It seems to be. It didn't get rid of the bites, but I don't think I have any new ones. Sorry about the smell. It fades when the skin absorbs it."

"I'll check the supplies and see if I have any ointment. Maybe something anti-itch or something with lidocaine. You need to stop scratching." He looked down at her shoes. "No open shoes. You have to worry about spiders and hookworm. The hookworm is absorbed through the soles of your feet."

"I know how you get hookworm. I am a doctor. These are for the shower." She turned, bending down to her drawer to grab some clean socks. He smiled as she hopped on one foot, getting them on. Then she slid into some trainers. "This better be worth losing nap time."

Izzy watched Liam as he led her down a path that she'd not traveled before. He had a flashlight and a knife on his belt. "You're armed."

"Aye, I am, and if you come here alone, ye should bring a machete or a knife. The jaguars don't usually come this close, but you need to be safe. You won't always have your bodyguard around."

"I don't need a bodyguard, but he's a good interpreter. He's been making me flashcards like a preschool teacher." Liam smiled at that. "Are you going to tell me where you're taking me? Is this like the Hansel and Gretel gingerbread house? You lure me here with sweets?"

"You're very impatient. Ye need to wait and see for yourself. Ye've got your prepaid phone with you, right? It's important you keep it close by, in case we have need of you."

"Are you dumping me off somewhere?" she said, but she stopped short as the path opened up.

Izzy looked around at the small clearing by the river. It was secluded and quiet. Lovely. The shacks were open air, hammocks hung on hooks and fishing traps underneath the pilings. All but one. One was enclosed. It looked fairly sturdy. She followed Liam, intrigued. He walked up the stairs to the porch of the tiny, cracker box bungalow. He pulled a key out of his pocket and said over his shoulder, "It's my little hideaway. I don't own it, though. It's for whomever has need of some solitude." She walked in and was immediately assaulted by cool, crisp, air-conditioned heaven.

"Wow, you have been holding out on me O'Brien." She looked at the bed that was at least double the size of her bed at the abbey. There were black-out blinds as well. She watched with curiosity as Liam seemed to observe a ritual. He looked under all of the furniture and in the bedding, using the flashlight as needed. Then up in the rafter, probing with a wooden staff. When he'd done a full inspection, down to the small cabinets in the kitchenette, he turned to her.

"Ye must do that every time. You saw the result of the wandering spider. There are lots of vicious little bastards that can make their way into even a sound, sturdy dwelling. Don't leave food around. Carry your trash out with you. Don't drink the water. Use the bottles, even for toothbrushing. The shower works. I just cleaned it."

"How did you come by this place?"

Liam told her all about the wealthy doctor who had put it in a trust for the abbey's use. She looked around, stunned at the gesture. Not of the man's, but of Liams. "And you're going to let me use it today?"

"We'll share it while you're here. It's a bit of a walk, but I manage to get down here once or twice a week. It wouldn't be right of me to keep it to myself. Sometimes you need a cool, quiet place to catch up on sleep. I love the kids and the sisters, but between football matches in the garden and that church bell four times a day, it can be hard to get some peace."

"I am going to roll around on that bed like a dog," she said, a cheeky grin on her face. "That nun cot is about a third of the size of my bed at home. Well, what used to be my home. I'm kind of gypsying it right now."

"Any thought on which hospital you'll choose?" Liam asked.

"None, I've barely had time to think. Now, not that I don't want to seem grateful...but I was promised a cookie."

"Oh, aye. Ye were." He rummaged in his backpack and came out with a foil wrapped bundle. "Gabriela's pumpkin cookies, with added chocolate chips to soothe your female soul."

"Chocolate does feed a woman's soul. Don't doubt that science for a minute." She took a cookie from his offerings and bit. Then she moaned. "Have mercy. They're so moist."

"It's the pumpkin and butter." He bit into one. "Christ, those are good. Better with the chocolate. It makes me think of my mother's baking." He seemed to surprise himself with that comment.

"You should try calling her on your own. It would make her feel good."

Liam nodded. "Perhaps in the morning before we head out."

"Head out?" she asked.

"Head out with the mobile clinic," he said, taking another bite.

"Another slum? I hate that term, by the way, but it seems like that's the name everyone uses."

"Yes, it is. It is maybe less derogatory here than it is in Ireland or America. But no, not the slum. Into the bush. You're going to see how the other half lives. Now, get a nap. Dinner is in less than two hours. Do you need me to call you?"

"Nah, I won't sleep that long. But I may curl up with one of those cookies and suck it like a baby bottle. Tell Gabriela she's a genius." Liam laughed because Izzy had a way with words.

He turned to leave and she called to him. "Liam." He looked over his shoulder. "Thank you for this." He nodded, meeting her eyes briefly. Then he walked outside and left her to her solitude.

The pillow smelled like him. It was distracting as hell when she first laid down, but then she let herself settle into the cotton bedding and soft pillows. Not hotel grade, but better than the abbey. With the masculine scent washing over her senses, she felt oddly comforted. It was a guilty pleasure. She hadn't had a man in her bed in so long, she'd forgotten that musky scent they gave off. The intimate one that came with sleep. The smell you only knew if you were well acquainted. She might not have a man in her bed, but she liked the smell of this pillow just fine. She drifted off, more peacefully than she'd slept in weeks.

Liam was intercepted on the way to see the spider bite patient by Sister Agatha. "Excuse me, Dr. O'Brien. The abbess would like to see you."

He knew this was coming. They'd been busy, and he hadn't met her for tea. She knew he'd been in contact with the family. "Tell her I'll be there in ten minutes. I just want to check on the forest worker." Sister Agatha nodded and made her quiet retreat.

The patient was doing well. He was lucid, the antivenin and antibiotics were doing their job. Pedro was taking blood as Dr. O'Keefe examined the flesh around the bite. "He looks good. No infection. I have to admit, this is my first spider bite. Bloody awful way to end up in the hospital." Liam agreed. The man had been in horrific pain. He looked weak, but the moaning had stopped.

"Pedro, let's give him the works while we have him. Blood and urine. Check his body for rashes, test for the usual, look for parasites, fungal infections, bacterial infections, everything. You know the drill. No reason to send him home just to have him back again."

"Sim, médico. Right away."

Liam turned to O'Keefe. "Adam said he'd cover the hospital tomorrow. I'd like you to go with us to the eastern village and into the bush. There will undoubtedly be some pregnant women that haven't made the trip to St. Clare's. It would be good to have you on board."

"Aye, of course. Looking forward to it. The eastern village, is that where Gabriela stays?"

Liam nodded absently. "I have to go see the abbess. Adam will tell you what supplies to switch out. There are things we'll need that we didn't take into the city."

"Landed in the schoolmasters office, did ye? You strike me as the sort of lad who spent some time there in his youth." Liam laughed.

"Aye, I did. This is different. It's a weekly thing with her. Part of my...arrangement for the long stay with the mission."

Seamus raised a brow but didn't pry further. "I'll leave you to it, then. I think our friend, here, is going to be just fine. Where's our young Yank? Having a lie-down?"

"Of a sort. She said she'd be at dinner, but by the look of her, I think she'll sleep through the dinner bell."

"Then you should take her a plate," Seamus said, giving him a sideways glance. "She'll need her strength. Gabriela wouldn't mind. She'd feed me ten times a day if she could." Liam laughed. Gabriela always gave Seamus extra helpings, saying he was a big, strong man. Needed to eat. Quite the change from that callous ex-wife of his.

The abbess was at her desk, deep in thought. Liam knocked on the doorjamb. "Have a seat, lad. I'm just writing a letter to the dioceses." Liam sat, staying quiet. "You did great work today, the whole team. Adam gave me a brief account of the mobile activity. Well done. You've been busy."

"We have. I'm sorry I missed our tea." He wasn't actually sorry. The abbess dissecting him on the shrink's couch gave him the scratch.

"Not at all. If I thought you were avoiding me, I'd have pressed the issue. How are you, Liam? I know you talked to your family."

He fidgeted in his seat. "I did. All is well. Two new babes, another on the way. Everyone is fine. I'm fine."

"You've done the hard part. Now you just have to keep the momentum going. Call once a week. You're not the only one hurting. How did your mother take it? The call, I mean."

"She cried a lot. I didn't know how to comfort her."

The reverend mother waved a dismissive hand. "I've seen you with the children and your patients. You know how. You're a wee bit rusty with the family. It'll come back. The words will come to you. And you should let her comfort you. Mothers need that, to feel needed. Now, how is our Dr. Collier settling in?"

"You'd have to ask her. She's a good doctor, I see that. She's got that commanding presence. It puts the staff at ease. They trust her, and that doesn't often come so quickly with a new foreign doctor. She was a good choice, despite my personal objections."

"Have you put those objections to rest? I assure you, I wouldn't have agreed to the three-month rotation if it had been about getting you to call your mother. She's got an impressive resume. She can treat under less than ideal circumstances. She's a decorated naval officer. Has she told you of her time in Iraq?"

"Not yet, we just haven't had the time. She's headed out into the tributaries with us tomorrow. So is Dr. O'Keefe. Adam will take the lead in the hospital. We're taking Antonio as well."

"Well now, that's a change. We don't usually get him twice in one month." Liam shrugged. She said, more to herself, "I don't suppose it's got anything to do with the new surgeon?"

Liam stiffened. It was subtle, but she noticed. She narrowed her eyes. "Where is Izzy? She usually comes to tea at the cantina and then gathers Genoveva for their…what did she call it? Ah, yes. Sweat therapy."

Liam barked out a laugh. "Yes, she was a bit tired. The first time in the slum is a bit taxing. It takes an emotional toll. I took her to the bungalow that you pretend not to know about."

"Cheeky lad." She gave him a crooked smile. "If she sleeps through dinner, have Gabriela set a plate aside for her. You visiting docs usually start dropping weight you can ill afford to lose. I don't know if it's the heat or the food."

"I'll take care of it," he said. Then something occurred to him. "Reverend Mother, do you happen to know her full name? What is Izzy short for?"

"Why do you assume it's short for anything? Maybe you should just ask her." But the look on the abbesses face told him everything he needed to know.

"She told you not to tell me, didn't she? Her medical screening didn't have her full name, but I bet your files have it. You have a copy of her passport. Why not just tell me?"

The abbess laughed lightly, which was as much mirth as you ever saw out of the woman. "Because I'm an old nun, and I can do what I want. And if she told you to call her Izzy, that should be the end of it."

He stood then, the moment broken. "If we're done here, I'm going to get ready for tomorrow. Gather the supplies. I'd like Paolo to go with us if you can spare him. Between him and Raphael, we should bridge the language barrier."

"Yes, Raphael has been a good addition. I'll have to give that some thought. Perhaps once Dr. Collier's agreement with him is over, I can petition the diocese to fund a full-time interpreter. He's a military man. Given the troubles to the northeast, it may not be a bad idea to have him along on the trips into the forest."

Liam's brow drew down. "You mean the deforestation or the drug trafficking? I wasn't aware it had come this far toward the abbey." Suddenly a tingling of fear struck him at the thought of taking the women out into troubled areas.

"It's inevitable, isn't it? The more they clear of the forest, the more access for trucks and planes. But don't you worry on that account. God will provide and protect."

Liam's disgusted snort came out before he could stop it. "Aye, like it did in Dublin? Forgive me if I don't leave our safety and wellbeing up to God."

The sun was low in the sky, having set beneath the canopy line. Liam walked carefully. He'd deny it with his last dying breath, but the spider bite had rattled him as well. Nothing like a full grown man wailing in agony to put you on alert. The only worse bite he'd seen was a brown recluse, a couple of days into it. The necrotic flesh looked like acid had eaten away at the man's leg. He managed the light and the plate of food up the stairway as the rain started to drizzle.

As he walked into the cool cocoon of the bungalow, he was surprised that Izzy didn't stir. The bathroom light was on, and he saw her still figure on the bed. He shut his eyes, trying to erase what he saw. She was sprawled like a toddler. He had enough nieces and nephews to know how they slept. When Cora was small, she managed to defy physics and take up an entire queen sized bed. Finn would be teetering on the edge, ready to fall off. Brigid on the other side, coiled around the available spaces in a distorted, amusing tangle. Cora's fingers tangled in her hair.

The thought overwhelmed him with affection...until he opened his eyes. Because that was where the similarities ended. Izzy was resplendent. In a tank top and tight cotton shorts, her arms were splayed out, showing every bit of what was under that thin shirt. Her nipples were tight peaks, her smooth stomach peeking out between her shorts and the shirt, which was riding up. She had long, toned legs. *Fucking hell.* A surge of irritation went through him. He was gawking at her in her sleep. He really had the worst timing with this woman. He cleared his throat. "Izzy! Wake up, lass." His voice was just brusque enough to break through, and she shot out of bed with a stick in her hand. "Whoa! Christ woman, easy now."

She blinked at him and lowered the stick that he used to check the rafters for snakes. She looked around, confused. Then looked at him, one eye still shut. "Sorry. Am I needed? I fell asleep harder than I meant to."

"No, but you missed the evening meal," Liam said. His tone a little less hostile. "Gabriela sent a plate."

"Shit. I'm sorry. Sometimes I don't know how tired I am until I hit the pillow. It was so cool and comfortable. I'll get out of your way." She stood and began putting her clothes back on. That's when he realized she wasn't wearing shorts. They were those boy-short style panties he'd seen in lingerie catalogs. The athletic tomboy's version of sexy panties. They covered more than a swimsuit would, but not enough to diminish the effect. He turned toward the kitchen. "Don't worry about clearing out. I'll stay at the abbey. Just set your watch alarm. We'll head out by nine o'clock, and you'll want to prepare and eat breakfast."

She came next to him and put a hand on the covered plate. "This was nice of Gabriela…and you. Thank you. I needed this break."

"It's nothing at all. Before I go, do ye mind if I use the shower? Alyssa was headed to the locker room when I left."

"Of course not. I'm still relatively clean. I won't need one until morning."

She was still clean, but not that freshly showered affect. That would have been easier to handle. The entire cabin smelled like her. It was only about two hundred square feet. It smelled like warm, clean breath. Like shampoo and clean, feminine body. A little earthy, probably from the bug repellent he'd given her. All in all, Izzy Collier smelled good. He suddenly had the irrational urge to smell the back of her neck. Right under where her hair was cropped.

His voice was a bit hoarse. "Why did you cut your hair? If I remember, it was quite long."

Izzy nervously played with the loose curls. "I know it's short. I donated it. I had a friend, a Marine Officer, I knew his family pretty well. We were neighbors in Virginia in the temporary lodging. The relationship stuck even after I moved into an apartment on base, and they moved to a house. His little girl is sick. She has a malignant brain tumor, AT/RT."

Liam cursed under his breath. She continued. "Anyway, she's in the middle of a treatment. They have these charities that you can donate your hair to make wigs for children. So, I cut it," she said with a shrug. "It was good timing since I was coming here. All that hair would have been a nuisance in this heat and I didn't just want it to get tossed in the trash at some beauty salon."

"You're a do-gooder, Izzy. It was a nice thing to do." He looked at her, really looked at her. "I'll only be a minute, then you can be rid of me for the night." He looked at the plate of food. "Eat up, while it's still hot."

Izzy nibbled on the chicken and rice that Gabriela sent. It was good. She hadn't eaten since lunch, and it must be at least seven at night. She swallowed several gulps of the bottled water, needing the hydration. She sighed with contentment. She'd slept wonderfully, and she was secretly overjoyed that he was going to give her the bungalow for the night. She was embarrassed that he'd caught her sleeping. She'd been so out of it, she hadn't even heard him come in. She heard rain on the roof and decided to take a peek outside to check the temperature. She turned the exterior light on and opened the door.

Liam soaped up his body, willing it to cooperate. The sight of Izzy sprawled all over that bed in a little shirt and panties, coupled with the fact that he'd seen her good and naked the day she'd arrived, kept running a play by play in his mind. His cock was screaming for attention, and he was disgusted with himself. It's not like he could take care of it himself. His choices were between doing it here, with Izzy in the next room, which was beyond creepy, and the worse alternative, going back to his room at St. Clare's... the charity mission... operated out of an abbey full of nuns. This was like some sick joke, the arousal unwanted and offensive to his conscience. He wasn't going to think about it, or her, anymore. He was just going to get clean, get dressed, and get the hell out of here. He soaped up his chest, then got under the spray to rinse off. That's when all hell broke loose.

Izzy took one step out onto the porch, breathing in the balmy air. Her front porch was the only light in sight, and it was kind of eerie. She knew Liam would never have left her here if he thought it was unsafe. Just as she began to retreat back into the house, she saw the motion. She looked down about ten inches from her feet and screamed bloody murder.

She leaped to the right, just as the little bastard scurried right through her front door. She ran inside, slammed the door, and went for the bed, hopping up and grabbing her stick. That's when Liam burst through the bathroom door, soaking wet, holding a towel in front of his business end.

He saw the spider and almost jumped out of his skin. "Holy feckin' shit!" He scooted toward Izzy, who was up on the bed screeching every time it scurried a few inches.

"Is that one of those frigging wandering things? It's huge! You didn't tell me they were so huge! Jesus, look at that thing!"

Liam took the stick from her with careful ease. "I don't want to scare it into a crevice. Then we'll never find the little fiend. It's a Goliath spider. It's not one of the really bad ones."

"I don't give a shit! Get it out of here! Smash the shit out of it, O'Brien!"

He laughed, "Do you mind if I cover my ass first?"

"Come on, Doc. I showed you mine. Don't be shy." She was trying to joke around, but he could tell she was scared.

"So, the fearless, bad-ass Izzy Collier screeches like a girl over spiders, eh? I'd never have thought it."

"That is not a spider. That is a bear with really long legs. Now get it done, O'Brien." She hissed.

Liam went at it and it reared up like a monster. He hopped from foot to foot, "Jesus, the little bastard is trying to fight me. Izzy, go open the door."

"No way, that's how he got in! I opened the door and he ran in!"

"Open the door, or I'll leave you here with the thing. And I'll take the flashlight."

"You wouldn't dare," she growled.

"Just try me. Now open the door."

"I am SO telling your mother on you." This made Liam crack off a laugh, despite the stress of the situation. Izzy tiptoed over and opened the door. That's when Liam struck. He launched the thing like a golf ball, right out the door and into the darkness. Izzy ran back over and slammed the door, flipping the lock. Then she looked at Liam, still dripping in nothing but a towel. That's when she lost it.

Liam O'Brien thought to himself that it was quite possible Izzy Collier was completely off her rocker. She was doubled over on the bed, laughing so hard that she curled into a fetal position. He tried to hold it in, be dignified about it, but she just had one of those contagious laughs. The kind you just couldn't hear without laughing yourself. He plopped down on the edge of the bed. "You're bloody insane, woman. Do you know that?"

"I'm sorry. I'm a nervous laugher. It's a condition!" She cackled, barely getting the last word out.

"You scared the shit out of me, woman. I thought it was a home invasion."

She was starting to simmer down. "That was the most ridiculous thing I've ever seen. You just nine-ironed a ten pound spider through the doorway in a towel." Then she started up again, holding her stomach until she wore herself out. She wiped her eyes, taking a big breath. "Thank you, by the way. I'd take on three fully grown gorillas before a big hairy spider."

"Yes, well, I spray the exterior regularly, and the crevices inside. You just can't invite them in by leaving the door ajar. I guess you learned a lesson about life in the rainforest. Don't tarry with the door open. Especially at night."

"Amen to that."

Before he left, he asked her something that he'd been curious about. "Why the Navy? You were done with the schooling for the most part. Why not just roll into a civilian hospital for your residency?"

"I guess I decided when I toured the Marine Corps Air Station in Yuma, Arizona. I was in medical school and the flight doc seemed like the coolest guy I'd ever met. And the pilots were sexy as hell. Cocky fly-boys. He hooked me up with a recruiter that specialized in recruiting for Navy medicine. I got a tour of a military hospital in California, then a big carrier. I was hooked." She smiled, remembering what it was like to be so excited about something. "It wasn't anything I'd thought about before then but it was the best decision I ever made."

"Did you have friends in the military or family?"

"After 9-11, several of the senior boys joined up. I was fourteen when it happened. Playing field hockey in first period when they pulled everyone into the school. It didn't fully sink in, what it all meant, until I watched the young eighteen-year-olds at graduation. You know, when they tell you their name and what college they were headed to. A couple of the guys were good athletes, good students. They could have had their pick of schools. But they enlisted. Most in the Marines, a couple in the Army.

"Why did you leave?" he asked.

"I've asked myself that many times. I think I got tired of saying goodbye. You move a lot in the U.S. military. It's hard to keep relationships going."

Liam wondered if she was thinking about that cowboy Marine she'd parted ways with, or if she meant relationships in general. When he'd met her in Ireland, so many months ago, she'd told them that she'd had a heartbreak. That the man had just recently been married. That she'd been the one to end it because she couldn't be what he needed. Did she still think of him? He didn't like how that felt, although he wasn't sure why. "Goodnight, Izzy. Sleep well."

11

It dawned on Izzy, part way through the morning, that Liam O'Brien was completely in love. Not in a traditional sort of way. It wasn't romantic love. It was something altogether different and surprising. Then again, it shouldn't be. She knew the O'Brien family.

She watched Liam loading the last of the equipment on the ATV trailer and the old, converted Land Cruiser that was owned by the abbey. His shadow, otherwise known as Estela, was a constant. He didn't seem to mind a bit. Some men didn't like kids under their feet, but he seemed to genuinely adore her. She was completely adorable, so who could blame him? She had long, dark hair. She was tiny. The smallest child that lived at St. Clare's, and the youngest, at three years old. When those big, soulful brown eyes fixed on you, you were done for.

Once he finished the last crate of supplies, he scooped her up and put her on his shoulders, taking her into the cantina. Izzy followed, unable to stop watching them. Liam approached the counter, where Gabriela was handing Seamus a large plate of breakfast. That was another weird thing. Gabriela and Seamus seemed to be on very friendly terms, and she wondered if the doctor was developing a crush on her. She was soft and pretty. They were both probably the same age, give or take a couple of years. She smiled at the interaction, but when she thought about it, she realized probably not. Seamus was just grateful to have women in his life who recognized his worth. She liked Seamus. If he'd been ten years younger, she might have had her own crush. She suddenly wanted to wring his ex-wife's neck.

"Gabriela, you feed me too much!" Seamus said.

"No, Senhor. Women no like the skinny man. You need your strength." Her English was fairly good, having worked with the Irish nuns for so many years. Certainly better than Izzy's Portuguese. Still, she was learning. Thankfully Raphael was willing to work long hours. He would quiz her during down times, demanding she speak Portuguese instead of English. Some people had an aptitude for languages. It came easy for them. She didn't, and she suspected that Raphael was going to be with her the entire three months.

She watched as Liam helped Estela decide what to have. She could have the banana cake and guava juice as long as she had some milk as well. He opted for the muesli cereal, and she watched as Gabriela topped it with the local cashews and açaí berries. Then she slid him a cup of that gorgeous coffee. She spoke up, "I'll have exactly what they're having." Liam laughed. "What? I like a big breakfast. Probably explains why my hips will never go down to 34 inches." Gabriela waved a dismissive hand. "No, Médica. You not lose your body. Men like a curvy hips. How will you find a husband if you make your body like a small boy?"

Liam was holding back his laughter as he took Estela over to the children's table, and deposited her breakfast in front of her. She always sat by Genoveva when given the choice. Then Liam joined the other doctors at the adult table. As they ate, Raphael and Paolo came in together. Followed by all of the sisters of the abbey. The Reverend Mother led the group in a morning grace, and they ate.

Seamus said, "Paolo needs help this weekend. He needs to make repairs to the wall. It's come down on the west side, near the school. I told him I'd pass the request on to the staff."

"Of course I will. I'm sure going out with us two days in a row is putting him behind on his other work. Whatever he needs." Liam quickly polished off his cereal and stood. "Izzy, could I use your laptop before we go?"

She warmed from head to toe. He was calling home. She could tell by his face. "Of course you can. I think that's a great idea. Tell everyone I said hello."

Liam departed, and Alyssa asked, "How did you know each other? I know it was through the family, but did you know each other well?"

Izzy shook her head, not knowing how much he'd told them. "Not really. I'm friends with his brother Aidan and his wife. His wife is an American as well. She's one of my best friends. I came for a few reasons, but Liam was one of them. His family…"

She paused, and Alyssa got her meaning. "Did they have a falling out?"

"No, not at all. Liam had some stuff happen to him. It's not my place to say. He just needed to get away. I think this has been good for him. His family just wants to find out how he is doing and now they know."

Antonio smiled, pointing a finger. "I think this smells of woman trouble. Did he get his heart broken? An unfaithful lover or bad parting?"

Alyssa elbowed him, and Izzy said, "Antonio, I'm very serious. Don't push him on the matter. If he decides to tell anyone what happened, it needs to be his choice. Just trust me."

Liam ended the video call feeling relief. His mother hadn't wept this time. He'd seen a few smiles, been teased a bit. More like the mother he knew. Then he'd talked to Brigid and seen the new baby, Declan. It had been nice. Before he ended the call, Brigid cleared her throat. "Ah, Liam. I have a message I'm supposed to pass on from Cora."

"Is she there? Perhaps she could tell me herself."

"No, she's playing down the road. She told me that if you or Izzy were to call, that it was important to remind Izzy of what she told her. The night she stayed with Izzy at Mam's house, she wants to make sure that Izzy remembers what she told her."

"And what did she tell her?"

"I don't know. I guess that's between Izzy and Cora." Liam could tell that Brigid was withholding. The hair prickled on his neck.

He knew that he needed to call Tadgh. He'd missed his wedding. And Michael, who'd had another child as well. He needed to call all of his brothers and his grandparents. He'd been so wrapped up in his own grief, he hadn't been willing to think about how his abrupt departure had affected everyone. Especially Seany. His father had gone to their apartment two days ago and cleaned it out. Loaded his belongings up like a dead man, and hauled them off to be stored in their garage. Liam rubbed his eyes, overcome with regret. He may not be ready to go back to Ireland, but it was time to start communicating with his family again.

Dublin, Ireland

Patrick ran to his cell phone, grabbing it off the counter of their apartment kitchen. "Hello, mam. How's everyone in the West?" They spoke for a little while, and she told him all about her conversations with his brother. Thank God for Izzy. She'd managed to do what no one else had. Letters, phone calls to the abbey, nothing had worked. "She's here. She's just getting out of the bath. She had a back ache. Let me see if she's dressed." He talked as he walked into the bedroom. "Caitlyn, love. It's mam. She wants to talk to you."

Caitlyn stumbled out of the bathroom in a pair of grey yoga pants and a t-shirt. She was starkly white. "Patrick," she croaked, just as she started to go down. The blood was everywhere.

Patrick's heart stopped cold in his chest as he screamed, "Caitlyn! Oh God, no!" he dropped the cell phone as the shouts of his mother went unanswered.

Doolin, Co. Clare, Ireland

Sorcha was in the car before Brigid had even reached her father. "She's gone, da. She reached him on the phone, just as the ambulance was pulling up to the building. She called Caitlyn's parents and then just left! Oh God, Da! I think it's really bad. He said there was blood everywhere. Jesus, da! What should I do? I feel so feckin' helpless!"

Sean's voice was strained. "Ye must call your brother Michael and wee Branna. I'll call Tadgh. He's at work. Then call Seany and Aidan. I'm headed that way as well. I'm headed to Dublin. Once we get the whole picture, I'll call the grandparents. I don't want to alarm them if we don't know the whole story. And pray, Brigid. Like you've never prayed before."

12

St. Clare's Charity Hospital, Manaus, Brazil

Liam walked into the surgery, then stopped, holding back to watch the activity. Izzy was drawing on everyone, on the inside of their arm. *What in the hell?* But as he watched her, he realized what she was doing. She was marking them with their own blood type. Jesus, what had she seen in Iraq? He knew soldiers kept their blood type on their dog tags, in case of emergency.

"Is anyone here allergic to any medications?" Alyssa raised her hand. He knew that she was allergic to sulfa drugs, but Izzy checked something off in her own notebook. "How about bees? We have epipens with us, but I just want to know now rather than later. No one? Great. Raphael, you'll stay with me and Antonio. Paolo, you will stay with Seamus and Liam. Alyssa, if you can be flexible, it would be good to have you float between the doctors."

She was impressive to watch. She noticed him. "Sorry, Dr. O'Brien. I hope you don't mind. We're leaving in ten minutes and I didn't want you to feel rushed." She was talking about the call with his mother.

"Not at all. Sounds like you covered everything. I'll check the supplies, just to get a fresh set of eyes."

As they all walked out of the surgery, she stopped him. "How is everyone?"

"They're all grand. Ma and Brigid said to tell you hello." He was going to talk to her about Cora later when they had more time. "You're a good leader, Izzy. I wouldn't have thought of the blood typing."

She lifted her chin. "My team comes first. Always. If we lose a doctor or nurse, everyone will suffer. I need to be ready if we have an incident while we're out. The field trauma kits are very complete. U.S. Government approved for combat situations. They each also include a field transfusion kit. That's not ideal, but if it comes down between losing someone and a donor-to-patient transfusion in the field, we'll do it. We don't have the capability of carrying blood and plasma in the mobile unit. Between drug traffickers, jaguars, killer spiders, bullseye ants, and whatever else can screw with us, I'm not going to get stuck out in the jungle with no options or missing equipment."

He laughed and interrupted. "Bullet ants, love. Bullet."

She smiled. "Bullet ants," she amended. "Are you ready to head out, Tarzan?"

"Yes, everything looks in order." He was looking through the supplies as they talked. He gave her a sideways glance. "Just don't let Antonio's flirting distract you. Are you sure you don't want Seamus?"

She waved a hand dismissively, "Nah. Antonio probably came out of the womb flirting. Italian men are like that. I need him to weigh in if we have surgical patients."

Liam disagreed. Antonio didn't flirt with everyone. He was friendly, yes. But he was laying the charm on thick with Izzy. He definitely had his eye on her. Which was fine. They were both adults. Then stupidly, he didn't drop the subject. "Not your type? I guess you do prefer the cowboys, now that I recall." He regretted it instantly. Her face held a smile, but her liquid brown eyes had a hint of sadness. "Yeah, sometimes. Literally and figuratively. It hasn't served me well. I should date accountants or male librarians." Her tone was light, but Liam could tell he'd hit a nerve. For some reason he didn't like to think too closely about it. He hated the idea that she was still hung up on that infantry Marine. So, he let the matter drop.

Paolo sat on the ATV. Antonio was behind the wheel of the Toyota Land Cruiser with Alyssa and Seamus. Izzy looked over at Raphael's Jeep and realized that they'd talked him into carrying extra supplies. Antonio yelled, "Room for one more!"

Izzy got into Raphael's Jeep and Antonio's face visibly fell. "You wound me, Isabella."

She laughed. "It's Izzy, now get your ass in gear."

Liam jumped into the backseat of the Jeep, stretching his long legs out over a box of mosquito nets, and they headed into the jungle, northeast of the river.

Dublin, Ireland

Sorcha walked through the car park at St. James Hospital in Dublin with her heels smoking. Her heart was filled with a dread she'd never experienced before. *Oh, Caitlyn.* She loved Caitlyn as much as her own daughter. She loved all of her son's mates this way, as she loved Finn with an unwavering sense of belonging. Once her children had married, that was it. They were family. She'd tried with Fiona, but that had never felt right. She'd tried with Eve…but she couldn't think about that right now. The women in her family were more than blood. They were the daughters of her heart. Aoife, Sean's mother, was the mother of her heart. And Katie…she'd loved her immediately. Both of them young and in love. She'd seen Katie through the worst moments of her life. Wanted to lay down and bleed with her, when she was sure that Katie would never get past her sorrow and take another breath.

Now Caitlyn. She'd been taken in an ambulance because she was hemorrhaging internally. There's no way the child survived that kind of bleeding, and second and third-trimester miscarriages could be dangerous to the mother. A wave of fear and sorrow went through her. She approached the nurse's station in the emergency room. "I'm sorry, Madam. They've taken your daughter-in-law up to the obstetrics floor. Your son went up as well."

"Please," her voice was hoarse and strained. "I'm a nurse-midwife. I need to be with my son. I don't know my way around this hospital."

The nurse's face softened. "Ginny, could you watch the desk. I need to take a walk with Mrs. O'Brien."

As they walked, she filled Sorcha in on what she knew. Caitlyn had suffered a placental abruption, cause unknown. The fetus was just about at eighteen weeks and hadn't passed out of her body, but they didn't detect a heartbeat. Then they'd done an ultrasound. The fetus had died in utero. She'd lost too much blood to put her through trying to deliver, and she was continuing to hemorrhage. She received a blood transfusion shortly after arriving. Her obstetrician was en route. The demised fetus would be taken by D&E, and they would try to save the uterus, and not do further surgery, as long as they could stop the hemorrhage. "They may already be done. They took her over an hour ago, started the dilation immediately. I know the doctor. He's a good man."

The tears poured down Sorcha's face. Then the nurse stopped in front of a pair of swinging doors. She turned to Sorcha and took both her hands. "I'm sorry for it, love. So sorry. But your lad is just past these doors." She squeezed her hands. "Time for chin up, Mam. He's going to need to lean on you." Sorcha, nodded, wiping her eyes. Then she pulled the nurse in for a hug. "Thank you."

As she walked through the doors, she saw Tadgh talking on his cell phone. Then she saw Patrick. His head was in his hands, bent over his knees, as he sat in a waiting room chair. Seany was next to him. Patrick looked up and saw her. The tears were silent, but a shudder went through his body. She tread lightly, like any sudden action would quite possibly shatter him. Then she crouched down in front of him, to get eye level. "It was a boy," he said on a sob, and he collapsed into his mother's arms.

Tadgh watched with haunted eyes as Patrick came undone. It was so unfair. He exchanged looks with Seany, who sat silently, witnessing his mother try to comfort Patrick. Patrick said, "We shouldn't have tried again. I should have made her listen."

"It's not your fault, my lad. No one could have predicted this. I'm a bloody midwife, and I didn't see this coming. I thought she was past the danger."

Tadgh looked toward the elevator, as someone got off. "Charlie," he said in a whisper. And then she was there.

"Oh God, Tadgh. I'm so sorry. How is she?"

"She's out of danger, we think. They haven't had to transfuse her again."

Tadgh took her hand, leading her away into an empty room. He flipped the latch on the door and his mouth was on hers. He was desperate, his mouth plundering hers. Wanting to feel anything but sorrow. "Oh, God. Just touch me. Jesus, Charlie."

She soothed him, mumbling lovers words, comforting words. "I'm here. Shh, it's okay." She kissed his eyes, his forehead, his cheeks, until his breathing started to settle.

"Oh, God. I don't know how to help them. The poor lass. Please tell me how to help them!"

"I don't know, honey. I wish I did. They didn't deserve this," Charlie said, sadly.

"Branna had trouble with the twins, and now Caitlyn. Jesus, Charlie, I know we talked about getting pregnant, but I don't think I could take it if you were in this position. Maybe we should just..." She put a hand over his mouth.

"Don't make rash decisions in the middle of a tragedy. I'm okay now. And when we decide to do this, I'll be okay then. I'm not ready yet, but when we are both ready, I'll be okay."

State of Amazonas, Brazil

Izzy was wide-eyed as they took the dirt road to the next village. Liam grinned to himself because she was so enthusiastic about the next part of this adventure. And it was indeed an adventure. Some people joined the military, some the peace corps. Some people jumped out of perfectly good airplanes. It was exciting, doing a foreign mission. He'd learned more in this last year than he had the entire time in medical school. He was monitoring bacteria levels, parasites, pesticides, and other pollutants from samples that he'd taken himself. Not out of some lab kit that the school provided, but out of both the rivers and drinking water that serviced the surrounding communities. He'd traced exposure and infection chains, attempting to find the source of outbreaks in villages or certain parts of the city. The doctor who had overseen him during the first three months had been a brilliant man. He'd worked in Peru, Columbia, and Brazil, as well as in Nairobi and Angola. He shared his knowledge freely, and Liam had become a better doctor than he could have ever dreamed. He'd also had to fill in during the occasional crisis. Doing everything from helping with the delivery of babies to reviving a drowning victim. Sometimes things were peaceful and uneventful at the mission. During those times, he'd done well-children checks at the orphanage.

Now he was almost envious, watching the excitement and adrenaline thrum through Izzy and Seamus. Seamus had signed up for this medical mission after an ugly divorce. He'd liquidated his practice to pay his wife off. His daughters were grown, and he wanted out of the town where his wife had made him a cuckold. So, at forty-seven years old, he'd stored his belongings at his parents home in Killarney, and taken off for Brazil. He was a major asset to the team at St. Clare's. They needed an experienced OB-GYN. Sister Catherine was a competent midwife. His mother would have loved hearing about her work in a developing nation, but even his mother knew that sometimes, it was time to call the doctor. Midwives couldn't handle everything.

Izzy was completely in her element. She'd been waiting for this. She wanted out into the villages. She was a surgeon, yes, but she didn't need to be cutting on someone 24-7 to feel like she was doing her job. After all, Liam had worn many hats during the last ten months. She wanted to help these people, whether it was well-baby checks, hangnails, dengue fever, or big, freaky, hairy spiders and their little fangs. She turned to Liam and he was looking up at the canopy. Raphael had the top off of the Jeep, pretty brave considering the rain was never far off. His hair was pulled back in a ponytail except for a few strands in front that were flipping around in the wind. It revealed that tan face, perfect bone structure, and stunning sandy eyebrows that arched up to a masculine brow.

He met her eyes, and her stomach flipped. Damn, but he was handsome. All the O'Brien men were. She'd thought herself immune to them, given the blatant flirting that had gone on with Tadgh and Seany. She wasn't here for that. Men were the last thing on her mind, but she wasn't dead. You'd have to be dead to look at Liam O'Brien with that shaggy, sandy hair, the accidental tan, and those dusty blue eyes, and not feel a surge of pure, hormonal lust.

She'd heard about the O'Brien men, about their inability to see anyone but their mates. A strange word for modern times, but she knew it was the right one. The relationships in that family were unlike anything she'd ever witnessed. And as much as she loved them, she envied them, too. Eve had been a lucky woman. She was sweet and beautiful and was taken away too young. And Liam was probably never going to get over it. She understood why he stayed. Why he'd walked away from Ireland. The same reason Seany talked about moving back west. Bad memories. This was Liam's fresh start, but he still had a family back in Ireland. And if she did nothing else while she was here, she'd help him find his way back to them. Even if it was just for a visit or a weekly phone call. They needed each other.

"So, Dr. O'Brien. You've got quite a backyard. You ready to show me how it's done?" She was delighted when Liam put his head back and laughed.

13

The small village they first came upon was a cluster of about thirty houses. Modest, small homes on pilings with glassless windows. Many of the men were fishermen or worked at the fruit plantations. There were plenty of children as well. Several generations of the same family lived under one roof or in clusters of houses. Currently, Izzy was staring into the mouth of a twenty-year-old man who was complaining of pain in the back of his mouth. Given the age, she could guess the culprit, but she gave him a thorough exam anyway. "Antonio, do we have access to an oral surgeon?"

"Yes, I'm afraid the waitlist is rather long. About six months if it's not an emergency," he said. He was examining an infected big toe. "Is it the wisdom teeth?"

"Yes, they're impacted. He's going to have to have surgery. These aren't coming out on their own. It really shouldn't wait six months. His gums are pretty inflamed and I'm worried about infection. They are going to push and shift his bite, and right now his teeth are in pretty good condition."

"I'll see what I can do, médica. I can push an urgent order through. I cannot promise, however." Antonio worked as he talked. "Enfermeira," he said over his shoulder. Alyssa came to his side. "I need the local anesthesia." Alyssa prepared the injection as he cleaned the site.

"Do you always speak in mixed languages?" Izzy laughed.

"He does. It's an odd combination of English, Italian, and Portuguese, but we've learned to follow along," Alyssa answered.

"Do you speak fluent Italian, Dr. Collier?" His eyes were flirtatious as he addressed her in the formal.

"I do. I've noticed the words are similar to Portuguese. It's made it easier and harder. I want to revert to Italian, and it doesn't always match up."

Liam ground his jaw as he heard Antonio pour on the honeyed tongue with Izzy in Italian. "He's quite the charmer, isn't he?" Seamus said as he worked next to him. Currently, they were examining two women. Liam's patient was an old woman who had an upper respiratory infection and Seamus was examining her pregnant daughter who was showing signs of the same problem. Liam ignored him, taking out the Z-Pack and giving the woman instructions for taking the antibiotics. "What, no comment?"

"None of my business. They're adults," he said dryly.

"Hmph, if I were your age, I'd be throwing my hat in the ring, crooning to her in the Gaelic. I thought you County Clare boys were weaned on Gaelic."

Liam smiled. "Aye, we were. I'm just not interested."

"Christ, yer a fool. She's lovely. I mean, in that rip your head off and piss in your skull type of way." Liam barked out a laugh, in spite of himself. "Have you seen her working out with wee Genoveva? She's one of those feisty, fighting American women that like to hand you your fecking ass on a plate. And you'd gladly take the whipping."

This was not helping. "Yes, Seamus. I've seen her. She was in the Navy. She's strong, yes, but she's a good doctor. That's why she's here. Not to thwart advances from the male doctors."

Seamus narrowed his eyes as he handed the pregnancy safe meds to his patient. He gave her instructions in Portuguese, and she took her mother and left. "It seems strange that you knew each other before this, that she specifically came to the mission that you were living on, and you are so disinterested. What is the story, I wonder?"

Liam turned on him, and the look on his face was fierce. "Leave it, Seamus."

To his credit, Seamus didn't shrink away. "I'll leave it for now, but unspoken issues between team members cause problems. They fester. You know it as well as I do." Then Seamus walked away.

Liam walked over to Antonio just as he was bandaging the big toe of a middle-aged man. "How's the patient?"

"It was an infected ingrown nail. I removed part of the toenail, gave him antibiotics. As long as he keeps it clean, he'll be fine."

He looked at Izzy who was examining a thirty-ish woman. "Liam, can you come here?" He sat on the stool next to Izzy. "Under the arm, just past the left breast."

He palpitated the lump. "Yes, she needs to come in for an ultrasound. Maybe a biopsy. I can send it to the lab in Manaus." This was the second young woman with a tumor. "It's similar to the other woman I told you about."

Raphael gave the woman instructions about going to the abbey as soon as possible for an ultrasound. She nodded, understanding. "Tell her she can bring her kids if that makes it easier. One of the sisters will watch them until she gets her test done," Izzy said. Then she turned to Liam. "Is it the water source?"

The woman left and he turned to Izzy. "Aye, I believe so. The deforestation upriver causes the pollution run off to be greater. No barrier to filter through before it runs into the river. And they've been dumping large amounts of pesticide into the rivers to kill the mosquito larva. They tell the people not to bathe or use the river water after a treatment, to use filtration systems or bottled water, but they don't have the resources in these smaller areas for that, and boiling the water doesn't solve every problem. I've seen another case in an indigenous tribal village upriver. They are closer to the areas that are being cleared for development. Some fecking hotel or some nonsense. We caught them dumping old accelerant from the controlled burns right into the river. They could give two shits that the people downriver are getting poisonous water. I've worked with the local government. They behave for a couple of months, then we find out they're doing some stupid, reckless shit again."

Izzy shook her head. "Like spiders, snakes, jaguars, and malaria aren't enough. They have to deal with this kind of willful ignorance. I'm sorry for it, Liam. You're doing important work, here. Really important. So, is that where we go next? To the same tribal village?"

"Yes. We'll head down the road a bit, then unload."

"It's that close?"

Liam laughed. "No, it's just where the next leg of the adventure happens."

A floating mobile clinic. Izzy was grinning so wide, she thought her face would freeze like that. The insects buzzed around them as they motored slowly up the river. She'd seen those pamphlets and promotion videos encouraging doctors to work abroad in developing nations. Rows of hammocks on riverboats. The difference was that those docs did a week or two, then went home. So they lived on the boats. This boat, however, was all business. It was full of supplies. Pre-treated mosquito nets. Coolers with perishable meds and vaccines. With pride, she looked over at the three field trauma kits and the mobile defibrillator they'd packed for today.

"You'll notice the traditional dress. It's the end of tourist season." Liam explained. "But when we get farther into the village, they'll be dressed in more concealing clothing." Izzy listened as he talked about the remote indigenous village. "They speak a dialect. That's why we brought two interpreters. Paolo knows some of the dialects, and Raphael told me he can follow some of them as well. Each tribe is unique. This is a big village. Most speak a combination of Portuguese and their own native language."

As they pulled the boat up to a thin dock, they were greeted by a man that was painted on his face and chest. "Grua! Olá!" Liam waved at the man, then leaned into Izzy and spoke out of the side of his mouth. "His name means *great spearman* so don't try to hit him with your wee stick."

"I'll remember that," she said with a crooked smile.

❧

Izzy was in love. The object of her affection, at present, was an eighteen-month-old baby boy who liked to reach down her shirt when she held him. His mother took him, scolding him in her native tongue. *Don't grab the nice médica's boobies, young man*, was what Izzy assumed she was saying. She laughed as the toddler immediately went to work, rooting and latching to his mother's exposed breast. Extended nursing was a part of life in most cultures other than uptight Americans. She ran a hand over his soft, dark hair. "Found what you wanted, I guess. Sorry, my man. These are ornamental at the moment."

Alyssa laughed next to her as she did a well-baby check on a four-month-old baby. "It's staggering to me that ye've not got a fella, Izzy. How is it that some handsome doctor or sailor didn't snatch you up and drag you to the altar?"

"I haven't had a relationship friendly lifestyle, I'm afraid." Izzy's tone was light, but Alyssa met her eyes.

"Well, now you're out of the Navy. Time to settle down, or are you one of those single for life lasses?"

Seamus, who was checking the blood pressure on a pregnant woman, chimed in. "Now that would be a bloody shame." Then he glanced at Liam who was studiously ignoring him.

Antonio was intensely listening, however. "You've never been close, Izzy? I find that hard to believe."

She glanced across the village, not focusing on anything. "I've been close. It just fell apart when we ended up on different coasts. He's married now, just had a baby. It was best for him that I ended it. He seems really happy."

Antonio shrugged dismissively. "His loss is another's gain. You're still coming to my birthday celebration this week?"

"Of course. I love to dance. Count me in."

"Seamus, Alyssa?" Antonio added. "O'Brien has no sense of fun, but you two will still come, yes?"

Alyssa handed the baby to her mother. "Yes, and Margaritte. Adam won't come, which is good. We need someone at the hospital. Between him and the local staff, they can handle things for the night."

Antonio looked curiously at Liam. "You are an Irishman. What do you call this fun time? Something like smack?"

Liam grunted a half laugh. "It's craic, brother."

"Yes, that's it. Craic. You've lost yours, I take it." Liam bristled. "Well, if you change your mind, you are welcome."

"Hey! I've got a great idea. I'll talk to Gabriela and we'll cook Italian food!"

Antonio laughed. "Gabriela would no sooner turn over her kitchen then she would her firstborn."

Izzy waved a hand of dismissal. "Just leave dinner to me. I have a very persuasive nature. We'll eat before we go out."

They all turned as an older child ran out of the forest. He was pointing and shouting. Raphael stood, grabbing his bag. Izzy knew that he had a large knife inside the pack, and a machete sheathed and strapped to the outside. He also carried a mahogany walking stick, that she knew was for bashing skulls, not for hiking or any kind of limp. "What is it?"

"Two children hurt. They are sick, and something about a tree. I can't catch the whole meaning. We must go!"

Izzy turned to Antonio and Alyssa. "Stay with the supplies."

Antonio protested, but Liam was up on his feet and running alongside Raphael as Izzy grabbed the trauma kit and Seamus the defibrillator. "Do as she says. You cannot leave the lass here alone!" Seamus shouted over his shoulder.

They followed the boy for about five minutes. He was panting, having run his hardest both to and from. As they came to a clearing, just near a stream that led to the river, they couldn't make sense of the scene. Izzy ran toward the smaller child, about nine years old. It appeared he was having a seizure. Liam ran toward the older boy.

Raphael barked out an order. "No! Stop, Médica!" He grabbed Izzy's arm. Liam froze as Raphael pointed up. "What the hell, Raphael! They need me!" Izzy yelled, struggling. "Look, boss! The tree!" She looked up and really focused. Then she looked down at the ground. The parachute was hung up in the high tree branches, attached to a large bound and wrapped parcel. A branch had pierced the side of the wrapping. The white powder covered the fruit tree, the baskets below, and the ground. Cocaine was dusted everywhere. And it was all over the two boys. They must have been in the tree, picking fruit, when it came down.

"Get them in the water!" Liam screamed. "And double gloves, goggles, and masks before you touch them!"

They all worked with efficiency, coming as close to hazmat coverage as they could get. Then Seamus and Liam took the older boy, shaking and twitching, to the creek. Liam turned to the boy who had run for help. "Can you run?" Raphael translated. The boy nodded. "Tell the village not to take water from the stream until I say it's okay!" The boy ran. They took the children quickly to the part of the stream that was up from the cocaine spill.

"It's been inhaled and absorbed through the skin. Izzy, do we have benzodiazepines in the medical supplies?" Liam asked as he attempted to wash the boy.

"Yes. It's back at the mobile unit. Jesus Christ, Liam. This kid's heart is racing like a freight train." She ran water all over his body and clothes. Then began stripping him down to his underwear.

The older boy started getting combative in the water. "Seamus, don't let him hurt himself. Let's get them to the village." He stopped, shushing everyone. "I hear vehicles coming up the clearing. We need to move!"

"Why? They can help transport!" Seamus said.

"No, they're a truckload of traffickers coming to look for that missing bundle. We need to get the fuck out of here right now."

They were met halfway by some of the village men. Antonio had sent hammock stretchers to retrieve the boys. As they raced to the village, Izzy shouted orders. "Seamus, as soon as we get there, help Alyssa set up the solar shower. I need out of these scrubs, stat."

Panic punched into Liam's conscious brain. "Did you get it on you?"

"We all did. I could feel it in the air. I'm just smaller, so I'm feeling it more. My skin is getting numb and twitchy and my eyes are burning." The goggles hadn't been airtight, after all. Antonio met them as they opened up into the village and Izzy started briefing him on the details.

"Gesù Cristo, Izzy. You should have let me go!"

Liam interrupted the back and forth. "Benzodiazepines, now Antonio! Both of them!" Raphael ran to the larger boy and held him in place as Liam ran an IV. Antonio did the same with the smaller child. Fluids started, they gave them the anti-seizure drugs and saline.

Izzy listened to the small boy's chest. "Heart rate is too high.Way too high, and I think I've got a broken rib. The lung is collapsing. We need an oxygen mask and to get him to the mission!" But just as she tried to finish the last word, her breakfast made an appearance. She leaned away from the child and vomited. Then she was off her feet.

As soon as Liam got that kid's meds going, he leapt into action. He grabbed Izzy, scooping her up into his arms. Seamus fired up the portable shower as Alyssa went to work with a scrub brush and soap.

Antonio was screaming over his shoulder as he tended to the small children. Raphael, worried but focused, told him the rest of the story. They'd all been exposed to some degree to a burst bundle of cocaine. Antonio's look of horror focused on the rest of the group. Seamus was pouring a five-gallon jug of bottled water over his own head while Liam and Izzy shared the solar shower. Then off came the scrubs. "Raphael! Get your ass over here!" Raphael was next, as was the boy who'd run for help.

STACEY REYNOLDS

Antonio and Alyssa monitored vitals on the rescue crew as they, in turn, monitored the three children. One father had come along, to assure the safety of the children. Raphael was on the one satellite phone that the abbey owned. He was calling his prior commanding officer in the Brazilian army to report the drug activity and toxic spill that was so close to the village. They'd left the remainder of their bottled water with the village, but until the mess was taken care of, the army would bring a mobile filtration system upriver.

"Your heart rate is coming down, Senhorita," Antonio said, the relief in his voice obvious.

"Check her blood pressure," Liam snapped. He started pacing up and down the deck of the boat. "That's it. Next trip out, Seamus, Antonio, and I go out alone. Paolo can translate."

Seamus's brows went up, a whistle escaping through his teeth. Antonio didn't have the same sense of self-preservation, however. Antonio said, "I agree. I can come more often. Now that Izzy is covering the surgery, I can..."

Izzy shook off his attempt to put a blood pressure cuff on her. She had fresh scrubs on, but her hair was still wet. The curls bouncing as she jumped out of her seat. "Wait one minute, you two!" Alyssa was right next to her, hands on her hips.

"Don't even start, Izzy. This is not up for discussion!" Liam sliced his hand through the air.

Izzy struck out at him like a cobra hissing. "Who the hell do you think you're talking to? You are not my boss and you don't order me to do shit, germ-boy. We all took care of business today. Did a smash-up fucking job, as a matter of fact. We took every precaution. And no one held the team back because they had tits!" She was screaming now.

"Christ, woman! You're so bloody minded! We're just trying to protect you! This isn't America. You aren't on a Navy base!"

Her tone was deep, and a hint of menace rolled off her. "Don't patronize me, O'Brien. I've got no patience for it. I was landing in a hot zone when you were sipping lattes with your college buddies in

Dublin." She turned to Antonio. "And I suggest you stand the fuck down, too. I had enough Italian men in my family talk down to me because I was a girl. I expect more from you, so get on board, or stay out of my goddamn way."

She took a deep breath, trying to quell the urge to actually punch Liam in the face. "We are not changing the team line-up based on gender, unless one of you cupcakes wants to volunteer to stay back. End of discussion." She sliced her hand across the air, mocking Liam.

He began a retort, but she cut him off. "Now focus, because we aren't home yet." She walked to the edge of the boat as they pulled up to the dock that would lead them to their vehicles. Adam was standing by, their only pediatrician. "You move fast, brother. How did you get here?" He pointed behind him to Gabreila's scooter. "It takes a man who is completely secure in his manhood to be seen on one of those." She smiled, trying to shake off the urge to drown Liam O'Brien in the river.

Once the children were settled with Adam in the pediatric unit of the small hospital, Izzy and the entire team were summoned to the abbesses office. Reverend Mother Faith rubbed her temples as the story unfolded. Then she said, calmly. "You did extraordinary work today. Truly. I'm humbled by your strength and bravery. And thank you, Raphael. It sounds like you were a crucial part of the team to-day. It appears…" she sighed, "that the reality of human conflict has breached our walls. The drugs, the deforestation, it's getting close to those villages we serve. We'll need to proceed with caution."

She turned to Paolo. "You will accompany the medical team on all excursions into the forest, as will you?" She turned to Raphael. She phrased it like a question, because Raphael worked for Izzy, not the abbey. "I'll petition the dioceses in Ireland for additional funds. We need our doctors to be more carefully guarded."

"Sim, Reverend Mother. It would be my honor to serve the church in this manner. Dr. Collier has paid me fairly, and her Portuguese is improving, but I would welcome a more permanent arrangement."

"Your English is exceptional, Raphael. It is a blessing that Dr. Collier thought to hire you." She turned to Liam. "Now, lad. Do you have a bullet ant in your britches, or do you have something to say?"

Izzy's body tensed, ready for a fight. It didn't go unnoticed. Alyssa was grinding her teeth. "Well now, is it a battle of the sexes we have going here?" The abbess didn't miss a thing.

"Seamus and I can work around Antonio and Adam's schedule. We can handle the village visits while Dr. Collier and Alyssa cover the hospital."

The abbess raised a brow. "I see."

Izzy's jaw was tight, keeping her mouth shut. Nuns were notoriously conservative and she didn't know which side Reverend Mother Faith was going to land on in this argument.

"What you meant to say was that you lads would go on ahead, and leave the women to tend the hearth. Is that it?" The abbess was not amused.

"This isn't about being a chauvinist. It's about safety." Liam said. Antonio, the traitorous bastard, was nodding along with him. Seamus, who had lived in a house with four women, safely kept his own counsel.

Izzy leaned in, so he heard her perfectly. "How about you and I go outside and go a few rounds, and we'll see who can protect themselves more efficiently?"

Alyssa smiled, "Aye, black belt aren't you? An accomplished fighter. Perfect." Alyssa pointed a thumb at Izzy. "I'm with her, Abbess. You can let the lads cover their own asses."

The abbess gave an amused grin before she continued. "The sisters of St. Clare carved this abbey out of the jungle decades ago. We've always run on a predominantly female staff. Yes, you boys are fine, strong lads. You're welcome here and of invaluable use to us poor women-folk. However, if you can't work with your female staff, I assure you that it will be you who is left back to tend the hearth."

She stood up. "That's all we'll say on the matter. Now, Izzy, love, if ye think you can find your way to the library without one of the male doctors showing you the way, your computer has been making some sort of ringing noise all day."

Izzy closed her eyes for a moment, letting her adoration for this hard-ass nun, roll over her. "Thank you, Abbess. I think I can find my way."

They filed out of the office and Antonio spoke first. "I'm sorry. She's right. We just...it is the nature of men. I'm sorry if that is not the modern way to think. It seems archaic, but it's hard to beat it out of us. Real men protect their women."

Izzy sighed. She prided herself on the ability to take care of herself, but she liked strong men as well. "I understand, Antonio. But your good intentions stop at the door when they interfere with my job. I'm not trying to beat anything out of you. I actually like men who have a chivalrous streak. You just have to treat the female staff with respect. You have to trust us as part of your team. We would never take unnecessary risks. We want to be right on the front lines with you. It's how it is. You need to accept it."

Antonio stared at her for a long time. "You are a stubborn woman, but I understand. We're a team."

Izzy nodded, satisfied that she'd gotten through to him. Then looked a Liam. His jaw was tight, his eyes shut. "Can you excuse us?"

The group left her alone with Liam. He opened his eyes, his face tense. Izzy knew where this was coming from. She'd never met a bigger group of alpha dogs than the O'Brien men, and that was saying a lot considering she was in the military. They protected their women. Liam had lost his. In a brief, horrible moment when Eve had been without him, he'd lost her. Having Alyssa and her there in the middle of a crisis had to have set off all kinds of triggers in his mind. She knew all about triggers, having loved a man who'd been in combat.

She put her hands on his shoulders and forced him to look at her. "I know this is hard for you, and I understand why. I also know that you weren't raised to be a misogynistic pig. Sorcha and Brigid would have beat you into submission." She gave a smile, trying to lighten him up a bit. "I'm okay. Everyone is okay. It just hit me harder because of my size. Thank you for taking care of me. I'm glad you were there today."

A shudder went through him. "I didn't like how I felt today," he said. His voice was hoarse with emotion.

"Neither did I. All that hype about cocaine is bullshit. I feel like hell. Not to mention that Antonio and Seamus have seen me in my panties and bra. There'll be no living with them now."

He laughed, "I'm serious. For feck sake, Izzy."

She took his face in her hands. "I know. Very serious." She dropped her hands. "Now, if you want to take care of me, get me some food. I'm getting hangry. If you don't get my blood sugar up, I may give you that ass beating you've been begging for."

After a quick dinner, Liam went to the hospital to check on a new patient that had come in. Adam suspected Zika. The disease was passed through the blood, so they hadn't quarantined the woman. They just double gloved it when she was having blood drawn. As he stood over her bed, she was so weak. He put a hand on her head. So hot and her color was off. "I'm sorry," he whispered. "I'm sorry I can't do more." He would try. It's why he'd come. Why he'd specialized in infectious disease. So many people needed help and they didn't have the resources to get it.

Across the garden, Izzy went to the library to check her computer. She'd left her video calling program open, and saw that she actually had a video message. She pushed play and saw Alanna's face appear. She was in tears. The message she left was brief and she had trouble speaking through her sobs. She ended with, *You need to tell him. I don't want someone else doing it through an e-mail.* Izzy wiped the tears from her own eyes away, but it didn't do any good. They kept coming. *Jesus. Poor Caitlyn.*

She closed her laptop and walked toward the hospital. It had been a trying day. Liam was on edge, twitchy either from a brief exposure to airborne cocaine or the stress of the crisis they'd dealt with. Now, this. She needed to find the right words, and then he needed to call home. The damn tears wouldn't stop. It was both due to sadness and a stress response. She walked into the lab where Liam was seated in front of a microscope. He looked up and his face fell. "What's wrong, lass. Is it one of the boys we brought in?" He jumped out of his seat.

She cleared her throat. "No, Liam. Please sit. I need to tell you something. It's going to upset you, but I need to tell you and then we'll proceed from there."

He frowned remembering where she'd been headed after dinner. "You checked your computer. What's happened, Izzy?"

A tear came down her cheek as she came around the table and took his hand. "It's Caitlyn. She lost the child." She didn't tiptoe around it. He needed answers, not horrible imaginings. "She's stable, but she's in the hospital. Apparently, it was a pretty severe miscarriage. They had to give her a unit of blood. She was pretty far along."

Liam started shaking uncontrollably. "Jesus. I thought you said she was okay?"

"She was. Second-trimester miscarriages are rare, but they happen. Luckily Patrick got an ambulance there and she's okay. I'm sorry, Liam. Alanna didn't want you hearing about it in an e-mail. The whole family is a mess."

She wiped away the tears, and Liam really looked at her. "I'll need to use your computer."

She nodded. "I'm sorry for your family, Liam. Especially for your brother. It must have been horrible for him."

Liam's shaking intensified, but he wouldn't let go. Wouldn't let the emotion come out. "It's okay, Liam. Whatever you're feeling is okay. Pissed, sad, scared, whatever."

He stood up abruptly. "Don't psychoanalyze me, Collier."

"I'm sorry," she said simply. "I'll leave you alone. My computer is in the library." She was gone before he could take his caustic comment back.

Liam stared at the empty screen for what seemed like hours. Finally, he heard the library door open. "Dr. Collier told me I could find you in here." The abbess sat next to Liam. "We'll say a mass for the child on Sunday when the priest comes. And I'll remember your brother and sister-in-law in evening and morning prayers."

Liam gave a bitter laugh, but she was used to his process. Bitterness and anger were mother's milk to him. "We've come a long way, you and I. I know you, lad. Better than you think. You'd best get the meltdown out of the way before you leave this room. I won't have you exploding on a proxy when you can't contain your emotions anymore."

"What the hell do you know about it?" he snapped.

"That's it, lad. Let's have it." Her face was so calm that it was maddening. He started pacing. "What kind of God fills that orphanage full of unwanted children. What kind of bastard leaves little Estela without a mam or da, then takes three children away from Caitlyn?" He growled. "Goddammit. I don't understand it! She's a good lass. The best. He's Garda, a public servant. They live cleanly, go to mass every week. They take care of themselves and everyone else. Why? Why can't they have a feckin' break?" He struck like a grizzly bear, swiping piles of books off of a nearby table. They flew across the room. "Tell me why!"

"I don't know. I wish I did." She was calm, but she understood his anger. "I ask myself the same questions. I ask God, but I don't have any answers. I could quote you something from the bible, but it wouldn't be an answer. It would be an attempt to seem like I have all of the answers, which isn't fair or helpful."

He met her eyes, surprised at her candor. She continued, "I don't know why horrible things happen. I don't know why Emilio's mother overdosed and his father sells drugs and doesn't take care of him. I don't know why Estela's mother died in childbirth after her father died of malaria. I don't know why the hell I can't figure out who sired Genoveva, so she'd have one parent to care for her before she turns of age and I have to turn her out!"

Her voice, usually calm, raised in anger. Then she slumped in her chair. "I don't know. And I'm sorry. I'm so sorry for all that you've lost. But you have people to turn to, Liam. You have friends here. Your family can't be here to comfort you and receive comfort from you. That's a hard position to be in, but you must learn to rely on your family here if you're going to make a life at St. Clare's."

She stood and approached him. She cupped his chin. "You need to let your body weep, my lad. Let it grieve and weep, and empty that toxic pot of anger and sorrow that boils within you. Empty it, or you'll never make room for new and better things." He stared at nothing as she walked away, her robes swishing in the silence of the abbey.

Liam opened the door to the children's room. The father had fallen asleep in an empty room next door, exhausted from standing vigil over his two sons. The other boy was sleeping in the orphanage, waiting to go home to his own family. Izzy was asleep in the chair, next to the youngest boy. She'd been unbelievable today.

He'd acted like an ass. He knew it. His mother would have boxed his ears for telling a doctor and a nurse they had to stay back because they were women. As he looked at her bent neck, her legs curled into herself, she seemed so small and vulnerable, and a wave of affection went through him. She was such a hard ass. She'd actually challenged him to step outside and see who would be the last doctor standing.

He smiled at the thought. She was feisty. Nothing new to him, given his family history. And the Reverend Mother hadn't batted an eye when she'd taken Izzy and Alyssa's side. *Deliver me from strong-minded women.* Still, he respected them all even more after today. He had to apologize to Alyssa, tomorrow.

The vitals on the boys looked good. The dry erase boards showed that they'd checked them hourly. For now, he'd let them sleep. Tomorrow, they'd check the blood to see if the cocaine was working out of their systems. He shook his head. Overdose by tree climbing. Jesus. What a scene. It made him want to take a vigilante group into the jungle and hack those drug traffickers limbs off and beat them to death with them. Their deaths would be preventive medicine for the people in this part of Brazil. And to the web of cities that those drugs would be distributed throughout.

He watched Izzy's soft breathing, and he was so weary. As if she felt his pain, she stirred and opened her eyes. "They're doing okay," she said. Her voice was groggy, her eyes sleepy.

"I didn't come to check on them," he said. She sat up, putting her legs down. When she met his eyes, there were tears welled up in their chocolate depths. It was like a kick in the nuts. "I'm sorry for how I've treated you today. On just about every fucking level."

"How are you doing, Liam? Really?" She ignored the apology like it didn't matter. Like all that mattered was whether he was going to twist himself into an uncontrollable basket case. *Let your body weep. Empty that toxic pot of anger and sorrow...*

He got on his knees in front of her. "I'm a mess, Izzy. And I'm tired of pretending I'm not." He watched her throat do an involuntary spasm like she was trying to keep a sob down in her belly. She pulled him to her, cradling him in her lap. She rubbed his back, soothed him as best she could. He never cried. Not a tear or a sob. He just melted into the contact, and that was something. She felt like he was letting something drain out of him. For now, it was enough. It was progress.

14

Liam woke in his small bed in the hospital staff quarters. He'd slept well. After Adam took over watching the boys, he and Izzy made their way to their beds. Izzy showered first, then he did. Washing off the sweat and bug repellent and sunscreen and every other bloody thing they'd come in contact with. The only time Izzy had spoken to him is when she'd said good night on the way into the locker room.

As Liam dressed, he stifled the feeling of panic he felt. He hoped to hell he hadn't given Izzy the wrong idea. She'd given him some comfort last night, yes. And there had been a sort of intimacy to it. He just didn't want her thinking things that she shouldn't be thinking. Women could get emotionally confused with physical contact. Nothing had happened other than her holding him for a bit, letting him take refuge in her embrace. There had been nothing sexual about it. Still, he really didn't need her getting all up in her head about him. He was about as emotionally crippled as a man could get without being a sociopath. She'd helped him. He was letting his family back in, slowly. And he'd been able to suffer through this grief with them. He'd talked to Tadgh, then Seany. His mother and Patrick were camping at the hospital. His da by his mother's side.

He walked through the hospital, determined to put a little comfortable, professional distance between himself and Izzy. Maybe he'd push Antonio a little further in that direction. Izzy was a beautiful woman, and they were both single. Perfect. So why did the thought of that make his gut twist?

He found Izzy in the surgery, and her scrubbing team hard at work. "In trouble again, I see." He looked at the boys, who were scowling as they scrubbed the floor. Izzy was all business. Genoveva was helping her arrange the surgical tools in the sterilizer. "Pedro got the results back for the first tumor patient. It looks like it's 100% encapsulated with clean borders. I called Antonio. Once the tumor is removed, we can test the surrounding tissue in six weeks and decide whether she needs radiation, but it hasn't metastasized. Looks really promising."

Liam let out a huge breath. He was such an idiot. He'd been expecting to come into the hospital today and see what, exactly? Izzy Collier all moony and glowing because he'd let her hug him? When had he become such an arrogant bastard? "Thank God. She'll be so relieved. I'll send word for her to come in. Did the other lass show up, from yesterday?"

"Not yet. Let's hope that it's the same type of growth if it is cancer." Genoveva finished beside her. "Médica, completo! Can we go?"

"Did Sister Maria say it was okay?"

"Sim, Médica. While the children play in the yard, I can work with you."

"Okay, rapazes. Go play with your little ball. You're done until after lunch."

Emilio stood up and pointed at Genoveva. "Why does this..." he thought about what he wanted to say in English. "She. Why do she get to work out with you, and we go with the smaller children?"

Raphael walked in just in time. "Raphael, explain to these boys why we don't invite anyone to work out with us."

When he explained in Portuguese, Liam barked out a laugh. Izzy looked at him, grinning. Liam translated. "The best I can interpret, he reminded them that they'd excluded Genoveva from the football games. Then he said that the workouts were much too difficult. That they were better off on the football field with the smaller kids."

Izzy gave Genoveva a fist bump. "And what's our mantra?"

"Strong is the new skinny," Genoveva said as she strolled past the boys with her head held high.

Liam walked into the garden area where he heard some *Imagine Dragons* blaring from an MP3 player. They weren't in the walled garden but beside it. Izzy was jumping on old tires from the Land Cruiser with Seamus at her side. He called it his revenge crossfit. It was done using refuse, and out in the jungle, like a real man. Not in some overpriced gym full of spandex wearing twats. Izzy was crying, she was laughing so hard.

Liam saw two figures staring around the hedge. Emilio and another boy named Henrico were hiding and watching. Henrico was a good boy. He didn't get in trouble like Lucca and Emilio. He heard them talking. Emilio was being his usual, snotty self. Henrico, however, was watching with the focus of a smitten young lad. He followed his gaze to see if the boy was getting an eye full of Izzy when he stopped short. *Wow.*

He wasn't looking at Izzy. He was looking at Genoveva. She had a lightweight bamboo staff and was sparring with Raphael. She was a big girl for her age. Probably about five foot seven inches. She'd always worn oversized clothes, but she'd traded that in for a pair of Izzy's workout pants and a fitted t-shirt. She was sturdily built, yes, but she was already whipping into shape. She wasn't skinny. She was built like a brick shit house. Fully into puberty, she had wide hips, strong legs, and more of a chest than Liam wanted to recognize. Not beauty queen proportions. More like a female MMA fighter. But whatever-Henrico saw, he liked. He was absolutely starstruck. Liam wanted to throw blinders on both of the boys. "Lads!"

The boys jumped in unison. "Get back to the play yard with the other students. This is invitation only." He said it in Portuguese again, in case they missed his meaning, and they slumped their shoulders and left. Izzy smiled as he approached. "You knew they were there."

"Of course I did."

"She's learning fast. Christ, look at her. She's like a different lass." Izzy glowed, wiping the sweat from her face with the bottom of her shirt. "And we've got Seamus working out. Seamus! What's our mantra?"

Seamus groaned as he leaped up onto the tire. "Strong is the new skinny. Christ, woman. I'm ready to puke."

Izzy laughed. "It's not a good work out until someone boots! Just don't puke on the tires!"

"You're an evil woman, Izzy Collier," Liam teased.

She smiled. "No, I'm a harsh but fair master. You wanna join us?" He gave her a sideways glance. "Maybe next time. Antonio called. She's set for surgery tomorrow. And I will be in there. She's my patient. I didn't shave the beard fer nothin'."

His accent was thick and she giggled. "I kinda miss that beard. You looked all caveman and rugged."

He rubbed his chin. "Aye, it was rather dashing."

She rolled her eyes. "Cocky bastard." Which made him laugh.

Liam watched her walk back to the tires and her latest victim. She had a beautiful ass and legs. She wasn't skinny, either. She was curvy and strong and had just enough muscle to cross the line between buxom and athletic. He'd seen it all, in living color, that day in the locker room. *Dammit.* Every time he thought he'd rid himself of that image, it came back. Her swaying breasts, the water running down her belly to the place between her thighs. He stirred to awareness as she continued over to where Raphael was instructing the girl.

"Careful, lad. That complete disinterest is showing as plain as day on your face." Seamus said. Then he jumped back up on the tire. Liam turned quickly and walked toward the hospital.

It was time to scrub in, and Liam couldn't find Izzy. She wasn't in the operating room. Then he heard a very unladylike curse word come out of the patient restroom across the hall. He knocked briefly and heard her grunt something like *come in*. He opened the door and stared dumbly, not sure what he was seeing. "What are you injecting into your leg, Dr. Collier?"

She looked up from the syringe and said, "Heroine. You want some? First shot is free."

"Very funny. What in the hell are ye doin'?"

"It's local anesthesia. My bites are itching like crazy. Nothing topical is going to last long enough to get me through this surgery. It's distracting and I really don't need to be twitchy while I'm cutting." She was currently trying to inject near a bite on her calf while looking in the mirror.

"Why don't you let Alyssa do that?"

She looked up, frustrated and annoyed. "Because she's prepping the patient who's scheduled for surgery."

"Jaysus, woman. Give me that before you do more harm than good." He took the syringe from her. "Come out into the light and lean on the exam table."

He knelt down, sticking her with the lidocaine near the bite on her calf. Then he stood. "All right. Where else do you have them? Did you get the ones on your arms?"

"Yes, I got a few of them. They don't really itch as much. They're older."

"So where are the itchy ones?" Silence…. "Did you not understand the question? Should I talk slower?" Izzy's mouth was tight. "Now, now. Don't be shy. I'm a doctor the same as you. And it's not like I haven't seen…"

She swatted him on the arm. "Don't finish that sentence."

He lifted a brow. "Your patient is waiting."

She let out a dramatic sigh. "Okay, but don't you dare laugh. I will seriously choke you out if you laugh."

He watched as she untied her scrubs, turned around, and leaned on the exam table. She had another pair of those shorty style panties.

They were black with… "Is that the house crest for Gryffindor?" She tried to turn around and he put a hand on her back, taking another look.

"They were a joke, okay? From a friend. And I'm behind on my laundry! Just get this over with and don't worry about my panties."

You could just take them off. Nope, he did not just think that. He leaned in, seeing the bites. "Okay. I've got two. One on the back of your left thigh that looks rather angry, and one in the crease under your butt cheek, right by the Quidditch broom.

She barked out a laugh. "Shut up! There is no broom! Just clean them and shoot me up!"

Liam was shaking with laughter as well. He swabbed them both. "Okay, here we go. Bend over the table Hermione, I'm going in."

Just before he stuck her in the ass, she said, "Is this the part where you tell me I'm going to feel a tiny prick behind me? Ow!" Then they were both laughing. Once Liam got started, he was laughing so hard that he fell to the ground.

She was bent over, crying as she laughed. "Hey now, you can't bend a girl over and leave her waiting like this. Get back up here and try again." The laughter took on a life of its own, filling the room to bursting.

Then Alyssa walked in. She stopped, jaw dropped. "Oh, excuse me!" She went to make a hasty retreat when Izzy yelled, "No, please!" She could barely talk she was laughing so hard. "Don't leave. I need your help!" Alyssa paused halfway out, then turned. Antonio was next. Izzy didn't even think about the fact that her pants were half-way down her legs in front of half the hospital staff. Alyssa cocked her head. "Are those Gryffindor knickers?"

Liam loved watching surgeries. Sometimes, he envied the profession. He loved what he did, but watching Antonio and Izzy tag team in the operating room had been a great morning. He trusted Antonio with his patients, but having Izzy there had been such a relief. And now they had Seamus for the birthing duties. He loved a full house. He said as much over tea with the abbess.

"Yes, we've needed them. I prayed for so long. Things have been hard these last few years. Less money coming in, fewer volunteers."

He set his teacup on the saucer. "You need to use modern marketing techniques. You may be a non-profit branch of the church, but you need to think like a businesswoman. I know you talked to Sister Agatha about this very thing. Why do you resist?" She waved a hand dismissively. "Reverend Mother, do you know how to remove an appendix?" Liam asked.

She furrowed her brow. "Of course not. What does that have to do with anything?"

"If someone came to the hospital right now with a ruptured appendix, would you let them die because you couldn't do the surgery yourself?"

The abbess narrowed her eyes at him. "Are you saying I have control issues, Dr. O'Brien?"

He smiled sweetly. "Yes."

She sighed heavily. "Giving me a bit of my own medicine, are you? Psychoanalyzing me?" He just sat back, arms crossed, challenge in his gaze. She changed the subject. "Have you thought about what I said? About making room for new and better things?"

He stared down at the delicate, porcelain cup. "I have. It's good in theory."

"I see. And what about putting it into practice is giving you pause?"

"It's not that. You're right. Letting go of some of the anger and sorrow, it's been good. I'm back in touch with my family. I'm even laughing on occasion, but don't spread that around." He had a crooked smile. "It's just not going to go any further than that. Some things can't be fixed. Some things are gone forever."

"Are we talking about love? What passes between a man and a woman?"

He nodded silently. "My family loves once. I had my shot at it. She's gone."

"Ah, I see."

"No, you don't. You have no idea, so you'll have to take my word on this Reverend Mother."

Her mouth tightened. "One of these days you're going to come down off of Liam O'Brien mountain and realize that there's more going on than you realize. Other people have lived completely independent of your personal tragedy. They've loved, lost, and hurt outside of your existence."

"What do you mean? If you want me to believe that, then spill it. I come here every week and suffer this head shrinking. Maybe it's time for you to share. Because from where I'm sitting, you are completely unqualified to counsel me on this matter." He knew she wouldn't. The number one rule of psychology. Don't mix your own experiences in with the patients. It's never about you. *I wasn't always a nun.*

She deflected. "So explain to me how it works. Why is it that you are so convinced that Eve was the only woman you'd ever be capable of loving? You never married. You were young. You've admitted to me that she was your first serious relationship. Admitting that you can love again is not denying her the honor of being your first love, Liam, my dear. What happened to her was so horribly tragic, that it's altered the path of your entire life."

She put her hands on the desk and leaned in, something like pleading in her wise eyes. "But she was taken away before the permanent joining was complete. You never married, never had children, never even lived together like so many young people do nowadays. What if... now hear me out..." she said as he began to protest. "What if she was the dream of a mate, unrealized? The potential that was cut short. Can't you see how that would make room for you to find someone else? After all, this loss has changed you. You talk of yourself as if you are two entirely different people. The man before the loss and the one after. Perhaps the man you are today needs a different kind of love. A different mate. Someone who can accept you with your tragic past, and love the man you've become in its wake."

She shook her head. "I hope very much that I'm right, lad. Because if you aren't going to become a priest, it would be a shame to see you live your life alone. God gave humankind love and marriage and the making of children as a gift." Liam's eyes were shut now, his body tense. "What I've said hurts you, doesn't it?" He opened his eyes, suddenly angry. "And when you're hurt, you get angry. It's how you're wired, but it wouldn't hurt if I hadn't struck a chord somewhere in that stubborn mind of yours." She gestured to his cup, abandoned on the desk. "Finish your tea, lad. Then hunt down Sister Agatha and send her to me. Apparently, she's been nominated to teach an old dog new tricks."

As Liam walked across the green space in front of the hospital, he caught the distinct scent of garlic, accompanied by the muffled sounds of dance music. The music wasn't coming from the area where Izzy worked out, so he followed his nose and his ears. As he approached the cantina, he paused to make sense of what he was seeing. Three lads. Lucca, Emilio, andHenrico. Lucca was holding a wooden crate in place while Emilio sat onHenrico's shoulders. At least they'd used a safety spotter. He had four brothers. He knew what this was about. Females.

He cleared his throat, and they all three flipped around, causing Emilio to start a rapid descent. Liam grabbed the lad by the collar just before he made impact. "I'm not going to ask. Just go."

They ran off as Liam heard laughing behind him. Seamus was smiling widely. "Boys will be boys."

Liam shrugged. "If it had been any building other than the cantina, I'd have taken them straight to Sister Maria. There can't be much to see in the cantina that would corrupt them." Famous last words. Liam tried the door to the dining area and found that it was locked, so he went around to the back, adjacent to the high window that the boys had been peeking through. He laughed as he heard the whistling start of a song by Maroon 5. He only knew the bloody band and all about Adam Levine from his sister. She had a thing for the ripped, tattooed lead singer. Rumor had it that this was the reason there was a tattoo crawling up Finn's left torso. The IT geek broke any stereotype about nerds. He was built like an O'Brien. Had long, black hair. The tattoos made him look more like a Pict warrior than a computer guy.

Liam noticed that Seamus was hot on his heels. The back door was locked as well. Liam had a key to the front, so they returned to the dining hall entrance and he opened it…only to be greeted by Raphael. He waved to the man and Raphael nodded. Seamus said, "Gabriela must be cooking up a secret recipe. It smells gorgeous altogether. Like a Roman holiday." Seamus loved Gabriela's cooking.

Then Liam remembered. Izzy had promised to cook Italian for Antonio's birthday. He made a shushing motion and approached the next door that lead to the kitchen. It was not locked, not that it mattered. He had a key to almost every door, being a staff doctor.

He gently opened the door, careful not to make any noise. Not that it would've mattered. Izzy had the music up so loud, it could have been heard in Dublin. Then his mind went blank as he got a look inside.

> …and it goes like this.
> Take me by the tongue and I'll know you
> Kiss me 'til you're drunk and I'll show you all the moves
> like Jagger, I've got the moves like Jagger

Liam pulled the door shut, putting his back to the wall outside the kitchen door. Jesus, Joseph, and Mary. He'd forgotten about the ass. That night in the dance club in Dublin, when they'd all first met Izzy. He'd laughed as his brothers and cousin watched Izzy Collier on the dance floor. She'd grabbed one of their friends, Alex. A safe pick for a dance partner because he was gay. The sight of those hips had stopped every man in their tracks, even Alex's partner, James. Somewhere between hula, belly dancing, and salsa. Izzy had ass shaking down to an art form, in all of its many nuances. Liam realized that he had blocked the entire scene out of his memory. Honestly, at that time in his life, all he'd seen was Eve. He was, and always would be, a one-woman man. But he'd have to have been blind and dead not to take an appreciative moment to admire the way the woman moved.

He heard laughing. He opened his eyes, remembering that he had an audience. Paolo was there now, as well. He elbowed Raphael and said something that Liam didn't catch. Raphael was more than happy to translate. "He says you are afraid of a senhorita." Liam looked at Seamus who was enjoying the hell out of the whole display.

He turned back, inching the door open again. The effect wasn't diminished with a second look. Izzy was singing into a wooden spoon, off-key and at the top of her lungs. Her ass was churning, hips rolling, and then she did a little gyrating motion all the way down to the floor, poised like a little, wiggling vixen over her feet. Then back up again. Gabriela was next to her, holding her own with a little Brazilian hip action.

> I don't need to try to control you
> Look into my eyes and I'll own you

He should not be watching. She'd kill him. That was his final thought before she turned around...and busted him red handed. Whatever reaction he'd expected, it hadn't been what she'd done.

She whipped that wooden spoon up to her mouth and pointed at him, not missing a single note or a hip curl as she sang. Before he had a chance to respond, a little fireball breached the space between his leg and the doorjambb. Estela ran at Izzy, and she scooped her up, placing her securely on her hip.

Izzy danced as Estela squealed with delight, raising her hands in the air and bouncing with the music. Next was Genoveva, shoving past him and joining the fun. When she started her own hip action, Liam's eyes bugged out. But Izzy was delighted. "That's it, girl! Shake it like you're not afraid to break it!" Liam burst into laughter as Seamus pushed past him, doing the saddest and funniest attempt at ass shaking he'd ever witnessed. That's when the music shut off abruptly. *Uh-oh.*

Reverend Mother Faith stood in the side door with her hands on her hips, one brow lifted. Sister Agatha was standing next to her blushing. The odd thing that was out of place was the iPhone in her hand. None of the sisters carried phones. But whatever. They were all standing frozen, waiting for the lecture about sinful displays of modern sexuality and vulgar music. None of that happened. "Antonio is on his way. Hopefully, you've managed to complete dinner, despite the fact that you've turned the kitchen into a nightclub."

She turned and left, and the giggling started with Genoveva. Then rolled through the group until they were all laughing. Izzy handed Estela over to Liam. "I am the corruptor. Time to go kiss a little ass and apologize."

"And would you mean a word of it?" Liam smiled, his eyes firing off as he looked at her flushed faced.

"Nope."

Izzy concentrated on catching up with the abbess so she wouldn't think about Liam watching her make a complete ass out of herself in the kitchen. She'd learned one thing well in the Navy. Improvise. She'd played it off effectively, but damn. She'd been working it overtime, thinking no one was watching. Raphael was supposed to have her back. She was going to kill him.

"Reverend Mother, can I speak with you?" she was panting a bit. The abbess stopped, saying nothing. "I'm sorry."

"For what exactly?"

"You know, for being me, I guess. For forgetting where I was. I had the door locked. We had a breach in security."

The abbess snorted. "Dr. Collier, since you've forgotten, I'll remind you. You're in Brazil. These children are shaking their bums right out of the womb. It's in the blood." She turned, really looking at Izzy. "You've done what I haven't managed to do in nine years."

Izzy cocked her head in question. Reverend Mother Faith looked at her indulgently, explaining. "You've managed to get Genoveva to lift those pretty eyes up to the world and see her own self-worth. The lass is changing for the better, Izzy. She's smiling. She's standing up for herself with those pushy lads in her class. Sometimes it takes a new approach."

"What will happen to her when she's legally an adult?" She almost didn't want to hear the answer.

"She'll have to leave. We will try to find a favorable circumstance for her. College or work. She's a smart girl. But I'm afraid that won't take care of the immediate issue of where she will lay her head at night."

"You can't just turn her out!" Izzy raised her voice.

"I know!" The abbess swallowed, reining in her emotions. She said, more calmly, "I know that. I've had no luck getting her to open up about her mother. She must have some idea who her father was, but her mother was a devout Catholic. She worked here for a time. The shame of an unexpected pregnancy may have colored her judgment about making arrangements for her daughter. She was near death when she brought the child to us. Ovarian cancer that had spread to her lungs and liver. She died here. Genoveva never left."

Izzy's eyes were tearing. The Reverend Mother took her hand and squeezed. "You have a way with her. Perhaps she'd talk to you."

"Izzy, this pasta is magnifico. I can't stop eating." Antonio was radiant, his eyes sparkling. He was so nice. A wonderful, talented surgeon. Izzy wished like hell that she felt a spark.

"It wasn't all selfless. I love my mother's recipes. They're simple and fresh. I have to mention that Gabriela helped. I'm accustomed to cooking for one."

"An unspeakable tragedy. If you promise to marry me, I'll let you cook as much as you like." Antonio winked at her.

"Gee, how can I pass up that offer? You're such a gentleman."

Liam wasn't sure if his stomach felt off from stuffing his gob with three bowls of pasta and a lemon tart, or if it was just Antonio mooning all over Izzy. He hated feeling this way because he actually really liked Antonio.

"So, O'Brien. Are you still going to stay home like an old maid? Adam decided to stay and cover the hospital, so you have no excuse." Seamus was such a shit, sometimes.

"I'll pass, but thanks. Antonio, I have a gift for you." He pulled a parcel out from under the table. It was wrapped in butcher paper from the kitchen.

"Liam, you shouldn't have. But I love that you did."

Antonio started opening it when Liam said, "I know how much you love watching the pro-footballer matches."

Antonio's face lit up...until he unfolded the shirt. He barked out a laugh. Then he read the shirt's tag. "Official jersey of the Republic of Ireland national football team. You are a swine, O'Brien." Liam was laughing into the back of his hand.

"I thought you'd like a jersey from a winning team."

All of the men were exchanging jibes, choosing a dog in the fight. Izzy smiled at Alyssa. Men and sports. They went around the table as Antonio received small gifts from the hospital staff. Even Raphael had brought something. A clay pot that his wife had painted. Raphael wasn't going out with them, but he'd stayed for dinner and was taking some leftovers home to his family.

Antonio grew serious. "I haven't had this many gifts in many years. Thank you all. It touches me, deeply."

That surprised Liam. Antonio was a handsome bastard. He was also a successful doctor from a well-off family. Antonio said, "Now before we head to the city, let's have a toast." The children and sisters had all left, and they had the Cantina to themselves.

Liam leaned in and whispered to Izzy. "I can't believe you've been sitting on a bottle of Teeling and didn't share it. Now you've gone and given it away."

She shrugged. "I told you I hit the duty-free. You were too busy pounding your chest and ordering me off your island."

He nudged her. "I figured you had some Jack Daniels shite from America. Not Teeling Small Batch."

She straightened her spine. "I do not drink Tennessee whiskey. I drink bourbon."

"What the hell is the difference?"

Izzy shook her head as Antonio put juice glasses from the kitchen on the table. She said, "I'm going to pretend you didn't just ask me that. You've got a lot to learn, O'Brien."

Antonio gave everyone a splash of Teeling just as Sister Catherine came through the door. She stopped dead in her tracks. "Is that Teeling? Who's been hiding that?"

Liam's laugh clapped through the room. "Dr. Collier has been. She's a selfish, sinful woman. Won't you join us, Sister Catherine?"

She looked behind her. "I shouldn't."

"Have ye lost all your Irish, here in this jungle? There's no sin in a wee sip o'whiskey."

Izzy smiled. This was the old Liam she'd heard about. The one who could have gotten Mother Theresa to drink. In the few days she'd spent with his family, she'd heard a lot of stories. He'd been the fun, carefree O'Brien. Past tense. But right now, he had mischief in his pretty blue eyes. Even Sister Catherine wasn't immune. And he was letting that accent fly in full force. She looked at Seamus, who winked at her.

"Aye, I suppose not. But just a sip, mind you." Sister Catherine was handed a small bit of the amber liquid. "God bless you, Antonio. You're a rare, fine Christian man. You're a blessing to us. Happy Birthday."

The whole group repeated the toast and drank. Sister Catherine closed her eyes. "That's as fine a sip as I've ever had. Thank you. I always said that midwifery was going to drive me to the drink." Everyone laughed as she left.

Antonio stood, "Time to be off to the city for some fun. Are you ladies ready?"

Izzy said yes, as Alyssa and Margaritte said no in unison. Then they looked at her. She was in a collared, cotton shirt and a pair of jeans. They looked at her feet. Sneakers. "Izzy, this is Brazil. You need help." Alyssa said as kindly as she could.

Liam watched the women emerge from the staff dormitory in single file. Alyssa was fresh-faced with a sundress and sandals. She was happily married, so it wasn't over the top. Margaritte was wearing a short, floral skirt and peasant top. More of a tropical flair to the fabric.

Then Izzy came out. She looked a bit uncomfortable, which surprised him. She seemed so comfortable with her body. But she wasn't a real girly girl. She was wearing a gauzy, pale blue dress that exposed her shoulders. It had a skirt below the knee that was loose and feminine. She even had a little lip-gloss on her lips. She was wearing a pair of comfortable, low-heeled sandals, which was more in line with what he'd expect out of her. But her skin glowed. Her shoulders and legs were a tint of olive and flawlessly smooth. Her legs were heavenly. She had long legs for her height, which made her seem taller than she was.

It was the legs, he decided, that did him in. Before he could stop himself, his gob was open. "I decided to join you!" Then he hopped in the backseat of the Land Cruiser. Because he was an idiot.

Liam watched with amusement at Antonio's gaping stare. "Are you sure she's not Brazilian in that family tree somewhere, or maybe

Columbian?" Antonio was eating his words as he watched Izzy shake her money maker with a group of local girls.

On either side of her were two men, but they weren't hitting on her. She'd zeroed in on the most unavailable men in the nightclub and asked them to dance. John and Tom were from southern Florida and on their honeymoon. After a while, she came to the table and sat down. Liam noticed that she did so after Antonio left to get a drink, and wondered if it was a coincidence. "Do you always find unavailable men to dance with? Last time we did this, I believe Alex was you dance partner."

Izzy laughed. "It's the perfect strategy."

"How so?" Seamus had joined the conversation.

"I love to dance. I've been shaking my bom bom since I was two years old. The problem is that a lot of men get the wrong idea. They think I'm trying to seduce everyone, but I don't dance for them. I dance for myself. No one puts Baby in a corner."

"You did not just quote *Dirty Dancing*," Liam said, dryly.

Izzy pointed at him. "Ah, but the only way you'd know that was if you'd watched it."

Liam rolled his eyes. "I was in love with a dance major. I was forced." Liam mentally recoiled from his own words. *Was? You are.* "I mean I am in love...or...you know what I mean." Izzy's face was so kind and understanding, it actually made him bristle.

The whole conversation made Seamus perk up. Izzy saw that he was going to start asking questions that Liam wasn't going to want to answer, so she cut him off.

"Back to my strategy. I find the gay guy in the crowd. He'll dance his ass off with me, and I don't have to worry about him trying to put his hand under my skirt."

"Bravo, lass. I may have to share that strategy with my daughters." Seamus lifted his drink and Izzy clinked glasses with him.

"Are ye sure it's not just a shield to protect you from meeting someone new? Ye might be putting off your future husband," Liam teased.

"I will not meet the future man of my dreams in a nightclub after two whiskeys. I have standards, man."

"I can see that. Two years, was it?" Liam jibed.

"Two years for what?" Alyssa slid into a chair and right into the conversation. Margaritte sat next to her, dabbing her forehead from dancing.

"Nothing. It's nothing." She shot daggers at Liam.

Seamus didn't scare so easily. "Two years since ye've been with anyone? A lovely lass like you? Christ, those American men must be fools."

"I doubt it was from lack of offers, Seamus," Alyssa chided.

"Thank you, Alyssa. No, it wasn't. I just don't sleep around. I mean, I'm thirty years old for God sake. I'm not some doe-eyed virgin. I just…need more than the physical stuff. Some things are worth waiting for. Now, if we're done talking about my pathetic love life, I need to get back to the abbey. I need my beauty rest."

Antonio came back to the table then, holding a glass of water. "I see you're cutting yourself off as well. We were getting ready to head out," Izzy said as she stood up.

Seamus added, "I'm sorry we have to call it a night. We have to work tomorrow. Paolo needs help and I've got an ultrasound scheduled for eight o'clock." Seamus shook Antonio's hand. Then they all walked out of the bar and away from the music. Antonio stopped Izzy as the others loaded into the car.

"Perhaps you can join me another night. Just the two of us." He looked down at her and she wished like hell that she was attracted to him. There wasn't a thing wrong with him. He was actually pretty perfect. "I'll take that as a no."

"I'm sorry Antonio. I'm not here for a fling. I'm here to work. I like you, but I just can't."

Antonio lifted her chin. "Is it because of Liam?"

She pulled back, her brow crinkled. "Of course not. Not at all. Why would you think that?" she said.

"Because, sweet bella donna, at this moment he's watching us like he'd love to rip my head off." Then he leaned down and kissed her on the cheek. "You're an extraordinary woman, Izzy. I'm not some casanova that is looking for a fling. I like you. But if it is to be friends, then so be it. Thank you for the beautiful dinner, and for the whiskey." He winked and she walked to the car.

Liam looked away just as Antonio lifted Izzy's chin. He just couldn't watch Antonio kiss her. Then, within a minute, she was in the vehicle next to him. Alyssa and Seamus were in the front. Margaritte had gone home to her flat in the city.

Alyssa broke the awkward silence. "Did you let the poor lad down easy?"

Liam's eyes shot to Izzy's. She was blushing. "We're friends. That's all I'm looking for. I've done the long distance thing. It never works. I'm sure he'll be over it by the time the next set of long legs walks by him. "

Seamus shook his head. "Some things a man doesn't get over so easily but it's probably best. Soap opera hospital drama is not what we need right now. We've got a great team. We work well together. Although, if you weren't trying to turn him on, you should have kept the jeans on. That dress sent the poor lad over the edge."

For the first time, Izzy looked at Liam. She hoped to God he hadn't heard Antonio's comments. He was looking at her, appraising her in the dress that Seamus was so fond of. She leaned over and whispered. "I'm still under here." Then she raised the skirt to expose her athletic shorts. Liam laughed and Alyssa looked back. "You sneak. Is it too much to ask that we get to doll you up for a night out? You're so pretty. It's a sin not to show those curves off every once in a while."

Liam disagreed. He'd be perfectly happy if she didn't wear that dress out around the other male doctors again.

15

Dublin 2, Dublin, Ireland

Patrick sat across from his mother, not drinking his tea. They were bringing Caitlyn home this morning. She was well enough, physically. Mentally was another story. "Thank you for staying, Mam. They need all hands on deck, tomorrow. It's some foreign leader visiting. I have to work. I wouldn't leave her otherwise."

Sorcha took his hand. He looked so tired and so very sad. "Are you sure you're okay. You've got to let yourself grieve as well."

His eyes misted. "I've got to be strong for her. It's worse for her. You know it is. She feels to blame. And, she'd felt it move. Told me it felt like a butterfly in her tummy." He closed his eyes, fighting the tears. He couldn't believe he had any left. "That was a couple of days before. How could everything go so wrong so quickly? I don't understand. She was so careful."

"I can't explain it. I wish I could. She's just made differently. Her body seems strong, but internally, she's got difficulties. If she tries again, they will have to take some drastic measures. There are things they can do, but nothing is fail-safe."

Her son recoiled. Then he stood, running his hand over his shorn hair. "She won't try again. We won't. I will not put her at risk. Better to have no child than no wife. She's not going to get pregnant again."

"Don't you think she has a say in that?"

He grit his teeth, feeling so helpless. "No. Her judgment isn't sound. Not when it comes to this. I have to protect her if she isn't going to protect herself. I will not get her pregnant again. Ever."

St. Clare's Charity Mission, Manaus, Brazil

The next week and a half went by quickly, everyone settling in to an easy routine, the excitement of the parachute incident fading. The boys had all gone home with their father, who had gone back to the village to retrieve a small boat. Liam had taken night watch, working on a batch of samples from the local creeks. The army had done a clean up of the cocaine spill, but no arrests had been made. He was checking not only pesticides and pollutants but mosquito larvae from different areas surrounding the eastern end of the city.

They were headed into the city tomorrow, where the other doctors would take care of the mobile unit. He had another mission. A new batch of Zika vaccines was being tested on human subjects. Two of the hospitals in the city were involved in the trial. He wanted in on it. They were small and non-profit. He didn't have any wāsiṭah in this town. A word he'd picked up from his brother Aidan. It was Arabic. He had no influence, no pull in the community. All he had was a stubborn streak bred from his mother's side. He would be heard. All he needed was maybe fifty samples. He could spread them out over some of the people at St. Clare's, some of the outlying villages, and some of the indigenous population. A small enough group that he could monitor the subjects on his own with Pedro's help.

Pedro came into the lab, and he looked up from his work. "Any news on that biopsy?"

"Sim, Doctor. Positivo. The médica said it was o mesmo like the other woman."

"English or Portuguese, Pedro. Pick one."

"Why, you understood me, yes?" Liam just laughed, shaking his head.

"When is the surgery?" Liam asked.

"Day after tomorrow. They'll bring her back when they visit the village tomorrow." Liam looked up, surprised at his answer.

"They're going into the city tomorrow," he said.

"Não, Senhor. There's a football match in the lot where we set up the clinic. The school's field is flooded, and there is a big match. So, they asked that you come next week. The doctors will go into the forest tomorrow."

Liam scooted the stool back and walked out of the lab, looking for Seamus.

"I can't go tomorrow. This meeting is important. You have to cancel." Seamus was taking inventory of his supplies, writing on a clipboard.

"I'm sorry, lad. We've already sent word. They're expecting the mobile clinic tomorrow at both locations. And Adam wants to check on the lads. You'll only be gone for an hour or two, in the city, so it will be up to you to cover the hospital. We've got Adam and Izzy. We'll leave Margaritte and Alyssa will go with us."

"I don't like it."

"In case you haven't noticed, Raphael and Paolo are both armed when we go. Paolo carries his machete, and Raphael has his little bag of tricks. I'm not worried. You shouldn't be either. The federal police and the army have been in the area. You're worrying over nothing."

Liam hated this. He hated that Adam was going in his place. Adam was a great pediatrician, but he was the most docile Australian that Liam had ever met. "Can ye wait? Until I get back? I've got a morning appointment."

"Wait for what?" Izzy walked in, carrying a box of bandages out of the storage unit.

"He wants us to wait for him tomorrow," Seamus said neutrally. "I suppose we could delay a couple of hours."

"That's not necessary, and it won't work," Izzy said.

"Why not?" Liam said pissily.

"Because we don't have Antonio to cover the hospital and we're taking Adam with us. He wants to see the boys that he treated. We need a doctor to stay back."

"Why don't you stay back? Why do they need a surgeon tomorrow?" he shot back.

She smiled beatifically. "Well, for starters, I don't have a morning appointment in the city. You don't have any other reason for not wanting me to go, right?" Her tone was docile, but her eyes were daring him to say one word about the females staying back. He swore under his breath. "Right, so we'll see you at dinner time."

Liam was ecstatic as he came home to the St. Clare's estate. The morning had been stressful. It had also taken longer than he thought. He'd won, though. He'd asked nicely, then demanded, then resorted to threats. Bad press and all that. The American CDC, along with a prestigious medical school, were doing phase 2 trials. The vaccine was successful in animal testing. When he'd threatened to call the press, publicly accusing those in charge of the trial of discriminating against poverty-stricken areas of Brazil, they'd miraculously changed their tune. The end result? They'd be delivering fifty vials of the vaccine in three weeks, along with a representative to oversee the vaccination and registration process.

He got out of the taxi and paid the driver, having had to get a ride back to the abbey. Paolo was with the team, deep in the forest. Estela saw him from the play yard and ran to greet him. Liam scooped her up and swung her around. "Hello, lass. How was your morning?"

"It was very nice. I learned my numbers to ten in the Inglês." As the little girl prattled on, he walked to the school where Genoveva was standing in the doorway. "Okay, you go along and keep working, love. I'll see you at lunch."

As he walked into the main entrance of their small hospital, he hated how empty it was. Hated like hell that they were in the outlying villages without him. Margaritte was coming out of a patient's room. "Sorry, I'm late. How was the morning?"

What a long day. Izzy was exhausted. Luckily, she'd had a good night of sleep the night before. Liam had offered up the bungalow, so that she could be well rested for the trip. It was a delicious indulgence, getting that little house to herself. The day had been productive and uneventful. She smiled as she thought about coming up the river to the rickety dock where they tied the boat off. One of the little boys that had been in the hospital waved enthusiastically, then ran to tell the others. As they entered the large, indigenous village, there were whispers. Some in their native tongue, and a few in Portuguese. Many eyes were on her, so she asked Raphael what they were saying.

He smiled knowingly at Paolo. "Anjo do rio," he said. "The river angel. Apparently, they've renamed you." Izzy blushed at the thought. Throughout the day, the young, eligible men of the village watched her, finding reasons to be examined. Hangnail, bad back. According to Paolo, they'd inquired about her and Alyssa's marital status, and zoned in on the single one. Okay. *Awkward.*

They'd been so kind, though. The old women patting her and touching her hair. It was getting lighter in the sun, her caramel curls glowing fairer at the tips. *River Angel.* She hadn't earned the name, but she couldn't say she disliked it. They'd fed them a hot stew, which she found delicious. Some sort of meat that she didn't want to know too much about, along with onion and dried fruit and the acai berries that grew in the region. Then a hot drink made of cacao and sugar cane. The original hot chocolate. The day was warm, but she was glad for the hot food that was cooked on the open flame. Hot temperatures meant less chance of a parasite. It wasn't like she was going to turn her nose up at the kind offering. As they'd left, the tribesmen loaded the boat with stalks of small bananas and all of those superfoods that grocery stores in Virginia charge an arm and a leg for. Delicacies like raw cacao, acai berries, camu camu, marakuya. It was their way of saying thank you for saving the young boys of their village and arranging for clean water.

Now she was leading the woman who would have surgery tomorrow to an empty room. Alyssa would go over some pre-op things with her, and Raphael would graciously help with the language barrier. What she needed now was some food.

Walking into the cantina, she saw Liam sitting with Seamus. "How were things at the barn, today?" She asked, approaching Liam from behind. She leaned an arm on the table, not sitting until she got her food. But she wanted to check in with him. Today had been an important meeting.

"Uneventful. Especially considering the morning I had." Izzy gave him a look, waving her hand in a gesture for him to continue. "After butting heads with the CDC and a pompous jackass that is the dean of a medical school, I bullied them into fifty vials."

Izzy let out a whoop and threw her arms around his neck, hugging him from behind. "You are the balls, O'Brien." She said it low, so no one other than Seamus and Liam could hear. Liam cupped a hand over her forearm, absorbing the contact before she pulled her arms away. She smelled good. She had a scent to her, even sweaty, that stirred a very primitive part of him. He hated that she had that effect on him, but he couldn't deny the reality. Seamus was giving him a speculative look as Izzy went to the counter for a tray of food.

Liam shrugged. "Don't give me that look. She's a hugger. There's nothing to it."

Seamus snorted. "I don't get you, O'Brien. What the hell happened to you that makes you so anti-female?"

Liam put his fork down. "I am not anti-female. I am very much pro-female. Just because I'm not trying to get in her knickers like Antonio, doesn't make me anti-woman. The rest is my business."

"So something did happen."

"What happened," Izzy asked as she slid next to Liam.

"Nothing. Seamus is just a nosey peahen. Now, tell me about today."

"I've got the patient with the tumor being prepped. We do it tomorrow. Antonio is working, so I'll need you to assist if you don't mind."

"Absolutely. The earlier, the better. I need to help Paolo with some wood chopping, and we still need to get the barrier wall fixed near the schoolhouse."

Izzy said, "Not a problem. I'll even help after we're done."

The cantina was buzzing with activity, whispered gasps and speculation rolling through the room. Izzy, Liam, and Seamus all looked up in unison to see what was causing the stir. Genoveva walked in, just then. She wasn't wearing anything outrageous. She was wearing a simple Nike t-shirt that Izzy had given her and a pair of track pants. But her head was up, and her eyes were forward. Her hair was the culprit for the change in focus from dinner to the doorway. Previously long enough to touch her waist, always in a ponytail, she'd shorn the long locks off to just above her shoulders. A chin-length bob that allowed her natural wave to bounce up around her face. A style that was very familiar.

Liam looked over at Izzy, wondering if she was responsible for the transformation of her protégé. Her jaw was dropped. She looked at him, then Seamus. "Don't look at me, I had no idea," she said defensively.

"It looks good on her. Look at that confident gait. Well done, lass." Liam was smiling, and Izzy thought he was talking about the girl. But he put a hand on her arm and squeezed. "Well done."

Genoveva walked by Izzy, putting a fist up, and Izzy bumped her. "Looking good, little sister. Did you do that yourself?" She shook her head. "Sister Maria did it." Her beautiful green eyes were smiling.

After dinner, everyone departed for their separate quarters. Exhausted from the day's work. As Liam made his way down the path to the bungalow, he let the sounds of the rainforest wash over him. He could hear the river as he got closer. The beetles and other insects buzzed, and a light drizzle started just as he got to the stairs of the house. As he walked into the small house, doing his routine check, the smell of the pesticide that he'd sprayed the exterior with faded, and the cool air from the AC replaced it. Izzy had left it on, knowing he would take the cottage tonight. He showered, shaved, and brushed his teeth before settling down for the night.

As he climbed onto the bed and stretched out, his body started to hum. *Holy God.* She was all over the bed. Her smell. A hint of soap, yes, but the strong scent of a clean female was all over the sheets and pillow. His body responded without asking his permission, his cock lengthening, and thickening. The sheets were soft, delicious on his skin, and he rolled his hips involuntarily. Jesus, he was totally sexed up. What was he doing?

He rolled on his back, removing his hot zone from the gliding surface of the mattress. He was a live wire, and the new position didn't help. He looked down at his body, his heavy, hard sex laying against his stomach. And it knew what it wanted. Some playtime with Izzy. How in the hell was he going to sleep like this? *Damn that woman.* Just to torture himself he inhaled deeply, and his erection kicked in response.

It's biology, he reflected. He was a young man. In his prime. He may not be capable of feeling anything romantic for a woman, but his cock didn't know the difference. The instinct to screw was at the very core of humans, and his body was waking up even if nothing else could be resurrected. *Approach this clinically.*

He needed to sleep. He was assisting in surgery tomorrow. He could do this. It was merely dealing with a physiological response, removing an obstacle. How many times had he done this as a lad? A billion? Okay, maybe not that many times, but how in the hell did young lads get through junior high? The younger Liam would steal a lingerie catalog or picture his favorite actress or model. But somehow, their images eluded him.

He curled his arm behind his head, raising one side of the pillow up as he inhaled. His hips surged in response. He grabbed his arousal, needing to just get this over with. That's when he was assaulted with pictures in his mind. That little cropped, dark triangle surrounded on all sides by smooth pink flesh, a taut stomach, round hips. Her wet breasts and pink nipples. The orgasm ripped through him within seconds, and he rode it out as her smell filled his nose.

Liam looked at himself in the mirror after his second shower. As disgusted as he was with himself, he fought the urge to picture Izzy on that bed, doing exactly the same thing he'd just done. Did she smell him on the sheets? It occurred to him that it wasn't just her smell that had aroused him. He'd slept on the sheets as well. There wasn't a washer in the house, so laundering only happened every two weeks or so. No, it hadn't just been her smell that had juiced him up. It was the unique blend of both their bodies that were contained on the one bed that had caused his cock to go into overdrive. The smell two people made when they shared a bed. When they did things in that bed.

He pushed off the sink as he felt another tingle of awareness begin. He was even more exhausted now. So he went down to the mattress, and this time he slept.

Liam was on the river's edge, looking upriver toward the stretching, green abyss. He felt, more than heard, the presence as it came alongside him. He turned and looked. His heart lurched up to his throat. "I've missed you. Oh, God. I miss you, so much."

Eve was beside him. She was wearing his big Trinity College shirt and leggings, like he'd just caught her studying in the library. She smiled. "I'm sorry, love. I'm so sorry I had to leave."

"I'm dreaming." It wasn't a question.

"Aye, it's the only way." Her face was so youthful. Her eyes so very kind and loving. Her hair a long, smooth wave over her shoulders and down her back.

"Then I don't want to wake up. I want to stay."

"You can't, love. You must go. Listen to me, Liam, my love. You must wake. And when the time comes, you need to go to the river."

She looked over the water. Then she turned back to him. "Remember."

Liam shot upright, gasping for air. He was covered in sweat, even though the air conditioning vent was pointed right at him. He ran a hand through his hair. "Eve, oh God." He was shaking. It had been so long since he'd dreamed of her. The awareness crept in slowly, as he looked around the little house. Then the guilt washed over him. What had he done? He plopped back down on his back, bringing his fists to his eyes. "I'm sorry, Eve. Oh, God. I'm sorry."

Izzy watched Liam come down the hall of the hospital, pass by his laboratory door, and go straight to the laundry area. He was carrying the sheets from the bed in the bungalow. A good idea, since it was about two weeks since they'd been washed. Between pests, pesticides, and warm bodies, even a few nights on them made them due. She did like the smell on the pillow. His spicy, male scent had its own lovely bouquet. But whatever. "Thanks for doing that. I'll get them next time." All she got was a grunt.

"Is the patient ready?" his tone was clipped. Okay. Maybe he didn't sleep well.

"Yes, Alyssa is standing by for anesthesia and Margaritte will assist as well. Adam and Seamus and the day nurse are covering the hospital rounds and intake. Let's do this."

Izzy was so careful and calculated with her movements. Had this tumor been a different sort, she wouldn't even be doing the surgery. But because it was completely encapsulated, she was able to remove it with very precise incisions. As she began closing, Alyssa spoke.

"Seamus said you used to do martial arts. That you are a fighter. Did you quit to protect your hands?" Izzy met her eye. "I quit competing. I adapted my training when I started my surgical residency. I haven't even done that in the last several months. I moved on."

Liam was silent, but he was listening. Last time he'd seen her, she was still training in martial arts. He hadn't realized she'd quit. "How so?" Alyssa asked. " Rather, what did you move on to? We've already established it wasn't a man," she said with a grin.

Izzy snorted her amusement into her mask. "Definitely not. I started volunteering. I taught women's safety and self-defense classes."

"Really? That's great. I think I'd like to learn some of those moves." Izzy froze over her stitching as an awareness cropped up between herself and Liam. Isn't that almost exactly the words Eve had used? "What got you interested in that? Was there a lot of crime where you were living?"

Izzy started stitching carefully, clearing her throat. "It was just something I felt like I needed to do. If you want to learn, then I'll make the time."

Several minutes later, she was tying off the last stitch. As they tended to the patient, and Margaritte began wheeling her to recovery, she gave her instructions for the aftercare. Pedro was sealing up the tissue, sending it to the lab in the city for further tests. "Thank you, everyone. That went well." Izzy said. Not meeting Liam's eyes. Then she pulled her surgical cap off and added it to the surgical laundry pile. "Alyssa, I'll be in the garden helping with some chores if she has any issues. Just monitor her pain as she comes to. If she gets really bad off, start a morphine drip. She's pretty tough, though. I'll have Gabriela talk to her family when she goes home tonight, as long as she's doing well. I want you to come get me if there's anything you're worried about."

Before they all went in different directions, a thunderous boom rumbled over the air. Liam watched the transformation in Izzy with confusion. She jumped into action. She whipped the used linens off of the operating table. "I need all hands on deck! Alyssa, I need a fresh surgical room, stat!" She bolted for the hallway, getting on the intercom as Liam heard another boom go off. She hit the PA system. "Prepare for incoming casualties. All hands on deck! All available staff report to the surgery, stat." That's when he understood. While he heard the dynamite blasts of deforestation, she heard bombs and artillery.

He put his hand over hers and turned the speaker off. "I need you to scrub in again, O'Brien." She walked back toward the surgery as a very confused group of staff came rushing down the hall. He put a hand up, urging them to wait. Then he stepped into the surgery behind her and closed the doors. She turned. She was completely clear headed. Hyper alert. "I need those doors open. Why the hell are you looking at me like I have a dick on my forehead? Move your ass!"

She did have a way with words. "Dr. Collier, there are no casualties."

"You don't know that. You can hear the explosions. We need to get ready. Where is Alyssa?"

He took her by the shoulders. "It's dynamite. From the deforestation, love. It's not what you're thinking." She stared at him for a minute, realization coming slowly.

Her brows went up. "No bloodbath?"

The question turned up at the end, and he barked out a laugh. "No, darlin'. No bloodbath. The only casualties today are trees. Maybe a few birds."

All of the tension went out of her body. "Didn't anyone think to tell a combat doc that there might be explosions going off in the area? Jesus Christ, talk about ringing my freaking bell."

"I'm sorry, Izzy. I didn't think. I've never heard it this close to the abbey." He watched her, hands on her hips, breathing and letting her adrenaline seep out of her system. He had the overwhelming urge to take her in his arms, especially since he'd seen the aftermath of war with his brother Aidan. Then she walked outside the surgery to the waiting staff. He wondered how she was going to handle it.

Alyssa's knowing face was on hers, checking for signs of a meltdown. Even though they were all right there, she grabbed the phone and activated the PA system. "This was a test from the emergency broadcast system. Great response time. You may now go back to your regularly scheduled program." The laughter started rumbling through the small group.

"Sorry guys, old habits and all that. Way to hustle, though. Seamus, you move fast for an old guy."

Seamus put an arm around her. "Christ, woman. I thought the Vietcong were coming through the jungle. Thanks for the excitement." Then he kissed her temple and released her.

16

And to serve that single issue, lest the generations fail, the
female of the species must be deadlier than the male. She who
faces Death by torture for each life beneath her breast, may
not deal in doubt or pity—must not swerve for fact or jest...

Rudyard Kipling

L iam watched Izzy from across the green. She was having the
children unload a cart of stones from the ATV trailer. Paolo
was mixing mortar in a wheelbarrow. Seamus was helping
them. She walked toward Liam and his skin prickled at the tangible
awareness between them. When she stopped, he put the axe in the
log in front of him. Then he wiped his brow with the bottom of his
shirt. The smaller kids were still in the classroom for five more minutes, then everyone would break for lunch except Paolo, who wanted
to get the stone work done before it rained.

She said, "I want you to know that what happened today wasn't a
problem. I know your brother had PTSD, but that isn't what was happening." Her face was a little defensive, even though she was trying to
play it cool. "I've dealt with PTSD on a personal level. Not with myself
but...with Jesse. My old boyfriend who was a Marine. I want you to
know that I wasn't having some sort of flashback."

Liam sat on another stump. "Okay, I believe you. You didn't seem out of sorts. You were utterly clear and focused. So…what was it then? Can you explain it?"

Her shoulders eased a bit. "I can try. I guess the best way to describe it is Pavlov's dog. You studied that, I'm assuming? Well, certain stimuli cause a chain of thought. Those thoughts lead to immediate action or a physical response. When you're working the trauma chute, you don't have time to mull things over. Seconds count. In Virginia, it was emergency cases coming through the bay doors or in the chopper on the roof pad. You assess quickly, get ready for the worst case scenario. In Iraq, it was even more of a learned response. You hear those explosions and you start prepping tourniquets, checking blood and plasma stores, and getting the limb saws ready. Everyone goes on high alert. You have to be good and goddamn ready when they bring those boys through the door. Indecision, hesitation, it's not in our make-up. Do you understand?"

"Aye, I think I do. I watched you that day by the river. You didn't hesitate. You left Antonio in your dust." He was smiling, now. "You're a talented doctor, Izzy. All of the staff sees it. You teach them something new every day. And the equipment you brought is just what they needed to be trained with. We won't always have you here on the river with us." *Go to the river.* Suddenly the dream he'd had assaulted him like a blow to the head. Then for some reason, he remembered Cora. Her dreams were something altogether different. *Tell Izzy to remember what I told her.*

Izzy felt satisfied that he understood the situation that had gone down in the hospital today, so she turned to leave. "Izzy, what did Cora say to you?" She stopped, not looking up. "She passed on a message through my sister. It was for you to not forget what she told you."

Izzy wasn't sure how much to share. She didn't need to set any triggers off with Liam, now that they'd reached an understanding. "She woke from a dream, that's all."

"I know about Cora's dreams. What did she say?" he said again.

"She said…*When the time comes, you must remember to follow the river.*"

The hair stood up on Liam's neck. "Is that all she said? No context? That's not usually how her dreams work."

Izzy shrugged. "She was half asleep. I don't know how it works. I'm sure it was just a dream."

Liam nodded as she made a hasty retreat. He shook his head, clearing himself of the unwanted feeling of dread that came over him. He heard the school house bell as the younger children came pouring out to play. He looked up to see his sweet Estela running through the yard toward him. It was staggering to him that she'd never been adopted. Babies never lasted long at the orphanage, yet she'd been here her whole life. It was the older children that were usually hard to place.

He knew the reason, although it was utter bullshit. Estela had been born with a congenital heart defect. Not a serious one, but enough to have gone through surgery. It was a small septal defect that had been fixed a little over a year ago. The scar was barely visible now, and she was healthy as a horse. But people in Brazil were having fewer children, just like in Ireland. They were letting careers and financial practicalities influence their family planning. The average had gone from six kids to two kids per family. The honest truth was that Estela was fine. It had been but a bump in the road. But people didn't want a child with even a hint of medical issues if they could get a healthy child instead. His heart squeezed in his chest, and he shook himself; suppressing emotion and focusing on his task. He started to resume his work when the scream broke across the green, making his blood run cold. It was Izzy, who was halfway between him and the school.

"Estelaaa!" her scream was blood curdling. He watched in horror as she raced toward the child, the jaguar poised at the ready, just on the edge of the forest. He grabbed the axe and ran, but he was too far away. *No!* The smooth cat sprang into action, heading for the lone, small prey. "Izzy, no!" he yelled as she closed the distance, those long legs pumping to beat the world's fastest mammal to the little girl.

Estela saw the animal and ran toward Izzy, her childish scream ripping into Liam. His tunnel vision only let him focus on Izzy as she grabbed Estela, whipped around, and put her own back toward the threat. No way was she going to outrun it, so she shielded the child with her body and dropped to the ground, just as the jaguar overtook them. Liam was six feet away when the machete struck the animal across the back of the neck. The cry from the beast was sickening as the blade met bone. The children were screaming, Raphael standing stoically over the animal's corpse, his breathing labored. Liam dropped the axe next to him, and dove for the huddled bodies on the ground. Izzy was wrapped so tightly around the child, he could barely hear Estela's whimpers. Izzy wouldn't let her go. She struggled, bracing herself for teeth and claws. Liam's voice croaked as he fought his own panic. "Izzy, it's me. It's okay. You're okay."

Her body started to tremble, but her head came up. Everyone was running toward them now. He saw Estela's face, fear stricken as she clung to Izzy. This child with no mother, no father, had been saved by a stranger who'd put her own life as a sacrifice to save her.

Izzy slowly raised up, still wrapped around the child. Then they both saw the carnage. She put the child's head to her breast. "Don't look, baby. It's over. It's all over." Izzy's voice trembled, not with tears. Just from the fear and exhaustion and whatever else she was feeling. "Let's get her inside."

As she tried to stand, her legs gave out. After all, she'd just done the sprint of a lifetime. A sprint that meant everything. Liam looked up at Raphael who appeared just as wasted. They all were. All running toward that common goal, praying to God they got there in time. Praying to God that Estela wasn't going to get slaughtered in her own backyard. And Izzy... more panic washed over him.

He didn't wait for her to argue or do the tough guy routine as she tried to stand again. As spent as his body was, the overwhelming need to do something gave him a surge of primal energy as he scooped Izzy up in his arms, the child still with her. Raphael exchanged glances with him, taking a step back. Understanding.

Paolo was dragging the beast into the woods as Sister Maria and the other nuns ushered the children back into the school. Reverend

Mother Faith was at his side now, and he wasn't exactly sure when she'd appeared. He'd been focused on the small players in this near tragedy. Raphael, Izzy, Estela, and himself, all colliding in this unfolding drama. The predator had been a female, signs of a recent litter on her underbelly. Liam's stomach rolled. Such a waste. Such a beautiful animal. But the rainforest was like that. As breathtakingly beautiful as it was deadly.

He walked into the hospital, Raphael holding the door and the doctors and nurses piling in behind him. *When did all of these people get here?* He adjusted the girls in his arms, walking into the elevator and passed the wheelchair that was offered. When he went to the second floor, he took them to an empty patient room and closed the door.

When he put them down on the clean bed, he watched as Estela burrowed into Izzy, like an infant searching for succor. Izzy turned into her, soothing her with soft words as the tears finally came down her face. "I need to examine you both, Izzy. Did either of you hit your head?"

Izzy didn't meet his eyes. "I don't think so. I had her head tucked into my chest." He started probing, looking for any sign of injury to either. Then he checked for any signs that Estela's heart had been stressed. He sighed with relief, and Izzy cleared her throat. "I'm not hurt, Liam. My legs were just done. I'm fine."

"Of course you are." His tone was sharp.

She tensed, then checked to see if the stillness in her arms meant that the child had fallen asleep. She slowly inched out of the bed, walking past Liam to open the door. Genoveva and three of the sisters were standing by. "I don't want her to wake up alone," she said to them.

They all nodded, coming in and finding a place to sit. Wanting to be of use. Raphael was in the hall. Liam wanted to kiss the bastard. "He killed the animal. He got there first. And thank God for it." Liam watched as Izzy fought the tears, walking into her sidekick's arms.

He patted her back so brotherly, it made Liam's throat seize up again. Izzy said, "Thank you, Raphael. Oh, God. Thank you." She shuddered and backed up, wiping her eyes.

"It's okay, boss. The médico was right behind you with the axe in his hand. You were very brave, Senhorita. Like a lioness protecting her cub."

Izzy wrapped her arms around herself. "I wish the animal didn't have to die. I understand the why of it. It's just sad. They're endangered."

"Paolo and I will find her litter. She wouldn't have gone far from them. We will call the conservation people in the city. They can take her litter to the preserve and care for them. They will reintroduce them into the wild. They need to track these attacks, and I won't be in any trouble. The animal was attacking a child." He stepped back, nodding to them both. "I'll go to do that now, from the abbess's office."

As he left, Izzy walked into an exam room and sat in one of the chairs. She was still a bit shaken. Liam followed her. "I'm okay. It's just adrenaline and muscle fatigue. I'm fine."

"That's a very solid, clinical assessment." Her eyes shot to his as she picked up on his tone. "Now what the hell were you thinking?" he bit out. She jerked at the question.

"What do you mean what was I thinking? That's an idiotic question! I was thinking that fucking cat was going to eat Estela!"

"You could have been killed, Izzy. People die every year from jaguar attacks. We lost a patient six months ago!"

She clenched her jaw. "I know that. What would you have me do, Liam? I was the closest one to her."

He paced around the room, pulling his hair up with his fingers. "Jesus Christ, Izzy. You can't take these kind of risks. Do you have a death wish? How many times have you said it? The team comes first. If we lose a doctor, everyone suffers."

She shot back, "This is different. This was a child. Is that what you're worried about? Having to look for another surgeon?"

He growled, low in his throat. "You are so bloody stubborn!"

She put her hands out, trying to tone the mood down a notch. "Listen to me. Because I'm going to explain this once. This wasn't about stubbornness. I didn't have time to think about it. I just saw that thing coming for her and I ran. I was on animal instinct every bit as much as that jaguar. You can't beat ten thousand years of breeding and animal instinct out of a woman with logic and lectures. I would do it again, in a second, if it meant Estela walked away."

"Even if you didn't?" he snapped.

"Some things are worth the sacrifice, Liam. One life for another."

"Oh, yes. That worked out perfectly for Eve! Right before that fucking van hit her! She died because she wouldn't put her own safety first! Deliver me from bloody-minded women!"

Izzy's tone was deep, and deceptively calm. "Don't. Do not do that."

"Do what? Say the truth?"

"Don't take away from what she did!" she spat out. "She gave her life to save that girl. They found those murdering psychos because of what she did that day. Don't you dare take that away from her! She earned the right to be called a hero. She was small and delicate and beautiful, but she was also pretty goddamn brave. Braver than some grown men would have been!" She sputtered, "What do you want Liam? A woman who would stand by and do nothing while watching another woman get abducted? Ignore her screams for help? Is that who you wanted her to be?"

She pointed at him, "You're not angry at me. You love Estela. You'd throw me in front of a bus. Hell, you'd throw one of these nuns in front of a bus to save that kid! This isn't about what I did for Estela or about you giving two shits if I got my throat gnawed out by some big cat. This is about Eve. Everything is about Eve, so I suggest you get off my case! Estela and I are fine. You are the one who's a mess!"

She stood up and tried to leave and he snatched her arm, pulling her to him. She wasn't sure what shift had happened in the universe or in this big man, but he was holding on to her like his life depended on it. He was shaking, putting his hands all over her. Like he was checking to make sure she wasn't bleeding or broken. His face was in her neck, his breath heavy. "I thought you were going to die, ye daft woman. I thought Estela was going to die. Jesus, Izzy. How could ye think I didn't care?"

Then she was holding him back, letting him squeeze and pet her and smell her hair. "I'm sorry, Liam. I can't be something I'm not." He had her against the wall, and he put his hands on either side of her head. He put his forehead to hers. "I know, Izzy. I know."

Izzy's body sprang to life when he touched her. A wave of lust almost buckling her knees. She wanted to pull him down to her mouth. She wanted him to rip her clothes off and push inside her. She wanted it hard and fast. She wanted an escape from the horror and fear and the tears in the aftermath of this day.

His blood was up, and she sensed that he would give her all of that and more. But he'd regret it. He denied it, but this was indeed about Eve, and it was about Estela. He was hurting and angry with the world, and even if he worked her out good and hard against this wall, until they were both blissed out...he'd regret it. And that would kill her. As much as she wanted him, she couldn't let this happen. He'd end up hating her for it. He wasn't ready, and when he was, it couldn't be her.

She pushed his chest, inching to the side and away from him. "I'm okay. I'm going to check on Estela."

"Izzy."

"Don't, Liam. Don't say it and don't think it. We can't go there. I can't be that kind of stepping stone for you."

He took a step toward her. "What do you mean, stepping stone?" Irritation creeping back into his tone. She looked at him, really looked, and his eyes softened. He took another step and she put her hand up. "I'm willing to put myself in harms way in a lot of ways, Liam. I just can't do it this way. I can't be a stepping stone in your path back to the land of the living. I'm tough, but I'm not that tough." This time when she turned away, Liam let her go.

The Reverend Mother looked around the dining hall and smiled. She'd decided that they all needed a night of fun. The day's events had traumatized not only the school children, but every person at St. Clare's. Antonio heard of the jaguar attack, having called to finalize his schedule with Margaritte. He drove down to join them for dinner. The concern for Izzy was palpable. She'd noticed the attraction. It was, of course, one sided. Izzy was a wonderful doctor, and as it turns out, a brave and fierce woman. But her eyes never lingered on Antonio when he was unaware. She only looked at one man. She was discreet, but it was there if you looked carefully. And it wasn't one sided. Some sort of door had swung open in Liam's mind when he saw that near miss unfold in the garden with the giant cat. He stalked Dr. Collier with his eyes. Where he'd been discreet before, now his gaze was urgent.

She should disapprove. She didn't allow fraternization. No hanky panky at the mission, so to speak. It was one of her many rules. But when she looked at the man before her, tuning up his guitar, he didn't appear as he once had those many months ago on her doorstep. A broken, shell of a man. Anger and bitterness in his every waking moment. Consumed by his work so that he didn't have to think about living. Now, he was changing. That tight, tense knot in his chest, where a heart used to be, loosening a bit.

Izzy held Estela as she bounced up and down. Liam was getting ready for the family sing-along, having been ordered by the abbess to remember his bloodlines and give this crowd a well earned tune. Izzy knew he would never do some of those bawdy songs she'd heard in the pubs in Ireland. She wondered what he'd choose. Henrico had a small set of drums from the school. Cristiano, pushing his glasses up on his nose, held a set of maraca-type things. He was still wearing his brace, but his collar bone was healing and all he had to do was shake the things. Izzy's heart squeezed because he looked so happy to have a part in this little performance.

"Are ye ready for a song, wee Estela?" Liam said with a wink.

"Sim, sim!" She was too tired to concentrate on her English lessons, and had regressed into all Portuguese. Izzy looked over at Raphael, who had gone to pick up his two children and his lovely wife. He'd said that he needed to see his kids. To hold them and his wife. She understood. The incident had affected everyone. Estela was the beloved child and youngest sister of everyone here. The children had spent the evening passing her around, kissing, and hugging her. She'd grown tired, however, and was now content to curl herself against Izzy.

When Liam started, Henrico played the drums in his lap. She smiled as he sang. Jack Johnson, *Upside Down.* The kids swayed and giggled. The older girls swooning as Liam sang. Izzy swooning as well, despite her best intentions. The little ones were twirling and jumping to the music. She looked over at Reverend Mother Faith, and the woman smiled. Nodding at her. Raphael had a kid on each arm, swaying to the music as his wife leaned in for a kiss. Seamus and Antonio were grabbing some of the smaller kids, dancing as well. Izzy just sat and watched. Content, this time, to be still. To hold this beautiful child and listen.

When he finished they all clapped. Henrico blushed as his classmates praised him. Liam picked up Cristiano and everyone clapped for the small boy as well. Liam leaned in and gave Izzy a wink. "Well now, Dr. Collier. It's your turn."

She laughed, throwing her head back. "I do not sing, O'Brien. Sorry."

"Everyone can sing a little. Surely you know some sort of song." He was calling her out in front of everyone, mischief gleaming in his blue eyes. The children joined in, begging for her to try. She leaned over to Alyssa and Sister Agatha and Sister Catherine. "I'll need some help, ladies." She handed Estela over to Genoveva, and grabbed a cup from the cantina counter. Everyone was silent. When she turned the cup upside down on the table, she started to tap on it, lifting it periodically in a familiar rhythm. She was swiftly joined by two nuns and a nurse, grinning as they ran to get cups and squeeze in next to her.

Liam groaned, "Come on. That's cheating. Every lass under the age of forty knows this song." Brigid went through a long *Cups* phase as a girl, and in turn, taught it to Cora.

Izzy said, "Shut it, O'Brien." Then she started to sing. *I got my ticket for the long way 'round.* Her voice was passable, in tune most of the time, but she didn't seem to care as she started to get into it. To Liam's astonishment, the children didn't seem to know the song. After all, they were isolated in this small area of the world. No TV, no internet, the sisters their only parents. They'd missed the resurge of this song on the radio. They watched with fascination as the sisters and Alyssa joined her, singing along and doing the little smack and lift with their cups. Surprisingly, Sister Agatha had a very pretty voice. Then again, she was Irish. They clapped the cups down, and Izzy said, "Take it Sister!" Sister Agatha took the lead, as the women sang along with her.

> *It's got mountains*
> *It's got rivers*
> *It's got sights to give you shivers*
> *But it sure would be prettier with you*

Izzy winked at Liam and he laughed when she sang, *you're gonna miss me when I'm gone.* When they finished, the children squealed and clapped. She did a little curtsy. She didn't win due to pitch or harmony, but she won for style.

They all slept in their dormitories that night. Not wanting to give up the feeling of family and security that had been thick in the air this night. Taking comfort in being under the same roof. As Liam lay awake in bed, he thought about what had happened. Izzy hadn't hesitated. She'd been completely at ease with her decision to sacrifice herself for a little orphan child she barely knew. He'd have done the same. He knew this. But something about watching Izzy, huddled with the child snug beneath her, shattered his heart into splinters.

He'd been a bastard to her, and she'd never wavered. It wasn't in her nature to let herself be dominated. To cower. She didn't wound her opponent unnecessarily, but she didn't stand down. He closed his eyes as he thought about what she'd said about Eve. The respect she'd had in her voice and in the brown depths of her eyes. *She earned the right to be called a hero. She was small and delicate and beautiful, but she was also pretty goddamn brave.* He looked out his window, to the stars above the canopy. He spoke out loud to her then, hoping she could hear him. "I'm sorry Eve. I'm sorry I didn't understand. You were so brave. So very brave." He'd been so angry at himself, at the world, but he realized that he'd also been angry at Eve. And with that realization, he was able to let some of it seep out of him. "I miss you. I love you. I'll always love you."

17

School had just started when Izzy heard the vehicle approaching. She'd dropped Estela off with Sister Maria after breakfast. She'd slowly been working to get the child's confidence back up. Get back on the horse, so to speak. She'd had a terrible fright, but she couldn't live in fear. She'd been very clingy to Izzy, and she loved the little girl. Loved her hugs. Loved when she took her hand. But it wasn't going to serve the child to offer a crutch or feed her separation anxiety.

She'd spent the week organizing the surgery, trying to keep herself from thinking about Liam O'Brien. Which was impossible. The man was everywhere. Chopping wood with no shirt on, muscles rippling. Helping fix the wall by the schoolyard. Pest control around the abbey in a tight t-shirt and low slung shorts. Singing in the freaking shower, for God's sake. It was like that night with the children in the cantina had uncorked his voice. And the man had pipes. Jesus, she knew all of the O'Briens could sing, but he was a true talent. A rich baritone, sexy and deep.

She hated the way she felt. It was muddied by sexual frustration and guilt. Guilt because this wasn't why she'd come to Brazil. Guilt because in some weird way, she felt like she was man stealing, which was crazy. You couldn't steal a man from a dead woman. But Eve had marked him both in life and death, and it made her feel like an intruder.

Maybe the fact that she'd been so long without a man in her life made her confused about her feelings. Was she really just sex deprived, and he was within close proximity? Was it that simple? She didn't think so. The reason being that she'd been in a male dominated society for the last six years, and hadn't had an issue with launching herself at a co-worker because she was horny. She didn't do that. Sex was great, but she'd never been able to remove her heart from the interaction. Which left only one answer. She was falling in love with Liam. Emotionally broken, unavailable, lives-on-another-continent, Liam O'Brien. And it wasn't like she could flee. She'd made a commitment to this mission. She didn't skate on her responsibilities, and she loved the work. Loved the staff.

The only solution was self-denial. She knew she could do it. That is… she thought she could. She'd been confident of that fact until the other night. His hands all over her, his breath on her neck, his smell. He'd been worried and stressed, and he'd reached for her. She could want him in secret, and she could live with that. But if he wanted her back on any level, she was really screwed.

What she'd said was correct. She couldn't put herself in harm's way, and it was harmful because of what it would really be about. She'd be a proxy for the woman he could no longer have. She'd be a soothing respite from his pain. A warm body to help him heal. But he wouldn't be hers forever, and he'd end up resenting her. Where would that leave her with Alanna? The entire O'Brien family, actually. She now considered them all friends. Almost family. It would ruin everything once it was over. She'd lose all of them.

Liam greeted the delivery truck, wondering what could be coming that couldn't go through the regular mail. The gentleman addressed him in Portuguese and asked him if he could sign for a package for the hospital. It was from a medical supply company he was familiar with, out of Shannon. He'd expected to see the abbess's name on it, or maybe Seamus. What he saw instead made him grin so wide, he thought his face was going to crack.

He grabbed the dolly from Paolo's garden shed, loading the large box. Then he wheeled it toward the surgery. As he came in the door, he sighed before he could bite it back. Izzy on her toes, reaching to tighten the new surgical lantern. It had been donated by one of the hospitals competing for her affections. She was in loose, white scrubs. And a sliver of belly was showing, because her arms were raised high. No more than an inch. But that's the way it was with her. It didn't take much to crank him up. "Ye've got a delivery."

She looked past the lamp and crinkled her brow. "I don't think so. I didn't order anything. How do you know it's for me?"

He smiled and read the label. "Doctor Isolde Collier, MD."

She groaned. Then she came around the surgical table and snatched the handle of the dolly out of his hand. "If you laugh, I'm going to beat the shit out of you."

"You're always threatening to beat me up, Is..." she shot him a look, "solde." He said with a mocking grin. She stopped and took a swat at him, not really meaning to hurt him. He grabbed her arm and pulled her forward, until they were nose to nose, her chin raised defiantly.

"Now how does an Italian, slash Welsh, slash German, slash American girl like you end up named after an Irish Princess?"

She narrowed her eyes at him. "My mother is a big Wagner fan. She was pregnant with me when she saw the Tristan and Isolde opera. I prefer Izzy. End of story."

Liam said, "Isolde is a pretty name. Too feminine for you? You'd rather have been named something like Knuckles Malone?"

Her mouth raised up on one corner. Then she extracted herself from him. She went to the package, reading the whole invoice. She was silent, staring at the piece of paper. Quiet so long that Liam came next to her and took the paper. She cleared her throat. "It's from your mother," she said softly. "Or rather, a donation from the birthing center where she works."

"Jesus, Izzy. It's a new ultrasound machine. How did she know we needed one?"

"She and I were talking about the lack of supplies, the substandard x-ray machine, the fact that we were using our crappy ultrasound machine to diagnose breast tumors as well as doing pre-natal scans. I mean, it was just general complaining. I didn't expect her to...."

Liam smiled, "She's a midwife, and she's had breast cancer. Then there's the whole Caitlyn thing. It obviously struck a chord with her, and she persuaded her practice to donate something. Seamus will be over the moon. Well done, Izzy."

"I didn't do anything. It was her. You should call her."

He nodded. "I will. But don't sell yourself short, love. You've really updated our equipment, and you did it by speaking passionately about our cause. You should put your head together with Sister Agatha. You're really good at reaching out and getting donations."

"Don't sell yourself short, either. You got your hands on fifty Zika vaccines," she said, smiling.

He laughed. "I suppose I did. We're a good team. Now, Seamus and I are going to the neighboring village and then to the far village in the forest to find volunteers for this vaccine. We'll need to draw blood on all of them to get a baseline. Do you mind if I borrow Raphael?"

"I'll do more than that, I'll come with you. We'll get it done faster if I come." She gave him a look that said she had every intention of going, invited or not.

"I'd like that. You can tell Seamus about the new toy."

At the first village, where Gabriela came from every day, they managed to get seventeen volunteers. Liam and Pedro would test their blood to make sure they weren't carrying the virus before they vaccinated them. Liam had two spare that would be alternates if someone wasn't cleared. As they made their way up the river, they smelled the smoke from the deforestation that was getting closer and closer to the village. Besides Seamus, Liam, Izzy, and Raphael, they'd been surprised to see that Sister Agatha was joining them today. She wasn't hospital staff, not even a full sister, but a novice. Then it made sense as Liam watched her taking pictures. Obviously the Reverend Mother had come around.

The smell of burning forest hadn't escaped Izzy. "They have to stop so many miles before, right? The tribes are protected?" Izzy couldn't fathom how this shit still went on in the world. After learning everything they had over the last thirty years, they'd started mowing down the rainforest again.

"Aye, they do. But if they can get them to move, then…" He shrugged. "Sometimes their convincing is more like coercion. Half the reason that jaguar was so close to the village is that they're driving the animals south, out of the denser jungle. They're trying to do the same with the natives. It's not just land that they want. It's the lumber. Mahogany brings a high pay off, and it's not getting replenished. Those trees are old and mature. They're taking forest that takes decades to grow, faster than the do-gooders can replant. It's all about money."

Raphael had been listening, and he added, "There is also the drug trade, boss. They can clear an airstrip by saying it is for the timbering or developing, then fly in drug planes full of cocaine. They are starting to cut roads for access where there never was access before. Roads that lead out of the bush and to trafficking points. They're permanently scarring this virgin forest for drugs. It makes me crazy to think about it. They supply other countries with cocaine, and this is the hub for the trafficking. And worse, a lot of it is staying in Brazil. Consumption within the country is high. They are poisoning their own people."

"So what's the answer?" she asked.

Liam's eyes were sad. "That's a larger problem than I can wrap my head around. I don't know. I just do what I can for the people here."

As they pulled up to the dock where a young boy saw them, he ran to the village. "What's he shouting?" Raphael looked at Izzy. Liam looked between him and Seamus, and then at Izzy, who was blushing. "Did I miss something?"

"Sim, Senhor. He's shouting that the anjo do rio has returned."

Liam looked at Izzy. "The river angel," he said softly, taking in the sight of her, anew. She was lovely, but she had a strength to her that held a different kind of attraction. Kind, liquid brown eyes, that had a hint of warm chestnut. She wore no makeup, but her skin was smooth and clear. She had the skin tone of her mixed heritage. Not the true Mediterranean, with the dark olive hues, but a lighter version. Fair, yet olive tones and touched by the sun. It made her glow. Her caramel waves almost touched her shoulders now, having grown in the time she'd been here. Short because she'd donated her long tresses. Now, it was kissed by the sun as well, golden at the tips. *River Angel,* he thought. It was a fitting name, by all accounts, but she was funny about names, wasn't she? She didn't go by her given name. Too exotic and feminine. So, he recognized the blush for what it was. She was embarrassed to be gifted such a nickname. "It suits you," he said.

Izzy got up, busying herself with the gear. "It's silly. I'm no angel."

"I think Estela would disagree," he said.

Raphael grunted an approval. Seamus added, "I certainly think you're an angel. Especially after having a new ultrasound machine appear from the heavens."

Liam laughed. "Shannon is hardly heaven. You'll have to come to my village. That, my friend, is heaven."

"How long have you been gone?" Seamus asked. There was speculation in his eyes.

"Ten months or so."

Seamus's brows lifted. "That's a far cry from the normal three month rotation. What made you stay?"

Izzy looked at him, then. She wondered what he would offer as an explanation. What he said surprised her. "I had something happen in

Dublin. I was ready for a change. And when I got here, I was needed. Everyone leaves, ye see. The sisters and the children see doctors come and go. They didn't have one single full time doctor. The pay is…all they can afford. Slave wages for a successful physician. But how could I go, when they needed me?"

"Well, now. It appears we've got two river angels, lad," Seamus said, with fatherly approval.

Seamus was disappointed, to be sure, to realize that the study didn't allow for them to vaccinate pregnant women. The virus was linked to severe birth defects. Microcephaly, in which the brain does not develop properly, and other brain abnormalities. Sometimes the defects were obvious, the child appearing to be missing part of the head. Skull deformities. But they didn't have the resources to scan every newborn, and sometimes the brain defects went undetected until they saw developmental and cognitive problems with the child. The problem had spread with the network of insects that carried the virus. Every mosquito was a suspect. And regardless of the precautions they took, everyone got bitten.

He looked at Izzy's arms, exposed in her *Naval Medical Center Portsmouth* t-shirt. She had numerous bites. He needed to verify that she'd taken a pregnancy test before leaving. Although, she'd claimed it had been two years since her last lover. He looked at Liam, who's gaze lingered on her often. Birth control. He definitely needed to read her medical records. Those two were headed for a collision. The horizontal, skin-on-skin type of collision. Neither would admit it, but you couldn't fight human nature.

As they walked into the village, the people gathered in the common area, an open-air shelter with a thatched cover. Then they began to work, having a couple of tribesmen who spoke fluent Portuguese get the full explanation from Liam and Raphael and interpret for the older men. As the tribal elders talked amongst themselves, they chose a group of men and women who fell within the criteria for receiving the vaccine. The men lined up to have their blood drawn, as the women went to a private area to take home pregnancy tests. As long as they weren't currently pregnant, they could participate.

They lingered, having a light meal and visiting with the villagers. The women loved to play with Izzy's hair and even drew some temporary tattooing on her upper arms. She sat with her sleeves pulled up, letting them pamper her in their own way.

Izzy smiled as she watched the toddler, wriggling in her mother's arms. She was a beauty. Straight white teeth emerging, and dark eyes. Raphael was equally smitten, making faces at the child to ease her as Izzy looked her over. Izzy had him try to explain, as best he could, what a hemangioma was. A bundle of blood vessels that were a harmless birthmark. It would lessen in size, as the child aged. If not, they could remove it. But best to let it be. When the mother didn't understand, she said, "Tell her it's an angel kiss. A mark at birth that shows that the child is kissed by the angels."

Izzy, herself, had a small hemangioma. It was on the soft skin that was under her right breast. Barely noticeable unless someone got up close and personal. They weren't anything to worry about and fairly common. Except if you were in Salem several hundred years ago. Then they would have called it a witch mark. Raphael smiled and translated. The mother's face lit as she ran a finger over the child's jawline, where the small, purple lump was located.

Liam was checking an elderly patient, who was having trouble with his breathing. That's when the stir in the village began. Liam and Raphael rose to their feet as they heard the vehicle. This dense jungle had no real roads, and it was a testament to how close the trouble was getting to the indigenous population. "Izzy, get in the huts with Sister Agatha and the other women."

"Like hell, I will," she shot back as she ruffled through her backpack. Liam's mouth tensed as he saw the large tanto knife emerge. It was in a leather sheath that Izzy put in her belt, pulling her shirt out of her pants to conceal it. Liam looked at Raphael, who just shrugged. "She wanted a knife, and she knows how to use it."

He looked for signs that the man was just appeasing his boss, but he saw none. Raphael trained with her. Not just in crossfit. He was trained in Brazilian jujitsu, and Izzy in Hapkido, so he'd seen them wrestling and teaching Genoveva some moves. That aside, he hated that she was here. He wanted her back at the hospital, safe.

Seamus said, "What's amiss, brother?"

"I don't know. If they're in a vehicle this far into the forest, they've either come from one of the logging camps or they're the owners of that missing parachute. Neither is good." The young to middle-aged males seemed to circle the clearing, standing at the ready. They had bows, spears, and machetes. Between hunting and the other dangers, they had to rely on themselves to protect their own. It wasn't like they could ring the Garda if there was trouble. A few minutes later, five men came out of the forest and into the north end of the village. They spoke Portuguese which told Liam that they weren't from this tribe. Many of the villagers were bilingual, but to each other, they spoke their native tongue. The clothes weren't right either, then he noticed the weapons. Raphael was listening intently. He leaned in. "This is not the first meeting. They're trying to get the tribe to move the village. They've refused."

They didn't have any weapons pointed at anyone. They were just using them for intimidation. The old man raised his voice, pointing in a way that let them know exactly where they could take their offer. His sons were standing, a strong presence beside him. One of the five men was eyeing Seamus and Liam. Then his eyes landed on Izzy. Liam tensed and Seamus said, "Easy lad."

As the man approached, he looked back and forth between them. Then his eyes rested on Raphael. Liam listened to the exchange. *Do I know you? You look familiar.* He could see Izzy getting nervous. Raphael had been doing counter-narcotics in the Army. He really wouldn't benefit from one of these shitbirds recognizing him. Then the man said something unexpected. *You know my son, Emilio at the Orfanato?* The hair stood up on Liam's arms. This was Emilio's father. The one who dumped him off after the mother overdosed. The drug dealer that couldn't be bothered to raise his own son. It looked like he moved up in the world from petty dealer to the trafficking end of things. Jesus, he really needed to get Izzy out of here.

The man looked at the supplies, and Liam wondered if he was looking for drugs. They didn't have any narcotics on them, like morphine or other opiates, but he really didn't want this dickhead rifling through those sterile blood samples he'd just collected. The man looked at Raphael and said something Liam didn't catch. Then he gave Izzy a very familiar look, a look that made the skin prickle. Then they were gone, filing back down the path from which they came. Liam exhaled. "What the hell did he say?"

"He said that we should talk to the villagers about moving."

"What is perigosa?" Izzy asked.

"Situação perigosa. It means..." he tried to think of the English equivalent. "Dangerous situation." Liam cursed under his breath. Izzy walked toward the area where the women were huddled with the children. Raphael turned to Liam, his face tense. "You must find a way to keep her back at the mission. These men are animals. They aren't above the most horrible tactics, including taking out women and children to break the spirit of the whole. To destroy the heart of a group. She will not submit to this, so you must do it discreetly. You and Antonio. Keep her busy on the day you must come back."

Liam's fists were tight at his side as he nodded. "If I have to gag and restrain her, I will. Did he recognize you, Raphael? Is your family at risk?"

"I don't know but I'll move them for a time. I can take them to my mother who lives just south of the city. And I'll call my contacts in the federal police. If it's not drugs, then there could be something else. Illegal gold mining or logging, perhaps.

"Emilio's father was a petty drug dealer. Trafficking fits," Liam said. Raphael nodded his agreement. "When I move my family, I'm going to move into the abbey if the Reverend Mother will allow it."

"Aye, it's a good idea. I'll make it happen. Even if I have to give you my room, and if you have weapons, bring them."

"The abbess would not like it."

"She's Irish, brother. Don't underestimate her survival instincts, or her willingness to do anything to protect the nuns and children under her roof."

18

They were eating dinner later that evening, when Liam heard a vehicle tear into the abbey from the east. They were laying on their horn. It was odd, because if they got vehicle traffic, it was usually to west, toward Manaus. Men were yelling. He jumped up as Sister Agatha came skidding into the cantina. "Dr. Collier!"

Izzy was already running, as were all of the doctors. Liam grabbed a limb as they pulled the first young man out of the flatbed. There was blood everywhere. "Oh God. Piatã's sons," Seamus said as he appeared next to Izzy.

"Get them in the surgery! And get Antonio here! Now!" Izzy looked at Liam. "I need help. I need another surgeon. We need to assess which brother is in worse danger and stabilize the other until Antonio gets here." They were walking as Liam helped them set the younger son down on the table. Then the other men that had driven the truck, along with Adam and Seamus, brought the other son in. The father was inconsolable. Shouting and waving his arms.

"You need to get him out of here. No unnecessary personnel!" Then she began. "First patient has a double GSW to the chest. I need an IV and oxygen, Alyssa." As she went on, she gave orders and assessed both young men. She was mumbling to herself, adding up the time that had passed between the shootings, and them getting the men on the boats, down the river, and into the truck in the neighboring village. "Too long. Dammit! Too long." The other young man had been shot in the abdomen and upper thigh. They'd put a homemade tourniquet on him that was barely staunching the flow. Adam worked with Seamus to try and get the GSW to the chest stabilized as the nurses ran fluids and started giving the one with the leg injury a unit of blood. Seamus wheeled him to the radiology room to get a chest x-ray.

The arterial bleed was the worse of the two injuries, which is how she made her decisions. "Any word on Antonio?" Sister Agatha was in the corner, staying out of the way. "He's in surgery, Dr. Collier. They couldn't interrupt him."

"Shit." Her eyes were pleading. "I can't be two places at once. Liam. Jesus, they're both his sons."

"You have to triage, Izzy. This injury isn't going to wait. We just have to hope his brother holds."

Izzy climbed on the table, straddling the man at the knees. He was moaning but staying still. She looked up a Liam. "When I say go, take it off."

When he did, blood shot out of the wound and all over Izzy. She pressed the wound down with all her weight until he replaced the tourniquet with a sterile one from their own supplies. She dismounted and said. "I need to clamp this off and then repair it. Alyssa, Liam, and Seamus get ready to assist. "

It seemed like decades that Izzy worked on the young man on her table. She fixed the arterial bleed, but he was still not out of the woods. The second bullet had nicked the left kidney. By the time she'd gotten the bleeding under control, it was fully night. She saw the darkness through the windows. "How's our other patient doing?" she asked Adam. He'd been doing his best to keep him stable, monitoring his vitals. But he wasn't trained to do surgery, especially with organ damage. Neither were Seamus and Liam. But they'd kept him going, hoping he could hold on until Izzy saved his brother. Liam assisted her as much as he could, suctioning, handing tools, adjusting her light, acting more like a surgical nurse than a doctor. Seamus only had experience with c-sections and hysterectomies, but he knew more than Liam about arterial bleeds and the needle and thread shit, so he went back and forth between the two brothers.

Adam answered Izzy's question. "His vitals aren't good. I'm not going to lie. Blood pressure is low, breathing is labored, oxygen levels are in the basement. Antonio just left the hospital and he's on his way."

She exhaled. He was still at least fifteen minutes out. That was before scrubbing in. She held her breath as she looked at the second bleed from his kidney. *Please hold.* When it appeared to do so, she started to close.

As she went to the brother, her heart lurched in her chest. Breathing was a struggle and his color wasn't good. Tension pneumothorax from a GSW to the chest. He was stripped and cleaned already, with bloodied bandages covering his tanned, youthful chest. Izzy refreshed her gloves and face shield, but couldn't take the time to change. She'd been sprayed over half her body with the brother's blood, but it didn't matter. This man couldn't wait anymore. She went to him and leaned in. "Your irmão está bem." Her Portuguese/English bastardization was awful, but he understood her meaning. His brother was doing okay. He nodded, then closed his eyes. That's when his chest heaved and he coughed, blood spraying into his oxygen mask. She started preparing for surgery. Once she stabilized him, they could try to transfer both the men to a bigger trauma unit in Manaus. They needed thorough scans to make sure the bullets hadn't hit anything else, and Izzy didn't have that kind of equipment.

Antonio came in just as she took the scalpel in her hand. Liam watched as they worked across from each other, Alyssa acting as the anesthetist and Margaritte as their nurse. Antonio said, "I'm sorry I wasn't here when you needed me. You did the right thing. You had to choose, and the other brother had to go first. They would have both died if you tried to transport them any farther. Honestly, it's staggering that they're still alive given these injuries." Liam heard the clink of each bullet going into the small metal dish. Once the lung was repaired, they sewed up a flesh wound from a bullet that had grazed the shoulder. Izzy let out a deep breath, so relieved. That's when all hell broke loose. The monitors ringing loudly. "No, no, no!" she yelled.

Izzy sat next to Antonio as he explained what had happened. A clot, most likely. Followed by cardiac arrest. Despite their best efforts they could not resuscitate him. They'd had a long journey to get treatment and then the other son had been more critical. They'd saved the younger son…younger by two years. His eldest son didn't survive.

The father asked to take his son home for burial, and one of the Brazilian sisters offered to help the father clean and wrap him. He would return for his other son in three days, but now he needed to take his eldest home to his mother, to his wife, and to his small child. The child with the angel kiss on her jaw.

Liam watched as Izzy stood, like a zombie. Antonio put a hand on her. "We did everything we could. I'm so sorry, Izzy. I'm sorry I wasn't here."

"It's not your fault. They were my patients," she said weakly.

Antonio's face softened. "Go get some rest, Izzy. You're exhausted. I will take first watch." As she left, the Reverend Mother came into the hall where they'd been talking.

"Antonio, thank you for coming so quickly."

"I'm afraid it was too late."

Liam spoke, then. "It sounds like they had another run-in with the men we saw in the village. The ones that are trying to get the village to relocate."

"I'm afraid times are changing in our little, green, isolated part of the world. I sometimes fear we are destined to fail. That I'll no longer have a place on this landscape. How will I protect the children and my sisters?"

Liam saw an opening. "We'll discuss that later, Reverend Mother. I've been speaking to Raphael about that very issue. But now I need to go check on Izzy."

He found her in the locker room. And as he walked in, he really didn't care at what stage of dress she was in. He knew her well enough to know that she was going to internalize this loss. She was a brilliant surgeon. She'd made a choice no one should have to make. A choice between two critical patients. A choice between a man's two sons. She hadn't done it based on whether one was single and one was married with a child. She'd taken the one who needed the most immediate care, because she'd been the only surgeon. She'd done her job. If she hadn't, then it's quite possible they both would have died. "Izzy," he said loud enough to get her attention and warn her of his approach. He heard the water running and prepared himself to quash his response at the sight of her naked. She wasn't, though. She was using a scrub brush to rid herself of all the blood. Her scrubs were covered, and it was probably from both of her patients.

She was crying silently. "I'm okay. I just need to get most of it off before they try to launder it." Her face was tight with pain and loss. Losing a patient was the worst part about being a doctor.

He didn't talk, he just went to her. He stilled the brush and soap in her hands. "It's clean enough, love. Let's take care of you." He was gentle as he took the scrubs off. First the top, over her head. Then the bottoms. She had a sports bra and tank top under the blouse, and those short style panties she favored. Liam took the soap and a cloth she'd put aside, and began washing her. Her eyes just kept tearing, not meeting his. But as he washed her, tended to her, her body loosened. He didn't touch her anywhere that was inappropriate. He washed her back, her shoulders, and her long legs. As he washed each calf, he felt her put hands on his shoulders, steadying herself. When he was done, he took the shampoo, squeezing it into his palm. Then he pulled her to him. When he tilted her head back and began to massage her scalp, she was fluid and soft in his arms. She sighed, and he soaked in the contact. Soaked in the feel of her wavy hair, thick in his hands. He wasn't sure when their eyes first met, but as she looked at him with utter despair mixed with a trust he couldn't wrap his head around, he fought like hell to keep his mouth from taking hers.

She had to have felt his arousal. It was a thick, hard length, pressing between their bodies. He shifted and tilted her head back further into the spray of water. Her body arched as she closed her eyes and he felt that warm, delicious feel of her sex against his. Nothing but his scrubs and her panties keeping him from her. He moaned before he could bite it back. She whimpered in his arms and his control snapped. Good intentions swirled down the drain with all that blood and soap and water.

He turned her and had her against the shower wall. Her face cupped in his hand as his breath mixed with hers. Then the evening prayer bell was ringing from the abbey and the reality of where they were permeated the fog of arousal. She put her hands on his chest, pressing. "I'm okay, Liam. Thank you...for caring for me." She stepped away, wiping the last remnants of tears off her face. "I'm okay, and we can't do this here." She shook her head, to clear it. "At all. I mean we can't do this at all. It's a bad idea."

Liam took her elbows into his hands. "You're wrong. This is exactly what we need." He pulled her close. "I'm tired, Izzy. Tired of hurting. Tired of the loneliness. Tired of not trying to feel anything. Tired of smelling you in that bed and imagining what you look like when you come. Wanting to be inside you when you do it." Her eyes were glossy, her breathing rapid. He felt like a predator. "Come to me. Come to the bungalow, tonight."

She squeezed the skin on his hard chest, clarity piercing the haze that had consumed them both. She squeezed so hard that it bit into him. His hips jerked, his arousal wanting out. He wanted her nails in his back.

"You aren't ready for this," she bit out.

His brow went up, confusion and frustration clipping his words. "I think you can feel just how feckin' ready I am."

"You think you are, but you can't even kiss me, Liam. You will regret this and resent me. You aren't ready for this, and it cannot be me. Even if I wanted to, it can't be me."

He palmed the back of her head. "It can only be you!" he said fiercely. "And if I get any part of my mouth on you right now, it's over. I won't stop until I'm in you." Then he pulled her to him, their mouths a hair from one another. "Come to me, Izzy."

There was a voice in the hall, then a knock. "Izzy! We need you in the hospital. The ambulance is on the way to transfer your patient!" Seamus's voice held no hint that he knew where Liam was.

"I have to go. He's my patient."

"Let Antonio go," he said, pressing into her. He nuzzled her neck. She shuddered.

"I can't. He didn't treat him." She pushed off the wall, taking him with her. "And we need to cool off. You need to think with a clear head."

"I am perfectly clear-headed."

"No, you're not. You can't trust your own judgment when you've got a hard-on. All the blood has drained south of the border. You're trying to comfort me, but this isn't the way."

"You want me. This isn't one-sided, Izzy. If I took you down on this tile right now, we both know what I'd find."

Cocky bastard. "You don't need to remind me that I'm a glutton for punishment or about the current state of my arousal. I'm ready to go wrecking ball on that freaking tile!" she hissed. He moved toward her, a growl low in his throat. She put a palm to his chest. "But that's biology. It's instinct. It's not real life. There are consequences in real life, Liam. After the sex was finished, you'd feel differently, and things would quickly deteriorate. I can't be a proxy, even for you." She grabbed a towel and was out the door before her words finally sunk in.

Izzy spent the night in the hospital. She hadn't meant to, but when they'd arrived with her patient, they'd put him in the hallway. Plugged his machines into an outlet by the nurse's station. They kept him on a freaking gurney in the hall. The public hospital was busy. They'd managed to supersede the waitlist for an abdominal and lower body CT scan, but the radiologist wasn't going to be in until 6 a.m. This was bullshit. There was no way she was going to leave him in the hallway and go home. So the nurses brought her a chair and she waited. By the time he'd had his scans and been put into a room with two other patients, the head of surgery had come in as well. They went over the scans together, and the surgeon had been impressed with what she'd managed to do with such basic equipment and no trained surgical team.

His English was very good. He was about sixty years old and at the top of his career. "It's surprising to me that you did not lose them both. I know this village. They came far before getting treated. The polícias will need a full account." Raphael was taking care of that today, and she told him so.

She sighed, so very tired. "I'll need someone to help with the translation. I think he knows Portuguese as well as his native language, but he has no English. We need to tell him about his brother."

Izzy washed her face in the hospital lavatory, trying to clear her mind. The young man had been devastated. His older brother died, and he was alive. Survivor guilt existed in every age, culture, and background.

She was so grateful when the night was over. She'd barely slept, nodding off in the uncomfortable chair. And in the place between sleep and wakefulness, she'd played that scene in the shower over and over again. In different circumstances, she'd have taken him up on those promises that his eyes held. Promises of pleasure and mind-bending sex, but one of them had to be the reasonable one. There was a power in their chemistry that was like nothing she'd ever experienced. Enough passion and need to burn them both alive. But it was the loss and pain that boiled within him that was the cause of that edgy desperation. Which meant this wasn't about her.

When the dust settled, he'd move on. She'd go back to America, he would stay or go back to Ireland and face his feelings about Eve's death. Either way, he'd be done with her. O'Briens waxed poetic about their mates. She'd heard all of the stories, including the fact that they only had one. If they lost her, they were ruined for any other woman. Even if she didn't believe it, Liam did. So she'd been right about being a stepping stone.

He was lonely and he was a sensual person by nature. He missed the intimacy. And she just couldn't bear the thought of being the metaphorical pool that he dipped his toe in before plunging back into the real world that lay outside of the abbey. She wished she was capable of no-strings sex. It wasn't in her makeup. Having him put that hard length to use would undoubtedly be a wild ride, and the thought of it pressed against her was almost enough to make her chuck her good intentions, but she had to be strong. Strong enough for both of them.

Liam spent the night in the staff quarters, sleeping like shit. He hadn't been able to get the feel of her out of his head. He'd also relived that parting shot over and over again. It had been like a shot to the balls. *I can't be a proxy, even for you.*

At five o'clock, he finally got up, heading to the abbey library. His intent had been to call his mother. But just as he'd started to do it, he found himself ringing Patrick. He hadn't spoken with him since Caitlyn had lost the baby.

Now, as he stared at the screen, he wanted to bash his head into the desk. Of course, Patrick was at work. Caitlyn was pale and thinner than he remembered. "I'm so sorry, love. That's all I can say." Her eyes were ruined. Tears misting and then quelled by an inner strength he both admired and wished she didn't need. Women were like that. She changed the subject, asking all about the missionary work being done at St. Clare's.

"An orphanage? Oh, dear. That must be difficult for you, Liam. How many are there? What ages?" She asked many questions, including about the school and Sister Maria. Before he realized it, they'd talked for almost an hour. He missed her, he realized. They'd lived in the same area of Dublin for a couple of years, and she'd always been quick with a smile and a hot meal. And she loved his brother to the depths of her soul.

"How are you doing, brother? It's been almost a year. Has your suffering eased a bit, with your new landscape?" He gave her a sad smile.

"I suppose. It's never gone, completely. I was out of my head for a bit, but I'm keeping busy. My work fulfills me."

"And do you have friends? Or maybe a woman?" He recoiled from her question.

"I have no woman. That's over for me." But even as he said the words, there was a big fat question mark at the end of that sentence. "You know that, Caitlyn."

"I don't know any such thing, Liam. If something happened to me, I would want Patrick to move on. I would want more for him than a life of mourning and loneliness. I knew Eve. She was dear to me. A good, kind, loving woman. If she can't get a vote, then I'll vote as her proxy. You should allow yourself at least the chance to love someone again."

There was that damn word again. *I can't be a proxy, even for you.*

He skirted the subject of himself. "Patrick would be a walking dead man if something happened to you, despite your feelings on the matter. Please, love. Please take care of yourself. Listen to your doctors."

"Weren't we talking about you?" she said stiffly.

"I just worry, deirfiúr." His eyes searched her face. Willing her to be okay in body and soul. She wasn't okay. He saw it in her eyes. Not okay at all.

He ended the video call, closing the lid on Izzy's laptop. Then he left to see if Gabriela had any coffee ready. It was still early, but she'd be hard at work in the kitchen. He walked into the main dining hall, smiling when he saw Seamus with a piece of cheese bread and coffee. "I have to tell you, brother. I've been drinking tea since I was a wee lad. This coffee, though. It's gorgeous altogether, and don't get me started on these little rolls."

Cheese bread was a Brazilian staple. Dough balls kneaded with cheese and baked to a light golden color. The residents at St. Clare's ate them faster than Gabriela could make them. He looked up as Izzy walked in, and his heart squeezed. She was exhausted. It was in her gait, in her sunken eyes, in her shoulders. She cracked her neck, rubbing it, and Liam wondered under what conditions she'd slept. He'd been at the hospital when the call had come in that she was staying with her patient until he was secured in a room, and seen by a doctor. There was such ownership in her work. He understood it. His relationships with his patients were a very real, personal connection. If he hadn't admired her enough already, it had grown exponentially over the last twenty-four hours.

She accepted a cup of coffee. "When is the last time you ate, Izzy?" His words were gentle.

"I don't remember. At the village, I suppose. I'd only managed a deep sniff of my meal at dinner before that truck pulled up." She cleared her throat, her voice hoarse with fatigue. "I could eat."

Liam got up, leaving her at the table with Seamus. "Stay put, lass. I'll see what she's got that is ready."

Liam worked alongside Gabriela, making a plate of food for Izzy. Fruit, yogurt, some granola. He snagged a few cheese rolls and some sliced ham. Gabriela gave him a sideways glance. "You are a good man, médico. Sometimes the woman needs someone to take care of her. She's too busy taking care of the others."

He blushed, shrugging. "It's just a plate of food, Gabriela."

She stopped, taking his shoulders and turning him toward herself. "I know what it is to lose, Senhor Liam. I lose my Luiz many years ago, but it still hurt me in here." She pointed to his chest. "I don't know who you lose, Senhor, but it's okay to feel something good." She hugged him. "You're a good boy, Liam. A very good boy."

Liam hugged her back, suddenly missing his own mother. Gabriela was about ten to fifteen years younger than his mother, but his mam had always been youthful for her age. And she'd always known just what to say, and just when to step in with a hug.

He walked out into the dining area and noticed that Genoveva had joined them. Normally the children sat separately, but she was early. And it wasn't their rule, it was Sister Maria's. Genoveva got up, palming Izzy's coffee cup. "Wait, lass." He turned to Izzy. "More caffeine isn't what you need. You have to get some rest, Izzy. Hydrate, eat and go to bed. We'll keep an eye on things."

Her instinct was to resist, but she waged a little internal battle and accepted the plate. "Just a nap. The federal police are coming in an hour with Raphael. Then we are headed to the village."

Liam couldn't believe his ears. "Jesus Christ, Izzy." As he said it, Genoveva crossed herself. "Sorry, lass." Then he turned back to Izzy. "You don't need to be there. You aren't a witness. Let Raphael handle it. Two people just got shot, for God's sake."

She slapped the table. "I have to see his wife. I need to pay my respects! He died on my watch. I owe it to them to face them."

Seamus's tone was calm, taking some of the bite out of the inter-action. "No one could have done more, Izzy darlin'. Ye did all you could. If ye hadn't been here, we'd have lost them both."

She shut her eyes, so tired and sad. "I know that. My mind knows that, but my heart is telling me to go be with them as they bury one of their own."

Seamus nodded. "I'll go with her."

"No, Seamus. I'll go. We need you here. I'll go," Liam said.

As Izzy finished her breakfast and left for a brief nap, Seamus whistled between his teeth. "She's got the heart of a lion, that one."

19

The Reverend Mother stared across from her two doctors and weighed the decision before her. "I'm not completely comfortable with this."

"Duly noted, but that's not a no." Liam sighed heavily as he watched Izzy wear her opponent down. "I just want to go pay my respects. And if they'll let me, stay to attend the funeral ceremony." Then she paused. "I mean…they don't practice cannibalism of their dead anymore, right? They bury them."

"Yes, but I doubt an outsider would be permitted to stay. It will be at least another two days of mourning. You can't be away from the hospital that long, even if they'd allow it, and the rain is coming. It's going to be a big one. I don't want you on the river when it happens, so you must only go for the day.."

"I understand. Thank you, Reverend Mother, for understanding that I need to do this."

Just then, Sister Agatha interrupted. "May I have a word?" Liam and Izzy tried to leave but she stopped them. "No, all of you. Please."

She came into the room. "The police are here. I just wanted to talk to you briefly. I downloaded my photos from the other day. I have a picture of the men who came to the village. I zoomed in on them when we were taking refuge in the huts. I know it may not matter, but I wanted your permission to give a copy of the photos to the authorities."

Izzy watched the Reverend Mother cross herself, rattled that one of her charges had been in the middle of this whole thing. "I think that's the best news I've heard all day, sister. If it's alright with the abbess, I definitely think they're going to want to see them."

Liam's eyes burned with emotion as he took in the diminutive figure before him. Sister Agatha was a delicate, pretty, little thing. Probably in her early twenties and very quiet. The thought that she'd taken the risk of getting caught snapping photos, of zooming in on those five men while they tried to intimidate the tribal leader and his sons... it unnerved him. He couldn't help but make the comparison. He was humbled by it. That a woman that could seem so delicate, so agreeable, so kind down to her marrow, could also possess bravery. He thought of Eve, alone in that alley. No, not alone. She'd been in the presence of true evil, and instead of running, she'd stayed. Her actions had saved that girl in the alley. "Well done, Sister Agatha."

"Yes, of course." The Reverend Mother finally found her tongue. "However, I must insist that you refrain from going into the forest with the doctors again."

"Should I do any less than Dr. Collier? My life is no more valuable. In fact, I would argue it is much more expendable. She heals the body, but perhaps I can offer some sort of spiritual comfort."

The Reverend Mother couldn't keep the pride out of her eyes. "I understand, Sister. But my decision is made. You will stay back where you are needed. There has been much turmoil in our small home these past few weeks. Perhaps you could join me in ministering to our staff, and to the children. We need to first tend to our own flock."

Izzy said softly, "The team comes first."

Raphael, Izzy, and Liam went in the boat with Paolo, while the federal police followed them in their own boat. Raphael spoke to the men who came to the dock, telling them why they were here. Then the father of the two men who'd been shot appeared behind them. He spoke something that Izzy didn't catch, then the men parted and led everyone, including the federal police, to the village. The matter was being handled by them, instead of the civil state police, due to the high probability that it was drug-related. The police, both state and federal, had a sketchy past and a rocky relationship with the people of Brazil, and even the remote-living natives knew to be cautious. Raphael seemed to think the men that had taken this report were genuinely here to help, which is the only reason he'd eased the way for them. As they dismounted the boat, the rain started misting.

Liam watched as the police officers walked with Raphael over to the men, who were seated in the common gathering area. Then he watched Izzy walk to the women, her head low. He remembered what Seamus had said at breakfast, and he was right. She did have the heart of a lion. She was going before the mother and wife of her patient to let them do what, exactly? Judge her? Condemn her for not saving both men? He took a step forward when he felt Raphael's hand on him.

"No, brother. You must let her do this."

Izzy's tears started as she knelt down to where the women were gathered. Their eyes never left her. "I'm sorry," she said in her elementary Portuguese. "I'm so sorry," she croaked again in English. The women moved closer, putting their hands on her. She couldn't understand their words, but their faces said it all. They didn't blame her. That's when Raphael and Liam joined her. Raphael said something to them, and the mother of the young men answered him.

"She said…that she mourned her sons at the moment she laid her eyes upon them. She thought surely to lose them both. It was beyond their medicine. So she sent them to the river angel, hoping that there would be a miracle." The tears poured down Izzy's face. The woman continued, and Raphael translated. His voice thick with emotion. "I had two sons. Then I feared I had none. You saved me from being…" he thought about the translation. "Mother to none."

The woman took her daughter-in-law's hand, a widow now. In one senseless act of greed and violence, she was a widow. Izzy met her eyes. The woman spoke through her tears. Raphael made a little sound in the back of his throat. Then he swallowed, blinking fast. Izzy looked at him. "She says she lost his body. But she keeps his soul within her." That's when the woman gave a sad smile, covering her belly with one hand. "He will live on in his son." The words held no doubt. She was convinced in her early pregnancy that the child she carried was a boy. Izzy put her hand over the woman's own and nodded.

As they continued through the day, Izzy and Liam were fed. Paolo had departed upon drop off, giving them the day to be with the family. When the police left, Raphael went with them. He had a meeting with his Army boss. He was a reservist of sorts, having been put out to pasture after his injury, but the Army helped with counter-narcotics and he needed to brief his commanding officer. It was almost instantaneous when the rain went from misting to a downpour. It was like standing in the shower. Izzy hadn't seen anything like it. And it didn't let up. If anything, it seemed to gain momentum. She saw Liam head to the riverside and she went after him, holding a palm over her head. When she realized it was doing no good, she discarded it. "Wow," she said when she came next to him.

"Aye. Just what the abbess was worried about. Although, it's a day early. Paolo won't be able to take the boat upriver in this." The river was swollen and rapid. A feeder river that drained into one of the Amazon tributaries. The dock was at water level now, and would soon be under water.

"Let's hope it eases up in an hour or so. If not, we may be stuck for the night." He turned to her, meeting her eyes for the first time in a while. That heat was back, for both of them. "Did you get what you came for, lass?"

"I don't know. I guess so. I'm not sure why I needed to come. I just needed…" she paused. "I needed to let them see me and to see their faces. I needed to apologize because I couldn't be what they needed."

"You're a brave woman, Izzy. You don't back down from adversity, even when you have an out. I admire you." He was closer now, and he touched her face, a sort of pain showing on his face. "You're so beautiful. It's almost too much to bear." He backed away then, taking her hand. "I'll talk to the boss. This happened one other time, and they put us up for the night."

It was fully dark and the rain continued. The women readied lodgings for the night, moving a family to another house so that the médicos had a place to sleep. Izzy swatted at the mosquitos until a small girl brought her some of the ointment that she'd been using at the abbey. It soothed and repelled. Mixed with the rain on her skin, it smelled kind of nice. Earthy. When she walked into the small, thatched house they'd prepared, she was surprised to find a sort of bed. She'd been expecting hammocks. Liam came in behind her and stopped as well. "It's the chieftain's quarters, where he stays with his wife. They honor us by giving us this house."

Izzy saw that a mosquito net hung from above, ready to be dropped over and around the bed while they slept. "I can ask them to get a hammock in here as well. You can take the bed, lass." His voice was rough, thick with some kind of emotion.

"You're bigger. I'll take the hammock." But he was gone into the rain before she could take it back. She didn't want either of them in that stupid hammock. When he'd touched her today, called her beautiful, it had been like a lightning strike. She'd almost pulled him down to her mouth. Because she was an idiot. She arranged the LED lights from her pack, placing them strategically, so that the room glowed with soft illumination. The structure was sturdy, built of wood except for the roof, which was well thatched to keep the rain out. The windows had board shutters that were propped open for circulation. It was so simple and modest. But she was beyond touched at the gesture.

She sat on the edge of the palette. A bed would have been a gross exaggeration. It was a large platform with legs. There was a cloth pad that seemed to be stuffed with cotton and dried herbs. She wondered if the herbs kept the bugs away. They smelled similar to her tonic. They'd spread some cloth over the pad and a fresh blanket that smelled of the river, trying to make it as clean and nice as they could. Tears pricked her eyes. That's when he came through the sheet of rain that poured off the thatch and through the only door. His scrubs were soaked, sticking to his body. His eyes were flames of blue ice, burning into her. His hard cock strained against his wet pants. She stood up as he threw the hammock on the floor like unwanted trash. Then he stalked toward her. "Liam, you...."

He cut her off. "Izzy, love. Neither one of us is ready for this." Then he took her head in his hands and kissed the hell out of her.

As soon as Liam touched Izzy's mouth with his, it was like ten thousand volts ran through his entire body. He broke the kiss, gasping as he looked at her. She was resplendent in the dim light. Her glossy mouth, flushed from his attentions. Her chest pumping like she'd run a marathon. Her chestnut eyes were bright, and that's when he knew she'd felt it too. "Oh, God. I need you. I need this. Tell me to leave now, if you don't want this." But she cut him off, pulling his head down to her as she wove her hands through his thick hair. The sounds he made were like someone else entirely. He heard the desperation and hunger in his own voice. Her's as well. He pulled her pelvis to his, taking one hand out of her hair and splaying it across her ass. He lifted her, and she was right there with him, her long legs winding tightly around his waist. He pressed her back against the wall as he found right where he wanted to be. The ridge of his erection finding her warm, inviting center. He was ready to come already;

she felt so good in his arms. Her round hips and beautiful ass fitting perfectly in his palms. He rolled his hips and she broke the kiss, moaning and whimpering. They were going to climax before they even got undressed.

Then she stopped, taking his face in her hands. "Liam," her voice was uncharacteristically gentle and almost sad. "Liam, open your eyes." When he looked at her, he couldn't make sense of the insecurity he saw in her eyes. She rubbed a thumb over his mouth. "See me. I need you to see me."

It took him a second to understand. Then he kissed her, soft and sweet, with his eyes open. "I see you Izzy, love." *I can't be a proxy, even for you.* In his battle to keep his wits about him, he'd closed his eyes. If he saw her face when she whimpered under his mouth and arched into his cock, he'd explode. But she'd misunderstood. She thought he was thinking of someone else. *I can't be that kind of stepping stone.*

How could she think he'd be thinking of anyone else? There was just too much Izzy to confuse things. She was larger than life. Beautiful and strong, and his heart tore a little at the thought of her feeling like less in his arms. Like a proxy. The truth was, he wouldn't have been able to do this with another woman.

He was a bastard of the first order for taking what she was giving him. His heart was dead, but his body sang when she was near him. He'd never felt such a primal pull to a woman. Like he was half animal. But she needed to know that he was fully aware of who he was with. He leaned in, his eyes never leaving hers. Hovering over her mouth, he rolled his hips. He moaned her name as he did it, over and over again, giving her light kisses, rubbing his lips back and forth on hers. "I see you, Izzy."

She palmed his face and kissed him. She held nothing back, and he knew that she understood. He wanted her. There was no one else in the room with them.

He pulled back off the wall and pulled her shirt over her head. Her breasts were beautiful, but that sports bra had to go. "I need to see you." She unwrapped her legs as he took the bra off next. Then his mouth was all over them. She was panting, out of her head as he flicked her nipple with his tongue, circling it and flicking again.

Izzy was so aroused that it overwhelmed her senses. Liam was soaked. His skin tasted like the rain, and the cold wet clothes he was wearing sent a jolt through her; his wet hair leaving droplets on her breasts as his warm mouth suckled her. He kissed down her stomach, nibbling her soft hips. Then he looked up, meeting her eyes. When he started to pull her pants down and a little moan escaped from her.

The scent of Izzy's arousal struck Liam so hard that his human brain flipped to pure animal. He buried his face at the juncture of her thighs, probing and licking. He managed to get one foot out of her pants before she came. He hooked a leg over his shoulder as she rolled her hips against his mouth. He drank her in, kept at her until her other leg was ready to give out. Then he had her on the bed. He pulled his scrubs off and he loved the way her eyes traveled over his body. Then he knelt and began his work again. He looked up from between her legs as her body rolled. He stretched his arms up to cup her breasts while he tasted her. She liked it, he could tell, because he felt her hips start to move faster. "That's it, Izzy. Again."

He rolled her nipples between his fingers as he flicked his tongue right where she needed him. He didn't need a roadmap. That little triangle she'd sculpted so beautifully had pointed the way home, and the blood roared in his ears as she came again.

"Liam, I need you." He nuzzled her, ignoring her pleas, and she cursed, electricity shooting through her core. "Please get your ass up here. Now, O'Brien!" He laughed, growling as he bit her inner thigh. Then he was above her, pressing. She arched her neck, closing her eyes.

"No, love. Fair is fair," he said as he slid a hand behind her neck, raising her face to his. "Open your eyes, Izzy love. I want you to see me when I do this."

She opened her eyes just as he sheathed himself to the base. They both cried out at the sweet invasion.

Liam's head almost exploded off his shoulders. When she looked into his eyes, the need to be inside her took hold of him so hard, he thrust into her. She was slick and tight, and she cried out as he took her. He knew he was big, that he should be gentle, but Izzy was tough. She could take him like this. Hard and unapologetic. He could see it in her eyes, feel her body trying to grip more of him.

He looked down at her as he began to roll his hips. Usually so aggressive, so dominant, she was different now. The sweet haze of arousal softening her face. Her eyes begging, her body soft and submissive underneath him. Like having him inside her was keeping her alive. He raised up on both arms, arching as he went deep, watching her writhe under him. She was utterly beautiful. During the day, she was a hard-ass surgeon, prior military. Sharply intelligent with an even sharper tongue. But in the light of this small room, with the rain pouring all around them, the smell of the jungle mingling with the scent of sweat and sex…right here and right now, she was all woman. Lush female, sexy, and delicious. Right now she was his.

His thrusts became wilder. She felt the shift in him, tilting her hips and raising her legs to take more of him. He felt her nails in his ass, pulling him deep. She arched up, climaxing again, and he swallowed her cries. Then he broke the kiss. "I need to come, ah fuck!" he screamed as her body milked him.

Her voice shook with desire. "Come inside me, Liam."

He drove into her as he released, moaning her name, saying other things she couldn't understand. His orgasm went on and on, cresting and building again until he seemed to come again. She didn't know that men could do that. Then he slid his hand behind her neck and was kissing her, his hips jerking and his erection kicking as he slowly came back down to earth. She could feel his heart pounding in his chest, her breast arched to him as his mouth moved over hers, not quite ready, she knew, to let her go.

Liam looked up at the window, and it was still black as night. He'd extinguished the lights, not wanting to attract any more bugs than there already were. The mosquito net did its job, shrouding them. They'd made love again, and the second time, she'd risen above him. Her breasts tight and full, her luscious hips molding to his body as she arched and strained.

He put his face in the back of her neck, smelling her hair. Tasting her skin. She pressed into him, still half asleep. He should let her rest. She had to be sore. He hadn't been gentle with her. When he came the first time, he'd been senseless, pounding into her, not able to get deep enough. They'd made love a second time. And when she'd ridden astride him, finding her own completion, he'd tossed her on her back and taken her hard as he finished inside her again. For now, he just needed to keep touching her. He couldn't seem to break the contact. She had her tank top and panties on again. Partial protection from the bugs that loved her so much. They were covered with a light cotton sheeting. The rain had cooled the air, thankfully. He found himself completely comfortable as he spooned her to his body. He rubbed his hands along her hips as he licked and kissed and nibbled her neck and shoulders. When she arched again, he slid his hand forward into her panties and between her legs. She hissed a bit and he backed off. "I'm sorry, lass. You're sore." But she pressed back into his erection. He started at the top of her sex and she put her hand over his as she moaned.

"Take me from behind, Liam." He rubbed relentlessly as her breath caught. "Don't stop," she said as she rolled on her belly and cocked one leg, opening for him as she pressed and rolled against his hand. Never one to leave a lady in distress, he shifted his hips, pulling the panties aside with a rip. He was suddenly desperate to be inside her. Like a never ending hunger. He slid into her until their hips were fused and moaned into the darkness. He was so deep in her, he was afraid it would hurt her, but she arched her back finding a rhythm as she stroked him from the inside. That's when he got serious. It was pitch black, complete sensory deprivation with the white noise from the rain. So he felt his way, completely in tune with her body. He met her strokes with his own until they were perfectly in sync. Him pressing down as she squeezed and released with every arch of her hips. He put a hand between her breasts, lifting her until she was tight against his chest. He answered her as he came in a white, hot flash. His sight lighting up from behind his eyelids. When he fell, limp behind her, she was trembling.

"Are you okay? Did I hurt you, Izzy?" Had he been too rough?

"No, God no," she croaked. "That was just..." words escaped her. And didn't that just make his chest puff up a little. He'd known they'd be great together, but he'd never expected this kind of connection. He fell asleep, still inside her and curled into each other.

Izzy woke first. Having shifted in the night, she was sprawled across Liam's wide chest. She crept off of him, wanting to let him sleep. They'd had an active night. She slipped her panties back in place, laughing to herself at the huge rip in one leg. She was sore and wet in places that hadn't been sore or wet in a while. She looked down at him, conflicting feelings running through her mind. He was an incredible lover. Intense, skillful, and a little bit feral. She thought back to the day they'd met. The man she'd been introduced to, with the quick smile and the cute girlfriend, was barely a memory. She hadn't really gotten to know that Liam very well. The student, the boyfriend, the younger brother. The man she saw now had sleek muscles, a harsh, beautiful face. He had a temper to match her own. But he'd been so generous in bed. He loved pleasuring her, loved watching her responses. *I see you, Izzy.*

She shook herself, not willing to dive into any emotions this soon after their night together. She looked at him one more time, magnificent in the early morning light, and resolved to take whatever he gave her. To give him what he was willing to accept. And to enjoy, for the small time she was portioned, to love Liam well. *Let it be enough,* she thought. She didn't want to leave this situation worse off than when she came. She didn't want to end up hurt and ruined. *Let it be enough for me.*

She walked to the cook fire, the rain having simmered to a light drizzle. Her scrubs were still wet, and she shook with a chill. Then she sat near the women. She eased down on her bottom, feeling the effects of the love marathon. It didn't go unnoticed as giggles rolled through the women. One of the old women touched her arms, noticing her bites. Then she said something to one of the younger women.

A lovely, curvy, long-haired beauty. When she approached, she took Izzy's hand. Another woman brought a set of dry clothes. A simple sarong type wrap and cotton top. The colors were vibrant, and the fabric was soft with years of washing. Izzy took the clothes gratefully. The beautiful young woman commanded her in Portuguese. *Venha comigo.* Come with me.

They walked along a worn path, into the belly of the forest. Izzy could hear water running, but they were walking away from the river. Then they came to a smaller branch, more of a creek, that had a rope bridge. The noise grew louder as they passed over the bridge and continued along the path. Then she felt a blowing mist that had nothing to do with the rain and more to do with the rush of water as they walked up a slight incline. As the path ended, she looked up at the beautiful waterfall. It wasn't big. And it seemed to come right out of the rock. The smell was different too. A mineral spring that poured out of the earth. She touched the water, a bit cloudier than the streams, but less muddy. The water was warm to the touch. And although she was in the tropics, the early morning damp and wet clothes had lowered her body temperature. She looked at the woman who'd brought her here, wondering if she would be permitted to soak. The woman gestured for her to enter the water. "Mãe Terra."

Izzy said, "Mother earth? Is this a special spring?" The woman didn't understand. She'd have to ask Paolo when he retrieved them. One thing she did know was that she probably wouldn't find any dangerous animals in here. It seemed to come out of the earth, and escape back down. No stream led out of it. The mineral smell was strong. She didn't waste any time. She stripped, leaving her clothes in a pile as she stepped into the water. She sighed as she sank her body into the warm, inviting water. "Obrigado, Senhorita."

The woman left her to bathe, and she rolled on her back, floating weightless in the warm water. It was heaven.

Liam went off in search of Izzy. She'd undoubtedly gone looking for breakfast. As he came to the fire where the women were preparing different foods, he asked where she was. A beautiful young woman smiled at him, blushing. He followed her up the path, unsure why Izzy would have a reason to come this far away from the village. The narrow path was walled with dense, lush forest on both sides. The sounds were mesmerizing. Unlike the path from the abbey to the bungalow, there were no sounds of children, no prayer bells, no landscaping tools buzzing in the background as he made his retreat. This was nature in its raw and musical beauty. Insects, birds, and frogs were singing their own unique ensemble. An occasional cry from a tamarin. Then the sound of rushing water was a constant hum that grew louder as the air grew wetter.

Then he saw her. The path opened up to a warm, cloudy pool, replenished by a spring that came out of the stone face above. The woman ghosted, leaving them alone. Izzy tilted her head back, letting the water pour over her. She rose out of the pool of water like Venus. Her curving waist and full breasts slick and wet. She opened her eyes and her smile was radiant.

When Izzy cleared the water from her face, opening her eyes, she saw that Liam leaning against a tree. He was watching her, and the way he looked at her made her feel beautiful. His eyes traveled over her body instinctively. "Good morning, médico. Would you like to join me?" Liam looked around him and she was a bit amused that he was worried about being seen. The indigenous tribes in Brazil weren't known for their modesty. She glided across the water, giving him just a peek of her ass. His clothes started flying off as she gave a husky laugh. Then he was stepping into the pool at the base of the waterfall, his arousal stirring again.

"Dr. O'Brien, that thing is like the Energizer Bunny."

Liam winked. "Aye, it is. Especially when it's properly motivated." She went to swim away and he grabbed her ankle. She squealed as he pulled her back to him. He kissed her temple, her shoulder, cupping her breasts as he rubbed his jaw stubble along her neck. He pushed them to a large rock formation, like a bench. Perfect for what he intended. He turned her body to face him and kissed her, slow and deep. "Come to me, lass." His voice was hoarse and demanding. "I need to feel you. I need inside you." He felt her slippery legs come around his hips. Then they were joined and he was surging in the water, pulling her hips up and down on his cock. His mouth exploring hers as he stole her breath and gave her his own. Her breasts were full and flush against his chest. His eyes bore into hers as he felt her start to shudder. The warmth around them was a sort of liquid presence. As if it was a living character in this tale of romance and lust. He wondered if this was some sort of holy spring for these people. It held power. It coursed through him as he stiffened and said her name, releasing himself into her again.

They finally came back to themselves, floating lazily, intertwined. "I called on the satellite phone. Paolo will be here within the next hour."

"Back to reality," she said wistfully.

"Back to a real mattress. Count your blessings, love," he teased.

"Do you want that? Once we get back, I know it will be different. The abbess has rules."

"You think I slaked my thirst, and now I'm done with you? Is that why you're asking?" His face was harsh.

"Of course not. I just didn't come here expecting this to happen. And I'm so glad it did, Liam. Last night was…beautiful. Every minute of it. I'm just trying to be okay with whatever direction this takes." She looked into his eyes. "I don't want to assume anything."

"Well, then let me be clear, Isolde Collier. I expect to have ye in my bed by nine o'clock tonight. I've got plans for you." Then he pulled her to his chest. "Absolutely devilish plans."

Izzy hugged the women, tearing up again as she said goodbye. "Tell them we'll be back next week. I'll want to check on Grua when the hospital releases him." Raphael translated as Liam and Paolo loaded the packs and fruit that the villagers had gifted them. "And tell them I'll bring the clothes back."

She started to turn away when she remembered to have him ask about the spring fed waterfall. He asked, and the old woman smiled, telling him. "It comes from the mother earth. Warm from her utero... no," he stopped, thinking of how to explain it, "her womb. Then it flows back to her so that it may regain its power." He blushed then, "This spring, they use for the fertility of the young women. It is like our holy wells."

Izzy gulped. Blinked. "Oh," she said lightly. "Well, isn't that nice. I won't be needing that, but thanks for the soak!" Raphael was suppressing a grin, but as Izzy looked over her shoulder, she noticed Liam was a little less amused.

As they went down the river, the mood was sedate. The water was still clipping along, higher than Izzy had ever seen it. Each passenger took an area, watching for logs and floating debris. As they pulled up to the dock and got themselves to land, Izzy went in Raphael's Jeep. Liam went with Paolo. *Real world,* Izzy thought. Not only was doc-on-doc sexy time prohibited by the Reverend Mother out of the boundaries of marriage, but it would probably make things weird with the staff at the hospital. She went right to the hospital, Raphael on her tail. He didn't ask, and she didn't share, but his eyes held that chastising look of an older brother. *What the hell are you doing, boss?* She changed into her scrubs and found a message that Antonio had left on her desk. Apparently the brother was doing great. Thank God. She heard a knock and looked up. Genoveva was standing in the door.

"I worked out with Doctor Seamus. Can you have time today? I like when you help me."

Izzy's heart melted. "Of course. I've missed my girl time. How about at lunch? You need to make sure you're leaving enough time to eat, though. You need to give your body energy so that you can be strong." She worried about the girl. It was a delicate age, and Genoveva had body image issues. "You should never skip meals, okay?" The girl nodded.

"Hey, do you think you could help me this morning?" It was Saturday, and she knew the girl didn't have school. When Genoveva's face lit up, Izzy knew that this kid was going to end up breaking her heart. She was so smart and sensitive. "By the way, have I told you that I absolutely love that hair style on you? It makes your neck look longer. You have to keep your chin up and your shoulders straight, though. That cut has some attitude." Genoveva laughed.

Izzy counted the supplies and gave her helper the number. Genoveva had a clipboard where she'd mark down the inventory. "You're good at this. Do you think you can help me make a list for the next order?" She pointed to a column. "What we use every month." Then the next column was how many they had left. "You're good with numbers. Do you get that from your mother?"

Genoveva shrugged. "She came to the abbey and worked for the Reverend Mother. She helped in the school."

Izzy stopped, looking at her. "Yes, she said that your mother worked here. She just didn't tell me what she did. I'm so sorry that you lost her, honey. How old were you?"

"Sete. Seven years. I remember her. I remember her voice and her face, but I forgot her smell. You never smell in dreams."

Izzy took the girl in her arms. "I'm glad you remember her, though. Maybe you could show me a picture sometime?" Genoveva smiled and nodded. "Did you get your green eyes from her?" Izzy knew she was pushing it, given the girl had finally opened up a little. "They're so beautiful. Such a pretty green."

Genoveva just looked down. "No, médica. Her eyes were brown, like yours."

"Well then, your father must have been very handsome. You never talk about him. He must have been tall and strong like you as well. And don't you think it's about time you started calling me Izzy? At least when the smaller kids aren't around."

"I didn't meet him, Izzy." The girl had a sweet smile like she was excited about the prospect of calling Izzy by her first name. Then her face fell a bit. "My mother told me about him, but she said it was a secret. I think she was ashamed of me. She said she never tell my papai about me. Maybe he wouldn't want me." Her eyes misted.

"Oh, honey. How could she be ashamed of you? You're beautiful and smart and so kind. She brought you here because she knew that Reverend Mother Faith would protect you." She took her arm. "Come sit with me, baby." By this time, the girl was wiping tears from her face. "Come sit with me and have some chocolate therapy. You and I are going to have some girl time right now."

"Is this like the sweat therapy?"

"No, it is way better. Chocolate feeds a woman's soul. I've got a chocolate bar in my desk for emergencies." Izzy grabbed the chocolate and put her arm around Genoveva. "Let's go to the garden and get some fresh air."

They passed Alyssa on the way out of the hospital. "Chocolate and long faces. Is this about a boy? They're terrible creatures, lass. Stay away from them." This got a smile.

Izzy said, "We'll be in the garden if you need me."

As they walked, Izzy said, "Did I ever tell you about where I grew up?" She told her about the apple and apricot orchard that her family owned. About her grandfather's ranch. About the heat of Arizona, and her first crush on a cowboy. By the time they'd settled in the garden, Genoveva was more at ease.

"Listen, sweetie. You have to understand. Your momma thought she was doing the right thing by not telling your father. I know you loved her, but it's okay to look at adults and realize that they can make mistakes. Did she tell you anything about him, or why she would keep you from him? Was he cruel to her?"

"No, she said she loved him very much. She said he went away. Back to his home. She was ashamed because they weren't married and they..." she blushed.

"I understand. She was with him, the way a man and woman are together. Do you know about that? About how a baby is made?" Genoveva just nodded.

"She said he was very handsome. She..." She paused, looking around nervously. Izzy took her hand. "She said she met him when she worked at Santo Clare's. That he was a médico. He was like Dr. O'Brien."

Izzy almost fell over. She swallowed, took a shallow breath, and hoped the kid didn't clam up. "You mean his work? Like with the microscopes and malaria and that sort of thing?"

"No, Izzy. She say he was Irish."

20

Izzy skidded into the abbey just before the lunch bell rang. "Sister Maria, I need to see the Reverend Mother!"

"Is everything okay?" Sister Maria was a pretty woman. She had a kind face and her skin had a deep tone, the color of toffee. Her eyes were dark as night, and she had beautiful white teeth. She was a wonderful teacher as well. The closest thing to a mother that most of the children had. She looked worried.

"Everything is great, but it's important. Sister, I think you should be there as well."

Sister Maria took her to the library, where the abbess was drinking a cup of tea and reading her devotional. Izzy closed them in, then she finally let go. She clapped her hands together and started jumping up and down. "What on earth has come over you, lass? Have you taken a fever?"

Izzy leaned over the desk with a smile so big, her face actually hurt. "Genoveva told me who her father was."

Both the nuns clutched at their chests. Then they started firing off questions. Izzy interrupted them. "This is what I know. Her mother met him when she worked here. He was a doctor, a family practitioner from what she described. He was tall, blonde, Irish, and he had big, beautiful green eyes. Genoveva was born in March of 2002. Her mother left because she was pregnant and he'd gone back home, or so she thought. When she was almost ready to give birth she panicked and tried to contact him. He'd left Ireland again and was volunteering in Africa, but she is positive that he worked here as a doctor and that he was Irish. All you need to do is look back in your records to see what doctors were here in the late spring or early summer of 2001 and you can find him!"

"And what if he doesn't want to be found, Dr. Collier? It would crush her," the abbess asked.

Izzy said, "She told me that her mother never told him. He didn't know she was pregnant when he left. The one time she tried to contact him was the only time. I don't know what happened. Perhaps they had an affair and he just left her, or maybe they had a falling out. She doesn't know any more than that. If we find him and he doesn't want to meet her, then we won't tell her. We'll say we couldn't find him."

"I couldn't lie to the lass!" Reverend Mother said, aghast at the notion.

"Then I will lie to her. The last thing she needs is more rejection. But Reverend Mother, what if he isn't a rat bastard? What if he's a good guy? He could come for her. She'd have a family! We have to try and find him."

Sister Maria nodded. "How many children have we seen come and go, who had no hope of ever having a parent to care for them? We can't keep them once they're adults. We do all we can, but Genoveva is special. She's a rare, beautiful soul. To think that she might have a father out in the world who might want her. Oh, Reverend Mother. We must try. Sim? We must try to find this man."

Reverend Mother folded her hands in front of her. "Once we have a name, I wouldn't know where to begin. It's been fifteen years."

"You'll have more than a name. You asked for everything but a stool sample from me when I applied for this job." Then she paused, cocking her head. "Actually, I think I did have to give a stool sample." The abbess gave her a chiding look. "Anyway, what I mean is that you'll have a copy of his passport and visa, his birth certificate, everything we need to hunt him down in Ireland. And I have just the man to do it. I happen to have connections in the Garda."

Sister Maria smiled at her. "God has sent you to us, Dr. Collier. You've done wonderful things here. And now this, for our sweet Genoveva." She covered her mouth on a sob. "Bless you, Izzy."

The Reverend Mother put her hands flat on the desk. "Now, Sister Maria. If you could get back to the children, and please send for Sister Agatha. We have a lot of paperwork to go through, and I'll need a younger pair of eyes."

The elderly patient that sat before Liam was going to break his heart. Upon bringing her into the hospital, the granddaughter had looked at him like he was a miracle worker. Like he could fix this situation, but he couldn't. They were isolated in the quarantine room he'd set up near the laboratory. It was through a secured door so that no one could wander in. Advanced bacterial meningitis was a death sentence. She'd let it go for a week. The bacteria was in her brain, spine, and due to lack of treatment, in her blood. All he could do is make her comfortable.

The United States had a C.D.C. office in Brazil who worked closely with the Ministry of Health. Unlike St. Clare's, they had more than a one-man staff and had dispatched their people to the section of the Manaus slum where the family lived. They needed to find the source of the infection. Poor plumbing was most likely the culprit. It appeared that the granddaughter was clear because she took most of her meals at the school. They'd narrow it down due to the urgency of the situation. This disease went fatal fast. The symptoms could appear as other ailments, like the flu.

The Reverend Mother appeared in the doorway and he sighed. This woman was going to be the death of him. He pulled his mask down. "Just because you have the key, Abbess, doesn't mean you can break quarantine."

"Well, I disagree. Who's going to minister to this poor soul in her last hours?" He'd had this argument with her before.

"Okay, but mask and gloves, please. Actually, you should put on goggles as well. She has a cough and we aren't sure what else she's got. Pedro is doing a full panel." Liam knew that the Roman Catholic church didn't allow nuns or sisters to give the last rights, penance, or the opportunity to confess. A load of bollocks in his humble, sinful opinion. However, she could pray with her. She could offer communion. She could also call a priest. She butted heads with a few of the local priests. She might wear a skirt, but she was alpha to the core. Not a quality some old-school priests appreciated. But there was a younger priest in Manaus that would come if she called and he was able.

"Did you call Father Pietro?" Liam asked.

"I did. He's on his way. For now, perhaps I could pull up a chair and sit with her." This was good, he supposed. As she sat, the old woman gave a smile, even though her pain was significant. She reached out her hand and folded it in the Reverend Mother's gloved one. *No one should die alone.* He thought about Eve, alone in that ally, and the grief stung him anew. Grief and the first surfacing of guilt that he'd felt since he'd been with Izzy. He'd thought it would crash over him immediately. It hadn't. As long as he was near her, it stayed away. He looked at the abbess and remembered what she said. That he'd spoken of himself as two different men. The man he was now, the rough edges and bitterness, would have most likely sent Eve running in the other direction. It was ironic that the very qualities that had been killed in him by her tragic death were the very qualities that had attracted her. He'd made her laugh, he was fun, he was successful. He was the extrovert that drew her out into the social scene of Trinity. He was also an artist of sorts. He'd worked the traditional music scene in Dublin, from time to time, for extra cash. But college was over, and he was just an overworked doctor with a tragic past. Too dark for her light. Too bitter for her sweet.

He didn't mean to make comparisons, but it was inevitable. Izzy was as driven as he was. She was passionate about medicine. She was independent and tough, both mentally and physically. She served a higher purpose. She could have slid into a well paying job in a good hospital, but she'd come here instead. For the work and for him. To help his family find their lost son. Izzy was strong enough to handle his rough edges. The hardness that was a part of him now. She didn't try to tame the beast. She liked the beast. Liked who he was now, even if she butted heads with him. And she did. She didn't hesitate to get in his face if he was being an asshole. He admired that about her. It reminded him of watching Brigid with Finn, or his mother with his da.

He got up out of his chair and rubbed his eyes. "I need to go see the granddaughter. Are you okay with her?"

She pulled the mask down with one finger. She hadn't submitted to the goggles. "Yes, lad. Go and then get some dinner and some sleep. Margaritte can help with her tonight. Her passing will happen in its own time, and someone will always be with her. She was raising her granddaughter. There's no next of kin. They were resettled in the city after the mudslides hit their village. It wiped out most of the family."

Liam cursed under his breath, then gave the abbess an apologetic look. "Will we take her in? She can't be more than eleven or twelve." Liam said, his brow tight.

"I'll speak with the city, but probably. We have the room. Once her tests come back clear, I will put her in the dormitory with the other children. Even if it's temporary."

Dammit. Another kid in this city with no parents. He couldn't help but think aboutHenrico, Emilio, and Genoveva. They were the oldest. Teenagers who would age out and have to leave. Genoveva with no idea who her father was. Henrico losing both parents. Emilio with a father that wouldn't quit being a shitbird long enough to take care of his only child. Liam knew this happened on every continent, every country, every city. People could avoid thinking about it because it wasn't right under their nose, but they needed to know. They needed to do better.

Liam came around the corner toward the locker room when he caught a glimpse of Izzy headed the other way. She was in a robe and shower shoes, her feet snapping as she walked. Her shower caddy in her left hand. He looked around, making sure they were alone. Just as she opened her door, he scurried into her room behind her and shut the door. She yelped.

"You scared the crap out of me!" she hissed, but she couldn't hide her smile as he pushed her against the door.

"Just a kiss, darlin'. I've been needing a kiss ever since we got out of that spring." He pressed against her, cupping her chin with one hand while he snaked an arm around her waist. His kiss was thorough and languorous. When she slid her tongue in his mouth he moaned. Then he broke the kiss. "Nine o'clock, Dr. Collier. Don't be late."

She cupped him between his legs. "You better go take a cold shower before you show up to the cantina with a tent in your scrubs."

His hips jerked, then he pulled her back to his mouth. "Careful, woman. Or I'll just part that robe and to hell with the rules." She giggled as he took her mouth again. "You like teasing me don't you?" Then, quick as lightning, he pulled the lapel of her robe aside, taking a nipple in his mouth. She arched and he started taking pulls on it as she put her fingers in his hair. He knew she had sensitive breasts. "Liam, you know I can't…ah, don't stop." He slid his hand inside her robe just as she started to spiral.

Alyssa gave Izzy a strange look across the table, turning her head to the side. "Izzy, love, did you get some sun today? Your cheeks are flushed." Liam had to stop from laughing as the nurse assessed her friend, putting a hand on her forehead to see if she had a fever.

He was trying hard not to think about the cause of the flush. He'd given her a small taste of what was going to be waiting for her in the bungalow tonight. Seamus gave him a sideways glance, so he kept his face passive.

Izzy said, "I worked out with Genoveva today. It's probably just from the heat and the hot shower." Then she changed the subject. "Liam, how is your patient? You just checked on her, right?"

"Yes, I did. I spent the last hour watching the abbess pray with her. She died about fifteen minutes ago."

"Oh, Liam. I'm so sorry." Izzy said. Seamus clapped him on the back.

"She was too far gone. I worry more for the little lass she came in with. She'll most likely be staying with us. They've got no kin."

"Ye made her comfortable and gave her some peace and a clean place to lie her head, brother. She went to her maker knowing her granddaughter would be cared for." Seamus said. Liam knew he was right. He just looked at the two old women. One there to hold the other's hand as she died. He missed his Granny Aoife and his Gran Edith. They were getting older, and he hadn't talked to them in almost a year.

"Liam, when you're done eating, I need a favor. Could you follow me to the library?" Izzy asked. He met her eyes and knew she was serious. This wasn't a ploy to get him alone and get him all juiced up as payback. She had news.

As they finished, they walked out of the cantina together. "You have news." It wasn't a question.

She didn't beat around the bush. "I found Genoveva's father." Liam stopped dead in his tracks. "I should say we. Sister Agatha stepped in to help go through the files."

"Jesus, you really found him? You're sure? And what files, from the orphanage?" he asked.

"No, Liam. From the medical mission. The file on Dr. Quinn Maguire of County Wicklow. He's Irish, Liam, and he has no idea he has a daughter."

Liam couldn't wrap his head around it. "How in the hell did this come about? I can't even conceive of it. How could the sisters not know?"

They walked into the library and she sat on one of the comfortable chairs. Liam sat across from her, leaning in and still a bit shaken by the news. Izzy said, "Her mother worked here. In the school. No one knew about the affair. She was obviously young and unmarried. For some reason, they parted ways. We aren't sure what the story is, but she found out she was pregnant after he was gone. Genoveva said her mother was ashamed. She was a devout Catholic. She left the school and didn't tell anyone why. She showed up when Genoveva was seven. She died of ovarian cancer in our hospital and the child never left. Reverend Mother Faith knew that I was tight with the girl, and asked if I could try to get any information out of her that she hadn't been willing to share with the sisters. Today, I got her to open up. She said he was a doctor, like you, on a medical mission from Ireland. She knew that her mother loved him, and told her a bit about him. He's blonde, tall, and has green eyes. I thought he was a family practitioner, but it turns out he was in pediatrics. Obviously, we could narrow the list down given the date of conception. The only doctor that fits the description and the time frame is this Maguire guy. Once Sister Agatha started looking at the files from that timeline, it was easy to figure it out."

Liam ran his fingers through his hair. "Jesus, did you tell the lass you found him?"

Izzy rubbed her top lip. "No. We need to wait. He may be married with kids. He may not welcome the news. I don't want her getting hurt. If he's a douchebag, then we'll say we couldn't find him."

Liam coughed on a laugh, "And Reverend Mother Faith agreed to that?"

"She doesn't like it, but I told her the lie would be mine. That kid doesn't need any more insecurities. I'll likely castrate the bastard if he rejects her."

Liam's face was grim. "Aye, I'll hold him down for you." He shook his head. "It's amazing, Izzy. I can't believe you managed to do what no one else did. The poor girl has been here for eight years, keeping her mother's secret. This is incredible. You're incredible."

Izzy squirmed, not sure how to accept the compliment. "Anyway, this is where I need your help. We have a name, date of birth, place of employment before he came, and a copy of his visa and passport. Apparently, he did missionary work in Africa as well. So, the question is, does he live in County Wicklow now? Is he out doing missionary work? Is he dead from a jaguar attack?" Her mouth turned up at the last.

"Don't joke about it, girl. It wasn't funny at all." He got on his knees in front of her. "You're a brave and foolish woman, Izzy Collier. And apparently an amateur detective. It's pretty late in Ireland, but I'll give him a call. Tadgh, not Patrick. Patrick has enough on his plate right now."

"I'll leave you to it, then." She handed him the file that Sister Agatha had left in the library desk. "Once we find him, I'll figure out what to do. How to approach him. I may do it in person. My ticket to Brazil was round trip out of Dublin. Once I finish my tour here, I'll go back. Spend a couple of days, then fly back to the states."

Liam's chest constricted. *Leave? Go back to the States?* Of course she would. It wasn't like she could stay here. She had a post-military career to start up. She had three job offers. His voice was hoarse when he finally responded. "Have ye given any thought to which hospital you'll go to? I don't think you ever told me where they were."

She didn't meet his eye. She walked over to a shelf, running her fingers along the spines of some old hymnals. "Phoenix, Chicago, and Denver." She walked along, touching things absently. "The one in Denver pays the best, but the cost of living is high. Same with Chicago. And the crime is awful in Chicago. I can't see myself settling there, even if the money is good. I'm thinking the one in Phoenix. It will be closer to my family. It will be strange to be back in Arizona. I just..." She paused, not sure whether to go on.

"Go on. Say what you were going to say."

She looked sideways at him. "I don't know. I see your family. They are all so close together. Even Aidan is only a few hours away, though he's in England. I envy them, I suppose. I don't have my own family. I mean, the husband and kid thing. So, maybe it's time for me to go home. Spend holidays at the orchard. Visit my grandpa when the cows are calving. Pitch in, see my brother and his kids. I never thought I'd move back, but I'm thinking maybe that's the best solution for me right now."

Liam wasn't sure what to say. He felt like he'd been kicked in the nuts, which was insane. He'd made it pretty goddamn clear that he was never going to have another woman in his life, and that he had no intentions of going back to Ireland in the foreseeable future. What did he think, exactly? That a night of great sex was going to have her mooning over him and trying to trap him into marriage? Not bloody likely. Izzy Collier didn't need anyone.

"It sounds like you've made up your mind."

She smiled. "Yeah, I think I have. Starting over in a big city with no friends or family just doesn't feel right." She clapped her hands together. "Anyway, I'll let you make that call. I'll see you at nine." She winked at him and walked out, and when she left, he felt like the color drained out of the room.

Liam walked the long way to the bungalow and thought about the conversation he'd had with Tadgh. God, he really missed him. They were close in age and Tadgh was like his own brother. He'd liked having family nearby when Tadgh and Patrick had relocated. Then the thing with Eve happened. The shame of it was what he'd done afterward. He'd lashed out at Tadgh for no other reason than he wanted someone to hurt as bad as he was hurting.

He looked good. Marriage suited him. That beautiful woman he'd married was one tough cookie. Kind of reminded him of Izzy in that regard. He thought about Izzy with that knife. Hippocratic oath or not, he knew she wouldn't hesitate to use that weapon or any weapon if it came down to survival. He loved that about her. As he got to the bungalow, he realized she wasn't there yet. He looked at his watch. It was eight-thirty. Just enough time to get the place ready for her. He had some citronella candles in his pack that he'd nicked from the supply cottage. Mood lighting and bug repellent. Win-win. He was exhausted. It had been a stressful day and he just wanted to be with her. To lose himself in her beautiful body. So shapely and feminine. So strong and smooth and responsive.

As he checked the house for critters, he lit the candles and took out a bottle of Argentinian wine that he'd been saving. Antonio had gifted it to him when he'd had a birthday here. He'd chilled it in the cantina, not willing to stick it in the blood and vaccine cooler. It was sweating, and he put it back in the small dorm size fridge that was in the galley kitchen. He'd hung a mosquito net over the bed, now that they were using the space more often. He fussed around, arranging the candles around the windowsills and in the kitchen. Then he looked around, freezing in place. What the hell was he doing? Setting up a romantic night? Like a boyfriend? He considered that and wasn't sure how he felt about it. He wasn't anyone's boyfriend and the candles were bug repellent. And…well the wine was a few months old. It wasn't going to keep forever. Not in this heat.

He shook his head, trying to stop the idiotic battle that he was having with himself. He was tired and his head was starting to hurt. So, because he'd already showered in the staff quarters before packing his bag, he decided to just lie down and wait for her. Just rest his eyes and try to clear his mind.

Izzy came into the bungalow and felt a sense of warmth and peacefulness come over her. He'd lit candles. From the smell of it, bug repellent candles. Romantic and practical. She looked over at the bed and there he was. He was barely covered, the thin linen covering him from the waist down. He was so beautiful. His hair was unruly on the pillow. The light cascaded over his smooth skin and tight muscles. She stirred, low in her belly. She was late. About twenty minutes late because Sister Agatha had flagged her down. She needed to be discreet, so no one knew they were both down here. She set her bag down on the table and went to him. He was sound asleep but she could see he was aroused. Not completely but enough to work with. If she was a nice girl, she'd let him sleep, but he looked too tempting, lying there waiting for her. She slid the sheet down just enough.

Liam was dreaming. He had to be because he was alone. But man, what a dream! His hard arousal bathed in warm wetness. Pulling. He rolled his hips, and that's when he felt her hands. One on his thigh, the other cupping him. He opened his eyes and moaned as Izzy's big brown eyes stared up at him. She had her mouth on him, gliding up and down. She was bathed in candlelight and so beautiful. He moaned her name.

"Stop, Izzy. I'm going to come. You have to stop!" She didn't. In fact, she intensified her efforts. He grabbed her shoulders, pulling her up and flipping her on her back. She was smiling with mischief. "That's one way to wake a man up." He dipped his head low, giving her a proper kiss. "You're late."

"I know, I'm sorry. I got nun blocked." He laughed against her mouth. "The candles are lovely. Was this just for the bugs?"

He didn't answer. He just rubbed his lips over hers softly. "I have wine," he said, kissing her smile on the corner of her mouth.

"I'd love a drink, thank you." She watched as he flashed his spectacular ass to her, getting the wine out of the cooler. He poured two glasses and brought them to the bed. She got the front end flash on his return. His magnificent arousal ready for anything she wanted.

"You're beautiful, Liam. You are a lot leaner and more muscular than I remember. Is that Paolo's doing?"

He laughed, "Aye, partly. And fresh food instead of pot noodles and take away."

She was propped against the headboard, appraising him with those come hither eyes. "You should have let me finish you. I liked you in my mouth."

He stretched toward her on the bed, taking her mouth with renewed zeal. She was in yoga pants and a t-shirt. "When I finish, you're going to be naked and I'm going to be inside you." He nibbled her collarbone and her breath caught in her throat. He pulled her shirt off. "Mmm, no bra. That's convenient," he said. Then he leaned over and dipped his finger in the wine, tracing a wet circle around her nipple. It was hard under the blast of air conditioning and he took it deep in his mouth. Then once again with the wine, as he traced a finger down her stomach. He lapped it up and her hips jerked in response. The pants came off next. Then he took a sip of the cold wine and pulled her hips forward to meet his mouth. His cold tongue was exquisite torture against her heat. She felt him swallow the wine, mixed with her own slickness and she reared up, burying her hands in his hair. He drew her flesh into his mouth and she screamed.

Liam pressed his cock into the mattress as Izzy came against his mouth. The wine and her taste making him drunk and out of his head. Then he took her, finally, hard and fast and he shouted at his own release, pulling her up to him, so he could see her eyes.

Afterward, they lay in bed and talked, finishing their wine. She nestled between his legs, with her head on his chest, as he stroked her hair and played with the curls at the nape of her neck. The curls that were hidden unless you pushed her hair aside. The ones that smelled like her. They talked like friends, like colleagues, and like lovers, he supposed. She got up, finally, putting the rest of the wine back in the fridge and walking to the bathroom to brush her teeth and wash her face.

Izzy patted her face dry and opened her eyes. Liam was behind her. She could see him in the mirror. He was smiling a sweet, secret smile, watching her. "You're staring."

"I suppose I am. I like staring at you. You are so lovely."

She looked away, suddenly shy and holding the towel in front of her. He came behind her and took the towel away, laying it aside. He looked at her in the mirror, his stubble coming up against her cheek. Then he ran his hands over her body. She watched him, feeling her body flush and come alive. Then he surprised her by taking her hand. He put his hand over hers and slid it between her legs. Then he started to move it, gliding their fingers together on her aching flesh.

She was wet with her own arousal as well as what he'd left inside her. "Liam," she whispered as her head fell back against him.

"Don't stop this. Please," his voice was rough. He watched her climbing as their hands worked their magic and her hips stroked in rhythm. That's when he bent her forward and slipped inside her from behind. He was torn between watching himself slide into her, and watching her face in the mirror as he did it. She gripped the sink with her other hand and arched as he took her, a moan ripping out of her throat as he filled her. One slick thrust and she started to climax, one hand keeping hers in place as they stroked her, with the other on her waist as he fused their hips together.

Izzy watched in the mirror as Liam weaved this spell over her. His face was tight with lust, his eyes devouring the sight of her. And she realized that she liked watching them, too. She looked like a stranger in the mirror. All curvy woman, sexy, feminine, and aroused. Her breasts were swaying as their hips came together, skin flushed, hooded eyes as she started to climax. She came so hard that she almost blacked out. Then she knew only the haze of bodies slapping together mercilessly. Then Liam's voice, yelling as he went over the edge.

Liam picked Izzy up before her knees gave out. He was shaking all over, and so was she. She was delirious in his arms. He put her on the bed and climbed in next to her. She was glassy eyed. He touched her lightly, petting her all over, trying to peel them both off the ceiling after the sensations that had ripped through their bodies. Every time they'd taken each other to the highest peak, the sex got even more mind-blowing. He pulled her to him, trying to stop her shaking and his. "I don't know what this is, Liam. It's never been like this."

He pulled her closer, not even sure what to say. He felt the same way. Felt things he shouldn't be feeling. So he just held her and eventually, they drifted off to sleep.

21

As Izzy sat on the bench seat of the cantina tables, she felt a delicious tenderness from the night before. She could barely think straight this morning. Like a sex hangover. He'd literally screwed her brains out. Hopefully she didn't have any gaping belly wounds or amputations on the surgical docket today.

Sister Agatha, always with the phone camera somewhere within reach, was explaining to them what the community health fair was going to involve. She was the newly appointed fundraiser and marketing guru. She was bringing St. Clare's out of the dark ages with social media, and wanted to do some outreach in the more affluent areas of the city. Maybe cash in on some tourists dollars. Antonio was helping her pick the best location, because Antonio was, himself, affluent.

As they planned it all out, her eyes would drift discreetly to Liam's. He was like the cat that got the canary. It was subtle but she saw it. All fat chested about having to carry her to the bed, after he'd given her a DEFCON five orgasm, bent over the bathroom sink. And who could blame him? She certainly wasn't complaining.

She'd known that this relationship was a horrible idea. Guaranteed to leave her for dead with her heart ripped out on the side of the road. What she hadn't counted on was that Liam O'Brien may actually ruin her in the bedroom for any other man. She'd never felt this much carnal compatibility with a man. She'd been having sex for twelve years. Well, maybe not twelve if you deducted the time between boy-friends. She'd had three lovers before Liam. Jesse had been fantastic in bed. Her first real taste of amazing sex with a generous partner. This, though...wow. The only thing she regretted was what she'd said afterward. Just because it was the best sex she'd ever had, didn't mean it was the same for him. He'd held her close and said nothing. Polite of him, and at least he hadn't lied.

She focused on the topic at hand, and started getting her head back in the game. A child and expectant mother wellness booth, a blood pressure checking station, and an infectious disease preven-tion and detection table with Liam checking vaccine cards. Given that she could hardly offer a surgery booth, she decided she'd be in charge of drawing the crowd. Music, kids dancing or doing soccer demonstrations. Maybe she'd put Antonio at a kissing booth. That would draw a crowd. Hmmm, maybe just hugs given the infectious disease issue. She found herself getting excited. This could be good for St. Clare's. They needed more funding, more equipment, and more doctors to volunteer. Maybe Sister Agatha could spruce up that pathetic website. The one that had contact information and one pic-ture. No drop menus, no interactive stuff, no videos. No pictures of hot doctors, either.

Two more days and she'd go upriver to check on her patient. They'd released him this morning, and she'd give him a couple of days to settle back in with his family. Liam's patient with meningitis had most likely contracted it due to an underlying infection. She'd had pneumonia the month before. Given that her patient had been used for target practice, she just wanted to monitor him and make sure he was bouncing back.

She looked over at Liam and her heart melted. Estela had crawled up in his lap and she leaned against him with her thumb in her mouth. A habit that had relapsed after the jaguar attack. She thought of little Cora. That smart, beautiful child with a big heart and a heavy responsibility. That talent of hers was a burden as much as a gift. *Follow the river.* The thought made her shiver. She really hoped it was just a dream because, for the next several weeks, she was surrounded on all sides by rivers.

❧

Liam was doing paperwork in his lab when Seamus came in. "How are you, brother? Any pending deliveries?"

Seamus laughed, "Oh, yes. We've got two in the drop zone. Any time now. I heard about your patient. I'm sorry. So we've got another child with us?"

Liam rubbed his eyes. "We do. Did ye hear about Genoveva?"

Seamus leaned in. "An Irishman. Bloody hell. I'll tell you, I almost hope he didn't know. The alternative will make me want to string him up by his balls."

"Get in line. Izzy's already planning to castrate him if he turns his back on the girl. She's close with her. It's how she finally got her to open up. Eight years and no one got her to talk until now. Jesus, it breaks my heart to think about it. Can you imagine having a child somewhere and not knowing? To find out she's been in an orphanage for more than half her life? What was that mother of hers thinking?'

Seamus sighed. "It's not easy being a woman. I lived with four of them. They're more vulnerable. People are either trying to take advantage or underestimating them. The woman had an affair while working at a Catholic mission. Her boss wore a habit. You can imagine she wasn't too eager for it to get out. Hopefully, the man's not a prick."

"Genoveva doesn't know why it ended. He just went home after his tour. Maybe it was just a fling for him," Liam said.

"Kind of like you with Izzy." It wasn't a question, and the tone was slightly judgmental.

"Leave it, Seamus."

"Aye, I probably should, but I won't. She's a good girl. She's beautiful, smart, and funny. She's wonderful with the children. She has a sense of duty that you don't see very often in a lot of people. And you're going to make a cock-up of things, aren't you? All because some woman broke your heart? Did ye a bad turn? What exactly happened in Dublin that made you so bitter?"

"You don't know what the fuck you're talking about Seamus!"

"Then bloody explain it to me! Why, Liam?"

"Because she died!" He slammed his hand on the counter. "No, that's not exactly accurate. She was murdered. I took my eyes off her for one goddamn night and now she's dead! And I died in that bloody alley with her! So do not preach to me about making a cock-up of things." He closed his eyes, fighting the wave of emotions. "I loved her, Seamus. I wanted to marry her, and she's just gone. It has literally been all I can do to get up every day and walk upright." He pushed off the table, shaking himself. Then he gave Seamus a direct look, "Izzy is a big girl. She knew how things were before she got involved with me. She doesn't need me and I am no use to anyone in the long term. I will never fall in love again. Ever."

Seamus's face was stricken. "Jesus Christ, lad. I'm so sorry. I'm such an ass." He scrubbed his face with his palm. "Murdered."

Liam swallowed, shutting his eyes. "Yes. When the Dublin murders were happening with the young women last year."

Seamus cursed. "Oh God, the girls that were tortured?"

Liam nodded. "She interrupted one of the kidnappings. Started screaming for help and called the Garda. She got the killers on video before they ran her down like a dog in an alley."

"I read about it in the paper. A Cork girl. Eve something."

"Doherty. Her name was Eve Doherty."

"And that's why you never went home? Do ye have family, Liam?" He just nodded. "And Izzy came here why, exactly? To check on you or bring you home?"

"It's why I have to go to counseling with the abbess once a week. I left for the mission three months early. I just fled. The counseling was part of the bargain."

"Has it helped?" Seamus asked.

"I don't really know. I was kind of stuck until…"

"Until Izzy came," Seamus said.

The sound Liam made in his throat made Seamus's eyes shoot to his. "You're young, Liam. You've suffered a loss that no one should have to. But Izzy's here, she's alive and right in front of you. If you don't go back to Ireland, then get on a plane and follow her back to America. Take it from a man who's had the shit kicked out of him by love. Women like Izzy Collier are once in a lifetime if you're lucky."

"You don't understand, brother."

"You're right. I don't. Not at all." He turned to leave, then stopped. "The man responsible, he was killed by the police?"

Liam nodded, "By my cousin who is in the Garda. Tadgh was shot in the line of duty, but he's okay. Luckily his aim was better."

Seamus thought about it. "Did you want to kill him?"

"With everything in me, I wanted to be the one. But I'm surprised you're not giving me the *first do no harm* speech."

Seamus's face tightened. "I've loved one woman. The stupid cow didn't deserve it, as it turned out, but I loved her nonetheless. And my daughters are the breath in my lungs. I'm a doctor, aye. But if anyone hurt my girls, that is the vow that will trump all others. I suppose if it couldn't be you, it was good that it was family. Some things are too personal to leave to someone else."

Liam sipped his tea as Reverend Mother Faith eyed him speculatively. "You're quiet today."

Liam shrugged, "No updates to speak of. Maybe it's time to stop the sessions."

She smiled. "I'm afraid we still have work to do. Have you thought about what we talked about? About there being a mate out there for you? One that can love the Liam O'Brien who sits before me now, and not worry over the man he once was?"

"How is it that a celibate woman who can't marry is trying to give me advice on dating? Don't ye think you might be a bit out of your depth?"

"Perhaps you're right. Have you considered talking to your father about it? He's an O'Brien man. Surely he's more familiar with how this whole thing works. Why not call him? Or better yet, take some time off and visit. I'll hold your position, lad. Perhaps it's time to go home."

"I can't go home. I've just convinced them to include us in the Zika vaccine trials."

"Aye, well. Perhaps in a month or two. Maybe you can fly back with Dr. O'Keefe and Dr. Collier. I'm hoping that we find some replacements before they leave. We lose Alyssa and Adam even sooner."

"Well, it seems like you should put your energy into helping Sister Agatha get that marketing campaign off the ground instead of trying to marry me off to some wonder woman who doesn't even exist."

"Doesn't she, now?" She cocked a brow, but he ignored the comment.

"Will you come to the health fair? Come to think of it, have you actually left this abbey in the last twenty-three years?"

She gave him a dry look. "You know very well that I attend mass once a week with Father Pietro. Don't get cheeky," she said, picking up her cup of tea.

22

They traveled upriver, glad to see the pace had slowed significantly. It was a well-timed visit. No significant rain forecast today, other than an occasional quick shower. Liam watched Izzy's profile as she stared up at the trees, watching the colorful birds. They'd stayed in the staff quarters last night, due both to the early morning, and the fact that if Seamus had noticed, someone else would eventually catch on. Part of him hardly cared. He'd lain in that dormitory room aching for her. Not just because he wanted her body, but because he missed her soft sighs, her breath on his chest as she slept, her wild hair and sleep flushed face in the morning.

He'd had the dream again. The one with Eve by the river. He was so conflicted. He woke up, consumed with guilt, but then he saw Izzy and it seemed to chase his demons away for a while. This morning, he'd watched as she cleaned Cristiano's glasses and put them back on his face. Then she'd leaned down and kissed his nose. The little boy was smitten. She was good with all of the children. She never failed to hug them all at dinner before they left for their bedtime routines. And she'd worked wonders with the older ones. Emilio was getting in less trouble and had started asking to volunteer in the surgery. She was getting a list of kids who wanted to do demonstrations at the health fair.

He needed her tonight. He needed her like he needed air. He was pulled out of his train of thought by Paolo's voice. It was clipped, calling to Raphael. Liam, Izzy, and Adam leaped to their feet.

"What is it?" Izzy said.

Raphael's face was tight as he moved his daypack to within arm's reach. "Maybe trouble, boss."

Paolo had to slow the boat as he saw the large net that went across the entire river. This end of the smaller river was more narrow, the width only about one hundred feet. The men were armed. One of them motioned for him to pull off the right river bank. "Who the hell are these guys?" Liam asked.

"More of the same. All from the same crew. They take the jobs with the logging companies and they run drugs through the jungle clearings, airstrips, and small roads. They've never been this far down. This little river is the only way to the village."

The men were ruffians to be sure. Eyes darting over the supplies in the boat, and to Liam's disgust, their eyes roamed over Izzy as well. He shifted, putting his body between them and her. She whispered. "Steady, Liam. They're trying to provoke you." He ground his teeth, hating that she was with them. Hating that she was in any way at risk. Raphael spoke with the dickhead in charge, the man that had come to the village the day of the shooting. Emilio's father was nowhere to be found. In fact, this was the only man he recognized. The arguing heated up. Raphael turned to them. "They said they're working upriver, and that we can't go any farther for our own safety. It's bullshit. They don't own any of this land. It's all tribal land." The group jumped as dynamite went kaboom in the distance.

"Tell that asshole that my patient is upriver, and to move that goddamn net!" The man swung his attention to her as Liam hissed at her to be quiet. "Screw this. I will walk from here if I have to. These are probably the same pricks that shot him," she hissed back. Raphael gave her a look she'd never seen before. Like he was ready to toss her in the river to cool her off. "Um momento, médica." His tone didn't leave room for negotiation. Then he continued in rapid Portuguese to ask them to cease the demolition just long enough for them to dock at the village.

Liam turned to her while they were distracted. "Shut yer gob before I gag you, lass. We aren't letting them provoke us, remember? They have guns. We don't. So shut it." His accent was so thick she almost giggled. Almost. He was right. It was the men who would suffer if she kept running her mouth. This was a very macho culture. Although she was confident that if it came down to mano y mano, she could take that smug, little fucker.

As the two men argued, she watched as a neatly dressed man emerged from the path leading into the forest. He was more polished than the crew in front of them. He walked confidently like he owned the world. He had that slick, dark, and slightly cheesy air about him that screamed white collar crime. *Shit.*

She glanced over and realized they'd cut a thin, rough road about fifty feet in. Enough to get one Jeep through. "Gentleman, please. There's no need for this." He smiled at Liam and then his eyes locked and held Izzy's. "These good doctors of St. Clare's are merely trying to help our community. Why else would they put up with the bugs and the heat? I think we can cease our activity and let them get by. After all, it was terrible what happened to the young men. We must do all we can to cooperate." That was for their benefit, in perfect English. Then he barked out a few orders in Portuguese.

The men acted immediately, untying the net at one side so that the other men could pull it back to the bank. Izzy watched Liam's shoulders ease a bit, but then he bristled again when the man looked at Izzy. "Such a beautiful woman, this anjo do rio." Liam shot her a look before she let her mouth fly.

She ground her jaw. Then she smiled, "Thank you, sir. We won't be long. About an hour, then we'll head back downriver barring any obstacles." He gave her a slight bow and turned, going back to the military-style vehicle he'd been watching from. Then Paolo untied the boat and they carried on.

They unloaded the vehicles, and everyone was tired, sweaty, and hungry. They headed to the staff quarters, wanting to clean up before dinner. Raphael was headed to his mother's home to see his family, but before he left, Liam pulled him aside. "This is escalating. Who the hell was that guy? The one in charge?"

"His name is Fuentes. He's not originally from Brazil. He's Columbian. He's a developer. Hotels, casinos, and he's dirty. He's very heavy in some bad stuff, médico. Drugs, illegal mining, and logging. He's got his hands in many things. He's very rich. He pays off police and military. We must reconsider these trips to the village, at least until I can work with my trusted contacts. Do you understand? Today was a warning. They were waiting for us. They don't want us interfering with their attempts to move the tribe. They don't want any witnesses that could make trouble. Americans and Europeans getting attacked in Brazil will bring a lot of attention. He's trying to avoid that by intimidating us. For now, we need to take the warning. You need to keep Izzy off the river."

Liam heard the words in his mind. *When the time comes, you must go to the river.* It was similar to what Cora had said to Izzy. It was time to call home. Not now, though. Right now he needed a meal and to be with Izzy. Today had taken a toll on him. The reason being that he would not have been able to protect her had those men had real mischief on their minds. They could have turned those guns on them and taken Izzy.

He walked down the hallway and saw that her door was open. He appeared in the doorway as she was toweling off her hair. "Shower's free. I'm just going to put my juju magic bug repellent on and head down to chow." She stopped, taking in his tense body. "We're okay. It was hairy, but we're all okay."

"I know, Izzy. I just don't like how that felt today. We were out-gunned and outnumbered. Raphael said that the trips to the village need to stop until we can get his friends involved. I know that's not what you want to hear, but we can't put the whole team at risk. We need to take a step back."

"You're right. He's right. That could've been ugly today. At this point, it should be emergency only." Liam raised his brows. "What? Contrary to what you might think, I do not have a death wish. I like my head right where it is. What does this mean for your vaccine trial?"

Liam ran his hand through his hair. "I've got a couple of weeks. Maybe we can pay some security if we need to go back, or Raphael can start carrying. He is military. He's not active duty, but he may be able to arrange it. If he can't, I'll see if the CDC will cough up some security. I'll figure it out. The team comes first."

She smiled, liking that he was repeating what she'd told him that first week. Their eyes locked, that connection forming that they tried so hard to conceal while they were with the others. His breath stuttered. "I'll come to you, Izzy. Tonight. I can't stay here tonight. Not after today."

She swallowed hard, trying like hell not to read too much into his words. He'd been triggered today, no doubt. She knew he cared about her, but when he was confronted with this kind of stressor, it was more about his past. About Eve. She understood it. She really did, and she didn't resent him for it.

Liam came into the little bungalow and smiled at what Izzy was do-ing. She was arranging some flowers she'd picked in the garden. She turned the vase toward him. "Not bad for a tomboy, eh?"

He set his pack down, leaning on the counter. "Positively domes-tic." Then he gave her that look that seemed to call forth something from the depths of her chest. He needed her. She could feel it rolling off of him. He needed the physical outlet and connection that their sex gave him. If nothing else, she could be that for him. She could be his tangible comfort. She braced herself for his passion, wild and raw. He surprised her when he just put a hand on her wrist. The one she had leaning on the counter. He turned it up, rubbing a thumb along her pulse. Then he brought it to his mouth and kissed the soft skin.

Liam just wanted to feel her vitality. The blood that pulsed through her veins. Her warm skin. Today had been a little slice of hell, but here in this simple, one-room cottage, he found the refuge he needed with her. In the depths of her liquid brown eyes. He turned her palm to his face, feeling her warmth. Kissing it. Then he kissed her, coaxing her gently to his mouth. "Come, asthóre. Come to bed." He walked over, taking her hand and pulling her along. Then he sat on the bed, looking up at her as the candles illuminated her face. She looked like an angel. He pulled her between his legs, wanting her close. She ran her hands through his hair, tilting his head up. Then she lowered her mouth to his.

Izzy was undone by this man. As much as he'd rocked her to her core the other times they'd been together, it was his gentleness, now, that undid her. His actions were so fluid, so thorough. He undressed her slowly, stopping each time he removed a piece of clothing to kiss what he'd revealed. He worshiped her with his hands and with his eyes, whispering her name as he moved his mouth over her. She was intoxicated with the feel and the smell of him by the time he pulled her astride him. He stayed upright, facing her, cupping the back of her head with one hand, the other hand on her hip, guiding their bodies together. They were joined in this small oasis, both in mind and body. Their sex had been amazing but tonight, as he made slow, passionate love to her, she felt her heart break irrevocably.

Asthóre, Liam thought as he felt her warm body, tasted her skin, smelled her hair. *Treasure*. And she was. She was precious beyond measure. She knew how broken he was, that this pleasure and intimacy was all he could give her, and she came to him anyway. Gave of her body to heal him. He was so humbled by this...by her. He didn't deserve this piece of heaven but he was a selfish bastard. So he'd take everything she was willing to give him. He pulled her to him over and over again. Her face was almost pained, as shattered as he was by this current manifestation of their passion. "Izzy," he said against her throat. "Look at me." He could feel her, ready to release herself to him. "Izzy, please." When she looked at him, he saw the misty tears in her eyes. "No!" he said urgently. He took her mouth as they both fell into the abyss together.

He should have never started this. A thought that rolled through his mind repeatedly. She'd tried to keep her distance. Tried to think with a level head, enough for both of them. But he'd been selfish, and pretty damn close to helpless, as the desire grew within him. There was no way he could stop this. It was too late. He'd never survive being close to her and not having her. It would only end when she left him. He curled into her as she slept. With the candles extinguished and the mosquito net shrouded around them, he felt like they were cut off from the rest of the world. In this space between his earthly body and the hell that was in his mind, he'd found a sort of heaven. A hiding place in the deep recesses of the jungle. A place where he could find a respite from his pain and guilt, the woman in his arms the only sustenance he needed. And in this peaceful cocoon, he drifted off into a deep sleep.

Izzy stirred in the night, rolling to adjust her position. As she did, she felt the warm body and soft breath as Liam slept beside her. She nestled into him, feeling the stubble on his chin against her forehead. He smelled good. She was really going to miss this when it was over. The smell and feel of him. His intelligent eyes as he spoke in the staff meetings, making a plan for the week. Or his soft looks when Estela was explaining some childish thing to him in broken English. Even his sharp eyes, the looks he gave when his temper flared. She'd miss it all. Time was ticking by, and she'd go back to Arizona and try to start a different kind of life.

"You're thinking really loudly, love. Do you feel like sharing?" Liam said in a sexy, sleepy voice.

She ran a hand through his silky, sandy-colored hair. She kissed the underside of his jaw. *I love you*, she thought to herself. "Nothing. I'm sorry I woke you. Sleep, Liam. It'll be morning soon enough."

23

T he common area in the city center was the perfect location, Liam thought, as he looked around at the setup. Antonio had found the perfect spot to interact with the tourists, and the suit and tie sector of Manaus. The hotels, restaurants, museums, churches, and other public buildings were bustling with activity. They'd been here since five o'clock this morning, setting up the different booths. Now the school van came, bringing a few of the children, a couple of the sisters who worked at the abbey, and Gabriela with finger foods to keep everyone fed. The foot traffic was starting to pick up, people stopping to look at the different booths. They had a large wooden box with a slit in the top for donations. Raphael was put in charge of watching it, but he'd chained it to the leg of the folding table to secure it.

As the day went on, the tourists started to emerge. Izzy approached him. "We need to liven this up a bit. The early lunch crowd and the hungover tourists are starting to pick up foot traffic. You mind if I get a little loud?"

Liam laughed. "As if you've ever asked for permission."

"You wouldn't know what to do with me if I was docile and obedient, Liam O'Brien." She winked at him and his eyes flared. She yelled, "Genoveva, can you get the portable speakers out of the day pack? And a marker and a piece of cardboard."

Seamus and Adam laughed from their well child/expectant mother check station. Izzy was playing Brazilian dance music, loudly. As the tourists and lunch crowd walked through the city center, they stopped to watch the young boys from the school dribbling the football and doing all the fun tricks they learned in lieu of watching a TV or rotting their brains on YouTube. Another group of kids was playing peteca, a traditional Brazilian game that was similar to badminton, but they used their hands to strike the shuttlecock. Next to them Izzy and Estela and some of the other children danced along to the music, grabbing people off the sidewalk to join them. Genoveva and Raphael were sparring with long pieces of bamboo, in lieu of a proper fighting staff. Izzy had signs all around. *Support the St. Clare's Charity Mission. Help the children of St. Clare's buy a telescope! Help St. Clare's Charity Hospital buy a new X-Ray machine!* But the best sign of all was at Antonio's station. *Hug a Surgeon, Donations Welcome!* Antonio was currently being bombarded, women lining up to hug him and steal an occasional kiss as they stuffed their Brazilian real into the donation box.

"Hey, lad. Why don't you line up with Antonio and double the efforts!" Seamus yelled. Liam was currently checking vaccine cards and selling raffle tickets for three decorative mosquito nets that the sisters of St. Clare had sewn in their spare time. "You go ahead, brother. You're just as single as the two of us."

Liam looked over and saw the crowd of young twenty and thirty-something men admiring Izzy. Probably hoping she'd start a kissing booth. As she danced by them with Estela on her hip, a couple of them blew kisses to her and one even dropped to his knee.

"I see the day is going well." Liam turned around as the Reverend Mother appeared out of nowhere. She walked over to Antonio's booth, just as a scantily clad woman with generous C-cups took him by the face and planted a kiss right on his mouth. Unfortunately for him, he hadn't resisted. When he opened his eyes, the abbess was standing in her starched, white habit. Hands on hips. Seamus and Adam were bent over in their chairs, laughing to the point of tears as

the Reverend Mother thanked the women for their generous donation and proceeded to pull Antonio down to eye level by the ear. He
was trying to look repentant, but the hot pink lipstick on his upper
lip spoke contrary to his efforts.

Then she came back over and took a seat behind Liam's table. "I
notice you didn't chastise the owner of the lipstick," Liam said, grinning at her.

"Not with a 500 real note in her fist. I'm principled, but I'm practical. Just keep an eye on things. I won't stand for prostituting out my
staff."

She looked over at Sister Maria, who was currently bouncing a
soccer ball off her head, passing it to Emilio. "This is a good day, isn't
it?"

Liam looked at her and she was smiling with her whole face. "It
must be difficult, being in charge of all of this. Heavy is the crown
and all that. How is the volunteer hunt going?"

"Not well. I have hope, though. Sister Agatha has been updating
the website. She's rather good at it all, actually. We've got a My Face
page as well, and something called Tweeter." Liam was suppressing
his laughs into the back of his hand.

"It's good, Reverend Mother. It will bear fruit. I'm proud of you."
The abbess was taken aback.

"You're proud of me? For what? It's not like I can work the bloody
computer."

"Yes, Reverend Mother, but you delegated the job to someone
else. You loosened the reins a bit and tried something you weren't
comfortable with. I think you're going to see that this leap of faith
will bear fruit."

"I hope so. We can't go on like this. The diocese in Ireland will
not supplement us if we don't bring enough funds in. We have local
patrons, but they're getting old, just like me. I suppose this tweeter is
the way to reach your generation."

"It's Twitter, and let's hope so. It's not just the hospital. These children need us. They need St. Clare's."

"How is the search going for the lass's father?" The abbess's face seemed tired. Older than her years.

"I'm going to call my cousin tonight. I'll let you know. But Izzy wants to wait to talk to the man in person if he's still in Ireland. She'll go back to Ireland first, then to Phoenix, and she thinks it's better to do the whole thing face to face."

The abbess looked at him so long that he finally turned and met her eyes. "Then she's decided. It's to be the one near her home. It makes sense. She's a wonderful woman. She needs to be somewhere where there are people who love her. She needs to settle down, find a husband. Have a child or two."

"Yes, I suppose she does," he answered, his eyes going back to Izzy who now had one child on her hip and one around her leg. "She'd be a good mother." They were interrupted by Sister Agatha who said, "Smile!" So he swung an arm around the abbess and smiled for the camera.

"Nine thousand, eight hundred, and ninety-one real. That's over three thousand dollars! Hot damn! "

"Dr. Collier, please! Language."

Izzy smiled, "Sorry Sister."

They were all smiling as Sister Agatha gave them the grand total for the day's effort. And the event had cost them nothing. The raffle entries provided them with about fifty names and emails, perfect for soliciting donations and sending a link to the new website. "You did well, Sister Agatha. I can't wait to see all of the photos you took today," Izzy said. Then she got up, stretching. "I need a shower and an early night. Goodnight everyone."

Liam stood, "I'll walk with you. I need to call home if it's okay to use your laptop again."

As they walked to the library to use the only internet for ten miles, Liam looked around him. No one was around, so he took her hand.

"You did well today. The music was a brilliant move. And whoring our local surgeon out to horny tourists brought in a lot of extra money."

Izzy laughed. "Everyone pitched in. It was really a great day." They walked into the library, and before she could turn the light on, he backed her into a corner. "If I donate to the cause, do I get to kiss a surgeon?" His mouth hovered over hers.

Then she closed the distance, giving him a slow, lingering kiss. "I have to go. I need to sleep. I have a surgical consult at eight."

"I'll see you in the morning, then. Two nights away from the bungalow. I don't like this trend."

She smiled at that. "I don't either, but..." She shook herself. "Anyway, goodnight." She pulled him in for another kiss, and when she pulled away his eyes were intense. He pressed her to the wall and took her mouth again. When they finally parted, she pressed her forehead to his. "It's okay. Don't think about it, Liam. Time isn't going to slow down if we dwell on it." She pressed one more kiss to his mouth and left.

As it turned out, Tadgh had been called into work. He'd left a video message, brief and to the point. So Liam decided to call Doolin. He wasn't sure who he was going to call until he found himself doing it.

"Hello, brother. Christ, it's good to see you." Brigid was smiling. She looked so fresh and pretty. Like she'd just washed up before bed. Given the time, she probably had. She looked so much like their mother. They talked for a bit but then he saw Cora lingering in the background. "Brigid, do ye mind if I talk with Cora for a bit?"

Brigid turned. "Come, love. See your Uncle Liam." Then she said, "I'll just leave you two and go check on the baby."

Cora sat nervously. "You're up late, darlin'. It must be eleven o'clock. Did ye have trouble sleeping?" Cora nodded, her eyes wary. "What's amiss, sweet girl?"

"Uncle Liam. Did you leave Ireland because of me?"

Liam recoiled like someone had slapped him. "What? No, darlin'. Why would you think that for a moment?"

"Because I didn't tell. When I had the dream about Auntie Eve I didn't tell. After she died, you didn't come to Christmas. Then you left and didn't say goodbye. I knew you were angry with me because otherwise you would've said goodbye. I had a present for you. I made it in school. I guess it was kind of stupid." She wiped her eyes, "I'm so sorry for what I did. Please come see Granny. She cries for you. I'll stay away and you can see her and mammy and the boys."

"Stop! Oh God, Cora. Stop, lass. Don't say another word." Then he saw her face and realized that had come out wrong. He wanted to jump through the screen and hold her. "I love you, my sweet Cora. I don't blame you. I never blamed you. How could you think such a thing?"

"I should have told. And you ran away. You didn't say goodbye or call or send a letter. It's my fault."

He rubbed a hand over his face, fighting the tears that would never stop if he started. "You're my bright and shining star, Cora. When I think of home, I think of you. Playing on the beach and throwing stones. Remember when I'd visit and take you to the beach?"

Cora sniffled, wiping her eyes. "Yes, Uncle. I remember. And we'd go to the parlor for ice cream and you told me not to tell Granny that ye'd spoiled my supper."

Liam laughed. "Yes. Listen, sweetheart. I was messed up when I left. I was so hurt, I couldn't think of anyone else but myself. But it was selfish and cruel of me not to call. I thought about you, though. Every day I think about you all."

"Will ye come home to us?"

"I can't right now, love. There's no one to take my place here at the mission."

"What's it like there? Are there many children? Ma said there's an orphanage."

So they talked. He told her all about St. Clare's and about the villages. She was fascinated to hear about the indigenous people and the boat rides upriver to treat the people from the remote tribes. Then he told her how they'd started calling Izzy the river angel. Soon he realized that Brigid was listening, perched on a kitchen chair. "It must be almost midnight, love. Best let your ma get to bed. I love you, mo chroí. Kiss your brothers for me."

"Uncle Liam, I wanted to tell you something. I don't want you to be cross with me. I don't really know how to control what happens to me. I just…I told Izzy, but I think I'm supposed to tell you as well."

"Tell me what, Cora?"

"To remember to follow the river." Her face was serious, wanting to make sure he understood how serious she was. "It's important. You must tell Izzy. She must remember."

Liam swallowed hard, then looked up into Brigid's haunted face. She couldn't protect her daughter from these dreams. "Cora, who told you to tell me that?"

"You promise you won't be mad at me?"

"Never, Cora. I will never be mad at you."

"It was Auntie Eve. She's come to me again. She seemed more urgent this time. It's important. You must tell Izzy."

Liam felt his stomach lurch, but he kept his composure for Cora's sake. "I'll remember." He watched as Brigid crossed herself. Then he ended the call.

Jose Fuentes slammed his hands down on his desk. In front of him, he had three men. More like three morons. His Portuguese was clipped as his anger boiled. "You three idiots are to blame for this! First, you give the wrong coordinates for a big shipment and it gets seized by the government. Then you go to the fucking village while the medicós are there! Then you shoot the chief's sons? You are incompetent idiots! We've got military and police patrolling from the water! Every other day I'm spending thousands in bribery money in order to keep the product moving. Thank the holy Virgin the road is finished or we'd be ruined." He stood, leaning over the desk. "You three will be sent into the city to move product. You've been demoted. You're fortunate I don't make an example out of you and put your heads on a spike. Now go!"

"Please Senhor," Raul said, putting his hands in front of him. "I can fix this. It's those fucking medícos and that guard of theirs. I know him. I couldn't place it before but I know I remember him. Some sort of military. I think he worked with the narcotics enforcement. He's the root of your problem. Him and that little bitch he follows around."

"You're sure about this man?"

"Yes. I have a son at the orfanato. He can get them off the property, alone. Once we remove the problem, the others won't be calling the government. The rest of those medícos will be too afraid to come up the river again."

"No! For God sake, you've done enough. You leave the American woman alone. We haven't seen them in a week. If we route around the village, for now, it won't be an issue. The police will get bored and move on. We just have to ride out your mistakes. You will stay out of this. Do you hear me? You will peddle the product, like the piss ants you are, and be glad you still have a job."

Then he stopped, thinking of what the man had said. "You've got a son in the orphanage? You left him there instead of keeping him with you?"

Raul nodded. Fuentes snorted his disgust. "You really are a piece of shit, aren't you? I suspect the boy is better off."

Liam folded his laundry on the bed of his cot, in the men's portion of the staff quarters. It was getting late, but Seamus and Adam were at the hospital. One of Seamus's patients had arrived an hour ago in heavy labor. Adam was standing by to help with the child when it was born. Sister Catherine, Alyssa, and Seamus were handling the laboring mother.

He was tired and missing Izzy like crazy, wanting to sneak off to the bungalow and have some alone time with her before sleeping. Sleeping with her curled against him. Her hair in his face, her smooth shoulder right in nibbling range. He loved the smell and taste of her. Not just sexually. He was comforted by the feel of her. In the dark, away from the stress of the hospital, he lost himself in her touch. In her soft gasps and hungry kisses, and in the depths of those warm, intelligent eyes.

It was when he began walking to the locker room that the strange feeling came over him. He heard something coming from the women's hall. Music. He took a few steps closer, and that's when a flush of emotions went through him. The *O'Brien Set* was playing from Izzy's room. The family song that was played at all the large family gatherings. Especially the weddings. The dance that was performed by his family and their mates. An old tune, generations old. *What in the hell?*

He marched quickly into her room and she looked up from her own laundry pile. She was prancing around as she folded. Her face registered confusion and he snapped at her. "Turn it off!" he said, pointing at her iPod.

She recoiled a bit from his tone. "What the hell is your problem? Don't order me around!" Then she really looked at him. Saw the rawness. She didn't understand it.

Liam's blood started pounding in his veins as the song started to transition to a quicker pace. This song. Jesus. It was like a mating cry. He ran his hands through his hair, getting ready to freak out. Getting ready to run or leap, he wasn't sure which. His body decided for him.

Izzy said, "I'm sorry. Okay, Christ Liam. I'll turn it off. I don't know why…" She was reaching across to hit the pause button when she heard the door slam behind her. She thought Liam had walked out, but then he grabbed her. He was on her in an instant, pulling her to him as he swung her body around and pushed her against the door. "Liam…" but he cut her off by taking her mouth. His palms were flat against hers, pushed against the wall on either side of her head. And he kissed the breath out of her as she felt his hips surge.

"Izzy," he moaned against her mouth. Then he let her hands go and cupped her face, kissing her deeply. She felt the kiss down to her toes. His hips were rolling, in rhythm with the music. Then her shirt was over her head and he was on her mouth again. "I need you. Your shorts, lass. Get them off before I tear them to ribbons." He didn't have to ask twice. She was nude in a flash and started working on his fly. "That's it, ah God." He put a hand on the door to steady himself as she stroked his freed erection. He lifted her, meeting her eyes as he slid inside.

Izzy didn't understand. He was out of his head. Something about this song that Brigid had loaded on her iPod. She watched his face as he pushed inside her. He was completely changed. He'd come to her angry, but something shifted. His eyes were so intense, so purposeful. A small grin appeared as he started to move, gliding back and forth inside her with the fast pace of the music. He was big and thick, and the pace had her climaxing with a few skillful strokes. He laughed on a growl as he started to go over the edge and she felt the warm jets spurting deep within her. She grabbed a fist of his hair as she bit his shoulder. His hips went wild against her.

Liam held her up, her legs around his waist, kissing her so thoroughly, so passionately in the aftermath. He was still inside her, even though they were both completely spent from the hard, fast sex. The song was over and she was so rattled by the whirlwind of emotion she'd witnessed. When he finally took her to the bed and withdrew from her, he leaned over her, kissing her gently.

"Liam, I don't know what just happened."

"Where did you get that song, Izzy?"

"Brigid loaded a bunch of traditional music on my iPod for me. I don't know anything other than that. It seemed to upset you. I'm sorry, I don't know why, but I wouldn't upset you deliberately." He kissed her one more time, and she noticed he was shaking. It was subtle, but she felt it. An adrenal reaction. Then he stood upright, tucking his erection against his stomach and zipping his shorts.

"It doesn't matter. I'm sorry, too. We said we weren't going to do this here. I just…I had to have you. I don't have another explanation." She smiled, and it lit something up in his chest. Something he thought was dead.

"It's okay. I'm not complaining. Everyone is gone right now. It was…incredible. I needed you too." She stood and reached for her robe. He took it off the hook on the closet and held it open. She put her arms in and felt him reach around her, bringing the lapels together. Then he tied it, his chin on her shoulder, his body pressed to the back of her. He pulled one lapel down and kissed her from the base of her neck to her shoulder, tasting and nibbling as he went. He let out a contented sigh that almost had her tearing up.

"Goodnight, Izzy love."

24

Being Irish, he had an abiding sense of tragedy, which sustained him through temporary periods of joy...

William Butler Yeats

I zzy checked her email, cursed. After her surgical consult, she needed to hunt down Seamus. *Dammit.* This was not a complication she needed right in the middle of her jungle tour. She closed her laptop, feeling the effects of last night's poor sleep. The truth was that she was spoiled with that AC in the bungalow, and the feel of Liam against her as she slept. They'd better get used to it, though. She only had a few weeks left. She sighed. Tomorrow was her official last day in the Navy. The time had flown by this autumn. The rain was more persistent, the temperatures dropping. The rivers were fuller. There was a part of her that could barely remember not being at St. Clare's. She walked into the hospital and was greeted by Alyssa. "The patient is here to see you."

Liam woke in a rush, looking around the room to get his bearings. That damn dream again. What did she want? Always same dream.

He thought about what Cora had said and feeling a little pissed off about the fact that Izzy had only told him part of the story. She'd neglected to tell him that Eve had been the messenger. Maybe she'd thought she was protecting him. He hoped that was it.

Still, he'd missed her last night. Even after they'd made love in her room, he'd hated going to his own bed. He missed her soft hip curved into him as they slept. He ran a finger over the tender spot on his shoulder. She'd marked him. A pink mark of unbroken skin where she'd bit him through his shirt. He thought about the feel of it. Her teeth and her fist in his hair. She'd fed off his wildness, wanting to devour him as he did her. She gave as good as she got and he loved that. Loved that he made her control slip into something a bit feral.

He dressed quickly, heading out of the staff quarters toward the main area of the hospital. When he rounded a corner, Sister Agatha almost ran into him. "Dia Duit, Sister Agatha."

She smiled, "Good morning, Dr. O'Brien. I've been sent to fetch you away to Reverend Mother Faith's office. She wanted you to have morning tea with her." Liam cocked a brow. This was new. First thing in the morning they were both usually too busy for idle chat.

"I'll head over now," he said, wondering what the issue was. As he walked across the garden, he entered the part of the abbey that housed her office. Her door was open. She motioned him in, asking him to close the door. He wished her good morning, then took a seat, waiting for her to reveal the reason for this early morning meeting. He squirmed under her intense eyes.

"How are you doing this morning, lad?" There was a kindness and softness in her voice that she rarely shared.

Could she tell he hadn't slept? Or perhaps she'd eavesdropped on his call with Cora? Not likely. It wasn't her style. He was feeling short-tempered this morning. Between that chat with Cora and the dream, his guilt meter was in the danger zone. "I just slept poorly. I'm fine."

"It's okay if you're not. I just wanted you to know that I'm here for you. Today is bound to be difficult. My door is open all day." He cocked a brow, not catching her full meeting.

"I've had losses in my life, Liam. Tragic losses. And the anniversary of that tragedy is always a particularly trying day for me. I'll understand if you take the day off."

The room closed in on Liam, like a suffocating squeeze. His vision tunneled to the calendar on her desk. The end of November. A wave of nausea rolled through him. "I have to go. I need to go." He stood up abruptly as the sweat started to seep out of him.

He walked rapidly out of the building, needing air. "Oh, God." He moaned as he put his palms to his temples. He'd forgotten. In the hustle and bustle of the hospital and health fair, in the thrill of newfound intimacy, he'd forgotten. One year ago, today. She'd died one year ago and he'd forgotten what day it was.

No! This wasn't possible. He had the day burned into his brain. He'd just not been keeping track of the date. The climate was different, the seasons less dramatic. The holidays in Brazil were different. He'd often found himself forgetting what time of year it was, having to think about what month they were in. The only thing he'd been tracking recently was how many days he had left before Izzy's commitment was up. How many hours until he could get her alone.

He groaned. "I'm sorry, Eve. I haven't forgotten. I swear it. I haven't forgotten you!" A flood of anger went through him. It was at himself, mostly. He was selfish and disloyal. Mainly because he'd woken up this morning, wishing he'd had Izzy next to him. He'd taken her unapologetically last night, during the music that should've been played at his wedding. Even after his beloved Eve had come to him in the night, he'd still woken up thinking about Izzy. The self-loathing rolled through him until he was almost nauseous.

Liam walked down the hallway, noticing Izzy's voice coming from Seamus's office. "So, I was wondering how much of a hassle it would be to just remove my IUD? Can you do that procedure here? Probably the sooner the better." Liam backed up, hitting the opposite wall.

What the hell? She was going to stop her birth control? Without discussing it with him? What the hell was she playing at? He marched down to his lab, feeling like he was going to go full mushroom cloud. The idea that Izzy was scheming a long-term plan for them was rattling his cage even more so than it already had been. Did she think to get herself pregnant? To what end? So that he'd leave Brazil and take her home to his mother? Marry her? Then he thought about Eve. He'd forgotten about Eve, too consumed with his own pleasure. Letting himself get seduced into forgetting what they'd shared. Comparing the two women, for God's sake. *Hell no.*

Izzy explained her concern to Seamus after the e-mail she'd received from the drug company that manufactured her IUD. An ironic conversation, considering he was holding a newborn. The little one had been born last night. Mom's milk hadn't come in, and Seamus was giving her a bottle.

"The recall was for the hormonal IUD that I currently have. I'm a little worried. I wasn't sent the notice as a doctor but as a registered consumer. I don't know all of the reasons behind the recall. If I can wait until I leave, that would be better. But if it's something serious that requires an immediate removal, then I need to know. I also need to know if it is unreliable. I mean, not that it matters right now. I just need to know if I should use a backup method, just in case Chris Pratt shows up." That got a laugh from Seamus. "Can you look up the reasons for the recall and talk to some of your colleagues? The doctor that placed the IUD separated from the Navy two years ago."

Seamus nodded, "Okay, Izzy. I'll do it today. I'll go to the library, then get right back to you. If you can wait, it would be better. I won't have a replacement here, and as you know, the procedure isn't pleasant. I'd hate for you to have to break it up into two sessions."

"I agree. Unless it's something serious, I'll wait to see a doctor in the States. Thanks, Seamus. I'm sorry to muddy the line between colleague and physician, but I don't really have anyone else I can discuss this with. You know how controversial the birth control thing can be with the sisters. I don't want to put Sister Catherine in an awkward position."

"Not at all. I'm glad you came to me. The team comes first, right? We need you to be healthy. If it is something that needs immediate action, I'm capable of separating our friendship from the situation long enough to resolve the issue."

As Izzy left the office, she headed down to the lab to see Liam. As she walked through the doorway, she saw Pedro's worried face. Then she looked at Liam. He looked like he was ready to self-destruct. She didn't know what had set him off, but he was furious about something.

He glared at her and she cocked her head, wondering if the man had lost his mind. Was this the same guy who'd held her hand on the way to the library last night? The same man that had come to her later in her room. His eyes never left hers as he said, "Pedro, could you leave us?" Pedro gathered a few things and left, closing the door behind him.

A feeling of dread came over Izzy. This was it. This was the bitter Liam, getting ready to take a blow torch to their current relationship status. *Dammit.* She'd thought it would come the morning after their first night together. She'd almost expected it. But he'd lured her in over the last weeks, and she'd let her guard down. Now it was game time. "Is there a problem?"

He barked out a bitter laugh. "Well, where to start?" Izzy crossed her arms as he let it rip. "Why didn't you tell me that Cora's dream was about Eve?" That hadn't been what she'd expected.

"Liam, you were pretty raw when I showed up. I didn't think you needed the details. Plus the fact that it probably meant nothing. I'm surrounded by rivers and it was just a dream. Why are you so pissed?"

"I'm pissed because I expected some honesty. I'm pissed because, on the one year anniversary of losing my one and only love, I hear you scheming to stop your birth control a month before you leave!" He stressed the word *only*, and it stung, even though it shouldn't surprise her. "Is that why you came here, Izzy? To play the supportive friend? Suck up to my family and secure a spot at the dinner table?"

"What the hell? Were you eavesdropping on my medical consult with Seamus? How dare you!" She growled and threw her hands up. "You are such an arrogant jackass. You have no idea…"

He kept talking right over her. "Then you lure me into that fertility spring. And again into your room last night!"

"Lure you! Excuse me? Have you actually gone insane? Are you listening to yourself?"

Liam cut her off. "Yes, I am. From where I stand, I'm dead on the money. You're thirty years old, alone, and admittedly envious of my family. Well, let's get something clear Dr. Collier. Although it's been a stupendous ride, being in your bed, you will never replace Eve. You can stay with my mother, befriend my sister and niece, you can even come here and screw my brains out, but I will love only one woman. If you're looking to find a sperm donor to marry you, try Antonio."

She recoiled from him. "That is not what is happening here, you bastard! Have you lost your mind?" She swallowed a chain of obscenities, trying to keep her head from popping off her shoulders. She did not need to draw a crowd to this unbelievably ugly scene. It was completely unprofessional. She ground her jaw, her voice hoarse with the effort of keeping control. "I realize that you are all up in your head today because of Eve. I'm sorry for that. I didn't realize it was today. I didn't find out about her death until a week after it happened. I didn't know the exact day. That aside," she leaned into her words, a hint of menace rolling off of her, "how dare you talk to me like that." She shook her head in disgust. "Why, Liam? Why couldn't you just let me go home next month and part on good terms? You didn't have to do this!"

"I've done nothing! Don't try to turn the tables, Izzy. I'm not the one who has been withholding information."

Izzy's throat ached, but she was not going to cry. She put her hands on her hips, breathing as she stared at the floor. Damn him. "I may be thirty and alone, but I would never do the things you're accusing me of. I was leaving, Liam. In a month I would have been gone. Why did you have to do this? Why did you have to ruin it? It was going to end, we both knew this. Why couldn't you just..." she paused, closing her eyes as the wave of sadness went through her whole body.

"Why couldn't I what?" he snapped.

She looked directly into his eyes. He was so unbending. No sign of the man that had loved her body so gently a few nights ago. "Why couldn't you just let me love you for this short time? I wasn't asking you for anything other than that. There were no strings. I know you don't love me back, and I was okay with that." Her voice broke, "I just wanted to be with you. To part ways knowing that you were better off because I'd loved you for a little while."

She shook herself in anger. Anger at herself for letting this little scene wound her so badly. She chucked her chin up. "I know I'm nothing like Eve. I never tried to be. But I am a good person, and I'm worthy of a whole hell of a lot more than this. Than some...some arrogant, angry, self-pitying dickhead trying to make me feel like shit about myself. So bravo, Liam. You got what you wanted. You wanted to crush the life out of something rather than let it die of natural causes. Maybe so that it would appease your guilt and keep you right where you love to be? Wallowing in self pity and anger? So you win." She dug in her pocket and slid the keys across the table. "I won't be needing these anymore, and do me a favor, Dr. O'Brien. Just stay clear of me for the next few weeks. You can't tear the hide off of me and expect me to spend unnecessary time in your presence. It doesn't work like that."

As she walked out of the door she didn't slam it. She just walked away and was wondering why she wasn't limping. She felt mortally wounded. Surely she should have a limp? The blood was pumping in her ears as she heard him call her name, but it was too late. He had nothing to say to her that she didn't already know.

He'd loved being with her. She had that at least. Their sex had healed him to a degree, helping him escape his inner demons for a few hours every night. But he had never been and never would be hers. She raised her chin up as the tears dripped off the end. Despite his opinion, she had not come here to seduce her way into the O'Brien family. She had a job to do, and this brief distraction had ended in a fireball.

2

Izzy stood before her patient in the exam room, trying to figure out the best way to handle this injury without causing him undue discomfort. It was early morning, and she was surprised to see that he was not only up and dressed, but had been playing. "Emilio, why didn't Sister Maria bring you to me when this happened?" Emilio had never been a good English student.

Genoveva was leaning against the doorjamb. "He said he visited his friend in the next village. He meets the boy part of the way when he walks to the school. The village that Gabriela lives in. He got hit with a football. He's okay, but it's not quitting bleeding. He say it's no big deal."

"Well, it is a big deal. You don't want to scar. Now, I am going to need to put a couple of stitches in this. Genoveva, can you go tell Nurse Alyssa I need her?"

As she started to clean the wound, she noticed he was tearing up. "I'm sorry. I know that hurts."

"It no hurt. You are a good medíca, Dr. Collier. Good to us." Izzy felt his eyes burning as he looked at her. She didn't understand. He was usually so aloof. He had the snotty teenager thing down to a science.

"Thank you, Emilio. Now just lay back and I'll take care of you."

Alyssa came in just in time to help her with the lidocaine. After two small stitches to the corner of his mouth, she helped him to sit up. "Keep it clean. I can't bandage it, because of where the cut is on your mouth. The little ones inside are okay, they'll heal on their own. You can eat what you want as long as you are comfortable opening your mouth. Make sure you are drinking enough water. Your teeth are okay, but one of them is a little loose. You need to leave it alone.

Use the other side for a few days, okay? It'll be fine after that." She pulled her gloves off, then removed her goggles. The boy left, and she sat down. Exhausted.

"You look tired, Izzy. For the last day, you've been walking around like you lost your best friend. What's happened, love?"

Izzy mustered a smile. "It's nothing. Today is my last day of active duty. It's just…an ending to a really beautiful chapter of my life." The tears threatened because that had a double meaning for her. The last twenty-four hours were an ending for two chapters in her life. "I'm okay, really. I'm just tired."

Seamus walked into the lab, not bothering to give a shit whether Liam was busy. When Liam looked up, Seamus took a step back. Jesus, the guy looked like all the blood had been drained from him. He'd gone to the abbess last night, after suspecting that Liam was headed for a meltdown. It was in his every gesture, his face, the set of his shoulders. She'd told him that yesterday was the one year anniversary of Eve's death. That explained some things. It didn't explain why he and Izzy were avoiding each other. Right now, he looked like he was being eaten alive. "What did you do?" was all he said.

"I don't know what you're talking about. Now if you don't mind, I've got these vaccines to inventory. I've just received the Zika viles."

He walked to the cooler and placed the first tray inside.

"Let me speak plainly, then. What the hell did you do to Izzy? She looks like she's slowly bleeding to death."

Liam swallowed down a sound of despair that tried to bubble up in his throat. He'd been out of his head the last twenty-four hours. At odds with what he knew to be right in his mind and what he felt in his heart. His fucking traitorous heart.

He'd spent the morning talking with his father. He'd used Adam's computer, for obvious reasons. The pitying look on his father's face had only deepened the pit in his gut.

You lashed out at her because you couldn't admit your feelings for her. You deliberately struck a fatal blow because you didn't want her to be able to forgive you. The real ball-shriveler had been the disappointment in his father's eyes. Like he didn't even recognize him. *Ye think that if you admit that you love Izzy, that you've betrayed Eve. But think on this, Liam. What if Eve had been watching? What would she have thought of the way you treated this woman?*

"Answer me, Dr. O'Brien. It was inevitable that you'd make a cock-up of this but it seems you've outdone yourself."

Liam's instinct was to go on the offensive. "Let me ask you something, Dr. O'Keefe. Were you going to tell me that Izzy was going to stop her birth control? Were you going to keep that little nugget to yourself when you knew what was going on between us?"

Seamus's face was oddly confused. He cocked his head. "What is it that you think you know about Izzy's health issues?"

"I heard her, Seamus. I didn't mean to hear it, but she was asking you to remove her IUD. The sooner the better. That's how she put it, right? Well, you needn't bother. She and I are done."

"You stupid boy. Please tell me you didn't accuse her based on a few words that you heard out of context? Since you obviously didn't ask her to explain and you didn't give her the benefit of the doubt, why do you think I should tell you?" He narrowed his eyes, pointing at Liam. "You heard what you wanted to, so you could take a hunk out of the lass. You were grieving and feeling sorry for yourself and you looked for an excuse to attack her. Jesus, when you decide to fuck up, you don't go halfway do you?"

He started to walk out but thought better of it. "You know what. You don't deserve her. And since she didn't tell you, I will. There's a recall on her IUD. She was worried that she couldn't wait until she got home which, as it turns out, she can. But she didn't want to wait if her health was at risk. She also wanted to know if hypothetically she should be using a backup method of birth control. It had nothing to do with you, you arrogant jackass. Do you really think she's the type of woman that would trap a man with a pregnancy?"

Liam sat there being verbally whipped by his co-worker as the second round of shame rolled through his whole body. He supposed he should be used to this. Before he'd left Ireland, he'd done the same thing to Tadgh. Lashed out at his nearest and dearest so that they hurt as much as he did. When had he become such a prick? He cursed to himself. Then he looked at Seamus. His whole body started to shake with rage. Rage at himself. Rage enough to consume him.

His eyes were pleading for something. A mercy killing, maybe? Seamus's face softened just a bit. "Why did you hurt her if you love her, Liam? And you do love her, in case you needed to confirm it. That should be a joyous thing after all you've been through. To find true love twice in a lifetime is more than most people get. It's more than I've gotten."

He swallowed, trying to keep his voice steady. "I fell in love with my wife when I was barely old enough to call myself a man. I thought it was the real thing, and maybe it was for that time in my life. She gave me three beautiful daughters." He shrugged, "But I'd give anything to have a woman look at me the way that Izzy looks at you. The respect, the passion, the light in her eyes. That was all for you... and you trampled that precious gift like it was a roach under your feet." He turned to walk away.

"Seamus," Liam croaked. "I'm sorry. I'm sorry I assumed the worst of both of you. I know Izzy will never forgive me." He closed his eyes. "The stuff I said to her. Jesus, Seamus." His eyes were bright. "I need you to be my friend right now. I need to know that I didn't burn both bridges."

Seamus smiled a crooked smile. "If I wasn't your friend, why would I be here?"

25

Doolin, Co. Clare, Ireland

Sorcha sat across from her husband at the kitchen table, getting a full account of what had gone down in Brazil "Holy Virgin, Sean. Izzy and Liam?"

"Aye, and he's gone and made a mess of things."

Her shoulders slumped as she felt a tremendous heaviness in her body. Then she looked up at her husband. "Can I tell you something that will never leave this room?"

"Of course, love. You can tell me anything."

Sorcha took a sip of her tea, needing to collect her thoughts. "You know that feeling you describe when you saw me for the first time. That pull?"

Sean smiled, "I do. The connection was instant. It was the same for our sons and my father. Well…not for Michael and Fiona, but that was different. She wasn't the one. When he met wee Branna, that's when he felt it."

"You're right. It was instant. Like we were all players in the universe that were supposed to be on the same team. Like we'd synced to our partner. I felt it too. But there is something else in my life that is almost as powerful." She set the cup down. "The first time it happened was when I met Katie before she and William were wed. I felt such a pull to her. Like a long lost sister. Like she belonged to me."

Sean reached across the table taking her hand. "And each time I've met another one, it's been the same. All of my children's mates. Your mother. Your sister Maeve. There's a rare bond between the women in this family. There were only two times I didn't feel it." The tears started to well, a small sound in her voice like it ached.

"Fio was the first. I just…couldn't put my finger on it. It made no sense. It just didn't feel like forever. It's why I tried to talk Michael into waiting. I just knew."

"And the second time?" Sean asked, willing her to look up at him. Her breath stuttered. "Oh, Sean. I can't believe I'm putting it into words. Even the thought of it has consumed me with guilt."

"Because you never felt it with Eve?" he said softly.

Sorcha put her face in her hands. "Oh Sean, it's awful to even think it. I tried. But she was never here long. She was so sweet and such a dear girl. I genuinely liked her and she made Liam happy. I just…I don't know. Maybe that connection didn't happen because we were destined to lose her."

"Don't cry, chuisle. It isn't your fault. And perhaps you're right. Maybe the fact that she would never marry our son, that she was destined not to stay with us…maybe that sync you felt with the others never happened."

"But I felt it again." She dabbed her eyes with her sleeve. "I felt it, Sean. In the most unlikely place. It's why I tried to fix her up with Tadgh."

"You mean Izzy? Oh, God. You felt it with Izzy?"

"What if he's really done so much damage that she stays away? He'll lose two of them. It'll kill him, Sean. And if it doesn't kill him, it will drive him further away from us. She's his way home. I know this in my heart."

Izzy and Raphael drove down the access road to the small neighboring village. Gabriela was in the back seat, currently complaining in rapid Portuguese. She'd cut herself in the kitchen, trying to debone a chicken after the breakfast rush. She needed some time off. The Reverend Mother had assured her they could get by with leftovers and sandwiches for the rest of the day, much to her horror.

"You need to keep it dry and let the skin start knitting together, Gabriela. Just for today." Raphael pulled up to her little shared house and helped her out of the car. That's when Emilio ran up to them, waving his arms.

"Emilio, what are you doing off the property again? I know your friends are here, but I thought you had school today?"

He started rapid fire with the Portuguese and Izzy couldn't follow him. Raphael said. "He said there's been an accident. Another jaguar attack. They were afraid to move the boy."

"A kid? It's a kid? Shit! Where, Emilio? Onde?" Raphael listened as the boy spoke, pointing.

"He said they were playing just to the North, on the new road. Some boys ran down from the village and told them to go get the anjo do rio. That they needed you. He's bleeding too badly and they need you now." Raphael stopped interpreting, holding a hand up. "We need to go back and get the satellite phone. We can't go out there without communication. Too much has happened."

Emilio interjected. "They say he will going to die, medica." The tears welled up in the boy's face as he attempted to speak to her in English, and she was surprised. Maybe despite the distance, he knew the boy that was hurt.

"We have a full trauma kit in the Jeep. We have your pack with the weapons. We can't go back. It's too much time with the traveling. Let's go."

"I don't like this. We've never traveled this road. It's a bad idea, boss. Let's go get Paolo and take the boat, then we will have the phone with us."

"I'm not going to let some kid die because we don't have a phone! And need I remind you what happened last time we took the boat up-river? Forget it. You either take me or I go alone and take your Jeep. Which is it?"

Raphael turned to the boy and spoke to him in Portuguese. "You go to the hospital. You find Doctor Seamus or Doctor Liam. Do you understand? You tell them where we are going. Tell them to come to the village with the phone. Hurry. Run as fast as you can."

The boy nodded, then he gave Izzy a strange look. Almost apologetic.Then he turned and ran back to St. Clare's.

Liam walked through the cafeteria and his heart squeezed so hard in his chest, he almost doubled over. The girls from the orphanage were trying to learn the cups song. Sister Agatha was singing, teaching them the routine. Then he noticed that two more girls had cropped their hair above their shoulders. He thought about that night at the sing-a-long. Izzy had winked at him as she'd sung, *you're gonna miss me when I'm gone.*

Oh, God. What had he done? He couldn't be here right now. He turned to leave, almost running into the abbess. She was not happy. "In my office. Now."

"What did you do?" she demanded, glaring at him from over her desk.

"Why is everyone asking me that today?" Liam said dryly.

"You know why. For mercy sake, Liam. Why did you have to screw things up when she only had a few weeks left? Why bother starting anything with the lass if you were going to do her a bad turn?"

Liam was stunned. "You knew." It wasn't a question.

"Of course I knew. Do ye think I've come this far with this place by not paying attention? I see all, Dr. O'Brien, but it wasn't going on while you were here on the grounds, and you're both adults. I decided not to intervene, because..."

"Why?"

"Because she was good for you, lad. I watched you stitch back together, right before my eyes. A few scars, yes, but you were becoming whole again. You seemed almost happy. How could you behave so poorly? I don't know what happened, exactly, but I do know that I expected more out of you."

"I couldn't, okay?" He threw his hands up. "I couldn't let myself have her. If I did, then it was like admitting..." he closed his eyes, the guilt overwhelming him. Guilt because of Eve and because of Izzy.

"If you admitted that Izzy was your mate, the one that all of you O'Brien men wait for, the one you cherish above all others... if she was your mate, then you'd have to admit that maybe Eve wasn't?"

"No! You're wrong! That's not it!" he stood to go.

"Running again? My, what a coward you are." The calmness in her voice undid him.

Liam spun around. "Eve was the one. I was going to marry her. She was perfect and kind and beautiful and I loved her!"

"I know you did. Nothing can take that away from you or her, but she's gone, Liam. People lose other people and they find a way to go on!" She tightened her jaw, reining in her emotions. Then those sharp eyes fixed on him like she was preparing to stay there all day and battle this out with him. "Let me ask you something. Was Eve a lot like the other women in your family? From what you told me, she seemed like such an agreeable sort of girl. Almost passive. The relationship was so easy, no rocky roads or rough seas. You're fortunate. Was it like that for all of the men in your family?" Liam swallowed, cracked his neck, didn't answer. "How about your mother? Is she the passive, agreeable type?"

Liam snorted. He couldn't help it. His mother's temper was legendary. She'd nearly pounded their father to dust before they'd finally come together. She'd fought him tooth and nail. "How about your brothers? Did they just fall flawlessly into these perfect unions?"

"I'm not them. It doesn't matter how it happened for them."

"Oh, really? Ye just take bits and pieces of this lore that suit you and leave the rest behind? Well, if you're going to live and die by it, lad, you've got to take the whole thing," she said with a nod. Then she beckoned him with her hand."So let's have it. What's the tale about the O'Brien man finding his one true mate? Let's hear the whole thing. Was it unheard of that he love someone prior to finding her? Because you told me that your brother had been married once before. Did he not love the first woman?"

"Of course he did, she just wasn't..." he ground his jaw. "That was different. She cheated. She didn't die."

"And although he loved her enough to marry her, she wasn't his mate. So continue. We've established that there's only one, and..." she waved a hand, encouraging him to finish.

"And he'll love her all of his days," Liam said hoarsely. She gave him a look that told him to keep going. "The O'Brien man never comes easily to his mate. The path to their union is a rocky one. The O'Brien line is drawn to strength and their women are fierce. And once he claims her, he'll love only her." His eyes were starting to tear and he choked them back. "And if he loses her, he will be e're ruined. Never to love again."

Instantly, the scene of Izzy running toward that jaguar to save Estela flashed in his brain. Then another scene of her getting in his face, threatening to beat his ass. Then of her straddled over a wounded man, closing off his artery, so he wouldn't bleed to death. The blood, sweat, and tears that were an intrinsic part of her makeup.

"I know you loved Eve. How could I not see it, as devastating as it was for you to lose her? But you are different now, and you need something different from your partner. You are allowed to love someone else, lad. Someone who can love you back with all of these scars you've gained through your trials. If Izzy is that woman for you, then you can either thank God that he's given you a second chance, or you can waste the gift you were given."

Raphael sped down the roughly cleared road, dodging tree stumps and vines and fallen timber. "We shouldn't be doing this. We don't know where we are going." He was getting very frustrated. As a military man, this went against his training. Don't go blindly into the unknown.

Izzy had a map out, trying to read it with all of the bumpity bumpity going on in the vehicle. "Okay, we usually go up this tributary and into this smaller river, then we dock on the east bank. Here is the village we just left. We are basically running parallel to the river that we normally travel. We will come up on the eastern side of the village if we turn left in about five kilometers. We just have to hope there is a road to the left. We are going due north, correct?"

Raphael stopped the vehicle, paying attention to the map. Then he looked up at the sun, and at the compass on his watch. "No, we are going northeast. Why the hell did we listen to a child? This can't be right!"

"Didn't he say the path would cut left? That's what you said! Let's just go up another five or six kilometers. If we don't find it, we'll turn around."

"We've already gone ten kilometers, Izzy. This is dense forest between two swelling rivers. It's raining. We will go five more. If we don't find the turnoff, then we go back. Surely the others have started up the river by now." That was the only thought that was keeping Izzy from going into a full panic. If they didn't reach the kid, then the others would. They were trained in field medicine. They could try to stabilize the boy until she or Antonio got to him. She dreaded seeing Liam, but she knew he wouldn't stay back. He'd never send one of the team off on their own. Couple that with the fact that they were doing more demo today. She could hear the dynamite in the distance. Nowhere near them. It was like a muffled, far away sound that set her teeth on edge.

"Boss, you aren't thinking clearly. This thing with the medíco is weighing on you."

Izzy closed her eyes. "I don't know what you're talking about. Now drive. The sooner we get there, the sooner we can get a plan together."

He started to accelerate again. That's when he saw it. A duffel bag on the side of the road. It was too late to try and stop, so he gunned it.

He swerved as much as he could, given the jungle on both sides. The IED exploded just as the tail end of the Jeep passed the bag. They flew sideways and up, the tail of the vehicle flying up and away from the explosion as the Jeep rolled over. The seat belts gripped them hard as the roll bars hit the ground, keeping their heads from being driven into their chest cavities. The Jeep landed on all four tires. Just as he began to get his wits back, he could hear Izzy grunting and swearing. That was good. She was alive. Then he saw them. The three men approaching, weapons in their hands.

26

The prickling sensation on Liam's spine was bothering him to distraction. He'd been looking for Izzy for about twenty minutes. Then he realized Raphael's Jeep was gone. He went into the cafeteria where Sister Maria and Seamus were handing out food with the help of Cristiano. "Where's Gabriela?"

"She cut her finger. Raphael and Izzy took her home for the day. Why? You don't like me in an apron?" Seamus said with a sideways grin.

"You're a bit hairy for my taste," Liam said dryly. He took a sandwich and a cold milk, making short work of it as he sat with Adam and Alyssa. He was on edge because he could hear the demolition happening. The explosions that meant more of the rainforest was disappearing. He wondered, also, how the background music was affecting Izzy.

Jesus, he fucking hated himself right now. He really did. He excused himself, feeling tight and nervous. The need to get to Izzy was causing brain fry. The shit he'd said to her…it was unforgivable. He lashed out, trying to drive her away. He had, in fact, meant to behave unforgivably. As he walked the grounds, heading to the surgery, he tried to think about the precise moment that he'd fallen in love with her. Wanting her? That was easy. Right out of the starting gate, when he'd seen her in the shower. The sight of all that skin and curve and beautiful woman? He'd have to be dead not to have felt that attraction. But sex wasn't love.

Had it been when she saved Estela? When she'd taken Genoveva under her wing? He thought back over the last couple of months and decided that it wasn't one thing. It was the totality of this woman. The chance to know her day to day. Her talent, her sense of humor, her passion. She'd seeped into his system day by day, penetrating the wall that he'd built around himself little by little. But the defining moment, when he'd realized the depths of his feelings, was when she'd defended Eve. The respect she'd paid her. *Don't you dare take that away from her! She earned the right to be called a hero.* And when the wanting got too much to bear, and he'd succumbed to his attraction, she'd given him all of herself. Something, admittedly, she didn't do lightly.

The thing that was driving him right now was not forgiveness. She'd probably never forgive him. He just didn't want her leaving with the idea that she hadn't meant anything to him. She didn't know that he loved her. She'd looked him right in the eye, and admitted that she loved him, knowing that he wasn't going to return the sentiment.

When he walked into the surgery, no one was around. He looked on the patient board. The last person she'd treated before Gabriela had been Emilio, for a lip laceration this morning. An hour later, Gabriela had come in and she had a treatment time of ten minutes. That must have been when they drove her back home. He looked at his watch. It was one o'clock. She'd been gone for over three hours.

Genoveva interrupted his train of thought by walking in and looking around. "Are ye looking for Izzy?"

She shook her head, "No, Dr. O'Brien. Emilio. He has disappeared. He didn't come to school after he left the hospital."

"Did you check his room? Maybe he didn't feel well."

"Sim. He's nowhere in the school or orphanage. That is why we are looking other places."

"Is it possible he went to the village with Izzy and Raphael? I know he has friends there."

"No, medíco. I saw them leave. He wasn't with them. I helped them pack some supplies that they were going to give to the villagers."

A pang of irritation hit Liam, out of pure male instinct. She should have told someone if she was going to stay gone. It wasn't like her. She stressed teamwork. At least she had until he'd taken a wrecking ball to the work environment around here. *Shit.*

"Well, I'm sure she's just busy at the village," he said, more to make himself feel better than anyone. "Let's look for the lad. He's probably trying to hide from English lessons."

Izzy saw the men at the same time Raphael did. She grabbed her sheathed tanto knife that was between the seat and her thigh, clipping it into the back of her pants as she unbuckled her seat belt. *Holy hell!* Her body was screaming. That rollover was going to hurt later. The seatbelt felt like it had grown into the muscles of her chest and abdomen. They were less likely to search her for weapons. They both started scrambling out of the Jeep. The equipment was scattered. Raphael's day pack had been tossed out of the vehicle, too far to reach. "Look for a weapon, brother." She whispered the words as the men raised their guns, smug grins on their faces. It was three of the men from that day at the village. They'd been missing during the latest altercation on the river, probably hiding out due to the shooting. Izzy's heart rate soared. *We are so screwed.* An image of Raphael dancing with his sons blasted through her head. This was her fault. She'd gotten sloppy in the head and walked right into this.

The man she knew to be Emilio's father spoke in angry tones to Raphael as he waved his rifle around. The other men had pistols in their hands, ready for some dirty deeds. She caught bits and pieces. *Do exército...narcóticos.* Holy shit. This wasn't about her. It was about him. She'd dragged him into the jungle to work for her. He'd left his safe job as a cab driver to interpret, and as it turned out, help protect her in this dangerous place. And someone had recognized him.

She listened as he grew angrier. "They blame us for the police and military patrolling the area. And for the seizure of the cocaine." As he translated, the man grew irritated. Probably because they didn't speak English and didn't know what Raphael and Izzy were saying. He butted Raphael across the jaw with his rifle as the others drew closer.

That's right assholes. Get in nice and close, Izzy thought. This was not intimidation. They were going to shoot them in the head and let the ants have them. Whether they were following orders from their boss, or they were rogue, they were going to kill them. They had to fight or she was never going to see her parents again. Never see Liam again.

Raul gave her an overly familiar up and down. Then he said something that needed no translation. His eyes said it all. He was going to get some alone time with the female doctor before he killed her. *How about hell no?* She thought. She was going to rip this guy's balls off if he took them out of his pants anywhere near her.

It happened almost in slow motion. Raphael was down on one knee, having been struck. He spat the blood out of his mouth and nodded at Izzy. Then he swung his free leg around. Izzy drew the knife as she watched him sweep the legs out from under his assailant. The man landed on his back as the rifle blared out a series of shots in the air. That's when Izzy felt the sting in her right arm. Right after she stuck the knife in the other guy's side. A quick jab while he was distracted. Then she brought the tanto blade down like a meat cleaver, right on his wrist. He dropped the gun and screeched in agony. She heard the third man fire a shot off. Not sure at who, but she brought the pistol up off the ground with her left hand and shot twice, tap tap, and saw one connect with the center of his chest. She turned the pistol on the other two men. One whimpering as he watched the blood gush out of his hand. Then she saw Raphael, rifle pointed at Emilio's father. The man was doing some sort of begging in Portuguese.

"Don't shoot him. Please, Raphael. The threat is over." She went to the man she'd shot in the chest and he was gasping, the gurgling sound of his punctured lung wheezing out of his chest. She took his weapon from the ground as well. When she turned around, she got a better look at her friend. "Oh, Jesus Raphael. You're hit!"

"I'm okay, boss. I swear it. I need you to find my toolbox. Now, Izzy." He was straining with the effort of staying upright. She looked at the crash scene with fresh eyes. The back of the Jeep was demolished. The tire was gone and there was gnarled metal where the rear panel used to be. Their supplies were strewn everywhere, even though they'd strapped it all down. Maybe that was a good thing. Thrown clear was better than burned and ruined. The first thing she saw was her trauma kit, bundled into a portable case. Thank God. Then she saw the metal box that contained his tools. "Get the duct tape and as many ties as you can find. You know, the plastic ties that lock into place?"

His voice was different, almost distorted. He was in major pain, but he was keeping it together. "Cable ties, got em! And a roll of duct tape." She knew where this was headed. She set the pistols near his feet. "If they budge, then shoot them."

One by one she quickly used the cable ties. First wrists, then ankles. Then the duct tape. Because she wasn't a masochist, she taped the one with the wrist hanging on by a thread differently. She positioned him so that he was sitting up against a tree. She put his arms over his head, to help with the bleeding. Then she proceeded to tape him by his biceps, tightly to the tree. He looked ridiculous, but she might actually be saving the fucker's life. Then she taped their mouths shut.

"Izzy, we need to go!" She grabbed all the supplies she could carry, then tried to take the rifle from him. "Wait, I need a moment." Then he walked up to Raul, the only one out of the five that wasn't injured, and rifle-butted him right in the forehead.

"We need to go to the east. It's not safe the other way. We must go east and travel off the road. If anyone heard the guns firing, they'll come. We don't want to be here when they do, Izzy. This is an illegal road. The only ones who use this road are more like them."

His accent was so pronounced, and he'd slipped into half Portuguese, but she caught his meaning. She put one pistol in his day pack and one in her pants, and they spirited away into the jungle. Her last thought was, *why the hell didn't you go back for that satellite phone.*

Liam knew something was wrong when he saw Genoveva's face. She was terrified and so angry, she looked downright dangerous. Bracketed between her and Paolo was Emilio, who had a swollen, stitched up mouth, and was crying inconsolably. Apparently they'd found him hiding in Paolo's shed. The girl was screeching as she waved her hands in the air, the tears starting in earnest.

"Calm down, lass. I can't understand you. Slow down and tell me what's happened." That's when Paolo interjected in his broken English. "The medíca. He sent her into the forest."

"What the hell do you mean? On the boat? They took the boat out alone?"

He asked the boy. "No Senhor. The Jeep. Down one of the illegal roads."

The terror washed the blood out of Liam's brain. He grabbed the boy. "Why? Why did they go?" The boy winced and groaned, even though Liam knew he hadn't hurt him. "Are you injured?" The boy was curling into his side and he coughed, wincing again. That's when Liam let him go and lifted his shirt. "Jesus Christ. He's been beaten." Liam scooped the boy up and started toward the hospital. "Get Adam to the first floor, stat!"

He took the boy into the surgery, which was the closest room with a bed when they entered from the garden side. He laid him down, and the boy sobbed. "Get Sister Maria in here. I need to make sure I understand him!" But as soon as he said it, she was there with Seamus beside her.

She leaned over the boy, getting the full account. Her face paled. "It was his father who beat him. He approached him several days ago.

Asked him to help get the doctor and Raphael to come down the new road. To make up a story as to why," She stopped, listening. "As to why they needed a surgeon. He told Emilio that they wanted morphine, that they weren't going to hurt them, but he didn't believe him. When the boy didn't bring them, his father took him at the village. Early this morning, he was walking to meet a friend halfway. Raul grabbed him, demanded that he help them. He didn't want to do it, so his father beat him. Then he told Emilio that he'd burn the orphanage and the abbey down while we slept." The boy hiccuped as he hyperventilated. "Oh, Emilio. Why didn't you come to me?" She said sadly.

Genoveva was crying in the corner, hugging herself and rocking. When the boy answered, the sister said, "He said he'd kill all of the children. All of the sisters. Even him." She leaned and kissed the boy's head, soothing him. Adam came in and started quickly assessing him.

Liam was about to go completely mental. "You can't take him until we find out exactly where he sent them. You are going to have to treat him here." Adam, nodded as he went to work. Liam turned to Alyssa. "Go tell the abbess to call the police and the military contact that Raphael left." Then he turned to Seamus. "Call Antonio. We need a surgeon on standby. We have no idea…" his voice cracked as fear seized up his throat.

"It's done, Liam. And don't you dare feckin' leave without me." As if he knew that as soon as he got a bead on where Izzy was, he was out of here. He would not wait for the authorities to gather a team. He watched as Seamus ran to the main desk of the hospital, grabbing the phone to call out.

Sister Maria continued. "It's a new road, cut to the east of the village. It goes deep into the bush. The entrance is at the mouth of the big river, about a kilometer east of the last homes. Okay, Emilio, I hear you." She looked at Liam, her eyes destroyed. "He said this is his only family. He had to protect his family. He is so sorry."

Liam looked down at the boy, now stripped to his undergarments. He was covered in bruises. He'd obviously hidden them from Izzy. Genoveva had told him that the boy claimed the lip injury was sustained from a football to the face. Had told Izzy that he wasn't hurt anywhere else. The man had beaten his back, chest, abdomen, and what looked like a shoe mark on his left hip, all covered by his clothes. He couldn't believe the boy had been able to stand, let alone walk back and forth to the village. But then again, there had been a history of abuse. He knew this from the boy's intake records. He'd come to St. Clare's because after beating him half to death, his father had abandoned him. It was a neighbor who'd brought him to St. Clare's.

Seamus came back into the room at the same time the Reverend Mother made an appearance. She crossed herself. "Oh, my sweet boy. Emilio," the tears choked off her words. She looked at Liam. "Raphael's reserve unit is calling everyone in unofficially. They'll be here within the hour. The police are sending another group."

Seamus added, "Antonio will be here in fifteen. He's off rotation today. He said he wants to come with us."

Liam looked at his old friend. Her wise eyes torn apart with regret. "Liam, you need to wait. Don't run off half-cocked."

"She could be dead if I wait. I'm going and I'm taking the Land Cruiser."

Paolo spoke up, having listened as the drama unfolded. "I will drive."

The abbess threw her hands up. "Deliver me from pigheaded men!"

"I have to go. I can't lose her. I will not sit here and wait for news. Tell the police and the military that the three of us will be out there already. We don't want them getting trigger happy." As he turned to leave, the boy said, "They want the man. Her man, Raphael. They want to make sure he come with her." His words were muffled from his fat lip, but he was concentrating hard on speaking English.

Liam thought about who they were dealing with, and what Raphael had done in the military. Jesus, maybe they'd used Izzy to get to Raphael. Two birds. One stone. He turned to leave and Genoveva was in his face. "I go with you. I can fight! I want to go!" She was hysterical, her face drenched with tears. He shook his head and she cut him off, "Strong is the new skinny! I am strong! I want to go! I will fight for her!"

He took her face in his hands, trying to calm her hysterics. "You are strong, sweet girl. So strong. You have to stay and help with the police. I need you to help protect the sisters and the children. You have to stay, lass. Izzy would want you safe. She loves you." His voice broke on that last sentence. "She loves you, Genoveva. I can't take you with me."

Her face crinkled in on itself, her tears flowing. He kissed her on the forehead, then they were gone.

27

"Friendship is unnecessary, like philosophy, like art.... It has no survival value; rather it is one of those things which give value to survival."

C.S. Lewis

"Y ou're bleeding badly, Raphael. We have to stop and look at that wound." He grunted a no, barely able to keep himself moving. "Okay, He-Man. I am bleeding badly. I need to look at my own wound!" she said pissily.

He stopped abruptly, taking her in. He hadn't even realized she was hit. She had blood dripping off her fingertips, starting in the upper portion of her right arm. She sat immediately, finding a mossy rock that didn't have any ugly looking bugs on it. "I can't keep carrying this rifle. We'll have to make do with the pistols." She opened the trauma kit, pulling out a tourniquet. Then she looked at the wound. It was bleeding like crazy, but she didn't think she'd been hit in the brachial artery. She was having mobility issues, however. She put the tourniquet back into the bag, pushing away the stabbing fear of losing her most important surgical tool. Her ability to use her right arm. She'd try to stop the bleeding without resorting to the tourniquet. She needed to keep some circulation going. "I need as much pressure on this as I can stand." She poured some sort of brown liquid over the area and hissed. "Holy shit, that hurts." The rain drizzled lightly around them, as they were covered by the canopy, and it felt good as the sweat broke out on her face. "You need to help me. Once I get this bleeding stopped, I'll take care of you. You need me not to pass out right now. That's the only reason I'm going first. Do you understand?" He said nothing, so she looked up.

He got down on his knees. "I'm sorry, Izzy. They recognized me. This is my doing."

"We are out here because I didn't listen to you. If anyone is to blame, it's me. Look at me!" His eyes snapped up. "We need to move. You are very pale. It looks like the bullet went right through your spleen and out the back. I need to treat us both."

As she bandaged her arm, she let him help her. "Tighter. I can't elevate and use direct pressure. We have to keep moving. I need the bandage tight. Press on the wound as you wrap. Ignore my reaction and just do it."

He did it, and Izzy ground her molars as he pressed on the entrance and exit wounds. Her body trembled, sweat breaking out all over her. "Don't stop. You're doing great."

Once he'd secured the bandage, she made him lay flat on the forest floor. "Lay down. I need to see what we are dealing with."

She examined him, did some calculations on his body weight versus his frighteningly low blood pressure. Then she cleaned the wounds and watched as the blood flowed out of him. His belly was tender and rigid. He was in good shape, so she didn't know how rigid compared to normal. The real answer was that he was bleeding out. She ran an IV, giving him fluids, but that wasn't going to replace his blood loss. She was already starting to feel the effects of that blast and the death grip of the seatbelt as it dug into her body. She could see the bruises already forming on Raphael as well. But the priority was the gunshot wound in his abdomen. If they made it through this, they were going to have to be checked head to toe, including a scan for concussion damage and hearing loss. She had a bump and shallow cut on her scalp, from God knows what, hitting her from the airborne supplies. She grabbed the gauze, packing it on both sides and wrapping him. "Okay, that will do for now. We need to put some miles between us and that Jeep." She unloaded the rifle and hid the magazine under a bush. Then she put the rifle in another spot under some foliage.

Raphael was sweating and his color wasn't good, but he got off the ground by sheer will alone. He checked his compass on his watch. "This way. About ten kilometers if I am correct." They started again, and something niggled at her. If they started looking for them, they'd never look in this area. They were way east of the small river that they normally took to the village. Probably a deliberate move to isolate them somewhere that no one would look. *Emilio.* That's how they'd done this. She thought of the split lip and somehow couldn't manage to hate the little shit. He'd obviously been coerced. That wasn't the worst part. "He's not going to tell them where we went. There was no jaguar attack. Emilio isn't going to send anyone. We're on our own. Even if they miss us, they'll never come this way."

"I know," he said grimly.

"I won't let you bleed to death. I promise you. You will not die today. Do you understand?" She looked at her watch. It was quarter past one. Still plenty of daylight. The problem was that they were injured and this jungle was thick. She kept tripping and getting scratched on the vines and brush. They couldn't go back to the road, though. This ten kilometers would easily take them until tomorrow at this pace.

As she tripped once more, catching herself on a tree, she swore as she scraped her hand on the bark. They couldn't do this all day. Then a thought pierced her conscious mind like it had been shot out of the clouds, into the top of her brain. She was lying next to Cora, the moonlight lighting up her face. *You must follow the river. Eve said, when the time comes, you must remember to follow the river. It's important. She wouldn't have come to me otherwise.* Then Alanna's intense, green gaze. *If she told you something, she did it for a reason. You heed what she said. You bet your life on it.*

"Raphael, on the map, we were between two rivers. How far is the one to the east?" He grunted as he stopped, taking a labored breath. He was in so much pain, but she couldn't medicate him. Even if they weren't moving, she didn't have any narcotics in her trauma kit. They carried limited morphine in the mobile unit and some oral pain meds. She didn't have anything like that. All she had were two bags of saline that she'd salvaged from the debris and her trauma kit. She knew at some point, she was going to have to do a field transfusion, but she needed to get them to that river first. The chances of being spotted by a fisherman or someone from one of the villages was way stronger. A boat would be fantastic right now.

"It is about two kilometers east." She nodded. "Okay, set your compass for southeast. We'll keep heading down as we try to meet the river."

"That's farther away from the village!"

"I know, but you are going to have to trust me on this. We can skirt the river and we might run into a fisherman. We've got the pistols if it's not friendlies. You just have to trust me on this. We need to follow the river."

The three men started north from the village. Emilio's second-hand directions had been mostly accurate but the road hadn't been in plain sight. The tire tracks from the Jeep were what led them there. The ground was soft from the rain, and the treads were more obvious, the closer they'd come to the river bank. As they headed up the road, Liam prayed like hell that the God he'd been raised to believe in was listening. They'd been on shaky ground since Eve's death, but there were no atheists in a foxhole, so he prayed like he'd never prayed before. Seamus put a hand on his shoulder. "We'll find them. There are only so many places that Jeep will go."

"You're assuming they're still in the Jeep." Liam's tone was clipped. They followed what could barely be called a road. Just wide enough to get one vehicle through. They probably used it to haul product to the river. A boat waiting to take it downriver. The boat traffic would become higher as the rainy season started. They needed a route inland that was better concealed and wasn't being patrolled.

They were going in blind. They had no idea where the road led to, but given the corruption that went on in the police and military, the bribes that were taken, he wasn't sure who to trust. And their response time was simply not good enough. He wouldn't wait. He looked at his feet, where on the ground lay the machete that Paolo had given him from the garden shed. They also had a good amount of medical supplies, some provisions like bottled water and electrolyte sports drinks. Horrible for day to day, but good for emergencies. If all had gone well, they'd come to the East side of the village and find them there unharmed. But he knew in his gut that wasn't the case. Either Fuentes or someone in his organization had planned this. Planned for what? He didn't know. His heart lurched in his throat at the slide-show of horrible possibilities that ran through his brain.

As if reading his mind, Seamus said. "I'm going to be honest with you, Liam. I'm scared out of my bloody mind right now. I'm afraid of what those men are capable of."

"Aye, I know. But they don't know our Izzy. And the two of them together? They're going to dread the day they fucked with those two." He said it with more bravado than he felt. "And they're going to pay in blood, my brother. If they've harmed a hair on her head, they will pay."

Paolo grunted his approval. "This medíca, she is um guerreira. She will fight." *A warrior.*

About nine kilometers into the forest, the smell hit them. Something had burned in this area. "I smell it, keep going." Liam took the weapon in his hand, ready to jump out of the front seat. The first sign that something was wrong was a jug of water from the hospital supplies. It was right in the middle of the road. They came over a crest and Liam opened the door before Paolo had even stopped the vehicle. "No, no, no!" He yelled as he ran. The Jeep was upright but had obviously rolled. Their supplies were everywhere. The rear, driver side panel was completely mangled, the tire blown completely off.

"Where the fuck are they?" He was out of his head with panic. Then he noticed that Seamus and Paolo were stopped; staring to the left. Liam was almost too afraid to look until he saw Seamus lift the machete and start stalking toward the trees. That's when he shifted his gaze and saw them.

One man was dead from what looked like a gunshot wound to the chest. One was trussed up like fresh kill, his arms above his head. His hand was almost severed off at the wrist, but he was alive. Then Liam saw the third. The only one who didn't seem to be gravely injured. Raul. Emilio's father. Liam yanked him by the hair, pulling him off the ground as he felt the tearing on the man's scalp. He squealed under the duct tape until Liam ripped it off, taking some facial hair with it. "Where are they? If you tell me, you may live through this."

The man snarled an obscenity in Portuguese and Liam pounded him in the side of the face with his fist. That's when the first vehicle showed up. He threw the man on the ground as he turned to face the new arrivals. "Fuentes," he said under his breath.

The men with Fuentes pointed their weapons. "Não!" he barked. "Suficiente!" Fuentes got out of the vehicle and stood within striking distance of the three men. *Pretty ballsy*, Liam thought with grudging respect.

Liam pointed the machete in his hand to the Jeep. "Where are the female doctor and her interpreter?"

Fuentes looked at the mess, then at Raul. "You imbecile." Then he looked at Liam. "This man left my employment three days ago. I had nothing to do with this. We heard the explosion and thought someone was logging." He looked over at the dead man. "Did you do this?"

"No, we found them like this. That one is close to death as well. This little piece of shit is uninjured other than getting clocked a good one."

He went back, yanked his hair until he bowed backward. "Where are they?" The man said nothing. "I will kill him right in front of you if I have to," Liam said to the bossman.

Fuentes shrugged. "Go ahead. He's nothing to me. He's a liability. I would never have authorized this. I am a businessman!"

"Why should I believe you?" Liam snapped.

Fuentes raised a brow. "Because if I was responsible for this, you'd already be dead, Senhor." He walked to the military-style vehicle and got back in. "Good luck, medíco. It seems this woman doctor of yours is a worthy opponent. If we find her, you have my word that we will do what we can to get her and her companion to the hospital." Raul yelled at him as they started to leave. The polished, older man said something back, and his tone was deadly.

Liam turned to Paolo, because the man's Columbian accent and deep tone lost some of the translation. "What did he say?"

"He told him that if we don't kill him, he will do it."

Seamus went to the man with the lacerated wrist, checking his pulse at his neck. Then he started working to get the man free. "She didn't waste any medical supplies on them. Good girl. Her trauma kit and Raphael's backpack are missing." He pulled the man up to him, nose to nose. He said, in better Portuguese than Liam possessed, "I will save you if you tell me which way they went." The man's head lolled to one side as he moaned. "He's barely hanging on." He got the smelling salts out of his bag, cracked it, and held it under the piece of shit's nose. The man stirred quickly. "Which way?"

Liam turned his attention back to Raul. He grabbed him by the shoulders and kneed him right in the balls. The man doubled over, hands and feet still bound, and fell face first to the ground. "I will eventually get this out of you. You decide how bad I hurt you."

That's when the next vehicle pulled up. Apparently, Raphael's friends worked fast. It wasn't the police. It was the Brazilian Army unit that had kept in contact with him about the evolving problem with the drug cartel. Paolo went to the group of eight hard-looking men. He briefed them and they immediately walked to the two men who were still alive. The officer in charge pressed a rifle barrel to Raul's forehead. Liam stepped in and looked at the man. "This one is mine. The woman he attacked is my...amor. Compreendo? He is mine." The man stepped back, giving a respectful nod. "Sim, senhor. It is your right."

Then Liam walked behind the asshole. With swift motions, he used the machete to cut the ties off of him. Then he cast the blade out of reach. The man scurried to his feet just as Liam hit the motherfucker with everything he had. The man stood up and dove at him, but no one intervened. This guy was his. Liam was twice his size, and before he could decide whether to shit or go sailing, Liam had him on his back, sitting on his chest with his hand around his throat. "Which way did they go and how injured are they?"

The man laughed. He actually laughed. Liam could tell he was jonesing. Being tied up, he hadn't had a snort in a while. "We shot them both. They will be dead before nightfall. The forest will kill them if they don't bleed to death." Liam understood him perfectly, a sudden clarity coming back to him. No need to translate that one.

"All that means is that you got bested by a girl. An unarmed, injured girl, you little pussy." Then he punched him again, not caring that the man couldn't understand him. Some of the soldiers obviously knew English, because the laughter rolled through the group. The next hit was even harder. He pulled the man up and got in his face. "That one was for Emilio." Then he let the guy lay there as he caught his breath.

The officer in charge went to the man that Seamus was treating. The man was in terrible pain, so he knelt down in front of him and said something about narcotics. Then he looked up at Seamus. "I assured him that if he told us everything, you'd give him something for the pain."

"Oh, yes. Absolutely." *Absolutely not*, thought Seamus as he wrapped the man's wrist tightly with a bandage. Bandages were one thing. He wasn't wasting the one vile of morphine they had with them on this dickhead. He didn't need to know that, however. The prospect of pain relief loosened the man's tongue. He explained that it was all Raul's idea. An attempt to get back in the good graces of the boss. They'd take out a drug enforcement officer, scare the mission into staying away by killing the female doctor. There was a fight, and he knows they both got hit, but he doesn't know who fired which shot.

He was wheezing by the end, and Seamus saw that not only did someone cleave his wrist, but they stabbed him in the side. It wasn't deep or fatal, but someone had gotten him good. "Who stabbed you?"

One word. *Medíca.* "That's my girl," Seamus said. The pride battling with the fear so that the tears pricked his eyes.

Liam looked back at Raul, and the man just had to pop off one more stupid comment. Like he knew he had nothing to lose. He'd either die now or die at the hands of his boss for causing this mess. He was banking on Liam being more merciful. *Fat fucking chance, shitbird.*

"You are a medíco. You don't have it in you to kill. Just like that little bitch. Even after we shot her she still let us live. You medícos are as bad as those nuns with your vows."

Liam got the healer gene from his mother, and if that was all there truly was to him, then he'd have to agree. But there was another half to him. The old bloodline of men who would do anything to protect their mate...or avenge her. He brought forth the word he'd been so afraid of, so ashamed to utter. Not about Eve, but about his beloved Izzy. "You tried to kill my mate. Luckily the O'Brien men have their own oaths." He punched him again, ringing the guy's bell until all he could do was groan, slack-jawed and bleeding. When Liam looked up, that's when he saw it. His gaze locked on that tell-tale mound at the base of a nearby tree. The bullet ants ebbing and flowing in the dirt. Beating the guy unconscious would be letting him off easy. He needed to die slowly, and in as much pain as possible.

Seamus watched as Liam went to the vehicle, stopping the punches long enough to take out a...Gatorade? Like he needed a drink? Seamus said urgently, "Liam, think before you do this. Let the authorities handle them!"

Liam turned on him as he poured the sugary drink all over the man on the ground, pressing his foot into his chest to keep him in place. "You said it yourself. Some things are too personal to leave to someone else." Then he dragged the man over to the tree, dropped him, and stomped the nest with his boot before Seamus could fully grasp what he was doing. "Perhaps we'll let the forest kill you as well. A fitting death, I think," he hissed in the man's face as the ants poured over him. The screams pierced the forest air, birds fleeing from their tree branches and calling out warnings to the sky. Then the man screamed no more.

Liam turned to the commander. "East. They likely started that way and then went south. You can call an ambulance for that one if you need to. I'm finished with them." He didn't break eye contact with the man.

He just nodded. "I will tell them that the poor man fell into the ant pile while he...what do you call it? Resisted, yes." He gave the one living man an appraising look, calling to one of his own men to get an ambulance to the area. He was leverage against Fuentes, so they needed him alive. Then he looked back at Liam. "Sim, south. We'll radio the polícia and get more people here. We'll get boats on the river as well. In case they doubled back to the west and headed toward the river."

When the time comes, you must go to the river. That didn't make sense, though. Not after they'd been accosted the last time they went. "How many rivers are within walking distance? Are there any others besides this one to the west?"

"No, Izzy. You cannot. This will weaken you." Raphael pulled his arm away as she tried to insert the needle. Her field transfusion apparatus was his only hope. The first saline bag was empty, hanging off the top of his backpack. Izzy looked at him. "I will not leave you. This will weaken me a little, but it will strengthen you." What she wouldn't give for an xStat right now, but the Navy Seal who'd invented the damn thing hadn't been able to get FDA approval. A syringe that pumped small sponges into the wound, stopping the bleeding in the field. She'd only read about them, but she'd try anything if it was an alternative to what she was doing now. Packing that wound with gauze had caused him to put a stick in his mouth and bite down as he growled in pain.

They couldn't move and do this. She'd made it to the river where they found a cleared bit of bank on which to sit. This river was smaller than the one they took up to the village. Only about fifty feet across. Still plenty of room for snakes and man-eating reptiles and fish to flourish. It was clipping along, and she wished like anything they had a raft or something that would help them ride the rapid without getting eaten. As it was, they were both a bloody, leaking mess. Perfect bait for some black caiman to sniff her out and bite her in the ass.

She cleaned her arm first, putting the donor needle into the juicy vein in her left arm. She fumbled, clumsy. Her hand was tingling from the wound in her arm. The realization that she'd be lucky to live through this helped quell the fear of permanent nerve and muscle damage. Her career with the scalpel was the least of her worries if she was dead.

She watched the blood drain into the transfusion bag, ready to roll right out the other side. There was a whole lot of science involved in blood matching. Reactions could happen even if the blood was compatible on paper. But when it came down to life and death, an O neg donor was a universal blood donor, which meant she could transfuse Raphael patient-to-patient. If she got through this, she was seriously going to have to rethink that job in Denver. That hospital had been the one to donate the military grade trauma kits. She cleaned off Raphael's arm next. "Izzy, are you sure this is safe? You are injured! You've lost blood too."

"You are not going to bleed to death on my watch. Do you understand?" Then he felt the pinch. She disconnected the end that was stuck in her arm, having filled the bag with a pint of her blood. Then she used the second saline bag on herself. She rigged the blood bag on his pack, making sure the blood was flowing steadily into him. Then she attached the saline bag to her bra strap with a cable tie. "We need to keep moving, brother."

28

Paolo was going to need to make some serious repairs to the suspension and alignment after this trip. Neither of them said a word. The Army men started in the forest on foot as they sped for their boat that was docked at the village. They'd cut across the Amazon River, going east about three kilometers, to the mouth of the small tributary. The remote tendril of the sprawling Rio Puraquequara. Seamus relayed their intentions to the abbey from the satellite phone. He didn't mention the fate of Emilio's father. After seeing the boy, beaten horribly, he'd made a sort of peace with what Liam had done. The man had fully intended to murder Izzy and Raphael. The roadside explosives hadn't done the trick, so they'd shot them both. It was amazing that they'd managed to get the upper hand…but then, he'd seen them fight. *Strong is the new skinny.* He thought. *God, please let that be enough.* She was smart. They both were and Raphael knew this forest. They'd stay alive. They had to. He kept praying as the raced for the boat, ready to start checking the river. For some reason, Liam felt they'd go toward the river.

Paolo steered the boat upriver, hoping like hell that it didn't start raining again. They were traveling upriver, and he didn't need any more drag on this boat. "What you did, Senhor. It was a sin, yes?" Liam's eyes burned, feeling the aftereffects of a whole lot of rage. He'd lost one woman to violence and had not been the one to take the life of the man responsible. Tadgh had done it, to save his own life, so he could live with it. But there had been only him in that moment. The man who had so eagerly been willing to snuff her life out. Being with Izzy Collier was as close to heaven as Liam was ever going to get. And the man had tried to kill her. So Liam had done the only thing he could, and he'd live with it.

"Sim, Paolo. It was a sin. And if I see him in hell, I'll do it all over again."

Paolo grunted, understanding in his old, wise eyes. "There are no sins that God does not forgive, my brother. But you would not have forgiven yourself, I think, if you had not avenged our medíca."

A sob boiled up in Liam's throat and he choked it down. "She's alive Paolo. I know it as well as I know that I still breathe. I feel it."

Eve, if you've got any pull up there, please help her. The guilt he'd felt over Eve was gone, like a fog that had finally blown out to sea. She'd come to him twice. She'd come to Cora. *When the time comes, you must go to the river.* So here he was. The police were headed up the other river, toward the indigenous tribal village. Checking the river for any signs that they'd crossed back over and tried to follow the familiar path. His search party had stayed east of the road. Raphael's comrades on foot, the rookie patrol on the boat that served as a floating clinic. Someone was going to find them.

Izzy stopped again, so tired that she needed to take a rest. They'd ditched Raphael's bag, transferring all of the supplies to the one that contained the trauma kit. One knife was kept, two power bars, a bottle of water, and a headlamp. The saline was gone. Almost all of the gauze was gone, too, because she'd had to pack and wrap Raphael's wound. She'd also had to change her bandage, as it was no longer absorbing, and she was leaving a small trail of blood. Manageable, but she couldn't keep leaking like this if she was going to be draining out of the other arm.

Once her bandage was changed, she looked at her partner's abdomen. There was a lot of blood. All down his pants on both sides and in his shoe. She repacked it with the last of the gauze and bound him as tight as she could around the abdomen. Then she set up the transfusion kit again.

He was too weak to fight her. "No, amiga. You cannot spare this for me. Please." His English was thickly accented like he was barely able to keep up the effort of sounding out the words.

She got face to face with him and smiled, trying to act braver than she was. "Amigos share everything. I wouldn't give it to you if I thought it would kill me." Not completely true. She'd been tracking his blood loss, not her own so much. It didn't matter. She was strong and healthy and her injuries were minor compared to his. As minor as a bullet hole could be. She'd just given herself a whole bag of saline. Her blood pressure was way below normal, but she could do this.

She took big gulps of water as she watched the bag fill up again. She was getting fuzzy, but not so much that she'd pass out. She had no idea how far they'd walked. If she could guess, she'd say maybe three kilometers. Only seven more to go. She closed her eyes, fighting the wave of panic. It was completely possible that despite her best efforts, Raphael was going to die. She let him sip a little water, but that was it. No food. Abdominal wounds were tricky. Nothing by mouth if you could avoid it. She sat still, willing the bag to fill quickly so that she could give him what he needed. When it was finished, she set the bag on the log next to him and opened his line. She walked to the river's edge, needing to wash the sweat off her face. The rain had stopped, and the temperature had risen. She loved the feel of the water on her face. If there were pesticides, parasites, and pollution in this water, she didn't want to know.

She thought about that night in the shower, when Liam had so gently washed her. Leaned her back and shampooed her hair. As his face came to her, she knelt at the riverside and wept. It was a stress response that she was going to allow herself, a moment of indulgence that would inevitably steel her resolve for the rest of this journey. After a few minutes just letting her body weep into the river, she heard a stick crack. She thought it was Raphael. "Honey, don't stand. You need to lie still and save your strength." She was wiping her face on her shirt when she saw two bare feet standing before her. She went for her pistol until she saw the spear poised at the ready. She closed her eyes and sent up a message to God. *How about cutting me a break?*

She raised her eyes, hoping like hell that it was a tribesman she knew. She frowned. Nope. They were in traditional dress. Like, really traditional. Painted patterns on their skin, piercings, a red loincloth where some pants should be. She looked at the fierce-looking man, a warrior she guessed. Younger than the man behind him. His necklace was made of some sort of animal bones. At least she really freaking hoped it was animal bones. She didn't recognize any of the men that were currently staring at her.

She put her hands up. "Please, we just need help." Nothing. She tried in Portuguese, even though she was working at a first-grade level. She looked over at Raphael and he was in the same position, but barely. Looking at him through fresh eyes, she could see that he was not doing well. Lifting his arms was taking some effort. He spoke not to the stern looking man in front of her, but to the elder. It was some sort of dialect. She didn't know what they were saying, but then she heard it. Not from Raphael, but from the leader. "Anjo do Rio." Then he looked at her.

He approached, and Izzy tried to stay put, showing respect without fear. He touched her sun-kissed hair and fingered her curls. Then he called across the river. She hadn't noticed the others. They had three boats. Canoes that were roughly carved from a large tree. One of the men on the other side took a fishing net out of one of the boats and they started to bring them all across. The man was barking orders. That's when two men lifted Raphael and started carrying him to the boat. He gestured for Izzy to get in. She grabbed their supplies and didn't argue. "Obrigado. Oh God, thank you." The man nodded. Then he put a palm on her head. When she didn't understand him, she turned to Raphael.

"He said that you just need to follow the river." Then they pushed them adrift with a pair of rough paddles laying on the floor between them.

They began to float downriver at a brisk pace, the rain having sped up the current. Izzy said, "Don't paddle, brother. You'll screw up your needle site. We need to drift for a bit." She looked at him and he was so weak, he was starting to fade as the paddle lilted to the side. She made quick work of the transfusion kit. *Just a little more. Keep him awake.* Then she laid him flat, trying like hell not to tip the canoe over. She straddled his thighs, distributing her weight, and she pressed on his wound. He groaned. "We need to keep pressure on this again, now that you are horizontal. I'm sorry. I know you're in pain." He looked up and saw that she was draining another bag out of herself. "We're going to get home, Raphael. Then your wife can bake me a big chocolate cake with the local stuff. Pure Brazilian chocolate and sugar cane, none of that powdered, boxed crap. And we'll have a drink and laugh about this. Right?" The tears were a surprise. Raphael was a hard ass. The kind you could approve of because he used all of that toughness for something good. But she watched in surprise as a tear left the corner of his eye, running into his hairline. "You killed a jaguar for me, so now I let you go all vampire on me. Our relationship is give and take like that." She was babbling, she knew this. And she was really happy she wasn't walking because she was starting to feel really, really woozy.

"Can't this feckin' boat go any faster?" Liam snapped.

Paolo chastised him. "You look. We go too fast, you can't look." He pointed out to the river bank. He was right. This boat was chugging along. It wasn't a damned speedboat and they were going against the current. He scanned the front as Seamus kept his head on a swivel. He narrowed his eyes. "Watch that log, Paolo. Up ahead and to the right."

Paolo looked. "Barco!" Boat. It wasn't a log. It was a canoe. That's when Liam saw a small figure hunched down. Her hands over another figure. "It's her!"

Izzy looked up, and her eyes were blurry. She heard a boat approaching and all she could think of was that she wasn't going to get this far and have more goddamn drug dealers try to finish them off. She raised her pistol, taking one hand off of Raphael's wound. Then she heard his voice. His beautiful, baritone voice calling her name. "Liam," she croaked. She dropped the gun as it fell in the water. Her eyes focusing. *Oh, God. Seamus and Paolo.* "Liam." Her voice was a bit louder this time. They were pretty far downriver, but she knew the boat and the voices.

She tried to paddle but she couldn't because her right arm wasn't able to form a solid grip. It was numb. She started shaking. How could she be cold? It was so hot in Brazil.

They came alongside her and *splash*, someone was in the water. Then another splash following closely behind. Then there were strong arms pulling her out of the boat.

"Wait!" Seamus yelled. "Jesus, what the hell is this thing hooked to them both? It's a blood bag with two needles."

Liam pulled the needle out of Izzy's arm. "Oh, God. Izzy, how much did you give him?"

She was so tired, but she answered. "Enough to keep us both alive."

Raphael got a surge of strength, grabbing Liam's shirt. He almost tipped them. He pulled his face up to meet Liam's eyes. "É muito. Too much! Três! Too much, medíco!"

All of the blood ran out of Liam's head, starting to thunder through his heart. "Three bags? Jesus Christ, Izzy. Get them in the boat!" he screamed.

Izzy felt herself being lifted, then another pair of strong arms taking her. She looked at his face. "Paolo, I'm really glad to see you."

29

Liam and Seamus started working to get the field transfusion kit set up. There was one in every trauma kit, thank God. And thank the baby Jesus that he was O-negative. He could replace what she'd so willingly given to another. Two sticks in the arm and they were linked.

"He needs it more. He's bleeding badly. I think the bullet nicked his spleen. Please, treat him first." That's what she'd meant to say, but her tongue wasn't working so well.

"Shut up, woman. Just be still. Antonio is waiting at the dock to care for him. Lie back, Izzy. You are going to black out if we don't get some fluids in you. Let Seamus take a look at your arm, darlin'."

They were clipping along, going with the current. Liam reclined next to her, pulling her close and letting his body heat warm her. She was like ice and shivering. She was so pale, she almost looked grey. But that's what happens when you lose too much blood.

Seamus hissed. "Right through the bicep. Looks like it missed the artery but it's still bleeding. Probably due to the exertion. Jesus Christ, her blood pressure's in the basement! It's worse than his!" Because she was smaller. Izzy looked at Liam. His face was desperate.

"Stay with me, mo ghrá. Please." That was the last thing she heard before she blacked out.

"Izzy! Wake up! Seamus, she's not responding!"

"She's going into shock. Where is that fucking dock, Paolo? Liam, keep her warm and just keep that blood coming. The saline and blood are the priority. I'm more worried about organ damage than her being awake. Just keep those needles right where they are and bleed for her." He cursed again. "Come on Izzy, get that pulse steady. Please, darling. Don't break our hearts." Seamus's voice broke.

Take it all. I will give you every drop. Please don't leave me, Liam thought. The thought of it made his mind just splinter down the middle as the cry ripped from his throat. "Noooooo, Izzy! You can't leave me!" He pulled her up to his face, her head falling back limply. "No!" The word was like a wounded animal, so loud and anguished that Seamus's body hair stood up on end. He looked down at Raphael, and the man's face was in utter despair. Paolo was praying steadily as he steered the boat, to some saint or maybe to God himself. It was a constant whisper that was at odds with the battle cry that ripped from Liam's chest.

"I will follow you! Do you hear me? I will not stay here without you! Izzy! Wake up goddammit!"

Liam felt the pull on him. Someone trying to separate him from Izzy. "No! She needs my blood! I can't leave her!"

And this is why doctors don't treat people they love, thought Seamus. He got in Liam's grill. "We are here, Liam. We need to get them to the hospital!"

Antonio pulled the needle out of his arm, setting the bag of blood on Izzy's chest as he lifted her. He was mumbling in Italian. "Bella. Oh sweet Izzy."

Liam didn't wait to argue. He got in the backseat of Antonio's Land Rover with her as they loaded Raphael into the other vehicle. Liam briefed him on both patients as he tore ass through the small road that led west to the abbey. "Her injury is not the issue. It's not life-threatening. But she did three field transfusions to keep Raphael going. She's in shock, Antonio. She gave him too much!"

Antonio peeled into the hospital without responding. Then the hatch flew open and Liam was running with her into the surgery.

Antonio tried to work but Liam was out of his head. "She needs more blood. Hook me back up!"

"She has banked blood in the cooler. You need to get out of my way, Liam!" Antonio turned to Seamus and Adam. "Get him out of here, I need to work!"

Alyssa was crying softly. "Tell me what to do."

His words were militant, controlled. His accent with its smooth words and rolling Rs sounded more like an Italian General, clipped and precise. "The ambulance should be here in a matter of minutes. They need to go to the big hospital. I need help. I can't operate on both of them. She's going into hypovolemic shock. She needs blood. Get me a thermal blanket." He turned to Margaritte. "Go to the lab and bring me the O neg with the letter *I* on it. She banked her own blood for transfusions. Send one of the sisters to meet the ambulance." He leaned down and brushed Izzy's hair back. Then his voice was soft and gentle. "Don't leave us, darling Izzy. Please."

Seamus and Adam restrained Liam against the wall as he thrashed and fought. "Enough!" A voice came from behind them. Reverend Mother Faith's voice startled all three of them. "They are needed in there, Liam. Calm yourself down this instant and let them go help Antonio!"

She nodded to the other two, who let him go. Liam was shaking with emotion. "Ye can't be in there, lad. You're too close to her. You know that. You need to let them work and you need to calm down. If you want to go in the ambulance with her, you need to be level-headed."

Her voice was so deep and calm, like someone speaking to a skittish animal. "Come, lad. To the chapel. Just for a moment." She took his elbow and led him to the small chapel across from the intake desk. When she closed the door, she waited. The explosion was inevitable.

The rage boiled up in him from the deepest recesses of his soul. No words, just a guttural scream that ripped through the hospital.

Then he looked up to the altar, to the ceiling above him, seeking an audience with the one he truly blamed. "Don't you do it! Don't you take her! Don't you dare take another one from me! Do you hear me, you bastard!" His fists were tight against his sides, ready to fight Almighty God himself. Face flushed with fury, the veins visible in his neck. "You can't have her!" The tears came in racking sobs, waves of despair rolling through his body. Then he was on his knees. "Oh God, please don't take her. I won't be able to live through this. Don't take her from me!" He felt the abbess's arms close around him as he finally let go. The grief poured out of him as he sobbed on the chapel floor.

Reverend Mother Faith had lived through decades of counseling the wounded. She'd lived through her own tragedies as well. But as she held this young, beautiful, broken man, all she could think of was that twice in one lifetime was too much for any mortal to bear. So she prayed. *Please, Heavenly Father. Please let them both live.* Because Raphael had a wife and two children. Surely with all the good deeds they'd done, God would spare the two strong, brave servants that he'd sent to her doorstep. *Merciful Father, let her live or you will surely kill him, too.*

Izzy opened her eyes, and she saw the lush green canopy of the rainforest. "Oh, God. I was dreaming. I passed out and I was dreaming!" she said aloud, followed by a few unladylike curses. Liam hadn't found her.

She looked around her. Where was Raphael? Then she looked to her left, to the river bank. There was a woman standing there. A slight, ethereal figure with long brown hair. "Eve?"

Eve turned to her as she approached. "Oh, God. Am I dead?"

She smiled so sweetly, Izzy's throat seized up. "No, love. You're not dead. 'Tis a dream, but you must go back. You must wake. You're fading." She ran her hands over Izzy's hair so gently, so sisterly. "You must go back to him. He loves you. He needs you to wake up." Izzy was crying now and Eve wiped her tears away with her lovely, graceful hands. "I'm happy for him, and I'm so very glad that it was you. You're so strong. Strong enough to love him forever. You must wake up Izzy."

Liam sat at Izzy's bedside, watching the steady beat of her heart on the monitor. Her surgery had been fast. Much less involved than her partner in crime, but they were both alive. She just hadn't regained consciousness. Antonio explained that her body had just shut down. She'd fought so hard, both for herself and for Raphael, and her body needed to rest. Her mind as well. Exhaustion, exposure, and major blood loss both from the gunshot wound and the transfusions. Her body had just let go, needing to preserve energy for healing. She wasn't technically in a coma. She just wasn't going to wake up until her body and mind were ready.

Liam put his arm across her belly, wishing he could hold her. Lie next to her and will her to wake. During the quiet of the waiting room, and now as he sat here, just watching her breathe, he'd run the gamut of emotions. Scenes from his time with Izzy flashing through his mind like a slide show. The scene with the Goliath spider, her saving Estela, her Gryffindor panties, her skill with a scalpel and a needle, the way she'd helped sweet Genoveva to bloom. He also thought about the nights they'd spent together. A raw and beautiful truth between them. Pleasure and passion…and there had been love. Love enough to resurrect his soul from the hellish grief and consuming anger.

She made him laugh. And in the stillness of this room, she made him weep. He pressed his face to her side and wept for her. For the suffering and fear that she'd experienced. For the incomprehensible bravery that she possessed. The thought of losing her had driven him past the edge of madness. He remembered those words he'd screamed on the boat. *I will follow you. I will not stay here without you.* As deep as his despair had gone for Eve, he'd carried on. He'd gotten up every day and kept on breathing. It had been hell, but he'd done it. *I won't be able to live through this. Please don't take her.*

He lifted his head, tears running off his face. "Izzy, my love. You were never a stepping stone. You were no one's proxy." His voice trembled, achy and destroyed. He put his head back down and said, "Oh God, Izzy. I love you so much. Please wake up."

Izzy woke slowly, barely cracking one eye. She heard the familiar hum of a busy hospital floor. Then she felt the weight on her belly. She opened further to find that a large arm was holding her by the waist. A face buried at her breast. He was crying. After all this time he was crying. And then she heard the words play back in her head. The ones that had finally broken through her deep sleep. She'd been looking into Eve's eyes. She was telling her to wake up, to go back to him. Then she'd heard Liam's voice all around them. *You were never a stepping stone. You were no one's proxy.*

She touched his hair as her heart broke from his sobbing. He snapped his head up, hardly willing to believe it. Then he was smiling, laughing like a lunatic, even though his face was covered in tears. He took the oxygen tube away from her nose and kissed her. He mumbled words against her mouth and she had no idea what he was saying. Gaelic, maybe. With their foreheads pressed together, she whispered. "I'm back. It's okay, Liam. I came back."

Antonio came into the room after the nurses had paged him. Izzy was sitting up in bed, having a bit of soup. "You are the most beautiful sight I have ever seen, bellissimo." He walked to her bedside, kissing her on the forehead. Then he put a hand on Liam's shoulder, meeting his eyes. *I understand, my brother. She was always to be yours.*

He checked her vitals, approving of her rebound. Izzy was so afraid to ask, the fear almost paralyzed her. "We need to talk about my arm. I need you to be honest with me. Did you do the surgery?"

"I assisted. I called the best neurosurgeon in the city on his day off. The wound will heal very well, I think."

"My hand was numb and tingling. I couldn't get it to move like I wanted." Her voice broke, "If I can't be a surgeon anymore, you have to level with me."

"The numbness and tingling were due to the blood loss and the fact that you weren't elevating it. You were too busy playing Wonder Woman in the jungle, Izzy darling. The bullet cut right through the muscle and went back out. You'll need to rehab, but there is no nerve damage. You are, and ever shall be, a gifted surgeon."

Izzy hadn't realized how scared she'd really been until those words came out of his mouth. She put her arm over her face and let out a sob. Liam soothed her, rubbing her other arm and offering soft whispers of comfort.

"I'm okay. I'm okay, now. Jesus, I couldn't think about it at the time, but deep down..." her breath came out with a shudder. "I'm okay. Thank you, Antonio. Thank you for taking care of me in that operating room."

He just nodded, blushing at her praise. Then he cleared his throat. "You need to keep drinking fluids and I want you here for at least three more days."

"I can't do that." Both the men stiffened. "What I mean is, I can't do that here. I've already been here almost a day. My medical insurance stopped yesterday. It was my last day in the Navy. I can tell just by the wallpaper that I can't afford this private hospital."

"Izzy, don't worry. If I have to pay for it myself..."

She cut him off. "I want to go back to St. Clare's. I want my team. You can come and check on me, right?" Liam personally loved that idea.

He sighed. "You are out of danger, even though that was a fool-headed thing to do. I suppose moving you is a possibility."

"Liam told me that Raphael is doing well. It was worth it. The risk was worth it. He has a family. Children and a wife. If one of us had to live..." She shook her head. "It was the right thing to do. Will he move to St. Clare's as well?"

"Yes, he's already started the paperwork for the transfer. He's very lucky he had you."

Something occurred to Izzy. "What about the men that attacked us? Did someone find them?" Liam didn't meet her eyes, and Antonio cleared his throat. "What?"

"They weren't treated here, but I'll ask around. I can find out what became of them."

As he left, Liam excused himself to follow. When they were alone, Antonio asked, "What happened on that forest road, amigo?"

"Justice happened," he said. Antonio just nodded.

"What will you tell her?"

"I'll tell her the truth. She's strong enough to hear it. Not today, though. Today I'm just happy she's back."

"I didn't know. The connection between you and her, I didn't realize the depth of your love for her. I hope you know that."

"I didn't know the depth of my love until I almost lost her. I know I never told you what happened to me in Ireland."

"Seamus told me. After you went crazy in the operating room, Seamus told me everything. A sorrow I cannot even imagine, my brother. You must never feel guilty for being able to love someone again. To have found such a glorious woman, and to have loved twice in a lifetime." Antonio shook his head, "You are very fortunate."

30

Izzy was taken in an ambulance, alongside her blood brother, to the St. Clare's Missionary Hospital. As they offloaded the two, the children were crowding around the pathway, being scolded by Sister Maria. "You can all see them in good time. You must calm yourselves."

After they were settled in a room, a shared room that broke a couple of rules in the hospital, Izzy finally relaxed against her pillow. "Man, I missed Gabriela's cooking. Hospital food sucks here just as bad as in the states." Right on their tail were Raphael's wife, Milena, and their two sons. She was carrying a covered dish. She didn't go to her husband, but to Izzy.

"Minha esposa say that I owe you this torta?" She unwrapped a big chocolate cake and Izzy's face lit up.

"A cake! Oh my God, you remembered that? You were half dead! How in the hell did you remember that?"

Raphael laughed softly. "I remember everything, amiga. Everything you did for me."

They exchanged glances. He looked as bad as she felt. Bruises and cuts from the crash. Bandages and tubes sticking out of various places. Then she looked at his wife. "Thank you for the cake."

"Thank you for my Raphael. My heart." The two women teared up as they hugged, then she took the children out so that they could run around in the yard with the other kids.

"Liam is getting us some lunch and some of that good coffee. It pays to have connections," she smiled at her friend.

"You are my blooded sister now, Izzy Collier. You took from your body so that I could live. I will never forget this." His eyes misted. "And now my children have their father."

A voice came from the doorway. "Out of the depths I cry unto thee, O Lord. Lord, hear my voice: let thine ears be attentive to the voice of my supplications." They looked up to see the abbess in her white robes, looking like a wise, old angel. "My favorite Psalm. I prayed for God to return you to us and though you're a bit worse for the wear, you are whole. How are you feeling?"

They spoke for a while, then the abbess did something unexpected. "Antonio said it is good for you to walk a bit after surgery. Would you walk with me a while, Izzy?"

She stepped in to take Izzy's arm and they began an easy stroll down the hospital ward. "How are you doing, really? It was quite an ordeal. You were injured, I suspect, both in body and mind."

"I won't let this keep me from my work. Drug traffickers or not."

The abbess smiled. "I understand you, although you may doubt that. I have never been one to run from a fight." And Izzy believed her. She wasn't cloistered in some convent in Ireland, praying her only life's work. She was, in her own way, on the front lines. "I don't know if they've told you, so I'm going to tell you. Because it's important and I think you have the right to know." Izzy stopped, meeting her gaze. "The man you shot in the chest died before they found them."

Izzy's eyes closed for a moment. Then she let out a breath and opened them. "I don't relish the thought that I took a life, Reverend Mother. It's important to me that you know that. But it was them or us. And in that moment, I wasn't ready to die or to let Raphael die. I made my choice and I will live with it. Just like the jaguar that died in that yard outside, these men were animals, hell-bent on murder. I would do it again to protect myself and my brother."

"I understand. And it may not sound altogether sisterly, but I'm glad you made the choice to fight, dear girl. For the world would be a darker place indeed, having had to part with you." Then she started to walk again, taking Izzy's arm. "And I feared that the loss of you would be the death of our Dr. O'Brien. In truth, he's become a sort of son to me. Like the lost children who come to our orphanage, seeking safety and succor. He came to me so wounded, I wasn't sure I could help him. Then I saw the light come back to his eyes. An ember that was lit by the love you offered him, even though he couldn't let himself return it. You know, they pulled him out of that operating room by force. He was so crazed and determined not to let you go. And as he screamed up to the heavens and cursed God himself, I felt sure that he would die from these wounds." She brushed a hand over Izzy's bandage. "I know he hurt you, Izzy dear. But ye must never doubt that it wasn't due to indifference that he lashed out, but out of fear."

"I don't know, Reverend Mother. Some of the things he said...I know that he was worried for me. I'm just not sure he will ever be able to give his heart to someone. I'm afraid too. There is more than one way to be hurt. I'm not invincible. Not when it comes to him."

Izzy came back to her room and Raphael was sound asleep. Liam stood. "He's had another dose of morphine. He's in a lot of pain, though he hides it." Izzy felt a stab of affection as she looked at her friend. His muscled chest was not so broad as the men she'd known. He was closer to her size, as a matter of fact. But size didn't always matter. He was a fighter. A warrior. And he'd held on when most people would have slipped away.

Liam helped her to bed. Her muscles were sore from that long, limping hike out of the forest. She felt like she'd hiked a thousand miles. "Do you need pain meds, mo chroí?"

She shook her head. "I took some Percocet. That will do." He slid the tray in front of her. Cheese bread fresh out of the oven, Gabriela's amazing chicken stew, and two pumpkin cookies with chocolate chips. Izzy's vision blurred as she took in the simple meal.

"A part of me thought we were going to die. I fought that line of thinking pretty hard, but the possibility dogged me. Or that I would live and he wouldn't, which would have been arguably worse." She looked up at Liam and his face was pale, starkly so. "I'm sorry. You probably don't need to hear this after what you've been through."

"This isn't about losing Eve. As hard as it's been, I've come to accept it, to realize that although she's gone, I'm still here. You were a big part of getting me there when everyone else failed."

"I'm glad for you, Liam." And she was. She was so happy that he was able to find joy in his life again and to reconnect with his family.

"I need you to tell me what happened the day we were ambushed. I know you haven't told me everything. You have a story to tell me, and I have one to tell you. I'm ready to listen. I need to hear it all." Liam nodded. Then he began. He held her hand while he did it, a warm, heavy presence keeping her grounded. He told her about Emilio, how everything had come to be, and the beating and threats that the boy had endured.

"That son of a bitch. I should have let Raphael kill him." She swallowed. "Reverend Mother told me that the man I shot in the chest died of his wounds."

"Yes, he was dead when we got there. He died at your hand, Izzy, and Raul died at mine." Her eyes snapped to his. "I gave him a sporting chance. After he wouldn't tell me where you were and admitted shooting you both, I untied him and gave him twice the beating he gave the lad. Then I finished it. You don't need to know the particulars."

"Yes, I do."

"Are you sure you want to hear it? Should it really matter?" Her gaze was direct, her chin up.

So he told her, without apology, how the man made his way to hell. "He didn't think I'd do it because I was a healer, but that's only one part of me. I'm an O'Brien. We protect our mates with the last drop of our blood. I couldn't be there to protect Eve. I didn't get a chance to avenge her. And I found myself in the same horrible situation. I wasn't there when you needed me, and ye had to fight that battle on your own. But I killed him without mercy because he'd tried to kill you. Because, a ghrá, if you were gone, I was dead already. And I'd suffer a thousand years in hell before I'd let him breathe one more breath."

She wouldn't meet his eyes, the tears coming down her face. "You don't have to say that. I know you care for me and I know that you were scared, but please don't say these things because you feel guilty or are caught up in this drama. I'm not as strong as you think I am, Liam."

He turned her face up to will her to look at him. "I love you, Izzy. It's why I behaved so unforgivably. Because if I admitted what was in my heart…that after all the pain and hopelessness and anger, that I'd finally found my mate, it would somehow negate what I felt for Eve. I loved her. With all of my heart, I did. But I'm not that man anymore, and she's gone. All I have to give you is the man I am now. And admittedly, I'm kind of a bastard."

Izzy laughed, wiping her nose with a tissue she'd grabbed from her bedside. Then she just looked down, concentrating on the wad in her hand. "I know you're sorry, Liam. I do. But the stuff you said…you had to believe that on some level. That switch flipped in you because of something you thought you overheard, but you were pretty quick to believe things of me. One minute you were fine, the next you weren't and I don't understand how you can say that you love me when…"

He interrupted her with rapid words. "I forgot." She looked at him, not following. "That morning, Izzy. I woke up after having a dream about Eve, and when I felt an ache in my chest, it wasn't for her. I was lying in bed thinking about you. The first thought of the day was that I'd missed you in the night. That I wanted you with me when I woke up. I wanted you in my bed at night. Not just because I wanted to make love to you but because I wanted to press against you and hold you. Feel your breathing and your warmth. I woke up feeling all of this love in my chest, aching for you, and I forgot. It was one year ago, that day, and I wasn't thinking about Eve. When the Reverend Mother mentioned it to me, and I'd realized what I'd done…ach, God. I hated myself. I hated myself so badly that I thought I'd burn up from it. So I lashed out at you. Not because of any of the idiotic reasons I gave you. I lashed out at you because you made me happy." His voice caught, and he placed his head on her side. "I was happy, Izzy."

"I was happy, too, you stupid jackass." They both laughed then, the kind of laughter that broke its way through your tears. He raised his head and she saw it. Utter love in his eyes. For her.

"If you decided that you couldn't forgive me, I'd have to understand and accept it, but I'll never stop trying and I'll never stop loving you. Even if you leave me in a month and lead a separate life, I couldn't let you go away thinking you were some sort of proxy for Eve. You were never a stepping stone, and I will love you, and only you, until I meet my maker. My blood is inside you, now, and I'd have given my last drop if it meant that you lived. That's the best and truest vow I can make to you." He cleared his throat, fighting back tears and emotion. "And if Eve could see us, I know that she'd be so happy that I wasn't alone. I never told you, but she came to me as she did Cora. She told me that when the time came, that I was to go to the river. It's how I found you. She wanted me to find you so that I wouldn't lose you. I don't know if you think that's crazy but…"

She cut him off. "I don't think it's crazy because she came to me as well." He crinkled his brow as Izzy let out a tiny sob. "I was fading. I thought I was dead when I saw her. She looked like an angel, so elegant and lovely. She told me that I had to wake up. That I had to come back to you."

Liam suppressed a sob in his throat and she looked at him, her own tears flowing freely now. He took her gently under the neck and kissed her. "I love you. Oh God, Izzy. I love you so much. I'll go wherever you want me to go. I'll move to Arizona. Please tell me I haven't fucked things up beyond repair."

She kissed him back, soft and sweet, their tears mixing as their faces touched. "We've got time for all that. Just get up on this bed and wrap your arms around me."

He did, squeezing his big body on the bed and pulling her across his chest. He held her, kissing her hair and just enjoying the warm vitality of her, alive and whole. When she settled, calm and feeling safe, she finally told him. The whole harrowing tale poured out of her. The explosion, that due to Raphael's sharp eyes and skill behind the wheel, had assured that the back end of the jeep took the brunt of the explosion. Otherwise, they could have been killed. When she inquired about the man that she'd trussed up like fresh kill, Liam told her that he'd been collected. And other than a ruined career as a pianist, he was going to live. One handed, but alive, which was more than he deserved. But Liam had let him live because he was too wounded to fight back. Liam may not be a warrior, but he had a code of ethics that was undoubtedly a throwback from centuries ago. She continued, telling him of their decision to go east so that they didn't meet any more of Fuentes's crew. The blood, sweat, and tears that it took to keep them both going. "My beloved Izzy. You are a fierce, brave lass." Then something occurred to Liam. "But you never told me where the canoe came from."

She lifted her head up and smiled, shaking her head. "You are never going to believe this story, but it's the God's honest truth."

Seamus gave a knock. As he came in, Raphael was eating and Izzy was fast asleep in Liam's arms. Raphael gave a sideways grin. "It's good to see, yes?"

"Yes, it is. It's about bloody time. I was ready to go for her myself." Then he looked over and saw that they were stirring.

"I heard that, ye tosser. Don't even think about it. O'Brien men don't share. Ever." Izzy gave them all a groggy grin.

"He's so cute when he goes all neanderthal. What's up doc?"

"Well, I've kept her out as long as I can. The lass is fit to be tied."

Genoveva came in, pushing past him. Liam was already climbing out of the bed. "Come here, little sister. It's okay." Izzy took the sobbing girl in her arms. "I'm okay, baby. We're all okay. Don't forget our mantra." Seamus and Raphael bellowed, "Strong is the new skinny!" Genoveva laughed. They all did. A beautiful sound as the dark cloud of tragedy finally cleared completely.

Antonio cleared Izzy's release from the hospital, and she was so happy to be out of that bed and back to her surgery. "Antonio, I want you to know how much I appreciate this. It's above and beyond to give up two weeks vacation."

"Bella, I have so much time accumulated, I could take three months in Rio."

"Then why don't you? Grab some eligible nurse or doc or cocktail waitress and head down south for some R&R." He smiled, and it held a touch of sadness.

"I am like you in that regard, I believe. Despite the playboy reputation that seems to dog me, I have no one in my life. There is a socialite aspect to the more affluent part of Brazil that I'm afraid I don't quite have the stomach for. The village where I grew up in Italy, it was very beautiful. Greve, in the Chianti region of Tuscany. Just close enough to Florence for a bit of fun and culture, but a small town. My family has a vineyard. Sometimes I miss it. But the pay is good here, and they have no need of my services in such a small town."

"Could you commute to a bigger city? It seems like you're homesick."

"Yes, I've heard of this term. To miss your home so much, that sometimes it's as painful as an injury or illness. Deep in your chest." Izzy understood. She was lucky that she got to see her parents regularly. When she was busy, they came to her. She wondered if that would change. Where to settle had been on her mind, despite her instinct not to plan ahead. She needed to have a final answer for those hospitals. More importantly, she had three weeks to help with recruiting.

She looked down at the raw ham hock. It had been Antonio's idea for her to immediately start practicing her dexterity with a scalpel and needle and thread. She was sore, and she found a labor to it that hadn't been there before, but she was doing pretty well. He would work with her and help cover the surgery for the next two weeks.

Liam came into the room carrying some fresh supplies. He kept an eye on the two of them as he put the contents of the box away. "He's watching me like a wolf, Dr. Collier. I thought he was a eunuch before you came, but now he's acting very jealous while pretending to be busy."

"I can hear you, Antonio."

Antonio was laughing, "I know. It would hardly be amusing otherwise." Liam gave him a sideways grin.

"Thank you, brother, for helping her and the hospital. You're going to need to take some of that vacation time after this."

"We were just discussing that. He misses home. I vote for him moving back, getting a villa in Tuscany, and inviting us to visit." Izzy's smile was disarming.

"Maybe for a honeymoon," Liam said easily. He gave her a sideways glance. Her hands froze in place.

"I think I'll go check on Raphael." Antonio made a quick retreat.

Liam stalked toward her as she put her work aside and took her gloves off. Then she was penned in by his thick arms, leaning against the table. "You look wary, lass. Like you're afraid I'm going to take something back." Then he leaned back. "Or like you don't like the idea."

"I just wasn't expecting it. I'm still getting used to…being more. I was afraid to hope for anything other than an affair. Then I couldn't hope for anything. I just want you to be sure before you ask."

"Do you love me, Izzy?"

"More than I've ever loved anyone. Despite the fact that you are kind of a bastard." She said with a cheeky grin. He smiled widely.

"I told you and I meant it. I'll follow you wherever you go. You don't have to stay here and you don't have to go back to Ireland with me. I'll get licensed in the States if that's where you want to be. Arguably, you're the only one with a job offer right now."

"My visa officially expires at the ninety-one-day mark. I have a one-way ticket to Dublin. I can't make you do anything, Liam, but I think you should come home with me to see your family. Once we do that, we can decide where to go. I can put those offers on hold if I tell them I'm recovering. If I lose the jobs, we'll deal with it. My bigger concern is who is going to step up and replace us. Adam and Alyssa both rotate out next week. Then they'll lose me, Seamus, and you."

"To quote the abbess, God will provide. We just need to give him a nudge in the right direction."

"Funny you should say that. I have a family practitioner that only needs a small nudge. Although, she might come with a bodyguard."

Liam cocked his head, then he caught on to her train of thought. "Jesus, you're brilliant. I didn't even think of her. Did she keep her license up?"

"Yep. She went back to part time after six months of traveling. I think she'd be perfect. But, Liam. I think it would seal the deal if you were the one to ask her. You've got a history with her."

He paused, feeling stupidly nervous about reaching out to someone from his old life. Someone other than family. "Okay, I'll do it." He exhaled, feeling okay for the first time in a long time. "And I'll go home with you. I'll be honest, it's not going to be easy. I'm sort of attached to this place. But I'll do it. I'll do it for you and for my family."

She pulled him to her, wrapping him in a warm, loving embrace. He gripped her and put his face in her hair. Smelling her earthy scent mixed with soap and bug repellent. A strange bouquet to some, perhaps, but it was heavenly to him. "Will you come to me tonight?" He pulled back just enough to see her face. "If you're not ready, I don't want you to feel pressured."

"I'm ready. More than ready."

He pulled the keys out of his pocket. "When you threw these on the table, it was like a sort of death. A self-inflicted death." Then he bent his head and kissed her. They were at work, and he'd really just meant to kiss her, but it quickly spiraled. She finally pushed him away. "We are not having sex on my operating table with a piece of sliced up pig next to us."

He took her palm and put it to his cock, thick and hard under his scrubs. "Eight o'clock. And wear the Hermione panties."

31

Izzy sat in the garden, trying to soak in the sun that was poking through the clouds. The rainy season was in full swing. She was tired, which was not unexpected. She'd take a couple of weeks to get back into fighting shape. Sister Agatha came into the garden with Genoveva by her side. "We have something to show you. You and Reverend Mother Faith, if you feel up to it." They sat on either side of her, looking at the beautiful garden in silence.

Surprisingly, Genoveva spoke first. "Do you think my parents sat in this spot together?"

"I don't know, sweetie. Maybe someday you'll get to ask your father." She rubbed a soft touch over the girl's hair, knowing that leaving her would break Izzy's heart. Just like leaving Estela was going to kill Liam. They had a rule about the doctors adopting. Izzy had been confused by it. It seemed ridiculous until the abbess had explained the reasoning behind the rule.

Think about it, lass. It's not like you've come for the day to see the available children. That is somehow easier on them all. They don't know those people and it's a short-term stress to endure. But you've lived here for three months. Liam for almost a year. Antonio has been with us for three years. Imagine the rejection that the others would feel. And imagine the stress that would come over the place every time a new doctor came. Like they were going to spend the next three months trying to audition, hoping to go home with the next doctor. The two entities must be separate.

That's when she understood. She didn't like it, but she understood. How would Genoveva feel if they took Estela home to live with them? She'd feel rejected and unloved. How would the boys feel if the girls got picked? She thought of Emilio, shedding the signs of abuse on the outside, but who was permanently scarred on the inside. When she'd finally gone to him, his remorse had been gut-wrenching. He'd cried so hard that his whole body shook. He knew he'd never be adopted. That he'd age out and try to find work. He knew his father was dead, but he didn't know how he died. He'd been relieved to know that his abuser was finally somewhere where he couldn't touch him. Where he couldn't threaten the only family who had ever given Emilio any love or security. As much trouble as he was in the classroom, he loved Sister Maria with a child's true heart.

They walked back to the library, where the abbess was waiting. Liam was there as well. Sister Agatha had a low end but serviceable desktop computer set up on the desk. One that had been purchased by the diocese and never set up. They gathered around and Sister Agatha worked nervously, starting the video that she'd been working on. "Genoveva helped a lot. She picked the music and worked on the timing of the slideshow." Then it began.

Imagine Dragons *On Top of the World* played as the pictures of the abbey, the hospital, and the orphanage popped up on the screen. Then the more candid shots started and everyone was smiling as pictures of the children scrolled to the music. *The Children of Saint Clare.*

Liam's throat constricted as he watched the pictures of the children come on to the screen. Especially the ones of Izzy and Genoveva, of him and his little Estela. Pictures of the boys hanging from trees or Cristiano reading his favorite book. Then a new portion of the show started. *The Sisters of Saint Clare.* Some of the pictures were funny, some serious as the strong, quiet women went about their work. The best one was of Sister Maria at the health fair, bouncing a football off her head to pass it. The music was upbeat, and the video took on a life of its own as it scrolled through the heart and soul of this mission. *The Doctors and Nurses of Saint Clare.* Izzy clapped her hands together, laughing at the picture of her and Seamus jumping on tires. Then of her with her arm around Genoveva. She did the same now, holding the girl close. Then there were pictures of Liam. Darkly handsome and brooding, looking at his microscope or examining a child in the deep green landscape of the forest villages.

Seamus holding a newborn that he'd just delivered. Antonio wheeling a patient down to surgery, his beautiful face intelligent and serious. Liam looked up at Izzy and she was crying now. Pictures of her with the indigenous tribe, letting the women paint on her arms. Holding a toddler and checking his glands. There were captions, of course, all geared toward being a part of this wonderful community. They needed doctors badly. And they needed money. The video was so well done. As it approached the end, the photos got more humorous. Antonio with his *Hug a Surgeon* booth, getting smooched by a buxom twenty-something, the next one of the abbess with her hands on her hips, giving him a chiding look, then followed up with her pulling him down by the ear to give him a lecture. Now Izzy was laughing, her tears sparkling in her joyful eyes. The scrolling words had proclaimed the handsome doctor to be single and searching.

The last one was of Izzy dancing with the children, white scrubs, no makeup, and Estela on her hip. Utter joy on all of their faces. The ending scroll read. *Be the heroes of tomorrow. Family Practitioners, OB-GYNs, Pediatricians, Infectious Disease Specialists, Trauma and General Surgeons, Nurses, Midwives, Radiologists, Anesthesiologists. We want you to make a difference.*

The website and contact information was also included. When the last image of Izzy faded, Liam gave out a whoop! "That was brilliant, Sister. Well done to you and to our Genoveva."

The reverend mother was a bit more contained. "I don't know. It seems a bit…provocative in some parts. Perhaps with a bit of editing."

Agatha's face fell, so Izzy intervened. "Send it to me, I'll see if I can clean it up a bit." Izzy's words sounded so sincere that Liam had to bite his cheek to keep quiet. *Clean it up, my ass.* Sister Agatha sent it and Liam watched as Izzy started typing furiously.

"What are you doing, Dr. Collier? Perhaps we can fill in some new photos and it won't throw off the timing," Agatha said helpfully.

Izzy smiled innocently. "No need, I've got this."

Another minute and Reverend Mother Faith started to get suspicious. "What are you up to, Izzy? Ye've got mischief in your eyes."

Izzy looked up, "I'm just loading the video up to Sister Agatha's new youtube channel." Sister Agatha gasped, covering her mouth.

"Isolde Collier, don't you dare push that…" Izzy looked right at her like a defiant child and pushed send.

"Oops."

"Yer not a bit sorry. Take it down, lass. We need to get approval. There are things to be discussed."

Izzy closed the laptop. "It doesn't need to come down. No one is going to go looking for a YouTube channel that I just registered. It'll just sit there until we promote it. Go ahead and do your boss-lady thing. It'll be fine." *Except for the fact that I shared it on the St. Clare's Facebook page and blasted it out on Twitter and Instagram.*

"You think you're rather clever don't you?"

"What are you going to do, punish me? Lure me into the jungle and leave me to die? Oh, wait…you already did that." Liam and Genoveva were openly laughing now, Sister Agatha with her head down, coughing to cover her own giggles.

"Don't tempt me, young lady."

It was just before dinner when Izzy and Liam called Doc Mary on the video chat. Much to their delight, Alanna was visiting with the children. Two minutes into the conversation, Alanna was crying. Liam had called everyone the day of Izzy's rescue, including her parents, but Izzy hadn't talked to his side of the family. She'd called her parents as soon as she was able because her father had been ready to rush a passport and visa and try to get to Brazil.

Alanna said, "I love you both, and I know you didn't call to talk to me. Please stay safe and come home to us. I'll come back with Aidan for your return."

After a tearful goodbye, Doc Mary appeared on the screen with Hans at her side. That's when the hard sell started. "I talked to the abbess. They'd be willing to accept Hans in an unofficial capacity. With all that's happened, she doesn't want to wait for the diocese to approve funding for security. And honestly, Raphael isn't up to full strength yet. You won't be able to carry a gun, but you'd be a presence. Just until they can get the funds to hire Raphael permanently."

Hans sighed. "I'm not worried about myself, Liam. I'll be honest with you. I don't know if I can take Mary into that environment. For fuck sake, Izzy sitting in front of that screen with a healing gunshot wound in her arm. How could I possibly agree to this if there's still a drug cartel working in your backyard?"

"Actually, there's not. They did a raid the next day. The entire area was saturated with military and police. Someone tipped Fuentes off, coupled with the fact that his three rogue employees exposed them. He's vanished. They abandoned some of the logging equipment, but the trucks, the planes, the drugs, and all of the men, everything and everyone is gone. The area was too close to civilization and they'd been exposed, so they moved quickly. The land has been seized by the government and will go up for sale."

"And you're sure they won't come looking for you or Izzy? Or try to take some kind of action against the abbey?"

"I really don't think so. Those three were on their own. The head guy, Fuentes, seemed genuinely angered that they'd made so much trouble. Their actions led to the government raid on his property. I think he's laying low in Columbia or somewhere deeper in the jungle. My gut tells me he's gone home. And after these incidents, the police and military are patrolling the area regularly.

Foreigners getting attacked is really bad for the tourism in Brazil, and politically."

Hans looked at Mary. "Can you give us some time?"

"Yes, brother. Of course. This work isn't for everyone. It's challenging. There are bugs and rain and primitive working conditions... but it has changed the way I view practicing medicine. It changed my life. I hope you'll at least think about it."

Mary said, "I'm interested, Liam. Really interested. You'll have my answer by the weekend." She stressed the word *my* with a sideways glance at her husband and challenge in her gaze. Hans was getting schooled on dealing with a stubborn Irish woman.

Izzy added, "Mary if you want to know more, go on our Facebook page. I think there's a video that you are going to love."

Mary ended the call and looked at her husband, then at her step-daughter. Alanna was grinning. "I've lost this argument already, haven't I." Hans was frowning, trying to weigh his odds.

"Don't get your knickers in a bunch, love. At least you get to come with me. You can do a panty raid in the women's dorm." He smiled as he pulled her by the waist. He kissed her. Just a peck because his daughter and grandchildren were watching. "You're a handful, Doc."

"Precisely why you love me."

"True enough. Now that we have that decided, let's get to the juicy gossip." Alanna looked at him confused. He and Mary laughed. "You really didn't see it? You must be kidding me. She totally hit that." Mary nodded in agreement. "He tapped that big time. It was written all over their faces."

Alanna covered her son's ears. "Do you mean HIT that, hit that?" she said, completely shocked. Then she thought about it. They were calling home together, sitting close. And they'd been glowing. How had she missed it? Her squeal almost blew the roof off of the small house.

Liam walked into the bungalow and was enveloped by the smell of citronella. The lights were off, and Izzy was coming out of the bathroom freshly showered. She was wearing one of his button-down shirts and the sight of her shot through him. She spread the shirt with her hands as she placed them on her hips. Her Harry Potter themed underwear hugging her curves. She let out a little chuckle. "Ten points for Gryffindor, Doctor?"

He was across the room in a flash, kissing her and grinning against her mouth. "Absolutely. Twenty points if I get to take them off with my teeth."

He kissed her long and deep, and the urgency built in him. Suddenly the teasing was gone and he was desperate for her. "Oh, God. I love you so much. I didn't ever think I'd be with you again." He made pained noises as he kissed her, letting that connection between them heal and spark anew. "It's never been like this for me either, Izzy. It's never felt like this. I need ye to know that, a chuisle."

He spread her across the bed, taking his time with her. The shirt undone, he licked her nipples, causing her to arch and moan. When he inched those panties down far enough, he groaned. "You are a little vixen, Dr. Collier. I see you've been back to the spa." The narrow triangle was back, her smooth sex calling out to him for some attention. He couldn't wait. He pulled her panties off the rest of the way with rough hands, splitting her thighs. She arched and rolled her hips as he tasted her. "Liam, get inside me. I want you." Even as she said it, she put her hands in his hair, meeting his mouth with her raised hips. She was so close to the edge.

"You don't seem very sure about that." He flicked his tongue and she threw her head back.

"Stop doing that. You're killing me!"

Then he was inside, raised above her with broad shoulders and his face tight with lust. She curled her feet around his calves and he propped himself up on his arms so he could watch their bodies. She was exquisite, her hips hungry for him, her body gripping him, taking what she needed. Her taut stomach and lower body finding its own pace. Her eyes were soft and sexy, her mouth flushed, and it was open just a little bit so that her gasps could escape. "Come, Izzy. I want to watch you."

Their eyes met and her voice was hoarse with desire. "I love you, Liam. I love you too." When she let go, she moaned and strained, the strokes going deeper as she spasmed under him. He saw it happen in the lines of her body, felt her take hold of him and start to contract. The sounds she made jacked him up. She was so beautiful and completely undone. Her legs let go and came up so he could dive into her, strong and hard. He lifted her hips with one hand, thrusting deep. When he did that, she rolled into another orgasm. She whimpered his name as she came that second time and his control snapped. "You're mine, Izzy. Mine forever." His eyes bore into hers as he let himself go.

Liam played with Izzy's hair as she caught her breath, sweating and flushed and satisfied as she lay sprawled across his chest. "You never answered my question, Izzy love. Will you marry me or will you leave me for dead?"

She lifted her head and met his eyes. She saw a touch of vulnerability in his eyes. "I love you, Liam. And I'm not expecting you to marry me right away. If you need time," He kissed her, then. Shutting her up.

"I need to marry you. I don't want to wait. Life is too short, darlin'. I'm as sure as a man can be. I want to get married. Will you have me?"

"Of course I will. I love you. This is it for me. You're the one."

"Then let's do it. This weekend. It won't be legal since we aren't citizens, but I think I could arrange it with Father Pietro. I just…feel like we should do it here first. With the sisters and the staff and the children. We can make it official later. Let's do it before Adam and Alyssa are gone."

Izzy laughed. "Did anyone ever accuse you of having impulsivity problems?"

He gave her a boyish grin. "A few nuns in primary school, perhaps. But I'm not being impulsive. Can't you just picture it, Izzy? Our girls with flowers in their hair? The lads in their wee bow ties. In the garden behind the abbey."

Our girls. That's what he'd called them. And in that moment, she knew. They'd be back. Maybe not right away. There were too many logistics. But in her heart, she knew that they would be back.

"I think that sounds like the best wedding anyone has ever had. And when the time comes to make it legal?"

"I'm going to leave that one up to you."

She rubbed a thumb over his mouth. "Thank you. If my mother gets cheated out of planning a wedding for her spinster daughter, she'll never forgive us."

Izzy ran to the laptop, just as the ringing stopped. Of course. She dialed back Alanna's number. She was squealing before Izzy could even say hello. Had she heard about the wedding? She and Liam had agreed to surprise them when they got back to Ireland. That wasn't why she was squealing, however.

"Oh my God Izzy! I can't believe that video! I cry every time I watch it! Those children are so beautiful and the cute nun with the soccer ball!"

"So Doc Mary showed you our video before you left, huh? Yeah, it is pretty awesome."

"What are you talking about? Mary didn't show it to me. I saw it all over the internet, and Patrick said it's on the Irish BBC. It's gone viral, Izzy! You have almost a million hits on YouTube!"

Izzy's jaw was dropped. Suddenly her grin was huge. *So much for editing it.* They'd been so busy trying to throw a wedding together, no one had been online to do anything. "I gotta go, Alanna. Thanks for telling me!"

Izzy sprinted for the cantina where the sisters and older children were making flower arrangements. Izzy skidded right inside the door. "Sister Agatha!" The quiet novice stood, alarm on her face. "That video you made, it's gone viral. Apparently, we made the news in Ireland!" She thought Agatha was going to faint. "You need to check the Facebook and the website. Where's the Reverend Mother?"

"She's been in her office all day. I believe she was having a phone conference with the diocese, but that was early this morning. We need to tell her. She might get a bit upset."

They walked together to the abbey, knocking on the half-open door as they heard the phone ringing on several lines. Reverend Mother Faith looked up from her call. "Thank you, Cardinal McBreen. I'll be sure to pass it along to the sisters. Oh, yes. I'll have a list waiting for approval. We've got plenty of plans for the extra funds." As she hung up, she gave them both a stern look, then a creeping grin surfaced. Then she clapped her hands and shouted. "Our video has gotten a virus! People have been calling all morning!"

"It's gone viral, yes. Dr. Collier told me! That's wonderful!"

"Yes, and that's not all. People have been using the donation link that you added to the website and apparently, we've had donations pouring in since yesterday. I called the bank in the city and we've raised fifty-two thousand Brazilian Real. Almost fourteen thousand euro in less than a day!"

"Hot damn!" Izzy barked.

"Dr. Collier, please. Language."

"Sorry, Reverend Mother. I need to go tell the other doctors!" Liam had spent the last two days distributing the Zika vaccines for the trials. Three locations and fifty patients. The CDC in Manaus, thankfully, had given him an assistant. But she needed to tell everyone else. Seamus was staying on for a two-week extension, because he had a high-risk patient that was due and he didn't want to leave her. Everyone was going to be thrilled about the extra funds. The x-ray machine might actually happen.

"Wait, there's something else. It is arguably more important."

"What's that?"

Reverend Mother Faith put her hand to her heart. "I've received five applications from doctors not counting your friend Mary Falk, as well as three nurses and one dentist who have applied to volunteer for a one, three, or six-month commitment. Oh, Izzy. I was so afraid we'd have no doctors. It is such a blessing."

Izzy went to her then and hugged her. "You're going to be fine. And if you aren't, then you're going to call. Liam and I will always be there for you. You're part of our family now."

As she began to leave she said, "You just wait until that video hits Canada and the U.S. I think you may be able to afford a married housing unit. And I definitely think that you'll be able to afford Raphael's salary."

32

The rain has ceased for a few hours, almost as if God himself was giving his approval. Liam looked around as the sun fell over the garden, causing the rain-soaked trees and plants to almost twinkle. All the boys were fidgeting in place, nudging each other and getting chiding looks from the sisters. But they were freshly washed and combed. Their Sunday best as clean as little boy clothes ever got. Then he looked at the girls. There were a few more girls at St. Clare's, which made him sad. O'Brien's treasured their girl offspring like precious jewels, rare and beautiful. Estela was holding Genoveva's hand. The girl who had stepped up and been a big sister to her when she had no family left. The Sisters of St. Clare were in their good frocks, the ones that were worn for special occasions.

Father Pietro had come in from the city, willing to do an unofficial blessing of sorts. More like a handfasting than an actual wedding. Because Liam and Izzy weren't Brazilian citizens, they needed to get married in one of their home countries to make this official. Whatever. He felt like he was getting married today, and so did Izzy, and that was the whole point. In this place that had brought them together, and the people who'd loved two strangers that had drifted into their little part of the forest, he couldn't imagine doing this without them. Couldn't think of any place more beautiful than the walled garden where weary missionaries went to find a little peace.

Sister Agatha handed her camera over in order for someone to keep the video rolling. Then she came forward, clearing her throat, and started to sing. A clear, sweet soprano, she started the hymn. *Blest be the Tie that Binds* ringing through this fertile, holy place. Liam's throat seized up as he felt Seamus put a hand on his shoulder. He looked to the entrance of the garden, and there she was. Raphael had insisted that he be allowed to walk. He would not walk Izzy down the aisle in a wheelchair. And her boy was rock solid, his face glowing with the pride of a blooded brother. His wife and children were there as well, smiling and waving.

Izzy was wearing that pale blue dress, the only dress she had with her, and she looked even more beautiful than the first time he'd seen her. She had flowers pinned in her soft curls, her hair touching just below her shoulders now, after almost three months of growth.

> *From sorrow, toil, and pain, and sin we shall be free.*
> *And perfect love and friendship reign through all eternity.*

Now she was taking his hand, and in that moment, all of the pain of the last year went down deep into his memory. Settling there and content to remain in the archives of Liam's life, instead of in his present and future. There was no forgetting it or Eve, and he wouldn't have wanted that. But he was ready to move forward, to build a life he'd never imagined for himself, and be so very grateful that he'd been gifted a second chance. He looked over at Reverend Mother Faith. She was blotting a tear from her cheek, looking at them both with such a motherly love that it almost took his breath away.

Father Pietro gathered their hands; putting them together and tying a silken ribbon around both of them. Then he spoke. His English was thickly accented, but his words were clear.

"This cord is a symbol of the lives you have chosen to lead together. Up until this moment, you have been separate in thought, word, and action. As your hands are bound together by this cord, so too, shall your lives be bound as one. May you be forever one, sharing in all things, in love and loyalty for all of your life together. Let us pray. Heavenly Father, we ask that you dwell in this place of beauty and peace, and bestow your blessings on this betrothal. That Liam Joseph O'Brien and Isolde Sophia Collier hold these vows in their hearts, until the day when they are wed."

Liam interrupted, "Sorry Father, she goes by Izzy." The priest grinned and Seamus and Antonio laughed behind him. "My apologies, Izzy." He nodded to her, then continued.

"I bless you both and all who have gathered here to bear witness to this special day. In nomine Patris et Filii et Spiritus Sancti. Amen."

Izzy didn't wait for an invitation, she pulled Liam to her and kissed him square on the mouth. The children all squealed and giggled, Adam and Alyssa gave a loud whoop! And Gabriela was sobbing into a napkin that she'd borrowed from the cantina. Then Estela broke from the crowd and launched herself at the both of them, hanging on to a leg from each. It was a beautiful, perfect day.

The banquet was in full swing. Gabriela had outdone herself. There was a spit of beef over the fire pit, where Paolo carved slices of meat that were marinated in her secret mix of spices. Cheese bread, sumptuous side dishes, a delicious, gooey mango cake, and cashew tarts. The children had decorated the hall, papering it with pictures and messages of good wishes and love. Before Antonio left, he gave them a card. "Antonio, thank you." Izzy felt the bulk inside the envelope. "We said no gifts."

"Indulge me, bellissimo. Something for my friends. Some of the best I've ever had."

She opened the card as Liam looked over her shoulder. A key? "I'm afraid Manaus is limited with luxury hotels, but this resort is to the west, right on the river. You've got reservations in the honeymoon bungalow. I know this is not your official wedding night, but I thought you should have somewhere beautiful and private, away from the abbey."

Liam grabbed him in a fierce hug. "Thank you, mo cara." *My friend.*

Antonio whispered into his shoulder. "Treasure her, always, my friend. Love her well."

Liam pulled back, meeting Antonio's eyes. "I promise you."

Then Antonio hugged Izzy, letting go of the feelings he'd had for her, shifting to something different. Something they could all live with. He kissed her on the forehead, then turned and walked away.

Izzy stirred in Liam's arms, the sun coming through the window as they peeked briefly from the clouds. It had rained through the night. A steady pattering on the roof of the beautiful riverside retreat. "Good morning, a chuisle." She smiled under his mouth as he kissed her, raising her mouth to his as she arched her neck. They'd made love for hours last night. Enjoying the king size bed with the luxury linens. Something neither had felt in months. Then they'd slept, a deep and peaceful sleep.

Izzy looked up at the mammoth mosquito net, beautifully detailed with embroidered flowers and birds. The place smelled of exotic wood and delicate flowers, which were strewn around the room. "Good morning." She ran a hand over his stubble, playing with the dark auburn hair.

"I'm sorry, I should have shaved."

"No, don't. I liked the beard. I kind of miss it." She shrugged, mischief in her eyes. "It tickles."

His eyes flared a bright blue. "Does it now? Any spot in particular?"

She wiggled away from him, "That's too easy. You have to find it." She squealed as he grabbed her foot, pulling her back. Then he was rubbing his stubbled chin against the small of her back as she giggled. He bit her hips softly, tasting her skin. "Well then. Let the searching begin."

Only after he'd tickled and rubbed his mouth and chin on every square inch of her, and loved her again, did they settle. "I'm happy, Izzy. I'm so happy I feel like I might burst from it. Thank you."

"You're welcome. I'm happy too, Liam. More than I ever thought I could be. This isn't what I came to Brazil expecting to find, but it's everything I needed. It doesn't matter where we go now, as long as we're together."

She felt him reach under the bedding for something, then he took her hand in his. "I should have done this sooner, I just…wanted us to be alone. I wanted the time to be right." Then he slid the beautiful diamond and Brazilian blue tourmaline ring on her finger. She was speechless, which was new for Izzy. "I wanted something Brazilian. The blue tourmaline is very rare, which is why they're smaller. I'm afraid my wage from St. Clare's is a bit modest." He seemed a bit shy like he wasn't sure how she was going to react. "But the diamonds and the platinum are from Brazil as well. Antonio helped me find a jeweler that used only ethical mines for their inventory." After all, illegal mines and horrific work conditions were an unfortunate part of the gem trade in South America. "I just wanted something that represented who we were, where we started, and how precious and rare you are to me." He stuttered, "If you don't like it…"

He finally met her eyes. She was crying, little tears welling like crystals and finally falling down her cheeks. "I'm sorry. You know I'm a crier. It's so beautiful. It's perfect, Liam." He smiled, lifting her hand into the light. The platinum and the glowing blue of the tourmaline bright against her skin tones. The emerald cut diamond twinkled on her beautiful hand. It really was perfect, he thought to himself. It wasn't big or ostentatious, but it was beautiful and unique, like his Izzy.

The day was gloomy, which was appropriate. Given the joy of the weekend celebrations, it was like the weather had shifted, knowing that the mood at St. Clare's had done the same. Alyssa and Adam stood in the cantina, their bags already loaded into the Land Cruiser. Margaritte and Izzy cried with Alyssa as the trio of strong, feisty women had to be parted from each other. "I'll look you up when I get to Ireland. I don't know how long we'll be there, but I want to see you."

Alyssa whispered in her ear. "Please call me when you find Genoveva's father."

"I will. I promise. I won't stop until I find him."

The men all gave Adam a man hug, thumping him on the back as he headed in a different direction. Back to Australia, to his wife and children. Then they were gone. The thought that this would happen in a couple of weeks for Izzy was almost too much to bear. As the crowd dissipated, she decided to go to the abbey offices and see the Reverend Mother. She'd been surprised that she'd not come out for the final goodbye, although she'd said her farewells to them in private.

As she approached, she saw Reverend Mother Faith coming through the door. A tingling went through her because the abbess didn't look right. She was pale and slumped a bit in the doorway. She noticed two things. Seamus walking fast from the other direction, and the abbess sinking to the ground as she slid down the doorjamb. She heard Liam cry out from behind her.

33

Shame on the body for breaking down while
the spirit perseveres...

John Dryden

Liam couldn't believe he was in this chair again. As he watched the monitor that showed the abbess's irregular rhythm, his throat was so constricted that it ached. *Please, God. She's the heart of this place. Please, don't take her.* She was sleeping now, having assured everyone that they were fussing for naught. As he held her hand, he marveled at how such a fierce woman could seem so delicate and frail right now. Her hand was thin, the knuckles knobby with time's wear and tear. The pale skin was spotted, the blue veins prominent through the tissue-like skin. He just wanted to see those pale eyes. The strength and wisdom ingrained in every speck of light and blue.

He felt her grip him as she woke. Then her other hand came to his face. "Don't weep for me lad. Don't waste your sorrow. I thought we'd decided you would put all of that behind you?"

He realized that he was indeed crying. "You can't leave us, Reverend Mother. This place won't survive the loss of you."

She smiled then, patting his hand. "And it won't have to. I'm not dead yet, my lad. Just a skip in the road, or in the heartbeat, as it were."

"How long have you known about the atrial fibrillation?" If his tone was pushy and demanding, she'd decided not to notice.

She shrugged. "About six months. I've been cheating on you, Dr. O'Brien. I've been seeing a cardiologist in the city."

"You should have told us. We could have monitored the situation from here."

She sighed, "Aye, I suppose I should have. It's not easy being in charge. You want to seem strong, even invincible. Is this the part where you remind me of my control issues?" Liam laughed. There she was. Those wise eyes full of stubbornness. She cleared her throat. "I'm okay, Liam, and apparently I'm going to have to start some sort of medication. I hate to admit that the time has come for me to start grooming another to take the lead. It's not going to happen over-night. There's a lot to this place. The three factors always vying for one's attention."

She sighed, looking so very tired. "The logical choice is Maria or Catherine. They've been with us the longest. They'll both need help if I'm to groom them and see who's the better fit. That's assuming ei-ther one of them even wants the job. But I'm getting old, my dear boy. I'm not ready to retire yet, but the Almighty may have other plans. I want to control any transition, to avoid the dioceses trying to stick me with some overeager rookie. Don't tell the rest of the staff, please. It may be a few more years. I just want to be ready."

The thought made his heart hurt. A-Fib wasn't uncommon at her age, and it could be controlled. He knew this, logically. She was turn-ing seventy-one years old, after all. She just seemed so strong, march-ing the grounds of the abbey bossing everyone around. But everyone deserved to retire at some point. She wanted to go out on her own terms, however, and he respected the hell out of her for that. She re-minded him a lot of his mother, and of his grandmother Edith. Two strong women who had carved out a life for themselves in the midst of adversity. "You don't happen to have any Mullen kin do you?"

She smiled, "Mullen is a Cork name. I'm afraid not. We go back in Sligo, Mayo, and Donegal for three hundred years. It's a bit hard to leave that west coast, once it gets in your blood." Liam had to agree. He'd liked Dublin, in his youth. It had been exciting and different. But the West coast of Ireland was like the siren's song. The craggy rocks, mossy cliffs, and roaring sea pulled you home, time and time again.

He felt it, even now. He shook himself, focusing on the abbess. "You should tell Agatha that she needs to post a new position on the website. It's time to start a volunteer position for the smaller children at the school, and if you can't find an OB-GYN, you need to look in the midwife community. My mother can help. The school is the first priority, though. Wouldn't you agree? We need two teachers in the school. Especially if Genoveva leaves."

"Do you really think he'll come for her when he finds out?"

Liam closed his eyes, remembering the fresh-faced, green-eyed girl with flowers in her hair. She'd been so pretty at the wedding. Looking more like a fifteen-year-old than he'd ever seen before. "I would. If it were me, I would come for her. I can only hope he'll feel the same."

"I remember him. Once we put the pieces together, I remembered him. He was a good man. Wonderful with the children. I think you're right. I think he'll come back to us." Then she cocked her head. "And what about you? Will you come back to us someday?"

He leaned down and kissed the top of her fragile hand. "I don't think I'm capable of staying away for good. I'm not sure what's in store for us, but I feel like we're not done, you and I."

34

Liam's heart swelled as he got out of the passenger side of the Land Cruiser. He pulled Doc Mary into his arms. "Ah, Christ. It's good to see you." Paolo grabbed her bags as she returned his embrace. "I'm so sorry about the problem with your husband's visa. I'm sure they'll approve it as soon as the letter from the ambassador gets sent. Tell Hans not to worry."

She waved a hand. "He's fit to be tied. Tried to get me to delay, which of course wasn't going to happen. The Brazilian government took one look at the Iraq/Afghanistan/Djibouti travel history and denied it. Some red tape engineer, as Hans called it. Didn't bother to check the employment history and references and see that he was retired military. So, once he appeals, he should be joining me."

"Well, now. Are you ready for some extreme doctoring?"

Mary laughed. "Lead the way, Dr. O'Brien."

That night at dinner, Sister Agatha stood and looked at Liam and Izzy. "The children and Sister Catherine and I have been working on something. We wanted your opinion on it before it goes on the website and Youtube channel.

Izzy perked up. "Fire away! I can't wait!" Liam nudged Mary, who was enthralled by everything to do with her new surroundings. Izzy noticed that Sister Catherine had the video going on the smart phone, the only camera the abbey owned. Sister Agatha looked at all the children and they started to giggle. Then they all reached under the table and took out cups.

They began and Izzy couldn't believe how coordinated all the children were. When had they found the time to practice this without her knowing? Then they started singing, and the waterworks started. It was in Portuguese. They'd learned the entire cups song in Portuguese.

When they finished she threw her arms around Sister Agatha. "That definitely needs to go on the website! Well done everyone!" She went around and hugged and kissed all twenty-three children, just like she did every night.

Three days later...
The goodbyes were difficult. Genoveva had been the hardest. The girl had cried in Izzy's arms to the point of hiccups. Then Izzy watched as Liam cradled his sweet Estela in his arms like she was a precious treasure. She'd pulled on his beard, telling him that she'd send him pictures. She spoke in Portuguese only, as she always did when she was stressed. Not having the mental capacity at such a young age to call forth the translations in her mind.

Seamus promised to come to Doolin for a visit. He was essentially starting from scratch upon his return to Ireland. Liam had tasked his mother with sniffing out birthing centers and hospitals that needed an experienced OB-GYN on the west coast. And now, they were headed home. Three days ahead of schedule. No one in Ireland knew that Liam was coming home. No one knew that they were engaged. It was two days before Christmas, and the long flight would land them in Dublin around teatime on Christmas Eve. Everyone would be home, and that old Liam that had been buried for so long emerged, alongside the new Liam. The one that had been playful and mischievous and liked to surprise people.

He'd taken the back seat, giving Izzy the front so that she could sit next to Raphael. The two were a mess. Like twins being separated. Both fighters. Both fiercely loyal. They were all three irrevocably connected now. Her blood coursed through Raphael's veins. Liam's coursed through hers.

As Raphael pulled into the departures drop off at the airport, he silently helped them unload their baggage. He hugged Izzy, reminding her to practice her Portuguese. "Come back to us. medíca."

They made their way to their gate, waiting in line at security to have their papers checked and their bags scanned. Something pricked Liam's subconscious as he looked up. The walkway for the arrivals was to the left of security. Hoards of tourists and locals finding their way to the immigration checkpoint. Among the dark hair, he saw a long blonde ponytail sticking out of the back of a ball cap. Then the woman was gone. "What's up?" Izzy asked, looking that way.

He shook himself. "I don't know. I just thought I saw someone I knew. I didn't see a face, it was just…a feeling." He shrugged it off, and they went on their way. Ready to start the first leg of the journey home.

35

Christmas Eve

Thee mood was sedate at the O'Brien homestead. The family poured into the house. Both from out of town and in the neighboring areas. Sorcha looked around, and her heart tried to be grateful. Most of her children were here. Although Liam wasn't here, he'd begun calling them on the video chat at least twice a week. So in a way, he'd returned to her. If not in body, then at least in spirit. And even through the screen of the computer, she'd seen his transition. She knew it had been Izzy. They'd been sworn to secrecy. Izzy and Liam had formed an attachment, then they'd parted under unfortunate circumstances. Then the call had come that Izzy had been injured, an unspeakable act of violence causing her to be stronger than she ever thought she'd have to be. But she was okay, and it seemed that she and Liam, if not together, had made a sort of peace. And who knew what the future held. Maybe that fat headed son of hers would come to his senses and pursue the girl after the dust had settled. She couldn't shake the feeling that Izzy was meant to be with them. She lightened at the thought of seeing the girl for a few days next week before she left for the States.

She scanned the room, looking for Patrick. He was seated in the corner, his face solemn. She ached for him. For the wounded husband, and for the father that he might never be. She couldn't protect her children anymore. As they'd all grown to adulthood, that task had been delegated to the fates. Something she hated about growing older.

"Dinner is ready, everyone. Cora, can you take the little ones to the sink to wash their hands? There's my lass." The kids started to line up at the double sinks, stepping up on a stool as Cora aided them. Everyone jumped as Cora screeched, "Izzy!"

Izzy widened her stance as the nine-year-old fireball launched herself into her body. She squeezed her tightly. "How's Miss Cora?" Everyone was elated at her early return, Alanna in tears as she held her old friend with one arm, a toddler with another.

"What brings you home early, lass? It's a blessing to be sure." Sean hugged the beautiful young doctor and thought about what his wife had told him. As he held her, he realized that he was a little disappointed that Liam had not found his way to this woman. He just hoped that her early departure wasn't because of Liam.

"Well, since I wasn't going to make it to Arizona for the holidays, I decided to try and make it here. I've brought a present for everyone." Then there was a collective gasp as Liam appeared. Brigid was the first to get to him, sobbing uncontrollably in her brother's arms. But Liam's eyes never left his mother's. As Brigid released him, the whole family watched as he walked to his parents. Sean's eyes were filled with unshed tears, as were Sorcha's. They looked as though they thought him a mirage. A vision that would dissipate before they could take hold of him. Then Sean pulled him tight against them. They wept openly, holding their son. Sean's hand was in his son's long hair, Sorcha reaching up, her arm around his neck as she stood on her toes. Everyone watched, the emotions high in the room as they witnessed the heartbreaking reunion. When they finally parted, Sorcha grabbed Izzy, starting a fresh round of tears.

Liam went to his brother, Seany. The apology obvious in his blue eyes. "It's all right brother. Don't think on it. I'm just glad you're home."

It was Branna who saw it first. She didn't know Izzy as well and was trying to wait her turn in line for the hugs, so she hung back a bit. Then the light caught the sparkle. She was too far away to confirm it, so she grabbed the stool the children had been using, trying to look over people's heads. "Hellcat, what on earth are ye doin' on a stool? What are you looking at?" Michael was used to his wife's unpredictable behavior, but it still amused him.

She looked at him, ready to burst. She took his chin in one hand and pointed with the other. "I'm getting a better look at that!"

Michael blurted out an expletive. "Holy shit. Is that what I think it is?" Everyone turned to look at him. Then they turned to Izzy and Liam.

"If you're wondering if that's an engagement ring on her finger, then yes brother." He looked at his younger brother Seany and winked. "Dr. Collier is officially taken. So don't go getting any ideas, little brother."

Seany let out a whoop and picked Izzy up, spinning her around. Then he set her down in front of Liam. "Now we're to be family, Izzy love. As we were always meant to be."

Sorcha felt her husband behind her. "Well, I'll be damned. You were right, Sorcha." She leaned into him, smiling through her tears.

"I told you. I felt it. I felt like she was ours." She watched as Liam walked over to Patrick, finally scanning the room. Feeling the change in circumstance. And her heart wept again. Not for Liam, but for her other son.

Izzy sat on the couch, curled up with Cora. "You saved me as much as Liam did, Cora. I listened. When things got critical, I remembered your words. I followed the river and I was saved. Someday soon, I'm going to tell you all about it. I'm going to tell you because it's important to me that you know how special you are. That gift you have? Don't ever hide it, baby girl." Izzy looked up and saw that Finn was listening, tears misting in his eyes. He just nodded at her, a sort of thanks.

Liam looked around, feeling someone was missing. Tadgh and Charlie were in Galway with Katie and his grandparents. They'd be here tomorrow for Christmas lunch. But as he looked at his brother Patrick, it hit him. He approached and hugged his brother. "Where is Caitlyn? Is she with her family?" Patrick's face was ruined. As if the energy of keeping upbeat for their surprise had finally run out. He shuddered and swallowed, blinking hard. "Patrick, what's happened?"

"She left me, brother. She's gone."

"What? That's impossible. Caitlyn would never leave you, brother. She loves you more than anything. If she's at her parents' house, you need to leave right now and go see her. You need to work things out. She's grieving, Patrick. She isn't thinking straight."

"Aye, that's what I said. She agreed. She needed some time to clear her head. That's why she's not at her parents' house."

"Then where the fuck is she?"

"I would have thought you knew. She's gone to Brazil."

Liam's vision blurred, then the image of that blonde ponytail punched into his mind. The woman from the airport.

"Apparently they need a teacher at the orphanage. She's gone to teach the children, and to get away from me."

"I swear to you, brother. She never said a word! I would have talked her out of it. She needs to be here with you. You need each other."

Patrick's eyes were so sad. "Yes, well, apparently she's decided to go it alone for a while. She told me that if I followed her, then it would cause a bigger rift between us. That I needed to respect her wishes. Honestly, the Garda would never approve me taking off for two months anyway. I burned a lot of my leave to take care of her. If I took off for two months, I'd lose my job and my wife."

Liam grabbed him by the shoulders. "I'll talk to the Reverend Mother. You have not lost her. I know that this has got to be killing you, but I really feel like she's in good hands. The abbess will send her back. She's not just an abbess, she's a trained psychologist. I swear to you that she's in good hands. And as far as I know, she won't be leaving the mission like the doctors do. She'll be safe."

He pulled Patrick to him, hardly comprehending this twist of fate. As he'd found his way home, Caitlyn had followed his horrible example and fled. But if he was going to pick a place for Caitlyn to go, he couldn't think of a better one. The thought of her teaching his little Estela for two months melted his heart. He was almost jealous. "Maybe this is just what she needs, brother. It's a special place with special people. Just don't lose faith in her. She'll come home to you, brother. I vow to you she will."

36

Izzy and Liam walked down the hall at St. James Hospital, toward the pediatric ward. It was ironic that the very place Liam had trained, a top-notch teaching hospital in the heart of Dublin, was where Tadgh had found Doctor Quinn Maguire. Liam had called ahead, introduced himself and told the doctor of their mutual connection, having both worked at St. James and done missionary work in Brazil. The man had been downright friendly, and eagerly accepted Liam's offer to take him to lunch. So, they were here. Ready to ambush the poor bastard with some life-altering news.

Izzy's heart jumped in her chest as she locked eyes with Doctor Maguire. Those eyes. Jesus, as if she'd had any doubt. The look of this man would have sealed the deal. She knew by his records that he was forty-four. He looked young for his age. Sandy blonde hair, fit, tall, and beautiful green irises. No wonder Genoveva's mother had chucked the rule book out the window. He brought them into the office, getting introductions out of the way. "Yes, we're engaged. We actually fell in love at St. Clare's, while on a mission together." Izzy saw a shadow flicker over the man's face.

"Well, that's a fairy tale ending, isn't it? Congratulations. Let me buy you some lunch at the cafe." Before he got up, Izzy put a hand out to stop him. "Before we do that, I need to speak with you about the real reason we've come."

Liam watched the man for signs of cardiac arrest. This was what it looked like when you turned someone inside out. Izzy said, "I'm sorry. I just couldn't think of any way to handle this other than in person."

The man was stunned. "You're sure."

"Obviously I'd recommend collecting some DNA, but I can tell you that I'm pretty sure. So we were right. She never told you."

He shut his eyes. "Her name was Angela. I loved her, but…we had a falling out. It was my fault." His eyes were desperate. "I was still married, you see. We were all but divorced. She'd moved in with another man. All I needed to do is show up and sign the annulment papers and court papers. We hadn't been together in two years." He rubbed his eyes, looking ancient. "But that didn't make any difference. We were still technically married in the eyes of the church. Angela was devastated. Once we got serious, I felt like she needed to know. I thought I could make her understand. The marriage had been over for a while. It was all done but the signatures. I wanted to marry her. I loved her. She broke it off. She was so distraught, she left the school and stayed away until my tour was over. I tried to contact her but she demanded that I respect her wishes. She never told me there was a baby! I would have come back. My annulment was granted. I would have come back for her and the child." Grief seemed to ripple through him. "How did she die?"

"Ovarian Cancer."

He rubbed his face, trying to keep it together"And the child? Is she with Angela's family?"

"No. Apparently they turned her out when she showed up pregnant."

He jumped out of his chair, "Then where the hell is my daughter?"

Liam stood as well, "Easy, brother. She's safe. It's why we're here. Izzy unearthed this truth during our time at St. Clare's. Your daughter, Genoveva, is at the orfanato. She's been there since she was seven years old."

Liam's gut coiled as he watched this man split down the middle. "Please, don't do this unless you're sure."

That's when Izzy spoke. "I have a video to show you, Doctor Maguire. I'll show you Genoveva. She's taller than the other children, lighter skinned. She's beautiful and powerful, and she has the most beautiful green eyes you've ever seen."

Izzy watched the man's heart leap and then break, every time he caught sight of Genoveva on the video. It was like watching someone being slowly tortured. When it was over, he put his fist to his mouth. He swallowed, trying to get to the point where he could speak without having a complete mental breakdown. She had to give creds to the guy, because she was pretty raw herself. She looked at Liam and could tell this scene had taken a hunk out of him as well. The man finally turned. "She's almost grown. Jesus Christ. She's almost grown. Eight years in an orphanage. Fifteen fucking years with no idea who her father was. Feeling ashamed…" his voice caught and he shut his eyes.

Goddamn, Liam thought. This was one tough bastard. This was literally gutting the man alive, but he was keeping his shit together. And he was pissed. Rightfully so. Fifteen years wasted, separated from his only child. He'd never remarried. Never had any kids of his own. He'd dedicated his life to taking care of other people's children. On three continents, no less. "But you've got her future, brother. If you want it, you've got it. And she needs you. When she comes of age, she can't stay there. Do you understand? They'll have to try and place her in a job or something. She'll have to support herself." Liam felt his own tears threatening. "She remembers little outside of that safe haven. She's not ready to be cut loose in that drug infested city. She can't live in those slums. She needs to be rescued, brother. As if her life depended on it. She thought no one wanted her, but she's so wrong. I would take her in a second if I could, but she has a father. It's your place to go and claim her and let her know that she has a family."

"I'll go. Of course, I want her. It's just...we can't tell her. Not right away. The courts will never let me have her until we establish paternity. I couldn't bring her here without it either. And if you're wrong, it will scar the child even further than she already has been. I need to go to St. Clare's and see the lass for myself. I'll figure out a way to get her DNA. The abbess surely will aid me, don't you think?"

Izzy laughed, almost giddy. "She will. Oh God, Quinn. You have no idea. I couldn't even explain it to you. You're going to fall so head over heels in love with this kid. She's smart and so sensitive. She helps with the smaller children. She's had some self-esteem issues, but I've watched her blossom into such an amazing young woman. I wish I could be there. Just please, make sure this is what you want."

"Of course I'm sure."

All of Izzy's cheerfulness faded in an instant, and she leaned toward him in her chair. "No, I mean you REALLY need to be sure. If you reject that little girl or break her heart, I will hunt you down like a dog. Do you understand me?"

The man leaned back, a little surprise and fear showing in his demeanor. He looked at Liam who just shrugged. "In this instance, the female of the species is most definitely more deadly than the male, my friend. Don't doubt it for a feckin' minute."

"Then you must understand me. If she's my daughter, I won't leave Brazil without her. If I have to pitch a bloody tent in the yard of that orphanage, I will not leave her. Ever."

And that's when Izzy threw her arms around the stranger and hugged the shit of out him.

Sorcha smiled as she watched the video again. She turned and looked at her son. She ran a hand over his beard, taking in how much her boy had changed. And that was the biggest change of all. The boy was gone. His face was beautiful but had harder lines now. His eyes were older, having lived through such devastation. "The way you talk about Reverend Mother Faith, I think I'd like to meet her someday."

He smiled. "I think you'd love her, and Sister Catherine. What they lack in equipment, they make up for in instincts. The staff is wonderful. St. Clare's saved me, in a way, at a time when I thought I couldn't be saved. It wasn't just Izzy, Ma. It was that place."

"Then maybe it will do our dear Caitlyn some good. God, Liam. I hope so. Patrick will not survive this if he loses her."

"I know, Ma. Just have some faith in Caitlyn. And don't forget that Mary is with her. Sometimes women do more for each other than the men can offer. She'll find her way back to him. She's suffered a terrible loss, but she'll find her way home, Ma. Just like I did."

Liam laughed as he watched Cora chasing Izzy with a nest of seaweed. They'd bundled her up and taken her to the beach, just like old times. She was so breathtakingly beautiful, it almost hurt to look at her. Long, chestnut waves swirling in the wind and the cold, the dark Irish genes that she got from her father. Her porcelain skin, so much like Brigid's, was pink at the cheeks and nose. He knew, now, why the legend of the selkies had endured for centuries. It was in the wild children of the sea, with the dark hair and eyes that held a touch of mystery. Children like Cora who would grow into indescribable beauty. She was wearing one of the sweaters Katie had knitted for her, made of warm, thick Irish wool, and she squealed with delight as she chased Izzy through the wind and the foam.

He thought of Katie, then. He hadn't been able to see her. She was in Galway with her parents who had the flu. It was more and more difficult for her to get away to her retreat on the island but she had a place to go now, thanks to Liam's cousin Daniel. He found himself wishing that he could take Izzy there to that little seaside cottage. He hadn't even seen it, yet. But his mother told him all about it, and he'd seen the pictures at Tadgh's wedding.

He'd love to take Izzy to the islands. The raw wind and punishing surf roaring in the air. The salty mist coating the windows as they nestled themselves by the fire. So different from the balmy air that settled on your skin in Brazil, and never seemed to leave.

They just didn't have enough time. *You'll come back. It's not forever.* He watched Izzy, her smile so big and bright against the grey winter sky and sea. Ireland suited her. He closed his eyes, wanting to remember this moment with her and Cora. Now he had two homes to mourn. As heartsick as he'd been to leave St. Clare's Charity Mission, a home hidden in Amazona, he'd miss Ireland as well. But it was the best thing for them right now. The right thing for Izzy. He owed her everything, and they had to live somewhere, had to work somewhere. For now, he was letting her take the lead.

Liam sat across from Tadgh and his father, a cold pint in each of their hands. It was so good to see his family again, Liam thought. He'd asked Tadgh and his father to meet him at the pub early. They sat comfortably. Then he finally said, "I brought you something. I suspect you'll find yourself sharing it with the others, but I couldn't afford one for everyone." He handed a large package to Tadgh.

"It's big but light. What in the hell did you bring me?" Tadgh said with a smile.

"Just open it, brother. I think you'll like it. A new challenge." Liam was surprised how nervous he was, wanting his cousin to love what he'd brought. He had a lot of making up to do, considering how he'd treated him, and that he'd blown off his wedding. "I missed your wedding." He shrugged. "The new babes were easy. Izzy found some shirts for the lads and all the girls got embroidered dresses. This, though...well, I have one as well, and I thought you'd like it."

Tadgh opened the package and pulled out the protective wrapping. Then out came a hard case that looked a lot like what you would put a musical instrument in. He took a deep breath, then he unlatched it, lifting the lid. Sean whistled from behind him. "Jesus, Liam. I don't know what to say."

The traditional, handmade Fado guitar was a thing of beauty. Tropical wood, hand painted and lacquered. It was a piece of art, really. "There's a heavy Portuguese influence, as you know. There is a man in Manaus who makes them by hand. He's a true artist. It plays beautifully. There's a CD and a music book in there as well."

Tadgh ran his hand over it. "I'll share it. It's too much, but you'd have to kill me to part with it." They all laughed. "But I'll share it. That's what brothers do."

Liam nodded, "Yes, they do. And of all my brothers, you've got the kindest heart of all of us." Tadgh stood, handing the case to Sean. Then he hugged Liam, the old wound between them finally healing. Liam knew that Tadgh had forgiven him a year ago, but he hadn't forgiven himself. And he remembered that scene Izzy had described. When Tadgh and Seany had gone to check his apartment, thinking he'd killed himself. "I love you, Tadgh. I missed you."

They sat for a minute, clearing their throats and reining in their emotions. "So Phoenix?" Tadgh asked.

"Yes, for now. I know it's far. It's hard to explain, but Izzy gave me my life back." Then he shook his head. "No, that's not right. She didn't give me my life back. She just gave me my future back. She gave me a new life. She gave me her love when I did not deserve it. I need to do this for her, just like you would have done for Charlie." Tadgh understood. Rather than let Charlie go, he would have left Ireland. It would have killed him, but he'd have done it for her and Josh.

His father said, "It doesn't matter where you go, son. We've got you home. If not in body, at least in here." He pointed to Liam's chest. "You've had your share of suffering. It's time for you to be happy. If that happiness is found in Arizona, then so be it. But that's not why you called us here, is it? Ye've got something on your mind that you didn't want to discuss in front of the others."

Liam gave a sideways grin. "You are too smart for your own good. It's two things, actually." He looked at them both, wanting them to understand. "I don't blame either of you for Eve's death. Despite how I behaved, I never blamed you."

"We know that, Liam. And no matter what you say, I'll carry her death with me always. We both will, but it's good to hear you say it nonetheless. Now tell us. What's the second thing?"

He hesitated, not knowing how to start. Then he just did it. He told them about what happened on that forest road. About the life Izzy took and the one he took as well. Not sparing them the details, he told them. He wasn't sure what he'd expected. Judgment, maybe?

"Ye took a life, brother. I know something about that. But you learn to live with it. It's all you can do. And if it helps you, I'd have done the same. We all would have. Some things…they have to be done or you can't live with yourself. And what happened in that jungle will be kept between us. No one will know unless you tell them."

"Are you sure Caitlyn is safe there, Liam?" his father asked.

"I'd be lying if I said there wasn't an element of danger to doing a mission. The disease, the snakes and bugs and other beasts, the crime; it's all a reality. I won't sugar coat it. But if this is what Caitlyn needs to do in order to come to peace with her loss…to make it home to Patrick…then we must respect that. They have full-time security now, and soon Hans will be there."

"And if she doesn't come home?" Sean asked.

"Then he'll go after her. He'll rescue her, even if it's from herself. Just like you did for Ma." As they clinked glasses, the first of the family members started piling in. His family usually filled up half of Gus O'Connor's Pub all on their own, but behind a steady group of tourists, others came in. Hans, Ned, Robby, Miriam, local business owners, fisherman, and musicians. Jenny was behind the bar, and it was a full house tonight. In that moment Liam realized that it wasn't just his family that he'd missed. It was this town. This would always be his home and Doolin would always be exactly where he left it, waiting patiently for him to return. The people would live their lives and change in small ways, but that sense of home was in his blood and always would be. A constant in an otherwise unpredictable world. The people who lived here were as much a part of him as his own family, and he was never going to forget them again.

NOTES FROM THE AUTHOR

This book was a challenge to write. Out of all of my books, this one took the most research. I'd like to start out by saying that I don't speak Portuguese, which is why I kept it to a minimum. It just needed to be Brazil. I don't have an explanation other than that. It's been Brazil from the beginning. Before the Zika outbreak, before the Olympics in Rio. Liam was going to go to Brazil. In the wake of this tremendous journey, I feel like I know the place. Maybe someday I'll travel the Amazon by boat, and maybe that boat will be driven by a sweet old guy named Paolo. That would be quite an adventure, despite the fact that I'm piss-pants scared of spiders and snakes.

I always said that if I had my life to do over again, I would study harder and go into medicine. I briefly considered nursing school but went another direction. I liked being a police officer for that short time in my life but I have so much respect for the medical profession and especially military medicine. My son is a Navy Diver Medical Tech. Like a corpsman, only with additional training.

The study of infectious diseases is an admirable one. Quite often, the populations that are ravaged by disease are the least likely to have good healthcare and affordable medicine available to them. Doctors and nurses that go to developing countries to volunteer are superheroes, as far as I'm concerned. If you know someone who is fundraising to go on a foreign medical mission, step up and donate. The travel expenses often come out of pocket for those volunteer doctors and nurses. Two such non-profits are Doctor's Without Borders (or Medecins sans Frontieres) and Catholic Medical Mission Board, but do your own research and find the one that suits you.

I dedicated this book to my brother, Randy. He died unexpectedly a little over a year ago. I think he would have gotten a kick out of my books but he never got a chance to read them. He died of bacterial meningitis. A complication of a broken rib that punctured his lung, tension pneumothorax, resulting in a case of pneumonia that he couldn't quite seem to kick. We suspect the exposure to the meningitis bacteria was during the time he was immune compromised after this injury, and most likely came from contaminated water in his pond system that supplied his drinking water. The infection masked itself as the flu until it was too late. My family was devastated. The lesson learned was to listen to your body, get your vaccines, and don't be afraid to go to the emergency room or call an ambulance for yourself. My brother died alone and in pain, and just like that, I never saw him again.

Internal medicine doctors and infectious disease doctors are on the front lines of human disease. Like fireman who run into a burning building, when everyone else is running out, some of these doctors walk into an active infectious disease outbreak, willing to put themselves in harm's way under harsh, dangerous conditions, in order to save those who can be saved, contain the outbreak, educate the community, run vaccine trials, and hold the hands of dying human beings as they pass. So in a way, I dedicate this book to them as well.

Much of my information about the diseases mentioned in this book was taken directly from the website for the Center for Disease Control.

I'd like to thank my husband, Bob, for his help with the maps of Brazil and his insight into the drug cartels and trafficking in Central and South America. As a young enlisted man in the Marines, he worked as a Spanish linguist, doing counter-narcotics in Panama. He saw his first combat during Operation Just Cause when the U.S.

participated in the military action to remove General Manuel Noriega from power and liberate the Panamanian people. As with book two and three, he's helped me get an insight into my antagonist and helps me keep my facts straight on the current and historical events.

As always, I'd like to thank my family for their support during the writing of this book. I'd like to thank my readers, who push me to do better, keeping the O'Brien storylines moving forward, and encourage me with their support and kind words. Finally, thank you to my beta readers and my wonderful cover designer, Christine Rasey Stevens of Stevens Design. The cover design for this book was way more grueling than the first three books. I love my covers and I wanted this to reflect the heart of this wonderful series while show-casing the unique and untamed setting where it took place. For my beta readers, I am so grateful. Finding good proofreaders has been a difficult journey. That first book was the test case, and I have since updated and reformatted *Raven of the Sea* to have a cleaner copy for future readers. I am so thankful to the friends who have stuck by me through this process, sharpening their red pens to help me get the best product I can onto the presses.

For my readers, I know I broke my own rule and gave you a little cliffhanger, but I really felt like Patrick and Caitlyn needed their own story. Through part of the next book, their story will run concurrently with this book as far as timeline, but it will be from their point of view. Don't worry, though. You haven't heard the last of Liam and Izzy. We'll peek in on them from time to time, as well as all of the other O'Briens. Because regardless of where they are, O'Briens stick together, just as family should. And speaking of family sticking together, I'm rooting for our sweet Genoveva. And maybe, just maybe we will see her again very, very soon.

89988921R00207

Made in the USA
Columbia, SC
23 February 2018